T...

It was the ultimate in Nam vet fraternities. But it... a club no one really wanted to join.

Everyone talked about the Dirty Thirty. Every soldier worth his salt bragged he was getting closer and closer: "Killed another Charlie last night while Lurpin' thru sector seven. That brings my count to over two dozen. Only a matter o' time before I'm in, before I'm a Dirty Thirty myself!" Few grunts actually came close to killing thirty enemy soldiers in hand-to-hand combat before they rotated back to the States. Green Berets, yes, but few Air Cav troopers . . .

Only maniacs like Brody the Whoremonger bucked the system, extended their combat tour another six months, and spent their time off in the Void in search of action and adventure. It was only a matter of time before Brody found himself eligible for initiation into hell's elite.

With a glossary of military jargon.

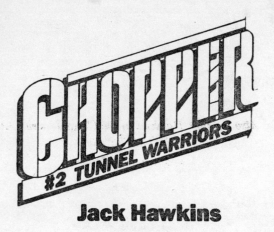

CHOPPER
#2 TUNNEL WARRIORS

Jack Hawkins

SPHERE BOOKS LIMITED

SPHERE BOOKS LTD

Published by the Penguin Group
27 Wrights Lane, London W8 5TZ, England
Viking Penguin Inc., 40 West 23rd Street, New York, New York 10010, USA
Penguin Books Australia Ltd, Ringwood, Victoria, Australia
Penguin Books Canada Ltd, 2801 John Street, Markham, Ontario, Canada L3R 1B4
Penguin Books (NZ) Ltd, 182–190 Wairau Road, Auckland 10, New Zealand

Penguin Books Ltd, Registered Offices: Harmondsworth, Middlesex, England

First published by Ballantine Books 1987
Published by Sphere Books Ltd 1988

Made and printed in Great Britain by
Richard Clay Ltd, Bungay, Suffolk

For Lt. Matthew Brennen (Vietnam 1965–1969) of the 9th Air Cavalry's Flashing Saber Blues, who flew over 400 combat gunship assaults with "The Headhunters." He deserved much more than simply a CIB patch, and he may now be finding that "special something" in the never-never land of Kansas.

This is also for Lt. Col. Harold Moore, commander of the 7th Cav of the First Cavalry Division, Artillery Commander Lt. Col. Earl Ingram, of the 2nd Battalion, 12th Cavalry, Col. Thomas Brown, Commander of the 3rd Brigade, and Gen. Harry W. O. Kinnard, division commander of the entire First Cav. But not for the reasons they might think . . .

Author's Note

The 10,000-day war in Vietnam, and the battle for Ia Drang Valley, and the siege of the Plei Me Special Forces camp in 1965 really happened. The 7th Cav of the First Air Cavalry really existed. But there is some disagreement among armchair commandos and military archivists as to whether or not there ever really was an "Echo Company."

Though the colorful Col. "Neil Nazi" Buchanan and many of "Brody's People" may remind readers and First Cav vets of soldiers they might have known in The Nam, this novel is a work of fiction. Other than well-known public and historic figures, any resemblance of its characters to persons living or Killed in Action is purely coincidental.

The following chronological account involves that elusive tract of time missing between Chapters 26 and 27 in Chopper #1: *Blood Trails*.

FOREWORD

First deployed to the II Corps area of South Vietnam, the First Cavalry Division was the only American division to engage the enemy in all four tactical zones below the DMZ. The First Cav participated in the first major confrontation with North Vietnamese troops—at the Battle for Ia Drang Valley in November of 1965—and the U.S. Army warriors emerged from the bloody clash victorious.

Three years later, the airmobile raiders rode their gunships north to the Imperial City of Hue during the surprise Viet Cong attacks of Tet 1968 and also reinforced the besieged Marines at the encircled outpost in the Khe Sanh.

In October of that year the division moved south into III Corps to defend the capital, Saigon, from impending assault by hostile forces. They spearheaded tactical ops shortly thereafter throughout IV Corps and participated in cross-border forays into Cambodia in 1970.

Airmobile troopers of the First Cavalry Division were awarded 25 Medals of Honor in Vietnam, 120 Distinguished Service Crosses, 2,766 Silver Stars, 2,697 Distinguished Flying Crosses, 8,408 Bronze Stars for Valor, 2,910 Air Medals for Valor, and 5,328

1

Army Commendation medals—not to mention a Presidential Unit Citation (the only U.S. Army division to receive one), from President Lyndon B. Johnson (for defeating the NVA at Ia Drang), as well as the Vietnamese Cross of Gallantry with Palm, and Vietnamese Civic Action Medal.

In Vietnam, the First Air Cavalry Division lost over 30,000 men killed or wounded in action—more than its 4,055 casualties sustained in WWII, and 16,498 lost in Korea, combined.*

By September of 1964, more than 400 U.S. Army aircraft were deployed in Vietnam in support of South Vietnamese soldiers. These included 9 CH-73 Mojave heavy-transport helicopters, 6 OV-1 Mohawk recon craft, 53 Cessna birddogs, 88 other transport aircraft, and over 250 UH-1 Hueys. Over 3,000 enlisted men, commanded by some 800 officers, operated these planes and gunships.

The first U.S. Army airmobile unit to see action in Vietnam was the 173rd Airborne Brigade, which arrived in June 1965. Two months later, the First Cavalry Division sent an advance party of personnel, and soon afterward, the rest of the unit followed. By late October 1965, the First Cav had over 400 helicopters and 1,600 vehicles in Vietnam, operated by some 16,000 soldiers.

This is the story of those men.

*Source: Vietnam War Almanac, by Harry G. Summers, Jr., Col., U.S. Army Infantry.

CHAPTER 1

Koy slid to a stop in the moist leaves, startled. She had nearly tripped across the strands of razor-sharp concertina—strands that were sparkling new, and must have been laid only last night.

Frowning, she dropped into a squat to contemplate her situation. The two large pails suspended from a pole across her shoulders flattened the lush green flora on either side of her. Water and several tadpoles rose above her bare feet. With frogs croaking in the distance, the tiny tadpoles wriggled against her amber toes, but Koy ignored them. Under normal conditions, she might scoop them up—a handful or two, at least—and save the lot for fishing bait back at the caves. But this was not safe land. Even now, she could see several of the long noses a hundred meters or so in the distance showing a squad of Montagnarde mercenaries how to properly erect a new guard tower. Koy's people had toppled the old tower the night before.

That must be the reason for this new perimeter of wire, the nineteen-year-old Mnong maiden decided, but she shook her head from side to side, amused. Did the Americans really think a couple of extra strands of barbed wire could keep out the sappers? The guard tower had been destroyed by a novice even younger

3

than herself.

Koy dropped back under some fronds as a gunship suddenly beat past overhead and flared in for an impressive landing at the Special Forces camp. She grinned at the recollection. Her comrade Tan was only fourteen but he was good with a Cambodian crossbow, and Bai had recently shown everyone how to wrap old rags soaked in gasoline around the tips, tie them in place with light fishing twine, and set them aflame before launching the arrow at one's target.

Tan had not hit the giant red-haired man wearing a green beret—he had missed the tower platform itself entirely—but the youth *did* manage to embed the projectile in one of the tower's support beams, and the dried-out wood was on fire and crackling like an overcooked stick of *satay* within minutes.

The American and his two apprentice lookouts had managed to jump from the collapsing tower as it was halfway to the ground, and none was hurt seriously. Koy was sure the foreigners at the Plei Me CIDG compound would never be the same again, and the thought made her giggle.

Reprimanding herself for the slip in noise discipline, the slender woman covered her mouth with dark fingers in the peculiar Oriental fashion restricted to moments of embarrassment or surprise. A large green-and-blue parrot dropped from branches high above and landed at her feet. Squawking loudly at her—Koy was not sure if the bird was protecting its territory or merely irritated at her unannounced intrusion—the parrot pranced back and forth, huge wings spread and chest expanding with each screech. Twice, the bird darted toward her, as if interested in sampling her dainty toes, and Koy had to shoo it away. Finally, she had to draw the pistol from her web belt.

Intending to use it as a hammer if the parrot charged again, her precaution was not necessary: This was one bird who knew his weapons. The sight of old steel and a four-inch barrel sent him flapping off into the branches

4

along the jungle's edge.

Koy glanced down at the two pails. Bok, her cell leader, had assigned her the task of filling the containers several dozen times before dusk. He would have people watching her.

Koy shuddered at the thought as she remembered the "tricks" Bok inflicted on the young women when he didn't get his way—when they didn't complete their tasks, contributing to the effort.

Koy had been a member of the local Viet Cong guerrilla force for over three years now, but it would be two more years before she could expect to advance in any manner, and then it would probably only be to assistant cell leader. Every assistant cell leader Koy had ever known was dead. Killed by ARVN, the Army of the Republic of (South) Vietnam. Those who had escaped death were rumored to be rotting away in prison cells in Saigon, where the *canh-sats* passed the time attaching electric field-phone wires to breasts and female genitalia, or starving to death in the tiger pits on Con Son Island.

Koy's parents were not dead . . . not victims of the war with the French and the Americans and the Viet Minh; they were very much alive, and living in a small village along the Cambodian-Vietnamese border. But when Koy was only nine years old, a devastating drought had been followed by a typhoon that wiped out half the region's rice crop. An old, bent-over Chinese man from the capital appeared in the village one day, and offered a handful of piasters for Koy and her older sister.

Her mother's sobs had brought Koy sneaking up to the bamboo shades that separated their meager hut into living and sleeping quarters. The sight of her older sister standing naked and humiliated in the middle of the room as the stranger examined her breasts and buttocks by candlelight brought a silent shock to the nine-year-old. Her father's head nodding as each *P*-note was counted and dropped into his palm was the last scene registering in her mind as Koy gathered up her few earthly possessions and vanished out the back window.

As were most dwellings in the Mnong villages, the hut was built atop stilts, and she nearly broke a leg dropping to the ground, but no one heard her.

Nobody except one of the older married men in her hamlet, a tall, husky hunter known throughout the valley for his skills with bow and arrow, who followed her, at a distance, out beyond the village's protective ring of campfires to the foot of the rain forest.

There Koy promptly halted, unsure where exactly she would go now.

A panther screamed somewhere in the distance. Her eyes locked onto the orange crescent moon riding the horizon, and an owl hooted down at her from the branches overhead. Backing away from the imposing tree line, Koy tripped and fell backward as something scampered up through the branches above her head. It was as if a thousand eyes were staring down at her from the veil of darkness, daring her to leave her hamlet and venture into the dark and into their hostile clutches. She scooted back on her haunches through the musky leaves, but the little girl knew she could not go back to her hut.

Even nine-year-olds heard the stories about the dirty old man from a place called Cho Lon, where the streets were made of black rock, glowing lights twinkled as far as the eye could see, and little girls grew into young women on their backs, or their knees—only to be tossed into the gutter when they could no longer perform, or their looks had deserted them.

Koy scooted back on her haunches through the musky leaves and bumped into the hunter's boots—boots he had taken off a dead Frenchman when hunting men was more profitable than hunting the elephants of the Central Highlands. Stories told of the hunter were even more distressing than those about the bordellos, and Koy was terrified of the man. But he was gentle enough

6

that first night.

"And where does little Koy run to in the middle of the night?"

He had clamped ironlike fingers along her elbows and lifted her off the ground from behind, then twirled her around in the air to face him.

"You wouldn't be trying to run away like Venn did a few days ago, would you?"

She broke down and told him everything: about the old man from Cho Lon, and how her sister was standing naked before him being *inspected* like poultry at market! And how she had heard stories that life as a prostitute was horrible, that old men in the big city liked little nine-year-olds even more than young women her sister's age. Koy was positive she would just *die* if destiny betrayed her so and she was forced into a life of pain and shame before she had even been given a chance to grow up.

The hunter had not dragged her back to her father's hut, as she feared he would. Instead, he gently led her back to his own home and told his beautiful wife to rise from the sleeping mats and warm some *pho* for the both of them.

Koy would never forget the hunter's wife. Even in the middle of the night, with little time to brush her hair or wipe the cooking fire soot from her face, she was so pretty: like the women on the cover of magazines her mother had shown her in Plei Me, at the open-air market. The woman was definitely not of this place. Perhaps the city—but not even Pleiku, or Hue, where the emperor and all the emperors before him lived. No, she was a southern girl. From Saigon. Or maybe even beyond the sea.

Koy had heard there were lands far away, beneath the dreamy clouds of dawn and sunset—the Frenchmen were proof of that. But this woman had dark, sloe eyes, the same as herself. Koy had heard of Hong Kong—all the girls had: That was where the magazines came from. But the hunter's wife spoke the local dialect as if born in the region, or at least having lived there several years. And she had surely been the woman of the hunter's hut for as long as Koy could remember. Someday, when she was older and wiser, and as wealthy or even more so than the village chieftain, Koy would venture to one of those distant cities with strange-sounding names: Singapore, or Malaysia, or Bangkok.

Her father maintained that there were no such lands—that Plei Me and the hills surrounding her had always been their home, had been the home of their ancestors, and was all they would ever need. The magazines she told him about were from Sin City, her father claimed. There was no such thing as Hong Kong. But Koy was mischievous and laughed in front of others, threatening to leave him when she was old enough to find out for herself. Her older sister had defended Koy, saying she just might go along if the old man kept them working in the rice paddies from down until dusk. Their father lost face over the incident, for Mnong custom, as in most traditional Vietnamese families, holds that the oldest daughter must remain in the home to take care of her parents as they age and become elderly, and he never allowed them to go to the open-air market to stare in awe up at the magazines again.

After the hunter had poured Koy her third bowl of soup—she was amazed and impressed: It actually had pieces of chicken in it, instead of just rice and sprouts—he began talking with the little nine-year-old about the world. He assured her there was indeed a Hong Kong, and a Bangkok and a Singapore—his wife was evidence a place called Phnom Penh truly existed—and he told her about France, and the Soviet Union, and the land called the United States, where the long-nosed, hairy-armed American came from. And he told her who were friends to The Cause, and who were not.

Then he told her about *The Cause*.

Vietnam had once been a very beautiful country, he explained. No bombs in the night. No helicopters in the air, disturbing the peace and serenity of the land of

8

their ancestors. No round-eyed, white-haired devils telling them how to live so that they could be more like the legendary U.S.A.

The hunter twisted history a bit to suit his needs, and before they were through their fourth bowl of soup, Koy hated not only all strangers, but also the old man from Cho Lon. She wanted to go back to her hut and punch him one—*soc mau* the old bastard—but the hunter and his wife convinced Koy that the pimp was not worth any more of her emotional anguish. In the morning, they would take her to a secret place, where there were other children her age . . . children who were really learning what life and destiny and worth were all about, and no longer had to work in the rice paddies from dawn until dusk.

The next day they took her to the tunnels.

For nearly a year she attended a sort of extended field trip, which taught her about survival in the wilderness, and also taught her about the world.

When she became eleven, she accompanied the hunter and his wife on a trek through the jungles to a mystical land of temples and incense and big buildings. Phnom Penh.

Koy attended school there for three years, where she learned to read and write proficiently in both Vietnamese and Cambodian. And then they taught her how to use a rifle.

At thirteen, Koy was sent back to the hills and valleys of Plei Me with several other children-soldiers. Dwarfed by their weapons, the youths took up residence with other guerrillas in the caves at the foot of the Chu Pong itself. There they would patiently wait and watch, until they were called upon and given a mission.

The Cause . . . Koy still didn't really understand The Cause, but the last three years harassing and ambushing the Americans and their Yarde strikers had been more fun than she could stand. And the "operations," as the hunter called them, enabled her to live the way men

9

lived: bold and free. And not as women in her village had always existed: passive and protected, confined to their huts, or the communal fires, or the washing streams. The raids around Plei Me were always meticulously planned by the hunter, it seemed, so that none of the youngsters ever really came closer to danger than a lucky tracer or two. Hand-to-hand combat was never on the agenda, no breeching of perimeters fell into their list of objectives. The teams Koy accompanied into the boonies merely hurled Molotovs, or fired rag-tipped arrows at the enemy from a safe distance. The hunter was building them up for something big, no doubt, but he was in no hurry. For three years, all Koy and her friends did was travel from isolated outpost to isolated outpost, taunting the Americans and their Montagnarde mercs. It was really no different from the hide-and-seek games she'd played as a child. Except once the hiding place had concealed a tiger, and the mine they played with now had blown off the hand or foot of more than a couple of her friends.

Koy stared down at the concertina wire again. There were only a few strands, and no poles or reinforcing whatsoever. Here and there the loops were nailed to a tree. It obviously all ran back to an alarm system somewhere. The hunter had shown Koy and the others how the Americans set up their early-warning devices, and how easy it was to breech them. Koy stared at the wires, then she glanced over at the empty pails. She reholstered her Chinese-made revolver and rose slightly, seeking out the helicopter again. It had landed within the camp walls, and she could no longer see the shark's teeth painted along the front snout, but the rotors were still slapping at the thick layers of muggy heat enveloping the valley.

The gunships . . . Cobras, the hunter called them. They had been swooping low over Plei Me for more than a week now, Plei Me and the whole of the Ia Drang Valley. The hunter and all the other cell leaders were at a loss to explain all the fly-overs—helicopters were not new to the highlands, but these "Cobras" accented American superiority in the skies of Vietnam, if not her jungles—they were of the latest design, obviously: more maneuverable and equipped with more firepower, though only two pilots rode them into the swirling shrapnel and billowing gunsmoke. These Cobras also signaled the arrival of a new kind of infantry unit: airmobile troopers. The United States Army was definitely up to no good. The nineteen-year-old woman dropped into a squat.

Koy stared at the sparkling barbs of razor chips on the concertina. She glanced down at the harsh khaki fabric against her chest—for once wishing her breasts had not matured so—then back at the wire. Sighing, she looked back over her shoulder to ensure she was still alone, then began unbuttoning the shirt. A few few seconds later, she removed her gunbelt.

Koy kicked her sandals off silently, dropped back onto her haunches from the casual squat, and slipped her trousers down over flaring, deeply tanned thighs. The trousers were of black calico—as harsh, if not more so, than the camou-streaked khaki—and Koy used them to wrap her other clothes with the crotch section. She then rose to her tiptoes and tied the pants legs around the highest branch she could reach, back behind the outer trees—out of sight. Pulling a small vial of bug repellent from a pouch on the pistol belt and setting it aside, she hid the holstered weapon inside a hollowed-out tree trunk.

Koy's hair was as black as the darkest lacquer-wood tray. Beneath the sun—or moon and stars—it seemed to sparkle like silk, a quality many Asian women of pure Vietnamese blood possessed. The long strands fell to her waist, and she pulled them together into a tight ponytail, which she held in place with a jade-and-ivory hairpin, one of the few items of jewelry the former peasant girl owned.

The preliminaries taken care of, Koy took a small

11

amount of the bug repellent in her palm and spread it over her upper arms and chest. The thick, oily substance took on a golden hue under the sun as the sizzling orb cleared the eastern horizon. A pair of dragonflies prowling the tree line spotted her and darted down to within a few inches of Koy's face, but she ignored them, choosing to spread the oil across her thighs and calves rather than disturb the omen. The Mnong believed dragonflies—especially greenish-blue ones like these—were extremely good luck if they arrived in pairs.

Lovers, she could still hear her older sister telling her the legends. *They carry the souls of dragons . . . and now they are lovers . . . .*

Koy spread a small amount of oil along the slope between her breasts, and she slowly rubbed it into her nipples, feeling them grow taut and erect as she closed her eyes against the harsh rays of the sun, and her thoughts drifted from dragons to the hunter, and the men she lived with but never touched. She thought about the American soldiers, and the stories her girl friends told about them in front of the midnight campfires . . . the fantasies they conjured up, despite their desire to kill all men with golden locks or eyes the color of the sky . . . fantasies they could never share when the hunter or his men were around.

Koy rubbed the oil in briskly, feeling the heat within herself grow, and her hands dropped to her waist and below, massaging against the heat, experiencing emotions that were new and pleasurable, yet strange. Emotions and feelings that had no place in this jungle, or did they? Only last night, they all laughed and giggled at the primitive roar and growl and erotic echoes of two tigers mating somewhere beyond the bamboo. *That* had been natural, but what was she feeling now?

Before she fled with the hunter, Koy could remember the girls of her village being traded into marriage at the ages of fifteen and sixteen. She could still remember, with crystal clarity, how her sister was sold to the man from Cho Lon when she was only twelve. How many young bucks she must have had between her legs before she even became a woman!

Laughing at the thought—and ignoring the pain in her heart that the memory brought on—Koy fell back onto her elbows. She opened her tightly clenched eyelids, feeling guilty now at her outburst. But it was true: She was nineteen now, had killed three men from a distance—that she knew of—but had yet to have one kiss her on the lips.

Not that the hunter hadn't tried several times in the past. Koy thanked Buddha the hunter's wife was ever-vigilant. A cold woman with icy eyes, she never smiled and rarely had a kind word for Koy. The hunter's wife kept a long, ugly dagger on her belt even when she wore a sarong. Koy was not sure if she was saving it to keep her husband in line or to gut the first female guerrilla who tried to take him from her.

Koy finished rubbing the last of the oil along the insides of her thighs, then brushed her hands off, closing her eyes again as she glanced away from her crotch—trying to ignore the tingle of pleasure and pangs of guilt wracking her body. The hunter *and* his wife would both go into a fit if they saw her like this: Training sessions involving tactics to breech and penetrate perimeter wire encouraged young sappers to strip naked if it was going to be a tight squeeze—barbs might catch onto long hair or clothing and go unnoticed until they triggered an alarm or pulled a trip wire. When naked, every inch of your body became a part of your surroundings. You *felt* everything that touched you. But even body parts could snag concertina wire. Bug juice or oil often allowed a sapper to slide beneath or through the barbs more easily, and the insulation sometimes prevented lacerations where the razorlike blades would definitely have gouged into the rough surface of unlubricated skin.

Koy lay down on her back and slid under the first wire without incident, but the others were planted closer to the ground. She was glad she had oiled down her breasts, hips, and knees, and not just her shoulders and buttocks, as the hunter trained them all to do in the past. The hunter wanted them all to breech the wire crawling along on their chests, but Koy felt more comfortable sliding through the dirt or leaves on her back. She felt safer when she could watch the sky—the gunships came from the sky. She could easily glance back to gauge her progress and the enemy in this manner; and should the day come when a guard or sentry killed Koy, she wanted to be staring up at the stars when it happened. The Mnong believe night stars are their ancestors smiling down on them.

She had just succeeded in getting both shoulders and arms under the second strand when the treetops began to shudder. Particles from the rotting jungle floor were lifted into a blinding whirlwind as if by magic, and suddenly her ears were filled with a terrifying *chop-chop-chop!* vibration. A downblast of warm air engulfed her body and forced the strands down against her flesh. A razor blade began to slit the nipple over her wildly racing heart.

Koy bit down onto her lower lip, but she could not help herself: She screamed as the monstrous metallic predator slowly passed over her—it was only a few meters above the swaying palms. Huge steel blades danced in a mesmerizing blur of silver, creating almost a halo effect, though Koy was Buddhist, and did not know what a halo was.

Koy did not know that the helicopter was a sky-crane—the most powerful rotored craft in the American arsenal—and she had no way of knowing that the olive-drab structure suspended beneath the chopper was actually a fully assembled guard tower, brought in from Pleiku to replace the structure Koy and her team of juvenile insurgents had destroyed the night before.

The bottom poles of the tower knocked the fronds from several trees as the skycrane dropped lower and lower for its landing within the Special Forces camp at

14

Plei Me. From the corners of her eyes, Koy watched the Cobra escort ship dart back and forth along the opposite tree line. She doubted its pilot could see her from this angle.

The strands of concertina wire Koy was trying to slide beneath were some type of warning system the Americans had devised. It was laid in place several hundred meters outside the main perimeter defenses, and far away from the actual chain link fencing that enclosed the triangular compound. Portions of this "warning system" could not be seen from the guard towers and bordered the edge of the jungle itself.

Koy lay naked and helpless beneath the concertina as the skycrane and its payload passed directly overhead. The craft's shadow covered her for an instant, but then a soldier was suddenly hanging out a side hatch. He was motioning someone else up to his position—a man armed with a submachine gun.

And now he was pointing straight down at Koy.

CHAPTER 2

Specialist Fourth Class Treat Brody glanced down at the treetops a hundred meters below the hatch opening, frowned, and shook his head from side to side. He leaned out a little for a better look at the payload dangling on cables beneath the CH-54 Skycrane and shook his head again.

"Your first trip on a Skycrane?" The PFC crouched on the other side of the hatch cradled an MP-40 submachine gun in his arms. He was leering at Brody with an almost demonic Death's-head grin.

"Yah!" Brody had to shout against the enormous roar of rotors overhead. The tremendous downblast seemed to carry his words straight down into the jungle— refusing to let them linger between mere mortals—and he was unsure the soldier across from him could hear anything. "But that's not what's botherin' me," he continued anyway. Brody was afraid the guard tower they were transporting to the Special Forces compound at Plei Me was going to snag one of the gnarled, fingerlike branches protruding from the triple canopy below. He was afraid the pilot was getting careless, and that they would soon be plucked from the sky and dragged down into the "Void Vicious"—as many gunnies called the hostile rain forest.

17

"You're afraid the boys up front are puffin' on pot or somethin' and we just ain't gonna clear them treetops with this goofy, no-account guard tower, right?" The private across from him nudged Brody with the cool barrel of the MP-40. Treat removed his helmet, forced sweat from his short, blond hair using his fingers.

"Something like that." Brody wondered if perhaps the pilots were flying low just to impress him. He'd been riding gunships for quite a while now, and even the old-timers with no more WO notches to climb had been known to blaze a trail through the top canopy in hopes of increasing the pucker factor of any newbies on board. He tugged at his thick mustache, which was always in need of a trim.

"Well, set your mind at ease, boy . . . ." The PFC's facial expression changed when Brody glared across the cube of dead space at him. "Uh . . . I mean Specialist." Brody had not been irritated by anything involving rank. He just didn't like being called "boy" by some hot dog a couple years his junior with half his experience behind an M-60. The clown wasn't even wearing a Hog Heaven patch on his flak jacket. "What I meant was that they always fly low like this on their approach to Plei Me. We've had some problems before with palm-frond snipers, and . . . ."

Brody waved him silent. "Fine, fine." *Asshole*. He hoped the kid read lips.

Palm-frond sniper, my ass. What the hell kind of new term was that? Something fancy for treetop rifleman, or what? And who did this dude think he was, acting so hot-to-trot righteous without having even half a Hog-60 in his hatch? What the hell did he think he was going to accomplish with an old German-made MP-40?

"That's what I get for volunteerin'," Brody muttered, leaning out again to get a look at the triangle-shaped installation a half klick ahead.

"Huh?" the grunt across from him shouted above the increasing clamor of monstrous blades overhead as the pilot changed pitch and began descending through a

18

break in the trees—trees that rose two, even three hundred feet off the jungle floor.

"Nothin'." Brody pulled a small pocket notebook from his flak jacket and opened it to the halfway point.

"*What*!?" The youth with the submachine gun leaned closer, and one of the Saigon phone books under his rump slipped from the teetering pile of others and plummeted down into the collage of rain-forest greens.

"I said that's what I get for volunteer—"

"You fucking volunteered to fly out here to Plei Me?" But the incredulous look on the PFC's face quickly disappeared. "Yah, I know what you mean. *Every*one wants to fly aboard a skycrane . . . at least once. It's got a meaner downblast than even a twin-rotored Chinook." He held his hand out the hatch and was almost jerked out into the void by the rotorwash. Laughing hysterically at the private little joke, he tapped the monkeystrap attached to the back of his web belt and locked his eyes with Brody. "Definitely a fucking lifesaver . . ."

"I hear ya, brother." Brody began writing something in the tiny notebook.

"Yah, definitely."

Fourteen July, 1965, Brody wrote at the top of a page. *Resupply run, Pleiku to Plei Me SF/CIDG compound. One guard tower. Workhorse: skycrane. Mindfuck to the max. Outpost manned by 415 Yardes, 14 LLLB's, and 12 Green Berets.*

"Say, what you writin' down there, brother?"

The grunt with the MP-40 had once been very stocky—Brody could tell by the way he sat hunched over—but the Nam heat, rigors, and long hours off the ground had caused him to lose forty or fifty pounds. His forearms and clean-shaven face were deeply tanned, but the patch of chest where his flak jacket and shirt were unbuttoned was white as snow. His hair, once brown, had been streaked blond by the tropical sun and was, against regulations, nearly an inch over his ears. Brody could not tell what color his eyes were because

19

he wore mirrored sunglasses above the shit-eating grin, and all the Spec-4 could see was the reflection of his own thousand-yard stare. "You keepin' a fuckin' diary or somethin'?"

"Something like that." Brody glanced up at him after finishing a sentence. He gave the PFC a tough, wanna-make-something-of-it look. It was a challenging look that revealed who was definitely the more seasoned vet. It was a grimace both pained and weary . . . a look that told the grunt with the MP-40 Brody ate punks for breakfast. What the hell kind of action was there to be found aboard a skycrane, anyway? he asked himself, wondering if the PFC had ever even fired the MP-40 in anger before. "Haven't you ever heard of a logbook?" After *12 Green Berets*, he scribbled in *Operation Detachment A-217*.

"A logbook?" The soldier looked dumbfounded.

"Yah . . . you know, a record of the flights you've made, and—"

"Only the peter pilots keep logbooks."

Brody bit his lower lip, trying to maintain control. He shook his head slowly, then gave up, deciding to simply stare down into the Void for the rest of the flight.

"Look, I didn't mean nothin' by it," the man across from him said after a few seconds passed. "What's your name, anyway." He extended a hand. "They call me Deadmeat."

A slight grin crept across Brody's features, and he looked up at the private again. "Deadmeat?" He laughed for the first time.

The PFC glanced away, nodding in the affirmative. "Yah, but it's not for the reason you might think. Has nothin' to do with my whanger . . . or the body count."

"I didn't think it—"

"We're used a lot for water buffalo removal," Deadmeat explained seriously.

"Water buffalo what?" Brody started with the routine handshake, but Deadmeat clasped his forearm instead,

20

Indian-style—at least, *TV Indian* style, Brody decided.

"You've heard of the problems we've been having with some of the jarheads lately, haven't you?" Deadmeat shook his head as if discussing an unruly student with the boy's father. "They hump the boonies day in and day out, makin' less and less contact the last couple weeks, except to get sniped at from the edge of this or that VC-controlled village . . ."

"So, anyway . . ." Brody was slipping the pocket notebook back into his flak vest.

"So anyway, some of the jarheads get real bored, you know? They get real bored with bein' shot at by chickenshit phantoms in black pajamas who disappear down into their spiderholes instead o' engagin' the guys on patrol with a little honest-to-God gunplay . . . ."

"I can understand the frustrations they must feel."

"Well, when the snipers beat feet and retreat and the jarheads spend several hours searchin' for ol' Luke but without success . . . well, naturally, tempers flare.
. . ."

"Right-o."

"And, since the zip-in-question was more than likely from the village where the tunnels run under, it's natural to assume the whole God-damned *ville* is Cong to the core, right?"

"Possibly, but—"

"Ah-*HA*!" The PFC pointed a finger at Brody as the skycrane began its landing, then abruptly pulled up and banked around for another pass. "A typical liberal lunatic!" he accused with a smile.

"Not necessarily." Brody was concentrating on the ground now—why had they gone around? Snipers? He knew he'd never be able to hear any discharges due to the roar of the chopper blades overhead. But no rounds had punched up through the floor of the craft, and Deadmeat didn't seem too concerned about the delay. Perhaps the pilot had come in on the wrong approach, or another chopper was ascending, or they couldn't bring the guard tower in from this angle, or . . .

"You thought I was gonna reveal the jarheads then proceeded to waste all the dinks in the commie-controlled hamlet, right? You thought I was gonna brag about some sort of hushed-up, never-heard-about atrocity, right?" Deadmeat interrupted Brody's thoughts again.

"Not really, but I'll bet you're gonna tell me something about water buffalos that's gonna get the SPCA in an uproar."

"What the hell is the SP—whatever you said?" Deadmeat stared at him from the corner of an eye.

"The Society for the Prevention of Cruelty to Animals."

"Oh . . ." Deadmeat pondered that for a moment. "Say, you aren't one of them college-edufuckingcated draftees, are you?"

"Naw." Brody tried to sound offended. "Just a door gunner from the Golf Course, pal."

Deadmeat recognized the camp nickname. "An Khe?"

"Yah. Rumor Control has it we're buildin' up to assault the Ia Drang, and I was spendin' some of my leave time checkin' out different places in the Central Highlands," Brody started to explain.

"You must like to travel." Deadmeat's words were laced with mild sarcasm.

"Cut me some slack, okay?" Brody took a splinter of bamboo from one of his flak-vest pockets and began running it back and forth through a slight gap in his two front teeth.

"You actually used up some o' your leave time to visit us out here in Pleiku City?"

"Well, I only had a couple of days left out o' my annual thirty, and I get my next thirty starting next month, and, though the Army don't have comp time, we sort of do in the 7th Cav of the First, if you know what I mean, and I just wanted to get it off the company books before Ia Drang or whatever fate takes us, because word tricklin' down the wait-a-minute vine has it we're

22

headed straight into a shit storm, and I don't want 'em to 'box me up and ship me home' unless I've used up all the leave time that's comin' to me . . . know what I mean?"

"Yah." Deadmeat seemed to contemplate what Brody had just told him. "And you're right . . . ."

"About what—Ia Drang?"

"Yep. They say that valley is just ass-crammed with Cong and NVA Regulars. Me—I'd just as soon finish out my Tour 365 escortin' skycranes on these shitless REMF resupply runs."

Brody noticed the Combat Infantry Badge patch sewn on the trooper's flak vest over his heart but didn't pursue the issue of skate jobs versus fire missions into the Void. "So anyway, about the water buffalos . . ."

"Uh . . . right, so anyways some of these jarheads get pissed about the snipers and no VC skullcaps to drink their boiling beer from, you know? So they draw a bead on the closest water buffalo and cancel the critter's ticket. Vietnamese value their damn water buffalos more than their wives and daughters, if you know what I mean." Deadmeat laughed.

"Kinda like the way *we* feel about our sportscars back in The World." Brody shrugged, resigned to playing the game.

"*Right!*" Deadmeat nodded, happy Brody was catching on so quickly. "But you know how Uncle Sammy is about things like that. He doesn't look at it as a case of getting even instead of insane."

"Uncle Sammy views it as a defeat for the hearts-and-minds program," Brody volunteered. "A setback for the Civic Action crap, psy-ops, and all of that."

"*Right-o*, chump! I can see I don't have to spell it out for you. So anyways, the U.S. Government pays off the farmer after he complains to the Saigon Government via his province chieftain, and we get this list of hamlets to visit where we got to set down and cart off the buffalo—or what's left of it—after the farmer and his family and half the villagers carve up the remains. *I* happen to be the sucker who 'gets' to drop down to the ground and wrap all the ropes and cables around ol' Mister Buffalo so the skycrane can hoist his butt off the ground, and back to the rear. That's why they call me Deadmeat."

"R.H.I.P." Brody spoke the initials as a two-syllable word.

"Huh?" Deadmeat cast him a quizical look. "'Our hip'?"

"Rank Has Its Privileges," he replied matter-of-factly.

"Oh, yeah . . . really. I don't mind the job, though. Despite the carcasses being alongside commysymp villages, I've never been sniped at while hookin' one o' the beasts up."

"Not that you know of."

"Huh?"

Using his thumb, Brody motioned above their heads, at the rotors. "It'd be kind of hard to hear gunshots unless you saw smoke, or tracers, or—"

"Or caught a round personally." Deadmeat made the sign of the cross as if knocking on wood.

"Right." Brody sort of changed the subject. In Vietnam, words—the mere discussion of a forbidden subject—were believed to possess actual power, according to the natives. Talking about something bad could actually bring the dreaded thing about. "So are you tellin' me Uncle Sammy actually has a mass grave or something somewhere where you guys and your skycranes dump the carcasses?"

"Yeah, but that's boring!" Deadmeat was concentrating on their final approach as the helicopter slowed considerably and treetops brushing against its support poles caused the guard tower to sway form side to side, which in turn caused the skycrane to roll slightly, like a ship in high seas. "I'd rather talk about something like pussy. None o' this local ying-yang, mind you—it's a bit too exotic for my . . . tastes!" He laughed above the increasing downblast. "But blond strands caught be-

24

tween my teeth, you know?"

"I think I catch your drift, Deadmeat."

"Yah, *ching-ching*, brother. Hell, they got this donut dolly up in Danang. I've only seen her once, but I'd wager a month's pay, including combat pay, that she's a true blonde."

"You're full of it, friend. Why the heck would she want to come over to Vietnam . . . unless she's a cherry girl with a taut tit for uniforms."

"Don't you wanna know how I know?" Deadmeat persisted, but Brody didn't seem very interested.

"Not particularly."

"Her underarms, man! The chick don't shave her underarms," Deadmeat revealed. "She's got these cute little blond curls under there. . . ."

"You're grossin' me out, Deadmeat!"

"No. Really, man! You've just gotta see her. Since you're jumpin' hops all around the Highlands, you just gotta visit the Doom pussies!"

"The *what*?"

"The round-eyes who hang out at the Danang Officers' Open Mess." Deadmeat beamed with the knowledge he, too, knew an acronym or two. "This one donut dolly, or Red Cross girl, or whatever she is—man, I *dreammm* about lying on the beach down in Vung Tau, and she walks by in her little itzy-bitzy see-thru bikini, and I just flash my best lizard-tongued grin in her direction, and next think I know she's sitting on my face. Sittin . . . on . . . my . . . face, man," he repeated the words slowly, as it it was important Brody understood completely. "You just *gotta* stop by and meet her when you get to Danang, dude . . . tell her you rode the big one—a skycrane—into Plei Me with . . . with . . ."

"Yeah." Brody smiled in anticipation. "What phony name did you use on her? Deadmeat?"

"I think . . . uh, I think . . ." Deadmeat pondered this sudden dilemma for a moment, then said, "Aw, just make up somethin' good, bud. A million guys prob'ly put the make on her every day. She wouldn't remember names."

"I'll ask her if she remembers the guy with the lizard's tongue."

Deadmeat laughed louder than before and slapped his knee. "Yeah, that's a good one, pal! Tell her *that*! Say, what was your name again?"

Brody shifted his chest to the right, so Deadmeat could read his name tag.

Deadmeat looked suddenly impressed. "The Brody?" he asked. "The Treat Brody from the 7th of the First? Brody the Whoremonger?"

"The one and only." Brody blushed slightly. He had no idea his reputation had traveled beyond An Khe. "Don't believe anything you've heard." He was expecting Deadmeat would bring up something about Treat's goal to bed down a cherry girl in every free country of the Orient before he completed his military service.

Deadmeat threw him a curve. "They say you're workin' on Numba 30. They say you're a real bad ass when it comes to hand-to-hand. They say you went on an FB last week to rescue a Khmer princess or something, and that you never found the cunt, but took out five Cong bare-handed after your rifle ran out o' ammo. They say—"

"It wasn't quite that dramatic." Brody was usually not so humble.

"They say there were bookoo witnesses." The awe sparkled in Deadmeat's eyes. "Lawless and Gunslinger. The Black Buddha's your crew chief, right? He was there, too. They all watched you take down Numba 29 in hand-to-hand, and the Stork told one o' our pilots about it, and *he* told the guys in my platoon, who retold it to me . . . ."

"Well . . ."

"That means you're one Cong kill away from joining the Dirty Thirty." Deadmeat swallowed with a throat gone dry, and, as if unable to control a yawn after watching someone else do it, Brody also felt his Adam's

26

apple scrape against the inside of his throat.

The Dirty Thirty was the ultimate in Nam vet fraternities. But it was a club no one really wanted to join.

Everyone talked about the Dirty Thirty. Every soldier worth his salt bragged he was getting closer and closer: "Killed another Charlie last night while Lurpin' thru sector seven. That brings my count to over two dozen. Only a matter o' time before I'm in, before I'm a Dirty Thirty myself!" Few grunts actually came close to killing thirty enemy soldiers in hand-to-hand combat before they rotated back to the States. Green Berets, yes, but few Air Cav troopers—they carried too much ammo and rarely had to resort to fistfights in the sticks, like the SF and Lurp types, who often traveled light.

A door gunner's best friend was his hatch M-60, which many gunnies took to calling Hog-60's, though the old-timers complained a hog was a gunship and not just a small piece of the gunship's armament; but the younger hot dogs refused to listen to what they considered "lifters," so the term "Hog-60" stuck, at least in Echo Company of the 7th Cav of the First Air Cavalry Division. And door gunners had something else to "shoot" for. If the Lurps and the Green Berets had their infamous Dirty Thirty fraternities, the troopers of The First Team had Hog Heaven. One hundred confirmed kills by hatch M-60 propelled a door gunner into Hog Heaven. The double-vets gave him a large patch to sew onto his flak jacket across the back, the prestige that accompanied it, a slug on the arm, but little else. Once one attained his place in Hog Heaven, there were few other cliques to advance to. Men who reached 100 kills were usually short as single-digit midgets anyway, their DEROS time was fast approaching, and before they had much time to contemplate the roadblock in front of them, they were boarding that precious freedom flight back to The World.

Only maniacs like Brody the Whoremonger bucked the system, extended their combat tour another six months, and spent their off-time accompanying spooks or SOG phantoms deep into the Void in search of action and adventure. It was only a matter of time before Treat found himself eligible for initiation into hell's elite.

But there was also a stigma attached to membership in the Dirty Thirty. As far back as anyone could remember, soon after a soldier killed his thirtieth Cong and his people went through the ceremonial tradition of spilling additional blood for good luck, drinking warm booze from VC skullcaps, and sacrificing the prettiest local maiden—if one was available—strange and eerie circumstances seemed to befall the man, not to mention the fact that he almost always was killed in action during the next couple of weeks.

Only two recipients of the Dirty Thirty badge were known to still be alive. One had "left military service" and gone back to the States—where it was rumored he promptly committed suicide, but a MARS radio-phone call from Mr. Krutch proved that rumor false. The other was a Green Beret assigned to the Special Forces camp at Plei Me—an ex-Cav trooper Brody had arrived in An Khe with. And a visit with this soldier was the true reason behind The Whoremonger's ride on Dead-meat's skycrane.

The Plei Me compound was a triangular-shaped collection of under a hundred huts and some administration buildings composed of connecting longhouses. Sand-bagged bunkers here and there broke the original symmetry of the camp before it had become a strategic hamlet of the Civilian Irregular Defense Group. Guard towers rose from two of the three corners along the perimeter, and trenches fortified with old helipad tarmac and cinder blocks could be seen crisscrossing the outer boundaries of the installation. The Plei Me compound was build on a slight rise in the gently sloping hill that cut like a sickle through dense jungle on three sides of the outpost. To the west, though miles away, the tree-tangled hills gave way to the mountains overlooking the Ia Drang, and this feature would have put the Special Forces camp at a distinct disadvantage were it not for the belief that enemy troops in the area had no artillery that could reach from the Chu Pong massif down into the outpost itself.

Chain link fence topped by sagging rows of rusting concertina encircled the camp. For a dozen feet outside the fence line, punji sticks of sharpened bamboo extended all around the compound like a feces-coated moat, and a second wall of razor-sharp wire served as a buffer in front of the deadly stakes rising from the ground in a diagnoal manner.

Brody could see that the men at Plei Me had burned out the vegetation threatening to overwhelm and conceal this second fence. A flat, blackened area of land extended for twenty or thirty feet around the camp, but as the slight gulley flattened out, vines, scrub brush, reeds, and elephant grass stretched out like probing fingers from the rain forest and quickly gave way to a wall of trees that marked the edge of the jungle. Two armed mini-camps provided added security on either side.

Brody could also see something sparkling down below—something meandering through the sharp reeds and scrub brush at the edge of the blackened portion: freshly laid concertina, he decided. Recently planted strands of razor-sharp wire undoubtedly attached to an alarm system of sorts—an early-warning system, designed also to rip some Cong flesh in the process. The concertina had obviously been unreeled in a haphazard manner—it climbed rocks and boulders, disappeared underground for a few feet, actually reached up into the low branches of a couple of solitary trees, then disappeared in the elephant grass again. And what was *that*!

"Did you see that?" Brody rushed over to Dead-meat's side of the hatch and nearly fell out in his zeal to get a better look at the ground.

"See *what*?"

"A girl—*a woman*!" Brody would never forget the way she had been frozen beneath the sparkling strands of concertina, flat on her back and stark naked—her

29

breasts settling ample and full across her ribcage . . . her chest . . . her *entire body* glistening with oil the color of amber . . . *beckoning him*! One leg out, against the ground, bent at the knee . . . the other rising slightly against the concertina as the skycrane's shadow fell across her and she panicked. "A nude woman down there! Lying in . . . or *under* the wire between those clumps of trees . . . *No*! Not the perimeter!" He pointed nearer the tree line, willing Deadmeat's gaze to follow his own. "Over there!"

Deadmeat was jockying about for a better position in the hatch, but he was unable to spot the woman. "*I* don't see nothin'!" he said skeptically.

"But—" And then the guard tower suspended beneath the skycrane passed between Brody and his beckoning amber Venus, and the Whoremonger lost sight of the woman and the wire, too.

CHAPTER 3

"You guys have to get an alert team together RIGHT NOW!"

The five Green Beret NCOs who sauntered up to greet the crew of the skycrane delivering their new guard tower stared at Treat Brody as if he were shit on a shingle. Who was this Air Cav screwball moochin' a ride into SF territory only to leap off his whirlybird rantin' and ravin' anyway? Not even bothering to shrug, they promptly resumed ignoring The Whoremonger.

Brody recognized First Sergeant stripes on a man staring down the hill toward them from the mess hall. "Top! *Top!*" he cried the informal greeting for an NCO with "diamonds" between his chevrons. "You just gotta get an alert team or a patrol or somethin' together—I'll go with you!—and search the outer perimeter along the southwest there . . . or is it southeast?" Brody glanced over at the rising sun, shielding his eyes with one hand.

"Whoa . . . whoa, son! Slow down! What's the skinny, anyway?" The tall, lanky first sergeant glanced over at a bewildered-looking Deadmeat, the huge idling helicopter cooling down behind him, then back at Brody. His eyes focused on the subdued First Air Cav patch on the soldier's right shoulder. "Who the hell are you?"

"Brody, sir! Treat Brody—Specialist Fourth Class. I used to be a corporal but after they busted me back from buck sergeant to E-4 they made me a specialist instead. But we're wastin' time, sir! We gotta get an alert team or something together, and—"

"*Where* are you from?" It was obvious to the first sergeant this enlisted man was not part of the skycrane crew.

"Echo Company, sir . . . 7th Cav of the First, and o' An Khe! *Pegasus* is my bird, Black Buddha's my crew chief, Snakeman Fletcher's my best buddy, though I don't know why sometimes, and—"

"*Sergeant* Zack's your crew chief, son?" Top put a large hand against Brody's chest as if to slow his heartbeat down.

"The one and only, sir!"

The first sergeant patted Brody on the back and turned in the direction of the mess hall. "What exactly is it you got your hemorrhoids all in an uproar about, son?" Two heavily armed Montagnardes were running down toward them, alarmed by the commotion Brody was causing, but the NCO towering over the Whoremonger waved them off. "Your skycrane pilot didn't radio my commo man in the CP about any trouble."

"That's 'cause they don't believe me, Top!"

"Believe you about *what*, son?"

Brody skidded to a stop, refusing to allow the first sergeant to lead him another step. "A woman, sir!"

"If you don't quit calling me 'sir,' I'm gonna give you a knuckle sandwich, son: I ain't no officer. I *work* for a living." Brody ignored the oldest Army line that had floated around military reservations since Christ was a corporal. Ever since he had been a boot recruit, first sergeants had terrified him. They were not commissioned officers, but they were sirs nevertheless, in his book. And this old-timer had been the first "top sergeant" to reprimand him for using the word. "We got a lotta women outside the wire, Specialist. Was she

32

hanging' AK's and Chicom grenades on her hips, or what?''

"She was naked, sir!"

"What!" The first sergeant rested his massive hands on his hips in a skeptical stance. Several of the jungle fighters who'd shown no interest in Brody's excitement earlier were now cocking eyebrows his direction, or falling in behind Top.

"Naked! She was butt-ass naked, and beautiful as a Tu Do street nude painted in neon on velvet!"

"*What*!?" Several of the younger Green Berets echoed Top's repeated question.

"And she was on her back in the elephant grass, down at the outer stretch of perimeter wire you got strung down there."

"What was she doin' 'down on her back'?" A short, stocky staff-sergeant with jump wings over his CIB cracked the remark, and several others laughed.

"Like I told Deadmeat back there—"

"*Deadmeat*?"

". . . She was slidin'; on her back *under* the concertina!"

The look of restrained amusement vanished from the first sergeant's face. "*That's* why she was 'butt-ass naked'!" He motioned for the Yarde strikers to double-time down to the location after all. He drew his .45 pistol, chambered a round, and waved the group of tired-looking Green Berets after him as he started down to the compound's main gate. "Was she oiled down, son? Or draggin' any satchel charges after her?"

"I couldn't tell . . . I don't think so—we passed over her too quickly. I just barely caught a glimpse of that heavenly set o' knockers, you know? I couldn't believe it at first. I don't know how the pilot missed her, even though I gotta admit I just barely caught a glimpse o' her through the two trees down there!"

"They were probably too concerned with getting the guard tower over the fence line." Top grabbed the mike from a prick-25 radio his CQ hustled up with. A few terse sentences later, he turned to Brody again. "A spotter plane was in the area just prior to your arrival, but he didn't see anything either."

"The Cobra!" Brody realized for the first time he was without a weapon, but he still followed the Special Forces squad through the compound gate as they hustled toward the southwest quadrant of the camp. "What about the WO piloting that snake that escorted us in? Surely he—"

"He was the *first* one I just check with," the first sergeant revealed. "Negative twice."

Once outside the compound, they fanned out in three fast-moving groups: The team led by the first sergeant kept along the wire but took the fastest direct approach through the mine field, going by Brody's directions; the second team, composed of five exhausted Green Berets fresh in from two weeks on an FOB Lurp patrol, trotted straight down the main access road to the camp, with the intention of heading off any sappers who were spooked by the choppers and attempting to retreat back into the rain forest; the third team was led by a soldier who appeared to be the youngest American there. He rounded up a half dozen Yarde Strikers who'd been loitering at the main gate and led them on a brisk recon of the perimeter entirely opposite where Brody had seen his "naked lady," just in case Charlie was using her as a decoy or distraction and was setting up to hit the other side of the camp.

They found no one.

A couple of Green Berets did locate two trees that most closely resembled the pair Brody had seen from the air, but there were no foot, sandal, or boot prints around them—which of course, meant nothing, assuming they were dealing with a hard-core commie female. Even the NVA's camp followers were taught how to "sanitize" an area.

The two Green Berets who'd spotted the trees were positive they'd also located haunch marks in the dirt, though. "And the nicest, roundest, most gorgeous buttocks impressions I think I've seen during my whole illustrious career with this man's army," one declared.

"Definitely a woman's ass," his buddy added.

"And a young one at that."

"No sag."

"Right."

"How the hell can you tell?" Brody dropped into an indigenous squat that brought a disgusted smirk to the lips of many of the men standing behind him. "To me they just look like—"

"Well, sure . . ." One of the jungle experts dropped into a squat beside the Whoremonger. "You can't go by the crescent moons here." He touched the impressions made by Koy's sliding haunches gently, as if he could feel her flesh by examining them in that manner. "A guy's butt don't look much different."

"You should know, *fella*," one of the squad members in the back of the group whispered with a faint lisp, but no one laughed. The first sergeant hadn't *cleared* anyone to laugh yet—there might still be hostiles in the area.

The jungle expert ignored the comedian. "What you gotta go by are . . . ahhh, yes . . . right *here*." He motioned Brody's face closer to the dirt, and, although the Whoremonger had been born at night and expected a practical joke, he hadn't been born last night, and he complied without protest. "You gotta go by these here tiny furrows in the dirt, my man . . . Is it clear to ya what I'm talkin' about?"

"I think so . . ." Brody scratched at his earlobe and glanced back at the others with an I'm-not-as-stupid-as-you-guys-think expression.

"Right *here*. These *furrows*, boy. Dual sets. Just like skid marks."

A chuckle arose from several soldiers clustered behind Top.

"*Those* furrows?" Brody wiped sweat from his brow with the back of his hand.

"Yah. Now get a good look at them, my man . . .

'cause you don't see tracks this distinct too often. . . ."

"Really?" Brody did not mock the Green Beret. He struggled to keep sarcasm out of his tone.

"Yeah . . ."

"Well, just what exactly made those there furrows, Sarge?" he asked, after the mandatory moment of suspense had passed without an explanation. This game was getting old. Bookoo old, *rikky-tik*.

"Them are clit marks, my man." The Special Forces sergeant licked his lips with a smacking sound.

"'Clit' marks?" Brody's voice rose, and a couple of the jungle experts huddled around them crowded closer.

"Yep. The bitch was quite a speciman."

"Huh?" Brody rose from his squat, suddenly exhausted—was it from the chopper ride, or this field trip lecture?—and wiped sweat off his forehead again.

"A true example of femininity and blooming womanhood. If ever I've seen one . . ."

"What?"

"He's tryin' to tell you those furrows were left by the lips of her . . . her you-know-what draggin' in the dust."

The first sergeant frowned slightly.

"Naw . . ." Brody shrugged his shoulders to cover the unexplainable shiver running through him.

"That's what he's tryin' to tell you, anyway." Top folded his arms across his chest.

"You sayin' I don't know my tracks?" The sergeant gave the soldier wearing yellow diamonds between his chevrons a hurt and insulted look.

"I ain't sayin' jack-shit, Ripper." The highest-ranking NCO there had taken to glancing back at the tree line behind the group. It was getting too quiet. Much too quiet. "I'm just repeatin' to the First Cav trooper here my current observations of this particular situation we got in front of us here, and it seems to me that—"

"Well, you're hurtin' my feelings, Top." The buck sergeant glanced away, back down at his vaginal mark-

36

ings, nearly bringing a grin to Brody's face. There was obviously no friction between the ranks here, despite the obvious game of mindfuck. It reminded him of the working relationship he and the Pack had with Zack. "You're truly hurtin' my—"

Someone yelling beyond a long clump of bamboo interrupted Sgt. Ripper. "Hey! Over fucking here!"

Brody recognized the voice instantly. Such luck! his mind laughed. He wouldn't even have to go searching for Nervous Rex. The man was right on the other side of that wall of vegetation.

Sgt. Ripper's chunky arms rose like a crucifix, shielding his tracks in the dust as the soldiers started toward the excited voice. "Whoa! Whoa, you dudes!" He had to push two of the younger Green Berets to the side, or they'd have trampled right over the "evidence." "*Whoa*! Gotta preserve the scene of da crime. Gotta preserve the scene of the crime . . . ."

Nervous Rex was nowhere to be found when they reached the other side of the bamboo. On instinct, the men fanned out, spreading away from one another, in the event they'd walked into an ambush, crouching low as they searched for the source of the voice.

Brody kept low within the reeds too. But surely they recognized Nervous Rex's voice, his mind raced. Surely they know it was Nervous Rex and not—

The Whoremonger nearly broke his ankle when one boot dropped down into the spiderhole.

Brody was convinced—though he was not thinking about it consciously at the moment—that the canvas hood of his jungle boot saved him from even spraining his ankle. The shock of dropping down into the unknown was so overpowering, he felt no pain—his only desire was to be free of the evil gobbling him up. Everything around him shifted into slow motion—everything except his boots, which had shifted into overdrive. But now the sides of the tunnel entrance were giving way, too . . . crumbling all around him . . . collapsing more quickly as he scrambled to regain his footing on the surface. "Over here!" Now he was yelling. "Over here!" He dropped his rifle the same instant his mind told him to use it as a brace—a lever to propel himself up out of the hole. *The pit*, his mind shifted gears on him as the earth drew him dowr deeper—nearly up to his shoulders now. *The pit gonna get you, boy!* He heard Sgt. Zack's laugh, and his months-old taunt. *If Void Vicious don' get you, the pit will! It gonna swallow you up whole, boy . . . swallow you up whole!* And Brody's mind flashed pictures of hell in front of his eyes as he dropped another inch . . . then a foot.

All this happened in the blink of an eye. And as the steel-plated sole of his jungle boot struck solid teakwood, he took his second breath. Brody hadn't been breathing at all, and as his lungs sucked in the humid, sticky air swirling through the bamboo, he realized for the first time that he wasn't dropping into Hades after all—his elbows were propped on the edge of the tunnel entrance . . . on its brim. And he was regaining his footing, and feeling a sharp pain in his ankle. But he was regaining footing. He was pulling himself out. Once again in control of his situation. The devil be damned.

Brody was in charge, and feeling the adrenaline course through his veins like encouragement from the gods themselves. He was feeling invincible in that second blink of an eye—indestructible, his biceps muscles bulging like a comic-book superhero's, in his imagination . . . . Any moment, he would ascend majestically over the patch of clearing. Under his own power, he would fly above the sagging coils of concertina, and—

And then the hand grabbed his foot. The hand from below. A hand that was massive. Massive and powerful. It was not the hand of a scrawny insurgent . . . a Cong guerrilla.

Brody screamed.

It was the first time he had screamed in front of other

men. In basic training he'd screamed a couple of times from pain and abuse, mostly. But in basic, he'd made the screams into motivation-charged yells—because in basic, boys became men. Brody was not embarrassed by the slip from self-control. He sincerely believed he was about to die.

"*YORRR steppin'* on my *FACE*, cunnnnnt-lips!"

It was as if the tracks of an APC had been lifted from his shoulders by the skycrane—Brody recognized the voice. Words flowed from his lips even before his brain could properly form them. Words flowed from his lips as he scampered up out of the spiderhole. "Is pussy all you guys talk about here?" he complained.

Back on the surface, Brody commenced dusting himself off, ignoring the rifle he'd been given back at the outpost. "Long time no see, Rex, ol' boy!"

"Screw you and the gunship you rode in on, Whoremonger!"

The man emerging from the tunnel did not seem in the best of spirits. Blood ran freely from the nose protruding from a charcoal-blackened face. "What kinda funky greeting was that, *anyhell*? Steppin' on ol' Nervous Rex's puss like that—*Christ*!" He wiped the blood out of his moustache with the unfolded sleeve of his fatigue blouse.

"I *tripped* down into that hold, pal." Brody brought on his most offended tone. "You gotta quit hidin' 'em in places like that. I wasn't even . . . I didn't even *know* you was down there!"

Without replying, Nervous Rex pulled a fragmentation grenade from his web belt, pulled the pin, nonchalantly dropped the explosive down into the spiderhole, then turned his back on it. As soldiers all around dropped prone or scattered for cover, Nervous Rex resumed conversing with the Whoremonger, as if nothing out of the ordinary were transpiring.

But Brody had disappeared. Brody was spread-eagled on the ground like the others. He was covering his head with scraped and bruised forearms.

Nervous Rex stared down at the soldier hugging the earth a few feet in front of his boots. As the muffled blast shook the ground slightly and sent black smoke billowing up out of the spiderhole, Nervous Rex reached down, grabbed Brody by the bicep, and hoisted him to his feet. "Now what kinda way is *that* to greet your long-lost blood brother, Trick-or-Treat?"

Crushing Treat Brody in a bearhug, Nervous Rex lifted the Spec-4 off his feet slightly, then dropped him back on the dirt. Swaying back and forth, Brody managed to keep his footing, and both men flew around as the distinct sound of someone moaning drifted up to them from deep underground somewhere.

"*Thought* I saw someone beat feet down into that spiderhole," Nervous Rex explained, handing Brody his M-16 as he drew a pistol from his web belt holster. "But I wasn't sure . . . ." From the agonized sound down in the tunnel, they couldn't tell if the exploding shrapnel had struck male meat, or female, or both.

"Was it a girl?" Brody spoke quickly as Nervous Rex started down into the spiderhole again.

"Was it a *naked* girl?" the first sergeant said loudly. "A naked Viet girl, with long black hair and—"

"Hey, cut me some slack, you bozos!" Nervous Rex dismissed them all with a wave of his free hand before disappearing down into the dark. "I already told you I wasn't sure what I saw."

Nervous Rex was a gorilla of a man. He stood nearly six-foot-four and weighed in at just under two-forty. He never would have made it into his MOS specialty—it had originally been armor—if the recruiter hadn't been hard-up for tank crewmen that month. Sgt. E-5 Nervous Rex Ritter was clean-shaven, with a jutting jaw that was both handsome and a bit comical—his buddies claimed it made him look like Dudley Doorlight, the cartoon Canadian Mountie—but his most outstanding feature were the places he was *not* clean-shaven: his biceps and legs. And his back. Nervous Rex was as hairy as a gorilla, and as big as the baddest. Normally,

40

his savage appearance was in contrast to his gentle nature and soft voice—traits that seemed to desert him when people stepped on his face.

"Sorry about the bloody nose," Brody said as he followed the monstrous tunnel rat down through the tricky spiderhole entrance.

"Don't worry about it, Trick-or-Treat," he growled. "Don't mean nothin."

Rex was the only living member of the Dirty Thirty left in Vietnam. There was one double-vet who had claimed the title and managed to escape the Orient with his life, but he was now hiding somewhere back in The World. Rumor had it the stress of achieving Dirty Thirty stardom and fame had been instrumental in driving the ex-Green Beret *dinky-dau*.

Legend had it—and the official record seemed to substantiate the stories—that shortly after an American soldier had killed ten of the enemy threefold, the odds caught up with him, Lady Luck abandoned him, and the man met a cruel death at the hands of either Charlie or the North Vietnamese. It didn't matter how good you were with a commando knife or an automatic weapon, or spook-'em tricks and booby traps. After you'd knocked off thirty phantoms in black pajamas, the eyes of the jungle were upon you. You became a most sought-after target . . . the object of every free, fire zone, the center of every sniper's scope.

That's why Nervous Rex was nervous. GI superstition and history seemed to prove he was a candidate for an olive-drab casket and a free ticket aboard the freedom bird.

Nervous Rex had no girl friends waiting for him back stateside. Not even a two-timing bitch who could write him a Dear John letter. And the local ladies couldn't bring themselves to fall in love with a man twice their size—who was sooo hairy! The only thing Sgt. Ritter had to fall back on in troubled times was his Green Beret unit, the brave fighting men who were his buddies, and his Vietnamese card-playing partners, who

41

rarely hesitated to call Nervous Rex a hairy monkey behind his back.

Though quite a contrast physically, nineteen-year-old Treat Brody exhibited courage and bravado identical to that of the soldier seven years his senior. Brody, whom the men called Whoremonger because his primary goal in life was to seduce a virgin in every country of the Orient and, failing that, bed down a bar girl in all the nations of Asia, stood an inch under six feet and, when the tropical heat didn't get him down, weighed in at around one-seventy. But his short blond hair—in contrast to Ritter's straight, black locks—and thick mustache made Nervous Rex and the Whoremonger an unlikely duo. The pair had been fast friends ever since a firefight outside An Khe several months before, though, and despite Ritter's transfer from the First Cav to Special Forces, the two had made a point of keeping in touch. Several weeks had passed before Treat learned Ritter had attained Dirty Thirty status and, now that Brody himself was on the verge of killing another commie for Christ, he felt it was imperative he seek advice from his old rice paddy daddy.

Brody hadn't expected their reunion to take place halfway down a spiderhole, however.

"I got about twenty meters up in there," Nervous Rex whispered as the two soldiers dropped onto the first horizontal level, "when I came across a whole spiderweb of trip wires."

"No shit," Brody muttered, the M-16 cradled in his arms against his side because of the cramped conditions. The Whoremonger's tone was not sarcastic. He was, in fact, awed by what he was seeing—it was his first real tunnel-clearing experience. And he was getting nervous himself now. It was dark down there. Dark and creepy. Water dripped in the distance somewhere, echoing like the eerie sounds in every Castle Dracula horror movie he'd ever seen. The moans had stopped.

"So I had to go back topside for this." Sgt. Ritter had grabbed a small satchel from the first sergeant. The

42

package contained a seismic device, he had explained. It would expedite their chances of locating a hidden passageway or secondary tunnel.

While Brody taped an L-shaped GI flashlight in the handgrips of his weapon, Nervous Rex set about warming up the small machine. Shoulda taped this sucker in place before ever takin' the afternoon off to go explorin', Brody silently reprimanded himself, but the maneuver only took a few seconds: The flashlight was hooked inside his flak jacket, and he always kept luminous tape in his first-aid pouch.

"What's the verdict?" The Whoremonger gritted his teeth after Sgt. Ritter had swept the walls, roof, and floor of the tunnel.

"It's a no-show," Nervous Rex muttered without emotion as he squinted to read a dial in the surrealistic beam from Brody's flashlight—the lens cap was red, permitting only a weak shaft of crimson to bathe the black box.

"Meaning . . ."

"Meaning I'm unable to locate any tunnels running parallel with the one we're in."

"Or even opposite."

"Right."

"Above and below."

"Sideways, upside-down, the whole kit-'n-ka-"

"Which means . . ." Brody prompted, frowning.

"Which means we get to maneuver the obstacle course Charlie's set up for us."

Ritter moved toward the unknown, away from the tunnel entrance, but Brody would not budge. "Why don't we just smoke 'em out?" he asked. He was upset with himself now. Both angry and ashamed that he suddenly wanted to back out on Nervous Rex, but his lips kept asking questions. "Why don't we just boogie on backwards and call in a tank . . . yah, a flame-throwin' tank."

"Waste o' time."

"A flame-throwin' tank that could drop its nozzle

down that spiderhole back there and fill this sucka up with napalm, or gasoline, or whatever they run off of . . . turn ol' Charlie into twice-fried guerrilla . . . make 'em all crispy critters, you know?"

Nervous Rex reached back and flipped the red lens off Brody's flashlight. "Let's go." He kept his voice low. "The more time we spend jawin', the more time they got to get away. And the more time we sit on our duffs, the longer they got to heave a claymore or somethin' our direction."

Treat Brody swallowed hard as the beam from his flashlight passed between a menacing-looking barricade of ankle-high trip wires. Fishing wire crisscrossed the floor of the packed-earth tunnel a dozen meters away from them. "How do I get myself into this crap?" he muttered under his breath, well aware he would have to go first since the flashlight was his— their guiding light was on *his* weapon.

"It's in your nature, Trick or Treat." Nervous Rex allowed himself a barely audible chuckle. ". . . A fluke of your personality, and—"

"Screw you, pal." Brody started low-crawling toward the booby traps, the muzzle of his M-16 leveled across his wrists awkwardly.

To Ritter, he looked like a terrified recruit, trying to negotiate a boot-camp obstacle course for the first time. "Sorry, fella . . ."—Nervous Rex poked the Whoremonger's rear gently with the business end of his .45 automatic—"but I'm not that kinda guy. . . ."

CHAPTER 4

"Hold up."

Nervous Rex Ritter tagged Brody's elbow as soon as they were nose-to-wire with the apparent booby traps. The Green Beret sergeant nudged Treat out of the way, pressing him without force against the reinforced wall. "Keep the light on the nearest wires," Ritter instructed.

The tunnel was a few inches over three feet high, with the walls slightly narrower. Every meter, stapled planks of flattened bamboo had been pressed into the dirt walls and held in place by railroad pikes. The wires seemed to be attached somehow to these yellow planks. Brody now held the rifle as far away from his body as he could extend his left arm. This rendered the weapon virtually useless as far as a defensive tool was concerned, but the vision of a rifleman down at the opposite end of the tunnel aiming at the light and sending a burst of tracer into Brody's face had become almost overpowering the last few minutes, and he wanted the beam to emanate as far away from his body as possible. He did manage, however, to keep the flashlight steady and to keep the beam on the wires Nervous Rex had pointed out to him.

Ritter placed the barrel of his pistol against one of the wires gently, testing its resistance. Squinting again, he examined the points along the bamboo planks where the wires passed through and disappeared behind tiny screw-eyes. He doesn't seem to be at all concerned about whoever is lying in wait beyond the wires, Brody mused as he watched the sergeant work. Maybe there isn't anybody down there, he decided.

Ritter was checking the packed dirt beneath the wires now and running his fingertips along the bottom of the first one, then two, then—breaking out in a grin now—*all* of the wires. "Let's go!" he announced suddenly, charging forward on his hands and knees—*right through the booby traps!*

Had the man lost his mind? Brody flattened out against the earth, shielding his head with his forearms—convinced that would be his last thought, convinced the explosion would turn what had once been Spec-4 Treat "The Whoremonger" Brody into just so much shredded and mutilated flesh—food for the rats. . . . Convinced his spirit would be flung backwards through the darkness, sentenced to wander the bowels of the earth for eternity . . .

But nothing happened.

Dust from the soles of Nervous Rex's jungle boots swirled back into his nostrils, and Brody nearly sneezed, but nothing more noteworthy than that occurred. There was no explosion. And now the Green Beret sergeant was fast disappearing down into the dark. Brody's arms and legs twitched a bit initially, as if ordered by instinct to chase after his more experienced buddy, but his brain took over, and he froze to the spot, dust in his eyes and hair now. What if Nervous Rex had merely cast fate to the wind and was playing out a death wish?

What if he was chasing a posthumous Medal of Honor and just didn't give a damn about anything anymore? What if Nervous Rex had decided he was already a dead man? Perhaps the antipersonnel mines were hidden behind the planks or up ahead, or even *behind* him. Perhaps they were waiting to go off! Maybe Nervous

46

Rex had just been lucky and had trampled across the wires in such a manner that they failed to trigger the explosives. Brody could surely never hope to duplicate such a feat. *He'd be blown to Hanoi and back*!

"Come on, Trick-or-Treat!" a voice from the dark chasm up ahead called back to him. "We ain't got all God-damned day!"

"But—" The meek protest left him like a sapling cracking in the humid Pleiku breeze.

"*Come on*! There ain't no explosives back there— take my word for it! Now get your no-account ass up here. I need some light!"

Nervous Rex was no longer whispering. And he did not sound nervous in the least. He was, in fact, yelling back at Brody in quite a commanding voice, casting all caution aside, it seemed—and the Whoremonger reacted accordingly.

Closing his eyes tightly, he rushed across the wires— his mind replayed the scene a hundred times in that split second: He was racing over them on finger-and toe-tips, spiderlike; when in reality, he knew he'd never been so clumsy, his knees numb and right wrist throbbing. Somehow he'd sprained it, or, at the least, twisted it badly.

Two seconds seemed like two *hours*, but then he was past them. One even snagged his heel, and he heard it snap, but there was no blast. No deafening explosion ripped his legs out by the roots, forcing his intestines out through his mouth . . . like in the nightmares.

His left knee flattened something spongelike, and he heard an ear-piercing squeal. He did not glance back as the rat fled toward the dim shafts of light dropping down, through the distant spiderhole entrance.

"Gimme some light right here."

Brody could almost detect Ritter's grin in the darkness as he spoke. There was a blur of an outline beside the sergeant—the hint of a lifeless shape.

The flashlight's beam fell across the disfigured snarl of a young Vietnamese man.

"*Jesus!*" Brody would have scooted backward if Nervous Rex hadn't already had a hold of his shirt.

"No sweat, GI." Ritter laughed. "He's dead as they come, champ."

Shrapnel had ripped his nose and one ear off. His face was a collection of deep and not-so-deep gashes. One eye was missing. The other hung from shreds of optic nerve against a gouge in his cheek.

"Your grenade?"

"Yeah," Ritter answered simply.

"Christ . . ."

"Yeah, those little superballs'll do a job on your smile. That's why I don't like carryin' 'em. Knew a guy over in Duc Co used to carry a whole shitload of the darn suckers. But one day he was on the shitter, you know? And one o' them little pins worked itself free. Next thing you know: kaPLOWeee!" Nervous Rex's hands flew up as he spoke, scraping moist dirt from the tunnel's ceiling. "Butt flesh and turds from Pleiku to Panama. I was on the crew that had to clean it all up." Ritter sighed. "Man, what a *shit* detail. . . ."

His hands were busy, searching the dead man's clothes for weapons. "He's clean."

The Green Beret pulled Brody's flashlight from the tape around his M-16 and directed its beam along the dirt all around the body. "AK buttplate." He pointed at a faint impression in the dust. "Somebody dragged this fucker's rifle away. And something else, too. Some kind of rucksack or—"

"Then—"

Nervous Rex made a three-level whistle not unlike the spine-tingling music in a horror movie. "Then . . . we . . . are . . . alone . . ." His teeth flashed white as moonlight over a cemetery, and Brody shivered again. He crouched low, hugging the nearest earthen wall, and waited for the sergeant to make his next move.

Ritter doused the flashlight. Both men immediately sensed something rapidly approaching them from the dark end of the tunnel. Something big. And inhuman.

The sergeant's pistol came up. He locked his elbow, and a moment later, the eerie silence erupted into a harsh snorting sound, then two discharges.

Blood splashed across the front of Brody's uniform, and the wild boar slid to a stop inches from his face. It was on its side now, but still snorting angrily with its last dying breaths.

"Jesus!" Treat scooted backwards on his haunches. Raising his rifle, he sent a burst of slugs into the wheezing hog's snout.

When the last echo from the discharges died away, the animal fell silent.

"Ham from Hanoi!" Nervous Rex laughed.

"What?" Brody glanced over at the Green Beret, trying to make out his face in the gloom—the flash of gunfire had temporarily blinded them both. "*What!*" Barely restrained anger coursed through the First Cav trooper. He had to send several mental commands to his hands before his fingers would flip the selector lever to SAFE.

"The pig, Trick-or-Treat!" Ritter sounded surprised Brody was so slow. "Them damn Charlies sicked a Cong hog on us, boy!" He flipped the flashlight back on and directed the beam over the porker's long fangs. "WhooEE!" The beam vanished. "He woulda done a royal job on your gonads, slick. They train them porkers to go right for your nuts . . . did ya know that?"

Brody wanted to reply with something about how disgusting he found Ritter's statement, but he remained silent.

"Yep, they train 'em to go straight for the scotebag, boy. Straight for the—"

"About those wires back there, Rex," Brody interrupted. His chest was heaving and it hurt to get the words out.

"*Them* wires?" Ritter flipped a thumb over his shoulder without looking back.

"Yeah." Brody's eyes remained set in the direction

the wild boar had charged from. "What told you . . . how did you know—"

"That they were decoy boobs?"

"We coulda been blown from here to—"

"But we weren't, were we?" As his purple vision returned, Brody could make out the gleam from Nervous Rex's satisfied grin.

"But we could have been," he protested.

Ritter sighed heavily for the younger soldier's benefit. "When I ran my fingers under the wire, they came away with dust clinging to the loops of my prints and—"

"The 'loops' of your *what*?"

"And that told me, since there wasn't a like amount of dust along the tops of the wires—which would result from debris falling from the ceiling, for instance—"

"I just wanna know—"

"The bad guys trampled over them wires ahead of us, Treat."

"What?"

"The scumbucket I ripped up with my frag," Ritter explained in his peculiar form of GI jargon. "He crawled right over the wires during his escape attempt, forcing them down against the packed-earth floor. They were a diversion, that's all . . . designed to slow us up."

"And—"

"And they did, didn't they, buddy?" Nervous Rex slapped the Whoremonger's shoulder heartily. "Now let's us diddy-bop on down into the dark and see if ol' Luke the Gook had any comrades down here who were waitin' to—"

At that exact moment, the tunnel erupted into a billowing cloud of black smoke and sparks as a projectile was launched at them from several dozen meters away. A screeching sound filling his ears, Brody hugged the earth as gold and silver sparks poured down on him when the twenty-inch homemade rocket passed over them. He heard Nervous Rex laughing in the background, then there came a loud *thump*! as the

50

aluminum missile bounced off a bend in the tunnel and slid to a stop only a few meters away.

"Oh, LORDy!" Treat imitated one of his old teammates, Abdul Mohammed, involuntarily. He glanced up at the multicolored flames still hissing from the rocket's nozzle and buried his face in the dust again. "This is *it*! This is *all* she fucking wrote. Good*bye*, Rex!" He envisioned the projectile exploding as he spoke, preventing him from giving his blood-brother the proper farewell. "Twas nice to know ya . . . It was fun while it lasted!"

Its solid propellant suddenly spent, the rocket sputtered and went silent without exploding.

While Brody gagged on the dense smoke, Nervous Rex rose into the push-up position. "Homemade jobber," he announced, reaching over to take hold of Brody's M-16. Nervous Rex sniffed at the smoke. "Not even black powder. I'd say the pud-pullers used crushed match heads, which don't pack no punch worth shit unless you've got good seals, and that baby," he motioned toward the source of all the smoke, "definitely had weak seals." As the last words left his lips, Ritter sprayed the tunnel in front of them with three short bursts of hot lead. The last burst was composed of glowing red tracers.

Brody watched them ricochet off an obstruction in the murky distance and burst into a shower of crimson sparks.

A muffled scream reached their ears—a man's scream—and then harshly whispered commands. Frantic footfalls followed.

"Shit," Nervous Rex muttered as the rifle's dustcover revealed an empty chamber. "Throw me another magazine, Trick-or-Grat. Make it a banana clip!"

"That's all I had, Rex!"

"What!?" Ritter dropped the rifle and drew his pistol again.

"It's not even my weapon. Top gave it to me topside!"

"*What*!? He didn't give you no bandolier?"

Brody frowned. How could any of them have anticipated real trouble and the need for extra ordnance? A moment ago, they'd all been racing to be the first to find the naked girl. And now . . . .

"Fuck it." Nervous Rex was grinning again. "Don't mean nothin.' Ain't no Cong cocksuckers gonna *cockadau* fraternal brothers of the Dirty Thirty, right, Whoremonger?" He was rushing past Brody, toward the sound of voices. When the Spec-4 did not immediately respond, he said, "Come *on*! Duty and country and godship awaits you! This may be your chance to join the ranks of hell's elite!"

They ran down the tunnel for what seemed like a hundred yards. They ran in a low crouch, but as the tunnel descended, it grew larger. They reached a bend in it, and Ritter held up his hand for caution.

Placing a rigid forefinger against his lips for silence, he unlatched another grenade from his web belt and slowly pulled its pin, then, moving in slow motion at first, he suddenly flung the frag around the corner. *So the dinks can't snatch it up and throw it back*, Brody's memory summoned one of Rex Ritter's old sermons on battlefield survival hints. *Especially when ol' Luke's in a foxhole or bunker: throw that frag hard. Make it bounce about so he can't grab it before it detonates*. The incident with the tripwires had reminded Brody of another rainforest recipe for survival Nervous Rex had taught him: *Don't use leaves like that for camouflage*, he had slapped Brody's helmet when he noticed the Whoremonger was placing the leaves on upside down. *The bottoms of leaves are a lighter color than their tops. You'll stand out like a sore thumb*.

You'll stand out worse than if you wore no camou at all. Nervous Rex was funny that way. He had all sorts of boonierat knowledge and tricks of the trade up his sleeve.

The grenade detonated with an earsplitting crack! and a dull secondary pressure thump sent the concussion

52

roaring past them. Nervous Rex counted to three silently—Brody watched his lips move—then rushed down into the next chamber.

The tunnel dead-ended there.

Brody and Ritter both expected it to branch out at this point into a maze of deeper tunnel. They'd had visions of being credited with a major cache find. But they'd reached a dead end. A dead end with two mutilated corpses sitting in the dark, their backs against the earthen wall. Their eyes were punctured by the blast— it had evidently gone off only inches in front of their faces.

"Holy Mother of—" Brody began as his flashlight beam played across the torn shredded masks.

"Mama Mary had nothin' to do with *this*, my man." Ritter dropped into a squat in front of the two guerrillas and placed the barrel of his .45 against the closest communist's forehead as he searched clothing.

"Let's get outta here, Rex." Brody scratched at his elbows and neck. "This place is beginnin' to give me the creeps." He rocked his eyes not to stare at the dead Vietnamese's faces. The blast had grotesquely disfigured them. It was the kind of sight one carries with him to the grave.

"Almost done." Ritter was checking the second guerrilla now. "It's not as if I were robbin' the deceased, you know." He flashed a set of bright teeth up at Brody. "Not as if I'm relievin' 'em of their valuables or huntin' for war souvenirs." Sgt. Ritter was obviously checking for documents, or maybe a war diary.

The air pressure within the tunnel seemed to change as a sudden hissing filled both American's ears. Something had dropped from the ceiling and landed behind them!

"CS!" Nervous Rex announced, believing he smelled teargas. He and Brody dropped into the prone position, but it was only a yellow smoke grenade. And a weak one at that.

After the device died out and the hissing stopped, a

weird clacking reached their ears. Brody's eyes were scanning the dirt ceiling, trying to find out where the snoke grenade came from, but Nervous Rex was staring at the bone-white skull which had appeared in the tunnel behind them. A bone-white skull with green glowing eyes and teeth gnashing wildly as the jaws clattered open and shut, open and shut so fast they became an ivory blur.

CHAPTER 5

Treat Brody's mind flashed back to every western shoot-em-up he'd ever watched at the movies when Nervous Rex's gunhand came up and his automatic began barking hot lead. Only three rounds came out, but they were one after another—nonstop—and the Whoremonger, if he used his imagination, was watching the cowboys on the silver screen fanning their revolvers as they fought it out with the Indians.

The .45-caliber slugs slammed into the glowing, cackling cranium with a ferocity that shattered Brody's split-second daydream. Shards of bone—or what appeared to be bone—rolled off to the side, spinning, as the main portion of the skull was knocked back, out of sight.

"Hey, you sonofabitch!" an American's voice boomed down from above. "You didn't have to waste the bastard!"

Brody rushed toward the source of the voice as Nervous Rex ejected his spent magazine and slammed a fresh seven-round clip home.

"My kid sister just sent me that, BOY!"

Treat Brody stared up at the grimy face peering down at him through the narrow ventilation shaft. Atop the face was mounted a green beret.

Brody wasn't sure how to respond. He wanted to direct his best obscene gesture up at the man—a *cao boi* favorite the Green Beret might not recognize but which, down in Saigon, would cost you your throat. He wanted to wave his fist too, and maybe point the M-16 up at the prankster, but instead, he merely sighed and stooped over to pick up the laughing skull gag. A corroded battery fell from the plastic insides as he picked it up. Brody shook his head from side to side with resignation.

Nervous Rex didn't seem in the least perturbed. His pistol holstered now, he rushed over to the air shaft, smile intact, and gazed up at the men crowding around the heavily camouflaged opening. "Hey, *hey*, Rory!" he chuckled. "Pretty good! You definitely had me worried there for a minute!"

"No shit, Nervous?" The voice boomed down again, like God.

"I wouldn't shit you, Rory . . . ."

"I'm his favorite turd," Brody heard 'Rory' telling the men clustered behind him. He could imagine the guy glancing around, nodding modestly as if reigning great pride in the designation.

"What's the fucking body count down there, Nervous?" The voice belonged to Top this time.

"Three, First Sergeant," Ritter called back. "*Four*, if you count this little mother." He grabbed what remained of the laughing skull and held it up over his head.

"You're at a dead end?"

"Yeah, Top!" Ritter glanced around and began slamming his fist against the earthen walls in an attempt to ensure he'd missed no hidden passageways or cosmetized hiding places.

"Thought at first maybe we had the tip of a real iceberg here." In fact, visions of multi-leveled tunnel complexes, complete with underground field hospitals and ammo caches, had filled his head when he and Brody first descended down the spiderhole. It was always that way with the dark tunnels. ". . . But looks like nothin' more than a shelter of sorts. Maybe—"

"Not even any rice?" The First Sergeant seemed disappointed.

"Not a grain, Top. By the looks of the bamboo braces down here, I'd say this sucker was put in by the French at least ten years ago."

"Oh, is that what you'd say, eh?" Top's tone turned sarcastic and skeptical, but Ritter seemed to miss the disrespect for his MI skills. "What kinda weapons were those Cong assholes carrying?"

"Two AK's and half dozen Chi-coms," Ritter called up, but he was still inspecting the tunnel supports. "Yah, Top . . . I'd say Charlie was just using this place to get outta the sun. Maybe take a break on his hikes between Pleiku and Phnom Penh, you know?"

The dirt walls around Ritter and Brody began to shake and tremble, and the two soldiers had to brace themselves by holding onto the bamboo supports. Dust fell from the roof of the tunnel. A grinding *clank-clank-clank!* reached their ears as it screeched down through the ventilation shaft, announcing the arrival of heavy armour.

"Tanks?" Brody locked eyes with Nervous Rex.

"At least one." The Green Beret sergeant smiled. He dropped into a squat beside one of the dead enemy soldiers and finished searching his body for articles of value.

"Get your—"

"We're coming! We're coming!" Ritter's grin warped into a frown.

"—young asses up outta there!" Top warned. "We got an M-48 full o' liquid strawberry jam up here waitin' to drop its load down your spiderhole. You get ten seconds, Nervous!"

Brody's eyes registered panic, as he stared at Ritter. *Ten seconds*? He'd recognized the slang term 'strawberry jam.' It was GI jargon for gasoline, or napalm, or whatever the flame-throwing tanks were carrying this week. Ritter wouldn't be able to fill his *pockets* within ten seconds, let alone sprint, bent over, back to the tunnel entrance.

"Don't sweat it." Ritter sensed the uneasiness exuding from the Whoremonger's aura. "Top wouldn't fry us. He wouldn't fry *me* anyway." He glanced up and winked at Treat. "'Cause I'm his favorite turd."

57

They dismissed Spec-4 Brody's discovery of a naked maiden in the wire as the product of an exhausted imagination—despite testimony by one of the jungle experts on hand regarding tracks left at the scene of da crime. They laughed off Treat's insistence he'd definitely seen a shapely representative of the local female persuasion attempting to breech the concertina in the buff, ". . . and she just might've made it 'cept them jugs o' hers were so full and firm she couldn't slide 'em under the razors without doin' irreparable harm to dual erect nipples the size of Sgt. Ritter's whanger." The last declaration was added at the Plei Me drinking hole most frequented by the jungle experts, after the Whoremonger downed his tenth skullcap of *ba-muoi-ba*.

"How would you know how big Ritter's ding-dong is?" Top challenged. Everyone laughed.

Brody thought he could hold his liquor. He'd drunk from VC skullcaps before—that was no big thing . . . it certainly wasn't mindfuck-to-the-max, as he was sure the Green Berets thought it would be—but there was just something about this Plei Me brand of Vietnamese beer that would have curled his socks and starched his shorts if he were wearing any. "Yes, gentlemen, she was a beeYOOtiful piece of leg! I swear it, by God! Wish I'd o' freefalled outta that skycrane right into her bones, I'm tellin' ya!"

"Well, awright!" An E-6 behind Brody slapped him on the back heartily. "A man after my own promotion!"

"I'm cursed now, gents . . . definitely cursed." Brody finished off the brew and whatever was floating around in it, and handed the skullcap back to the ancient mama-san mixing the concoction.

"Cursed? How's that?" one of the men asked innocently between belches.

"She put a spell on me," Brody sang the clue to his riddle in the fashion of a tune currently popular back in The World.

"Huh?" several of the NCos chimed in in unison. Brody was the only enlisted man there.

"We locked eyes—she was beautiful," the Whoremonger

58

sighed. ". . . And she put a spell on me. I'm cursed to have wet dreams about her for the rest of eternity. Hell, I can feel a hard-on coming right now as we speak." And the men all laughed again as more beer sloshed around.

Strange, Brody thought, well aware his mind was playing tricks on him. Strange how he knew every outline and curve of her body now, it seemed. Every detail of her face . . . the length of her silky hair, the color of ebony. Yet he knew, at best, all he'd really seen was the swell of breasts and then suddenly treetops, as the skycrane quickly passed over the outer perimeter of concertina. *An ample swell of breasts*, and then palm fronds. Yet he really *could* remember every detail about her!

Was he just desperate for female companionship? Was he really so hard up for a lay that his mind was manufacturing this all up to satisfy his current state of perpetual, normal-for-a-GI, lust?

Mindfuck to the max. . . .

He'd just read something about the brain and how it recorded everything we see. The article had claimed every person has a subconscious recording system that stores every detail scanned by the human eye. A system that remembers and, sometimes, later recreates entire scenes unfolding around that specific object the person was actually concentrating on.

The 'data' could usually only be 'extracted' through hypnosis, the article pointed out, but was it really that farfetched, Brody asked himself, to believe his mind had recorded everything about 'her'? She'd had the high cheekbones of northern royalty, he was convinced. And sensuous hips accented by the manner in which one leg outstretched and the other bent at the knee as she froze when the chopper passed over. *And her crotch!* The memory brought a smile to his face. *What a bush that woman had!*

"What ya smilin' about, boy?" Nervous Rex had finally arrived at the watering hole after turning in the war diary to the C.O. Ritter had found a tattered journal, embedded with chunks of shrapnel, beneath the shirt of one of the dead Cong, and though such items were prized souvenirs among

jungle experts, this particulr diary was difficult to read—
the pages couldn't be turned because of the shrapnel—so he
surrendered it to the captain.

"He's havin a wet daydream about that bitch he supposedly saw back down in sector seven," one of the Green
Berets chuckled unkindly. "He's makin' her out to have a
forty-six chest, Nervous."

"Naw . . ." Ritter wrapped his arm around Brody's
shoulder as if challenging the accusation.

"I never said nothin' about her measurements," Brody
said defensively. He leaned closer to Ritter, however, and
whispered, "But she *did* have some nice knockers, Nervous
. . ."

"Big boobs?" Ritter exploded for all to hear.

Brody's shoulders sunk. "Jesus," he muttered.

"Why didn't ya say so, chump?" He stood up.

"Sit the fuck down, Nervous!" Top dismissed Ritter's
antics with a loud swig of beer.

But if she had big boobs, we oughta mount a search
party. Whoremonger here's next-up on the ladder into the
Dirty Thirty, Top, and—"

"What?" The First Sergeant and the others seemed
suddenly interested in the First Cav trooper again.

"Yeah," Ritter added matter-of-factly. "Ol' Treat *cocka-
dau'ed* 29 Charlie so far, hand-to-hand, but that ol' Numba
three-zero keeps eludin' him."

"Documented?" Tops eyes narrowed suspicously as he
examined the C.I.B., airborne wings and subdued horse-
head patch sewn onto Brody's fatigues.

"Definitely," Nervous Rex answered for the Spec-4.
"Notorfuckingized by the Black Buddha himself."

"Zack?"

"Yeah." Brody sighed again. He was getting tired of the
notoriety. All these months in The Nam, and local superstitions were beginning to rub off on him. He didn't want to
attract too much attention to himself about this Dirty Thirty
business. It was kind of like a Vietnamese parent's concern
over showing too much attention to a handsome newborn—
he feared the demons lurking nearby would be attracted to

the boy by all the fuss, and, next thing you knew, the kid was history before he even had a chance to carry on the family name.

"But anyway," Ritter continued. "That's not what's got Whoremonger's hemorrhoids in an uproar."

"I ain't got no fucking hemorroids, Nervous!" Brody protested quietly, grinding his teeth.

"Ol' Whoremonger here has this rather commendable goal to fulfill before he completes his time here in the Orient. . . ."

"Oh?" The First Sergeant cocked an eyebrow in Treat's direction. "And what might *that* be, young man?"

Top wore a small crucifix and Saint Christopher's medal on his dogtags chain, and Brody swallowed as he prepared for Rex's recitation—one that was usually improved upon with each re-telling.

"Ol' Whoremonger here's hopin' to pop a cherry in every country from Thailand to Taiwan, Top!" Nervous Rex did not look nervous. He looked proud.

"He's hopin' to *what*?"

"Snatch some closed-clit from cunts wide and Far East," an anonymous voice in the background translated. Assorted snorts and wheezes followed.

The First Sergeant frowned. He slowly shook his head from side to side, then locked eyes with Brody, who immediately glanced away. "It's already been done . . ." He rose from his seat and started over toward the Whoremonger.

"Wh-what?" Nervous Rex asked, incredulous.

Top slugged Brody's arm solidly on his way out into the night. "By me." And then he was gone, without waiting for an analysis or commentary from the jungle experts gathered all around.

"Well, I'll *BE*!" Nervous Rex burst into unrestrained laughter. "A man after my own heart!"

"Faggot," the interpreter from earlier reacted to the statement, but Ritter ignored the jest.

The Green Beret sitting on Brody's left rubbed the spot where the First Sergeant had slugged him. "Looks like Top likes you," he grinned. "Or your style."

"He's a good man to have on your side." Ritter nodded, making a mental note to press the ranking NCO about his affairs with Asia's girls of questionable virtue.

Three days passed, and there were no further incidents at Plei Me. No attempts to breech the perimeter. But the local magic man read warnings in the rain clouds. There were powerful bad omens in the sky, he told the Strikers, who in turn told Nervous Rex and the other Green Berets. The gods had something in store for the Americans, and he suggested they say a prayer or two for Plei Me.

"That old fart's full o' shit," the First Sergeant dismissed the warnings lightly.

That night one of the Yarde tribesmen playing with his spotlight in the new guard tower, caught a half-naked male, wrapped in explosives, attempting to crawl through the primary perimeter wire. The tribesman's burst of tracers detonated the satchel charges, taking out an entire section of concertina and punji sticks.

The only thing left of the sapper was a piece of his lower jawbone and a chunk of mangled flesh Nervous Rex claimed came from the guerilla's heel.

CHAPTER 6

An Khe, one week later . . .

"One hundred and twenty-nine years ago, your grandfather's grandfather fought the white man on Comanche land . . ."

Broken Arrow saw himself laying in the river grass, at his mother's knees, listening to her re-tell the stores as she prepared the trout he'd caught for her only that morning. Blue mist creeping up from the river seemed to enshroud his mother's long, beautiful hair, and hummingbirds hovered mere inches beyond her shoulders.

"The fiercest battles took place over the hill behind your grandmother's homestead, but the fighting ranged across all the plains, really . . . across all that the white man eventually named Texas. . . ."

"Where is that goddamned crazy Indian?"

An abrasive voice scraped at the spell, destroying Broken Arrow's vision of his mother, ruining his karma, bringing a sense of loss to the full-blooded American Indian.

And someone was gonna pay.

He rose from his prone position beside the murky pond, glanced around and began shaking his head slowly, trying to clear his thoughts. Something was not right. The trees . . . the land—even the clouds floating along on the horizon. *Especially* the clouds: they were dark and ominous-appearing, like great sky monsters on the prowl for a sacrifice. Wisps of blue rainfall trailed after them as vast shadows moved across the jungle in the distance.

Broken Arrow glanced in the direction of the intruding voice, trying to focus on the figure approaching him, hoping his eyes did not look as dazed and cloudy as they felt.

A gaggle of choppers burst forth from the nearest treeline, passing low overhead—the *thump-thump-thump!* of their rotors beating into his ears, pressing his face down against the earth again. And he remembered where he was.

Vietnam.

The name alone worried him. Saying it sent a chill through him. There was something . . . *evil* about the three syllables, as if repeating them over and over was an incantation summoning demons from hell.

Be our defense against the wickedness and snares of the devil . . . as he prowls about the world for the ruin of souls . . . The Chaplain's words, as he prayed to Saint Michael, the soldier's guardian, at that morning's nondemoninational service, came back to haunt Broken Arrow as he watched the gunships disappear over Void Vicious. Arc-Angel, defend us in battle. . . .

"Shoulda known I'd find a crazy Injun the likes o' you goofin' off down here by the lake."

"It's a pond," Broken Arrow corrected the stocky weightlifter without meeting his gaze.

"What?" A set of spit-shined jumpboots slid to a halt in front of his nose.

"I said it's a pond."

Broken Arrow took a lungful of the sticky, afternoon breeze. "There's quite a difference between a lake and . . . a . . . pond. Would you like me to explain it to you, Hatchethead?"

"Well, it's an *OFF LIMITS* pond!"

The soldier with the axe-shaped haircut spat into the calm waters. "You know that. Top says the locals piss and shit in it so the clowns like you who go skinny-dippin' out

64

here end up with skin rashes or worse, and—"

"Does it look to you like I've been swimming?" Broken Arrow's voice showed no emotion whatsoever.

"I'm not sure *what* you've been doin' down here, dude." Hatchethead sniffed at the air suspiciously. "All I know is that Top sent me out lookin' for you. The C.O. wants you in the CP yesterday!"

"Fucking *OKAY*!" Two-Step, who got his nickname from surviving the bite of a bamboo krait viper—whose venom was so powerful its victims were lucky to get two steps after being bitten before collapsing dead—lost his cool. He stood up, nearly blacked out, staggered, then slowly dropped back into a squat, seeking some semblance of self-respect. *Mean mushrooms*, he thought to himself. That was one *mean batch o' mushrooms*! "Okay, Monrovia. I'm like officially fuckin' notified, okay? Now clear outta my space, *dude*."

His mouth looking like a crescent moon with its points pricking the horizon, Hatchethead executed an about-face, and started back up the hill leading to the 'Golf Course,' as the First Cav company area in An Khe was known. A sour taste in his mouth, Broken Arrow frowned too as he watched the giant with the funny hairstyle fading in the distance. *At least he didn't get it cut in a Mohawk . . .* The thought brought a smile back to his face.

It wasn't that Broken Arrow feared Hatchethead. That was not the case at all. But the reason he didn't cannonball the big oaf backwards, off his feet, and into the pond was because this morning he was not sure of himself. He was not in full control of his faculties.

Two-Step, whose given name was Chance, but who was called that only by officers and top sergeants, was going on his third year in The Nam. He wasn't afraid of anything of anybody. Except the rain forest at night perhaps. And maybe the wind gods, as his mother called storms. He had seen a typhoon wreck Wanchai on his last R&R to Hong Kong, killing hundreds of people, and had never been so glad to get back to Vietnam.

Oh, that's not to say he didn't know his limitations. There

were obviously bigger and badder men in-country than he, who had also weathered countless mortar and rocket barrages and a couple thousand snipers, and Two-Step knew that, given the right circumstances and a dose of luck or drugs, even a newby with babyfat on his cheeks could pound him into the clay—if he was big enough. But Two-Step feared no one. He would fight the meanest boxer TDY from the Marine Corps, or compare machetes with any commando ARVN could field, without emotion in his eyes. He would never back down.

But that last batch of mushrooms had screwed-up Two-Step Broken Arrow's reflexes.

He had taken to mashing up the dried-out mushrooms and smoking them in a corn-cob pipe after an evening of boredom led him to the discovery of their mind-altering potence.

Two-Step had never tried drugs before, but the stories and films and documentaries depicting his ancestors smoking peyote around the campfire had always intrigued him, and in a small way, his experiments with the mushrooms brought him closer in tune, he felt, with his heritage.

Two-Step rationalized that, since his pleasure with the mushroom dreams—they were really hallucinations, which were experienced while wide-awake—was not a result of ingesting narcotics purchased surrepticiously on the street (or the backalleys of An Khe), then all was natural and alright. The visions that came to him only elevated Two-Step closer to the gods his mother had spent so many hours telling him about: the nature gods, the earth gods. The dreams seduced him, took him away on the feathers of winged horses, away from the killing and dying, away from this evil land whose mere name was an incantation to Satan.

That's not to say Broken Arrow despised The Nam. After all, he'd extended so many times he'd almost lost track. But one did have to get away from all the gore and high-tech death now and then, and the mushrooms provided an inexpensive escape. Usually, if he could avoid interruptions, he could avoid a hangover, too—which one could not guarantee when it came to alcohol. And alcohol brought on the drunks. It was as social a disease as the black syph, and what Broken Arrow sought was solitude. Solitude, and dreams about the old days, the days before the reservation, and the white man, when the plains belonged to the Comanche for as far as they eye could see and yet no Indian dared claimed he owned the land.

Two-Step wondered what the top sergeant wanted. The Brass harrassed him. He always kept his uniform tidy, finished all the shit details well ahead of deadline, and volunteered without fail to manage the range when the troops were trucked down to VC Valley for weapons qualifications. He was a damned good soldier. A damned good soldier, but, an Indian. Always 'an Indian,' in the eyes of the military hierarchy. They had to keep an eye on him. At least that was how Broken Arrow felt. Maybe they feared him because he was going on his third year in The Nam, and more than a couple Tour 365's in-country usually changed a man. Changed him for the worst, some said.

A damned good soldier . . .

Two-Step had to give the United States Army credit for one thing: it had taught him the fine craft of soldiering. He felt in charge with a rifle in his hands . . . in control of the situation. And he was good with a weapon. Damn good.

But the fun started, Two-Step grinned at the thought, when he managed to get a squad leader who voiced no objections over him carrying his crossbow into the field. Two-Step always volunteered for the most dangerous position on the patrol were few and far between, his sergeants rarely hassled him about the bow. Especially Zack. Leopold Zack had even taken an interest in the weapon, asking Two-Step to let him shoot it a couple of times, but his aim didn't seem all that good—he allowed Broken Arrow to beat him in their off-the-record bullseye contest, anyway—and he hadn't mentioned the bow in several months.

Two-Step jogged in place for a couple minutes, attempting to get his blood flowing again—trying to clear his head.

Viewed from afar, he was an impressive figure: very muscular—though none in his platoon had ever witnessed him working out—but they were finely toned muscles arranged quite symmetrically, so as to be unimposing, yet emanating obvious power. Two and a half years under the tropical Asian sun had lent a smooth, bronze tint to his already dark skin. The young man kept his hair short, but he also kept a full-length, ceremonial wig at the top of his rucksack for his off-duty jaunts down into the villes. And for occasions like the one that had brought him down to the pond today.

Two-Step whirled around—what had happened to the wig? Had Hatchethead spotted him wearing it?

He trolled back down the hillside, over to the pond's edge, visions of his ancestors sweeping down from the hills into settler's camps at midnight still swirling about in his head. *Night raiders . . . . They had really been a band of courageous night raiders, defending what was rightfully theirs . . . .*

He found the wig beside a clump of the blush-silver mushrooms. *Truly a meean batch o' mush!* Today's dream hd been something about wrestling with a Texas Ranger—had he actually fought with Hatchethead, losing the wig? He honestly couldn't remember. . . .

Two-Step quickly folded up the wig and slipped it into his thigh pocket as thunder along the horizon reached his ears. *Manmade thunder.* He watched the long-range bombers—mere specks in the distance to the naked eye—slowly grow to be rumbling, metallic predators.

He ducked as a dozen of them flew over, black plumes of oily smoke drifting down across the land from their massive engines, bit at his lower lip to surpress his rage, then sprinted back up the hill, in the direction of the command post.

"I like your style, Corporal Broken Arrow." Col. Neil Buchanan handed the case over to Two-Step after returning his salute. Inside the case was another Purple Heart, from the rocket attack two weeks earlier. "Refusing to accept the medal in front of the men. Saves me bookoo time. Saves you bookoo time."

"Saves us *all* bookoo time." The company clerk glanced back over his shoulder at Two-Step, flashed the thumbs-up, then resumed typing notations into the corporal's 201 file.

"I wasn't trying to be disrespectful, Colonel." Two-Step wiped at his nose with the back of his wrist out of a need for movement: he feared no man, but officers and Orderly Rooms made him nervous. "But I just didn't feel the wound rated a Purple—"

"It certainly did." The company clerk spoke without looking back this time.

"Anytime you get four chunks of shrapnel in your back, and it takes a medic like Doc Delgado six hours to pry em' out . . . well, that's definitely Purple Heart material to me . . . ."

"T'was a million-dollar wound, if ya were to ask me." The company clerk kept typing.

"Well, no one *was* askin' 'ya, Private-with-no-time-in-grade—"

Broken Arrow interrupted the Colonel before he could say the soldier's name. "Sir, if you don't mind . . . I think I'll be on my way, sir . . . ." He felt as if he was going to black out any minute.

"No, no, no. Corporal Broken Arrow." Buchanan had just taken his seat, but he stood up again as he spoke. "The Purple Heart's all fine and dandy, but that's not why we've called you in here this afternoon. It's not why we've called you in here at all."

"Certainly not," the company clerk added with a laugh. He stopped typing, and slowly turned around to direct a you're-in-hot-water-now look in Two-Step's direction.

Broken Arrow could not recall anything he'd done in the last few weeks to merit the C.O.'s attention. Surely Hatchethead hadn't turned him in for seeking spiritual refuge down by the OFF LIMITS pond. "But sir. . . ."

"You just have a seat there, Two-Step." Col. Buchanan stepped out from behind his makeshift C-rations desk and slid a three-legged stool over to Broken Arrow. "While I get jizz-for-brains here going on his way over to—"

"'Jizz-for-brains'?" The company clerk, a PFC in his early thirties with cotton-like blond hair and a receding hairline, stood up, mock insult narrowing the eyes behind his wire-rim glasses.

"*Over . . . to . . .* the psyche-shack to pick up those documents I want you to run over to Plei Me for me." Buchanan stared at the company clerk as he spoke to Broken Arrow.

"Plei Me, sir?" Two-Step was dumbfounded.

"Right, Plei Me. You know it, don't you? The SF camp out west that plays stinky finger with Cambodia every time the sun goes down. . . ."

"Uh . . . right, sir. . . ."

"Well, I want you to run some documents out there, son. Think you can handle it?"

"Uh . . . yeah, of course, sir." Broken Arrow didn't feel so ill after all.

"And while you're out there, see if you can round up your buddy Brody." Buchanan lit up a cigar but didn't blow smoke in Two-Step's face, as the Indian expected he would.

"Brody, sir?"

"Yep, Brody. You know Brody: the Whoremonger or whatever he's calling himself these days. You guys and your nicknames." The Colonel, who preferred to be called The Bull, laughed lightly as his company clerk paused in the doorway.

"Uh . . . right, sir . . . ." The last time he'd seen Treat, the Spec-4 was riding *Pegasus* into a firefight twenty klicks east of Pleiku City.

"He begged a three-day pass outta me to go visit his boyfriend Green Beret over at Plei Me,"—both Buchanan and the company clerk snickered at the joke—"and that was last week. Tell 'im if he's not back in forty-eight hours, I'm placin' his no-account ass on the AWOL roster, and it's gonna be *Friday Nights At The Fights* when he does stagger in. Got that?"

"Got it, Colonel." Broken Arrow saluted, and turned to

70

leave the CP.

"And you!" Buchanan pointed a rigid forefinger after his company clerk.

"Me, sir?" The PFC's grin vanished.

"When you get done with *that*, set yore ass back down behind that typewriter and start working on your transfer papers."

"Transfer, sir?"

"Transfer! *Do I stutter, son*? Recycle your ass back to boot camp."

The company clerk swallowed so hard all three men in the room could hear him. He wasn't sure if Neil Nazi, as the troops called Buchanan, was serious or not. And, though he preferred nearly any dirty assignment outside of Vietnam, he wasn't sure if he'd trade eight more months in An Khe for another eight-week cycle of Basic Combat Training.

CHAPTER 7

Koy spent a few moments watching the crescent moon dart about behind the silver clouds before attending to the matter at hand. She had already shed her clothing, and now stood beneath in the trees, naked except for the silver beams upon her body. Slowly Koy lifted her sparkling black hair up off her shoulders and piled it atop her head. Using the jade and ivory hairpin to hold the long strands in place, her nimble fingers worked blindly as her eyes fell to the slopes of full breasts and the way shadows from the clouds danced across them, making her chest appear larger than it was.

It was muggy out. Steaming hot and muggy, but Koy giggled—she could not help herself—as she applied the oils to her flesh. The oils were cool. They made her skin tingle, and her nipples grow taut. The oils were cold as ice coffee. It was not as refreshing as when she applied them during the heat of the afternoon.

Leaving her clothing and weapon in a hollowed-out treetrunk again—the pistol's main purpose was to see her safely from the caves to this point in her mission and would do her little good under the wire—Koy stooped to pick up the pole with its two pails.

She was emerging from the treeline at a point approximately five hundred yards from the place where she had been spotted by the skycrane two weeks earlier. Pausing to sniff at the air, she found the only odor was of GI bugjuice swirling down from the CIDG outpost. Koy heard no sound rustling either in the jungle or up at the camp. So she began running across the clearing.

Carrying the pole balanced over her shoulders and the two empty pails swinging wildly on either side, she sprinted toward the outer strands of concertina as soon as another long patch of clouds covered the moon.

The soldiers had not reinforced the perimeter since the earlier incidents. They did increase their patrols, but Koy had been monitoring them for three nights, and quickly learned their routine, despite army regulations decreeing there would be no routine. The soldiers—two Americans and three Strikers—passed by here every forty-five minutes or so, though sometimes their patroltime stretched to a few minutes over an hour, and that was only when the mess sergeant brought midnight chow down to the main gate.

No tripwires snapped beneath her barefeet after she longjumped across the gleaming concertina. No flares shot skyward.

Never slowing, Koy's narrow, rough-bottomed feet took her to a clump of reeds, several hundred feet from the main, fortified perimeter fenceline, where she dropped prone against the earth, chest heaving, and waited.

There was no sound. Not even the call of barking deer, or parrots irritated by her antics. Only the gentle swirl of air as the breeze went about its nightly ritual of exploring the rain forest.

Koy's objective this evening was not to breech the secondary ring of barbedwire. Her goal was not to attempt to penetrate the minefield or fifty feet of punji-sticks. Such missions were left to the veterans—the hardcore cadre—not wildflowers, like herself, as one of the cellblock leaders had referred to her only the month before. And look what had happened to him. Showing-off for Lanh, no doubt, Koy decided, as she recalled the fool's attempt to rush the outpost with his body wrapped in satchel charges. His place in revolutionary history had been assured, the

74

hunter told Koy after the tragedy, but she still did not know his name.

Her primary job tonight was to continue what she had been doing for the last seven nights: help dig the series of trenches local guerrilla leaders wanted to have surrounding the Special Forces camp by October. Not tunnels. Trenches.

There was a difference.

The trenches were to be four to five feet deep, and fifteen to twenty meters in length, each trench separated by fifty meters. Time permitting, they would connect them all by a network of tunnels, but if it came right down to the deadline, the sappers would have to do just as Koy did: vault the outer perimeter, sneak up to the trenches, then surprise the Americans with an all-out, well-entrenched, assault.

Waiting until she got her breath back, Koy waded down through the reeds until the earth became soggy, tickling her toes. Elephant grass rose all around her, up to her shoulders. The Americams were funny that way. They would clear wide sections of land all around the outpost, but leave patches like this every few hundred feet. Perhaps the bogged-down gulleys were just too waterlogged to work with.

Running the mission in the nude tonight had been a lark for Koy. Breeching successive fencelines was not in the plan, and she had longjumped the outer perimeter—there would be no crawling under the wire . . . no need for her flesh to feel out every object around her. Or would there?

Running nude beneath the moon invigorated Koy. It made her feel more in tune with the countryside . . . more a part of the wilderness. More animal. Prowling the elephant grass without clothing, so close to the Americans' barracks, she could hear some of them snoring. It was thrilling. Having sharp reeds slice into the outer edges of her breasts as they swayed side to side while she moved through the jungle, bent slightly at the waist, excited Koy. Yet she was a woman who had never slept with a man— Vietnamese or foreign born—she was a girl who had never

75

been kissed. That would all change, though. Tomorrow. Tomorrow, Venn would take her into the open air market in Plei Me. They would shop for the cell, and they might even pass the open-air cafe on their way back to the caves . . . the open-air cafe frequented by so many Americans. And Venn could show her how to play their little game.

But that was tomorrow. Tonight, there was work to be done. The soles of her feet fell across something hard and smooth, and Koy stooped to remove the series of planks covering the trench.

Already it was three feet deep, and several meters in length. And they were a day or two ahead of schedule, by Bok's calculations. Koy set down the pole with its pails and frowned. Carrying the dirt away was that part of the job which she disliked the most, but she understood the reason for it. The Americans were very observant, if nothing else. They would notice a pile of freshly dug earth no matter how well it was camouflaged. The group had been ferrying the pails of soil to the stream a half kilometer away.

Koy checked the position of the stars. Then she dug.

She filled the pails, and packed them tight, and filled them some more, until it was almost time for the soldiers to return. Then, carefully mounting the pole across her shoulders, she trotted back down toward the concertina.

Soaked in perspiration by the time the strands came into view—there would be no longjumping this time—she followed the concertina downwind to a point where it crossed a dry gulley, and began sliding the first pail beneath the protruding razors.

A pair of hands reached out from the other side of the depression and began dragging the pails away from Koy.

The concertina was a few extra inches off the ground here, due to the rough terrain, but she still had to slide it on under her back. Once again, a barb caught the nipple settling over her left breast, and a sharp cry—but an instant in length—left her lips.

"What was that?"

The voices were only a few meters away. Where there had been only silence before.

76

"It sounded like a girl. A child, maybe."

"Sounded like a fucking bird to me."

"No, it was definitely a chick."

"That's what I said: a fucking bird, doofus!"

"Quiet, you guys!" A commanding voice silenced the two other Americans, and soon a trio of charcoal-faced Lurps appeared where there had only been shadows between trees a moment earlier.

Koy froze midway to the other side of the concertina. The Lurps were not part of the guard patrol. These men were returning to Plei Me from several days reconning the jungle. They were ragged, exhausted, and hungry. She doubted they had little patience left for prowling or laying dog, so close to the CIDG outpost.

The barb had snagged her nipple, but she remained unmoving—frozen beneath the gleaming razors the shape of miniature guillotine blades. She would 'lay dog' herself, for as long as it took. And though she was not sure she really believed in him, Koy prayed to Buddha. She prayed the soldiers would continue on their way without discovering her, for she had heard stories about what men who'd been in the jungle for long periods of time without women did to prostitutes down in the ville. They snap their necks while making romance to them, she could still clearly hear Venn's voice. That makes them 'double vets.' Koy could only imagine what they would do to a new girl, like herself. In Vietnam, new girls were virgins.

Blood dripping from the slight puncture wound down onto her breast, Koy listened for any sound from Venn and the others. Perhaps they would throw a rock far away, causing a distraction. Maybe they would ambush the Americans. But that would only bring unwanted attention to the project they were working on and possibly set back the surprise attack several months. Koy knew Venn and the others would wait. And if the soldiers found her, they would probably let them take Koy away, unchallenged.

"Let's beat feet," one of the men finally said, after croaking frogs and a wave of cicadas brought a dull crescendo of chirps against the night silence.

"Yeah, fuck it."

"Fuck her."

"Who?"

Koy's throat tightened. Had they spotted her? With one hand, she grasped the nearest strand of concertina wire, planning to slash her wrists before she would let them violate her. Alive.

"That boom-boom girl the supply sergeant's got held up in the hooch where he keeps all the blackmarket whiskey and—"

"Ah, thaaat 'her.'"

"Right-o, amigo!" All three members of the long-range recon patrol laughed now.

"Come on, let's move it or lose it."

Koy listened to them stomp off through the bush, no longer observing noise discipline with the lights of Plei Me so close.

"She's got a dry snatch, but big tits and—"

"You've actually balled that   that creature?" One of the men sounded aghast.

"Whatta ya mean 'have I actually balled her'? Sure, I've actually fucking balled her!" He sounded as if he considered his intelligence offended. "What else are you supposed to do with free pussy?"

"The sarge didn't *hire* her to give quickies, stupid." His tone changed, as if he was turning to face the other soldier. "Christ, I thought *every*one knew she's only good for skulljobs . . . ."

"But she's got big tits. *Whoppers*, bud! Certifiably of the weather balloon size."

"Silicone jobs, Norm."

"Huh?"

"More than a mouthful is just a waste o' boob, Norman. Didn't ya know that?"

"You guys gotta be puttin' me on."

"We're tellin' ya, Norman, you don't wanna be spendin' your time humpin' that ol' bitch, my friend. Next thing you know, your pecker's done shrivelled up and rotted away."

"Huh?"

"Or fallen off."

"*What*!?"

"Why do you think even the sarge calls her *Co* Claptrap, Norman? Huh? Why could that possible be?" *Co* was Vietnamese for '*Miss.*'

Their voices were growing fainter, but Koy refused to move until she could no longer hear their jungle boots trampling through the elephant grass.

"You don't mean . . ."

"The black syph, Norm. The cunt has got the black syph."

"No fucking way, dudes!"

"You remember Joe Numba Two?"

"The Joe from Brooklyn."

"Right-o."

"Yah, I remember him."

"Well, poor old Joe didn't get medevaced-out 'cause of a self-inflicted gunshot wound to the foot, like everybody thinks."

"You mean . . . ."

"*Yep.* Ol' Joe was never one to listen to the rest of us, you know."

"I remember. . . ."

"Ol' Joe dabbled in danger, and word tricklin' down the wait-a-minute vine has it poor Joe stuck his wick in *Co* Claptrap's little box of exotic delights, my friend."

"*He* said she was dry too. But he huffed and puffed and he burned his wick off. . . ."

"But he managed to get his rocks off too."

"You guys are shittin' me, right?"

"Ol' Joe . . . he was so impressed with *Co* Claptrap's bushy little rush—"

"Transplanted, dudes. Let's get the record straight."

"What?"

"That he took a dive, face first, into *Co* Claptrap's dried-up pleasures of the flesh. . . ."

"I heard she rubbed his face around in it."

"That's what I heard too."

"And anyway, that very next morning poor ol' Joe

79

Numba Two woke up screamin' and carryin' on. . . ."

"Joe Number Two? *Our* Joe Number Two?"

"Yeah. And Top and the C.O. and Doc Delgado went runnin' into his hooch, and you know what they found?"

"I think I've heard this one before."

"But the suspense is killin' *you*, right, Norman?"

"Right, *right*!"

"Well, ol' Joe Numba Two's eyes were swollen shut."

"Nawww. . . ."

"Yes they were. Truly, they were. Swollen shut with a mean dose of the incurable black syph."

Norman made a groaning noise but said nothing in reply.

"Doc Delgado had to cut his eyelids apart with a straight razor."

Norman groaned louder. "Spare me the details."

"There was blood everywhere. Squirtin here . . . squirtin' there. Worse than if a whole limo full o' whores on the rag was hit head-on by a semi-truck in the middle of the Golden Gate Bridge in San Francisco."

"You think they gave ol' Joe Numba Two a ticket to board his freedom bird, Norman?"

"I didn't give it much thought until right now."

"Well, they fucking didn't. They sent ol' Joe away, Norm."

"Away?" Norman's voice seemed to rise an octave.

"They sent him away to the island. To join all the others."

"The others?"

"The others who experimented with *Co* Claptrap's *ying-yang*, only to have their ding-dongs fall off."

"I don't think I've heard of this 'island' before, guys. . . ."

"Sure you have, Norman. It's where they send all the guys who catch it. They're all quarantined there, until someone discovers a cure for the incurable black syph."

"Oh. . . ."

"Say, Norman. We warned you in time, right? I mean, you didn't dip your wick where it don't belong, did you, boy?"

80

"Uh. . . no, no, *no*! Not me, fellas. You know me. I got a girl waitin' for me back home. We're promised an' everything."

"That's good, Norman. We wouldn't want to have to send her a note statin' you was missin' in action, or something. Missin' in action, and presumed fucking dead. . . ."

"Until they find a cure, that is."

"You guys don't have to worry about me. I promised Lucille—swore up and down—that I wouldn't even *look* at a VeeyetnaMEEZ girl!"

"That's good, Norm. Real good."

"We was just checkin.'"

"Say, Stormin' Norman, what do they call a girl in Tijuana who don't charge for it?"

"I don't know."

"A *frijole*, stupid."

"Oh. . . ."

CHAPTER 8

Broken Arrow spotted the Whoremonger even before his helicopter set down.

He'd heard strange stories about this Special Forces camp at Plei Me, so on the AC's final approach, he funneled all his attention toward inspecting the patches of woods and elephant grass outside the perimeter—but Plei Me looked just like any other godforsaken outpost erected in the middle of nowhere, deep in the heart of Void Vicious.

Brody was sitting in a gunjeep with two other troopers when Two-Step jumped from the twin rotored Chinook. All the soldiers except Brody held onto their helmets as the powerful downblast sent red clay across the camp like an Arizona dust devil.

"And just how the hell do you rate hoppin' a ride 'board a Jolly Green Giant, Comanche-san?" Treat was smiling, with hand outstretched, as Two-Step trotted away from the monstrous craft, legs rubbery from the brief ride.

"Neil Nazi sent me out to drag your ass back to An Khe!" The Indian had to yell above the roar of the hovering chopper. Men inside the craft were pulling pallets full of supplies out the back cargo door.

"I was afraid you'd say that!" Brody was laughing as he motioned Broken Arrow aboard the vehicle. "Hop in back!"

Two-Step pointed to the narrow packet under his arm. "Top-secret shit here!"

"I'm impressed." Brody's teeth flashed brighter. They seemed almost evil.

"Bring it along." The big, hairy soldier behind the steering wheel grinned too. "We could use some readin' material down in the ville. . . ."

"Between short-times." The man crouched behind the M-60 gave Broken Arrow the thumbs-up. The Indian responded with a skeptical frown. His eyes told Treat they were both in enough trouble already, and he didn't want any more.

"Two-Step, meet Nervous Rex and—" Brody began.

"Nervous Wrecks?" The stocky, dark-skinned trooper's hand was extended.

"R . . . E . . . X," Brody corrected him. "As in Tryannoraurus."

"Rllght." Ritter clasped the Indian's hand. Both men shook softly, neither feeling the need to impress the other.

"And this is Stormin' Norman."

Two-Step shook the second soldier's hand too, nodding cordially. Stormin' Norman didn't look ready to attack anything. Slightly overweight, with red cheeks, a pencil-thin mustache, and wrinkled fatigues, the twenty-five-year-old looked like he was suffering from a perpetual case of hardcore hangovers.

"Meet Two-Step," Brody introduced Broken Arrow.

"You a dancer or something?" Nervous Rex's eyes narrowed suspiciously. He obviously disapproved of the nickname.

"Chance survived a krait viper bite 'while back," Treat explained. "You know, the ones that—"

"That rarely let you get more 'an a couple of steps after being struck," Stormin' Norman cut in.

"Then it's casket city: a bodybag back to Baltimore." Ritter's smile returned. "Or wherever you're from."

"Can I see the scar?" Stormin' Norman was checking out Two-Step's lower legs.

"Well, I really better get those documents over to . . . say, where exactly is the—"

Brody's back went rigid as he snapped to attention in his seat. His hand flew to the side of his head in a crisp salute as the three enlisted men around him froze on instinct.

"At ease, at ease, gentlemen. . . ."

Broken Arrow turned slowly to find that three Green Beret captains had appeared behind him. He recognized two as former passengers on the Jolly Green Giant that had brought him into Plei Me.

"It appears you have a package for me." The ranking officer's hand was outstretched. It seemed all seven soldiers were smiling, but Brody was not sure if they were smiling about the same thing.

Broken Arrow was not so quick to surrender the documents, however. He leaned forward slightly, eyes searching for a nametag. But on the tiger-stripe fatigues, he could find no markings or identification whatsoever.

"Uh . . . I'm sorry, sir, but . . . *name*, sir?"

The captain laughed lightly. "Of course, of course. Very good, soldier." He made a show of checking Two-Step's nametag. "Uh, very good, Corporal . . . *Broken Arrow*, is it?" His hand came up, smile still intact—almost as if military formalities were a pain in the posterior but a necessary evil.

"Yes sir, that's correct: Broken Arrow." The slightest hint of a suspicious grin creased the Indian's features. He didn't trust these Special Forces types. They were always in search of a laugh.

"Cherokee, is it?" the captain asked, sounding genuinely interested. But where had Broken Arrow heard *that* one before.

"No sir . . . it's—"

"*Comanche*!" the captain added quickly.

Broken Arrow seemed slightly taken aback. "Why, yes sir . . . uh, that's correct."

"But you don't have a Texas accent." Was the captain's smile growing slightly? Was he—Two-Step—being set up to take a fall?

"I don't know any good Comanche who does, sir," Broken Arrow's face was expresionless now, but all three Green Beret officers, and the two troopers sitting with Brody, broke out laughing. Only Treat and Two-Step were left bewildered.

Forcing a serious look in his eyes, the captain moved closer to Two-Step. "Comanche are good people." His lips became a horizontal line, and Two-Step saw Indians on horseback ripping the scalps off white men in the reflections of those eyes. "I spent seven years at Fort Sam Houston . . . been all over the plains down there. You should be . . . *proud*, Broken Arrow. Very proud."

"I am, captain. . . ."

"The Comanche peoples have a rich heritage. They've always had *my* respect, and always will." He glanced back at the other two officers, who nodded agreement, their smiles gone.

Broken Arrow wondered if there was a drunk-Indian joke coming around the corner. "Thank you, sir."

The officer's hand was out again. "Now, about the packet, corporal . . . ."

Broken Arrow didn't pull any punches. He grinned uncertainly. "I'm afraid I still didn't catch your name, sir." He glanced down at the sign-over sheet on the documents folder, wishing he'd asked Col. Buchanan for a physical description of the man he was supposed to turn everything over to. But how many times did a courier get *that* specific? Then again, how many times did messengers without SF combat patches on their shoulders drop into Green Beret territory uninvited?

"The name's Stryker, son. *Captain* Stryker, as a matter of fact." He made a show of checking his watch. "Now, if ya don't mind. . . ." the officer glanced over both shoulders, as if watching for someone, "I'm kinda runnin' behind schedule, son, and. . . ."

Broken Arrow was checking his authorization list. He couldn't find any 'Stryker' on it. "Your uh . . . serial number, sir?"

"*Jesus*, man!" The captain swallowed hard and, for the

86

first time, Broken Arrow felt, strangely, like he was in control of the situation.

A clacking, scraping noise in the distance announced jeeps in need of new suspension springs were approaching from two different directions. Without warning, the three Green Beret 'officers' rolled into the back of the first vehicle as it went past—without another word to Broken Arrow or his companions.

Two-Step and Treat Brody's friends were saluting as the second jeep rolled slowly through the billowing dust of the first and coasted to a stop in front of the Indian. A full-Bird Colonel stepped from the vehicle gingerly, whipping a snappy salute. "Was that who I think it was?" He seemed to be directing his question to Nervous Rex. "Was that Sgt. Stryker?"

"I'm not sure *who* those guys were, sir," Broken Arrow said slowly, as both Ritter and Stormin' Norman shook their heads from side to side behind him. He really didn't want to know why the 'officers' had captain's bars on their beret sashes, but this Colonel here was referring to the apparent ringleader as a sergeant.

"Wonder what they were up to?" The Colonel gazed off at the dust cloud rising from the rapidly disappearing jeep. He seemed more irritated than worried, as if trying to intercept Top Secret documents before the C.O. could read them was a customary tradition at Plei Me.

This officer *did* have a nametag on his uniform, and, while he was talking, Broken Arrow was scanning his authorization list. The Colonel's name was on it. Broken Arrow glanced down at the jeep's front bumper. A blue sign about eight by ten inches in size was attached to it, along the left quarterpanel, and emblazoned in big white letters was the man's last name, below a Colonel's insignia. His driver looked official enough, and the Colonel himself appeared years outside the typical range for a prankster—even in the Green Berets. Broken Arrow held out the documents.

"Oh, of course . . . of course. . . ." The Colonel was bringing out his wallet. "That's what I left the CP and

87

came out here for, wasn't it . . . ." The man forced a smile.

Broken Arrow felt his own importance suddenly lifted: this officer was actually pulling out his ID card before taking custody of the folder. "Uh, that won't be . . . I don't think that will be necessary, sir."

"Nonsense, nonsense." The Colonel held the small green card in front of Broken Arrow's face, allowing it to waver before his eyes as long as it took for the corporal to match the photo with the face in front of him. "Rules is rules, right, son?"

The Colonel nodded appreciatively, accepted the documents after signing Two-Step's clipboard, then saluted the men before they could bring their own hands up, and was off in his own cloud of dust.

"Who the hell *were* those guys?" Broken Arrow asked Brody's friends later, as Nervous Rex was guiding their jeep down the narrow winding road into one of the villes below the CIDG compound.

Stormin' Norman made it a point to laugh louder than Ritter. "Those were three of my fellows . . . NCOs," he explained.

"*Sergeants?*"

"Yeah. . . ." Nervous Rex was still laughing. "They're always tryin' to get the word on happenings in and around Plei Me before the Colonel does. It's always been done . . . long before I ever arrived here."

"Hell, long before them three clowns with phony captain's sashes got here too." Ritter shook his head from side to side in mock resignation.

"Can't they get in trouble for that?" Broken Arrow's lower jaw was dragging on the jeep's floorboards. Practically.

"What—here in Vietnam?" Stormin' Norman cast Two-Step an incredulous frown. "In *Plei Me*?"

"No way," Nervous Rex added. "At least I don't think so. The Colonel respects his men. They live . . . on the edge, so to speak," he tried to explain.

"When you've spent nine out of ten nights out in the

bush, it kind of turns you into. . . ."

"An animal," Ritter coached Stormin' Norman. "The Colonel's got enough problems, what with Charlie sleepin' in the trees, takin' pot shots day in and night out, always connivin' about this or that. Wait 'till we show you the VC heads mounted in front of the club."

Broken Arrow sounded more surprised by the existence of a drinking establishment than any commie skulls lined up in front of it. "You have a club out here?"

"Sure we have a *club* 'out here.'" He feigned hurt feelings. "Whatta ya think this is—Bamfuck Egypt, or something?"

"Well . . . ." Broken Arrow was eating dust as they took a sharp corner on two wheels and veered down a back alley running behind the ville—and now they were actually rolling across smooth, steaming blacktop. The sound of rubber against the substance caught both Brody's and Two-Step's attention simultaneously. They leaned out their respective sides of the jeep and stared at the ground.

"What's *that*?" Brody's shock was genuine.

"Asphalt, idiot." Nervous Rex nudged him in the side.

"But this is . . . this. . . ."

"Like we was sayin', slick. . . ." Stormin' Norman began the chant and Ritter finished it.

"This . . . ain't . . . Bumfuck Egypt!"

Brody and his First Cav comrade were leaning down, halfway out of the jeep now—their faces mere inches above the ground, the sound of spinning rubber on blacktop music to their ears. "*Goddd*, I miss Bronson," the Whoremonger muttered to himself, ecstatic. 'Bronson' was the name he'd attached to his convertible back in The World. It was almost a tradition in the Brody family to tag nicknames to their cars—names which were normally uttered only in vain when the vehicle suffered a flat tire or wouldn't start. But Treat had a special relationship with his '61 Galaxie 500. He'd chopped the top off himself, and customized the car until it was a one-of-a-kind, souped-up hotrod, with two-toned candy apple red and royal purple paint job. He thought he was the envy of everyone in Hollywood, and he probably *was* the talk of the town in Los Angeles, where he lived across the Harbor Freeway from Chinatown. But if he missed 'Bronson,' Treat Brody had found a replacement for his emotions to zero-in on: The Nam. Brody loved Vietnam. He loved *Pegasus*, and all the other gunships, and he hoped he never had to leave. This Dirty Thirty business, however, kept a perpetual chill running through his spine, and he hoped to have it over with soon. The Whoremonger didn't like having monsoon storm clouds following his military parade. Either rain or raise Cain, but *di di mau* or die!

"So where are you maniacs taking us hostages?" Broken Arrow finally asked, after they'd driven around in circles for nearly an hour.

"It's been awhile since we been down here," Nervous Rex said, "and it's kinda tricky findin' the right cut-off that leads down to Mama Moi's pleasure palace."

"Yeah, them combat engineers—they're the dudes who put that little unofficial, unauthorized strip o' asphalt in back there—well, they're always fuckin' with us . . . you know: tearing out a half-klick o' blacktop here, addin' a new swirl there. . . ."

"Tryin to keep us confused," Nervous Rex translated Stormin' Norman's ramblings.

"They think they got dibs on Mama Moi's pleasure palace," Stormin' Norman explained further, "but this is a fuckin' free-fire zone, man. Nobody's got 'dibs' on nothin'!"

"Mama Moi's?" Broken Arrow's eyes were lighting up. Though they were only passing through row after row of ramshackle, barely standing huts, he envisioned a glittering palace rising up out of the trash and debris any second now, complete with prostitutes in day-glo hotpants and see-thru halter-tops waiting at the bottom of the steps in provocative poses to greet them.

"Aw, Mama Moi's is the local whorehouse." Nervous Rex didn't seem very enthusiastic.

"She charges a little more than *Co* Claptrap back at the compound," Stormin' Norman said, "but—"

"*Co* Claptrap don't charge nothin'," Ritter corrected the younger Green Beret, "unless she's started with *you*!" He glanced over at Stormin' Norman disapprovingly. "Moi' is Yarde lingo for 'savage,' you know," Nervous Rex turned to tell Broken Arrow and Brody.

"Does that mean she's a savage *fuck* or savage when it comes to rippin' off the GIs?" Brody asked.

"She *looks* like a savage." Nervous Rex laughed, and the others joined in.

"Aw, double-fuck," Stormin' Norman announced a couple minutes after Ritter finally found the correct turn-off and started down into a crackerbox collection of delapidated structures.

"Kee-riste!" Nervous Rex swung the steering wheel hard to the left the instant he spotted the four military police jeeps parked in front of Mama Moi's pleasure palace.

"Do you think they saw us?" Stormin' Norman kept glancing back over his shoulder as Nervous Rex sped in and out of several dead-end straight-aways, trying to put as much ground between them and the MPs as possible.

"You'll know if ya hear sirens," Ritter replied dryly.

"What's the big deal?" Broken Arrow was still waiting to be impressed.

"Mama Moi's has been OFF LIMITS ever since Colonel found out about it," Stormin' Norman explained.

"He 'found out about it' when one of the guys got his pecker bitten off by Mama Moi's queen cunt!" Nervous Rex added.

"She was Queen *Cong*, if you ask me." Stormin' Norman wiped his lips with bruised knuckles. Broken Arrow wondered if he was remembering the incident.

"'Got his *pecker* bitten off?'" Brody wanted to know the whole story.

"That's what the Colonel told us anyway." Ritter shook his head from side to side as he took a succession of left turns and brought them out on what appeared to be a main boulevard of sorts. "Nobody ever saw the wound—one of the medics was partying with him . . . had him covered with a poncho-liner when the troops arrived. They had the kid med-evaced out *rikky-tik*."

"And the medic was so short he had to climb a ladder just to reach the piss tube," Stormin' Norman said. "He *di di mau'd* that night and was on his freedom bird back to The World by sunrise."

"The Colonel wasted the bitch himself. Mama Moi pointed her out to him, and the old man smoked her without a truth-or-consequences session."

"Blew her right out of her Ho Chi Minh sandals with one shot."

"It was great," Nervous Rex agreed. "The MPs . . . they don't usually fuck with us over pussy—"

"They usually look the other way when it comes to payin' for it off-post, even though the UCMJ bible prohibits it."

"But somebody musta sucked a dose o' rank snatch."

"Or contracted crotch rot, or—"

"They're probably just checkin' VD cards, or countin' cockroaches—"

"I'll bet every swingin' dick flew out the back window." Stormin' Norman burst out laughing again as his mind formed a mental picture.

"So we are just gonna play global policeman and patrol this parasitic slum in the 'suburbs' of Plei Me until The Man beats feet, or what?" Brody was getting bored.

"Just hold onto your gonads, son." Nervous Rex was eyeballing a cluster of young women gathered in front of a roadside ice cream vendor. "I can smell untouched cherry-girl meat a mile away and—"

"Cherrygirls?" Stormin' Norman sat erect in his seat, shielding his eyes from the sun. "*Where?*"

Brody became more alert also. His main goal, after all, involved seducing and conquering females of the virginal species, and he'd yet to get a cherrygirl in South Vietnam to give him the time of day.

Three of the girls—they were young women actually—were staring at the approaching jeepload of GIs long before they themselves were ever spotted. Brody locked eyes with a slender, long-haired lass whose dark, mysterious orbs were already appraising his build. As the Americans grew closer, the woman glanced away, giggling.

"The ice cream's on *us*, ladies!" Nervous Rex was hoppin out from behind the steering wheel even before the jeep's sliding wheels came to a stop. Bowing, he removed his green beret and swung it under his body from left to right, like a knight saluting his queen.

The girls giggled again, but the three who had been so observant initially did not seem to hold the foreigners in such awe. "No speakee English." The woman who had locked eyes with Treat earlier viewed him through the corners of her eyes then dropped her gaze to the ground as she slowly licked at the vanilla ice cream cone.

Stormin' Norman and Two-Step were mesmerized by the actions of her long, glistening tongue. The woman picked up on this, turned her back on the four soldiers, and continued licking. Was it Nervous Rex's imagination, he wondered, or were the sounds being made by her tongue suddenly louder. He rubbed his crotch, warning to be taunted and teased in—

"Speakee *French*?" Brody challenged the woman.

"No talk GI!" she responded without hesitation.

"We don't have to talk soldier slang." Brody was feeling juvenile.

"Let's just talk S . . . E . . . X." Stormin' Norman was feeling rowdy. "How much?"

The young woman licking on her melting scoop of Vietnamese ice cream looked up at Stormin' Norman and frowned for his benefit. Brody noticed that, no matter how deep the creases went along her chin, she remained extremely beautiful. When she didn't respond to his new friend's insult with profanity or an obscene gesture, Treat realized he had someone special standing in front of him.

"Please excuse my friend." He smiled at her, bringing clasped hands to the front of his face, Thai-style, seeking forgiveness. All of the girls giggled again. All of them except the one he was speaking to.

Slowly, she raised her eyes to meet his, and a smile returned. "I talk you," she said innocently, the typical schoolgirl. "But I no talk *him*!" She flipped a thumb in Stormin' Norman's direction without really acknowledging the man's presence.

In Vietnamese, Brody said, "My name is Treat. What is yours?"

Intrigued by his command of the language, she tilted her head to one side, at a loss for words.

"My . . . name . . . is . . . Treat . . ." He repeated the phrase more slowly, afraid he must have mispronounced the words.

"I understand you." She stayed with English. "You speak good Vietnamese. My name is Koy."

"Probably alias." Stormin' Norman exhaled loudly and folded his arms across his chest.

Koy ignored him. "Do you know what it means?" She spoke in Vietnamese too this time.

The squealing of tires down at the end of the street kept Brody from replying. All faces turned to see two military police jeeps speeding toward the Americans "Ohhh, SHIT!" Nervous Rex had dived back into his misappropriated vehicle. Stormin' Norman was right behind him.

"Come on!" Ritter yelled, as he flipped the starter toggle, firing up the motor. "This jeep's hot as a whore's hole on Saturday night, boys!"

Broken Arrow somersaulted into the back seat as the rear tires began spinning. A blue cloud of burnt rubber appeared between Brody and the vehicle. He saw Two-Step's arms outstretched, ready to grab hold of him.

Treat gently grasped the woman's hands and looked into her eyes. He saw himself in their reflection, and the sight sent a chill through him, but he still could not leave her. "I'll be back, Koy. I promise."

"Go now!" She released his fingers and watched the MP jeep grow nearer. The driver activated the siren now.

"But I promise: I'll be back!"

He turned and sprinted for the jeep. Koy feared he would not make it—and she was furious with herself for caring one way or the other—but she felt her hands trembling as the scream of the MP's siren filled her ears.

Brody leaped for the back of the jeep, and Broken Arrow took hold of his wrists. It would have been an easy feat to accomplish, but Nervous Rex chose the same moment to shift gears, and when he popped the clutch, the Whore-monger was suspended in thin air.

Koy screamed as she watched the American tumble across the ground. She screamed because the military police jeep was not slowing. It looked like the MPs were going to run right over him!

CHAPTER 9

"Your grandmother's grandmother moved with her family to the Comanche plains in the summer of 1836. When she was only nine, she was kidnapped by the father of your grandfather's grandfather. . . ."

Chance Broken Arrow stirred slightly. This part of the dream always was the most unsettling. This part of the dream always left him feeling hollow deep in the pit of his gut . . . hollow and haunted. And he could never remember much of this part of the dream.

". . . She was the ten-plus-seventh girl taken against her will that summer. Fighting between our people and the new hunters was growing more vicious by the day. Weekly massacres were not uncommon. One newspaper covered the whole of Texas then. We never read it, of course, but I saw a picture on it once, and this of which I'm speaking was taken from the seller your grandfather's father traded skins for seed—the picture was of a terrible atrocity. But the new hunters committed atrocities against we Comanche, too. The newspaper never printed that, though . . ."

Smoke rings sneaking up his nose roused Broken Arrow again. He turned to his right. The doorway leading from the small cubicle was filled with bamboo beads and more smoke. To his left were brass flasks and a tangle of hoses leading from the opium to a pad beside his knee.

He noticed for the first time that he was naked. Except for a young snoring woman who appeared to have passed out with her face in his lap, Two-Step was alone. He felt the tingle of panic somewhere beneath the pit of his gut, far, far away, and he tried to rise, but his motor responses were not cooperating with weak signals on the edge of his brain. His body was sending him its own message: mellow out. *Never mind, GI. No sweat . . . we take care you, Joe. . . .*

He remembered Nervous Rex and Stormin' Norman now. They had passed on the offer of opium, and had disappeared down a winding corridor toward the sound of bedsprings in action, voluptuous little *business girls*, with long hair flowing down over their shoulders to cover shapely haunches, under both arms of each Green Beret.

He glanced down at the woman in his lap, giggled involuntarily at fleeting memories-lost, and watched his hands clasp her cheeks gently. The hands were lifting her face out of his crotch now.

Something milky-white drooled from the corner of her mouth, and he watched the hands release her. The girl's face plopped back down without sound or feeling.

Broken Arrow watched himself turn away in disgust.

"*. . . The new hunters tried to make slaves of the Comanche people, and your ancestors killed many of them. Though the customs of the kidnapped girl and your people were much different—they were a band of the Staked Plains in what became northern Texas, and she was from a land to the east called Virginia—young Cynthia Parker was adopted by our tribe. The tribe had many roving bands, and Cynthia Ann Parker grew up among them, travelling the width of the crimson mesa, as she became a young Indian woman. . . .*"

Broken Arrow had started to lean back, relaxing, as his mother's soothing words returned to his again, but suddenly he sat bolt upright. His eyes were wide open.

"*. . . Your grandmother's grandmother . . . when she was only nine . . . she was kidnapped . . .*"

Broken Arrow glanced around at his surroundings again.

He shook his head violently, trying to clear it of the magical smoke, but his mother's voice would not leave him.

". . . *Your grandmother's grandmother . . . the tribe had many roving bands . . . young Cynthia Ann Parker was adopted by our tribe. . . .*"

A tear tumbled down Two-Step's proud cheek. He wiped it away so roughly a red welt slowly appeared under his right eye. His chest expanded, and he let out a terrible war-cry, but the girl in his lap failed to stir.

"*. . . Cynthia Ann Parker . . . your grandmother's grandmother. . . .*"

"Damn!" he muttered under his breath, pushing the young woman aside, onto the sleeping mats. The sound of boots and tongs and bare feet running down the corridor toward his cubicle reached Broken Arrow's ears, chasing away the already fading image of his mother down by the riverbank, telling him stories as a child.

"*Damn!*"

The opium must have done it, he decided.

"Chance! Hey, Two-Step!" Nervous Rex and Stormin' Norman were crowding through the doorway's bamboo drapes, worried and concerned looks on their faces. "You alright, dude?"

"It sounded like that chick done sliced off your ding-dong with a rusty straight-razor, boy!" Stormin' Norman had his pistol out, and seemed disappointed he was not going to get a good reason to use it.

"I think you guys got the wrong room." Two-Step's presence of mind returned sufficiently to conjure up a story.

"What happen?" An old mama-san with breasts big as watermelons but thighs the size of rolled-up sleeping bags pushed both Nervous Rex and Stormin' Norman aside. "What you do?"

"I think it was the guy down the hall," Two-Step maintained. "The Marine with the black Cambodian chick."

"She Filipino," the mama-san corrected him, waving her finger accusingly.

"Filipenis-scheanus!" he snapped in reply. "Get the fuck outta my face, bitch!"

Everyone in the doorway cleared out, and it wasn't until then, as he watched two sets of pale buttocks bounce back down the corridor, that Broken Arrow realized the two Green Berets were naked from the waist down. Naked but unembarrassed. The sight brought a smile to his lips. The two men had gone out of their way to watch him all day and—

Broken Arrow's legs flew over the side of the bed as the shifting of thoughts made him remember Brody. The movement nearly made him pass out as the opium in his brain sloshed about like pond ripples during a storm.

Poor old Treat. The last Two-Step had seen of him, the Whoremonger was lying in the middle of the street, forearms folded over his head—a speeding military police jeep on a collision course with his cranium.

He had almost bit through his lower lip waiting for the MP driver to hit the brakes . . . waiting for the jeep to begin its skid, then the vehicle—at the last moment—was swerving around Brody on two wheels. One of the Viet cherrygirls was darting out into the street to help Whoremonger up, and by the time the MP jeep slowed enough for one of the army cops to jump out and start running back after him, ol' Trick-or-Treat was history: he and the girl had vanished between two of the ramshackel dwellings constructed of C-rations crates and flattened beercans.

"Whoremonger can handle himself," Broken Arrow decided, leaning back against the headboard of the cheap, PX bed. He had not even noticed that the woman who prepared his first pipe for him was no longer on the sleeping mats across the floor but snuggled up beside him.

Her fingers curled around his penis and began stroking him slowly. Broken Arrow smiled—she must have thought he said something about a handjob. "I not whore," she protested softly without looking up at him. "I opium den dancer. . . . You want I should . . . dance for you?'

Without emotion, Two-Step removed the woman's hand and gently replaced it with her mouth. She did not protest.

100

"Do the dancing with your lips, opium girl. . . ." he said softer than she had spoken. Merely shrugging her shoulders, the woman sighed and went to work, as if only the tasks had changed but not the boss.

Broken Arrow put the opium pipe to his own lips and inhaled deeply. The woman in his lap was gagging now, but he felt nothing below the throat—no sensations whatsoever.

The bamboo beads became long, breezy wisps of weeping willow leaves beside a riverbank a million miles away. Indian children were laughing and yelling as they floated past on homemade rafts and innertubes. The reservation was his entire life. He had never heard of Indochina, or a smaller place called South Vietnam.

". . . *Cynthia Ann Parker . . . your grandmother's grandmother. . . ."*

He heard his mother's voice again . . . far off and distant, this time.

"Damn!"

He heard his own voice cursing his discovery; the realization that . . . The opium must have done it. Unlocked the doors. The doors of his mind. The doors he had tried to keep sealed for so long. The memories he had refused to think about. The truth he did not want to accept.

". . . *Cynthia Ann Parker . . . the new hunters . . ."*

The new hunters were settlers. White people. His grandmother's grandmother was Cynthia Ann Parker. Now he remembered where the first name 'Chance' came from.

Chance 'Two-Step' Broken Arrow had a white woman in the family tree. He was not a full-blooded Comanche Indian after all.

Two-Step groaned. He turned his head to one side on the plush, satin pillow, trying to bring back visions of the riverbank, and the plains extending as far as the eye could see beyond his childhood treehouse. But all he could see was the slowly turning blades of the ceiling fan overhead. There was no roar of rapids and waterfalls mingling with the trickle of freshwater springs in the crystal caves. Only the slurping sound of the woman over his lap, trying to clean up the mess she had made.

The bullet ricocheted off the corner of the building on the other side of the alley, but slivers of brick reached him, stabbing into his elbow as he ran.

"Jesus!" Treat Brody slapped his hand across the wound. *Why is the guy shooting at us!"*

A gasp left Koy's throat as five more rapidly-fired rounds bounded off the concrete gutter beside them and zinged skyward. Brody tightened his arm around her, but she was trying to push him away—to be free of him. They both knew they'd make better time if they split up. At least, that's what Brody was thinking.

He was about to release her when she surprised him by taking a hold of his hand and guiding him down a hostile-looking corridor suddenly. So abruptly, in fact, a bolt of fear lanced down through Treat's insides: was she leading him into a trap?

A bullet split the doorframe behind them at that very moment—perhaps her movements were guided by instinct too.

Brody listened to the MP eject his empty clip and slam a fresh ammo magazine into the pistol's butt. The MP sounded a half block away—far enough for Brody to risk a challenge.

"Why the hell are you shooting at us?" he yelled. Brody was certain the military policeman was alone.

Sounding slightly out of breath, the tone told him the MP had been surprised by the question. "Deserters in *this* area of operations face a jury of two, asshole: me and Mista Colt!"

"We aren't deserters!" Brody yelled despite Koy's hands over his mouth, pleading for silence. Terror in her eyes, and her lips pulled back as if she expected to burst out crying at any second, she tugged at his arm, guiding him toward the fire escape of an old French factory.

The MP did not sound as if he were in the mood to debate. "You were in a stolen jeep, scumbag! That's a felony offense! That makes you a fleeing felon! That means I can pop a cap on your ass, and I'm low man on the totem pole this month for poppin' caps, *asshole!"*

Brody did not respond. He quietly followed Koy up the ladder.

When they reached the roof, Brody rushed over to the edge. The MP was slowly walking right below him, gunarm locked out at the elbow, pistol waving back and forth as he passed each series of doorways in the narrow corridor.

"Here," Koy whispered, nudging his elbow. She was holding a cinderblock the size of a large filebox.

Brody shook his head in the negative. His eyes narrowed trying to convey his disapproval.

"Then *I* do it."

"No!" His whisper turned harsh as he grabbed her wrist. Their eyes dueled, but by that time, it was too late—the MP was out of range, down the alley.

From the rooftop, they had a good view of much of the surrounding terrain, and Brody and Koy watched the military police jeep chase Two-Step, Nervous Rex, and Stormin' Norman up through a hillside maze of alleys and sidestreets.

Ritter must have been a grand prix driver in a past life, for it quickly became apparent he was only toying with the MPs. After driving circles aorund them a couple times— the jeep he'd 'borrowed' from a visiting Chaplain was brand new and the MPs' probably had an odometer that'd turned-over twice—Nervous Rex pulled away from them on a straight away and disappeared down into a stepping-stone network of lush ricepaddies that eventually came out on a plateau leading to Highway 19.

Brody and Koy waited until the MP jeep returned to pick up the disgruntled military policeman on foot, then, after the vehicle disappeared down a bend in the road, they climbed back down the fire escape.

"Now I'm up shit creek." Brody stared at the setting sun, wondering what time curfew in Plei Me was.

He was sure Koy would ask "what is shit creek?" but she surprised him. "Why you no kill MP?"

"He try kill *you*." Neither looked at each other as they slowly walked down the narrow corridor, Koy following

Brody, though she had no idea where he was going.

"He wasn't tryin' to kill me, dear . . ." The last word was spoken sarcastically.

Koy slapped his elbow lightly, and Brody recoiled. "*OW!*" he protested, jumping away from her.

"What call *that*?"

He could tell by her tone she was grinning, but he refused to look back at her. "A lucky shot," he answered.

"You should have killed him," Koy repeated. "Next time you do it. You kill him."

"You're talking like a VC. Jesus, the guy was just some hotdog REMF who wanted a reason to pop some caps somewhere besides the shooting range. No big deal . . ."

"Maybe I *am* VC."

Brody slid to a halt. "Not funny." He waved his finger in front of her small nose for reprimand.

"Not want to be funny. Maybe I kill many GI. What you think about *that*?" She resumed walking, taking the lead now

"I don't think anything about it one way or the other." Brody followed her without further protest.

"What mean . . . 'remf'?" she asked without looking back.

"Rear Echelon Mother Fucker," he answered matter-of-factly.

"And . . . 'pop caps'?"

Forming his hand like a pistol, he placed his forefinger against the small of her back. "Bam! You die, *du ma VC!*"

"Oh . . . I see . . . ."

"Really . . ."

Koy turned to face him. "Yes. Reawwy." She trilled the L's on purpose. With *her* forefinger, she touched the fabric over Brody's left breast. "You have good heart, GI."

"Me?" He feigned intense doubt.

"Maybe. You have chance *fini* MP, but you . . . let him go."

"Maybe we Americans just have this thing about watching out for each other." The grin returned to his face and she tapped his wounded elbow sharply. "*Okay!* Okay . . ."

A sound not unlike a dozen kernels of corn popping far, far away erupted behind them, high in the darkening sky. A starburst exploded in brilliant streaks of red and green, and a few seconds later, two silk parachutes with flares suspended beneath them began floating down between low clouds. Zigzagging from side to side, they threw flickering shards of golden light across the rooftops.

"Where you go tonight, GI?" Her eyes were smiling at him.

"I have a name." Brody stared down at her, realizing for the first time how close they really were to each other.

"So do I." Koy touched his knuckles, then ran her fingers up through the hair on his left arm.

"It is Treat."

"Tuh . . . tuh . . ." She was having trouble placing the R behind the T.

"Treat."

"Where do you go tonight, Treat?" Her lips smiled this time, but Brody did not immediately answer the question.

"I know your name." He remembered it, despite all the excitement following the earlier introductions. "You are Koy."

"Very good." Her eyes seemed to sparkle a bit at the realization he actually remembered her name.

"But I do not know what it means."

Glancing up at the drifting flares, Koy seemed to reflect on an earlier phase of her life . . . a part of her past. The smile seemed to fade slightly. "It means . . . evening flower," she said with little enthusiasm.

"Ah . . . 'evening flower. . . .'" Brody gently clasped one of her hands and slowly backed her into a doorway.

"Yes. . . ."

"You mean, like, one that blooms only in the dark. One that hides its beauty until after the sun sets. . . ." He dropped to one knee and, with much ceremony in his movements, kissed the top of her hand. "I am pleased to meet you, Koy, my evening flower . . ."

She glanced about nervously, as if fearing someone might be spying on them in that dimly lit doorway. She was

105

embarrassed by his behavior, but she didn't want to embarrass *him*. When he rose, she realized she was also touched.

Koy's heart began beating furiously, and she felt her face flush as his eyes slowly rose above hers again. Her surroundings no longer seemed so important.

"Where . . . you . . . go . . . tonight, GI?" She was not taunting him—not really, though he might have thought he detected a tease in her voice. Koy was still unsure of herself . . . unsure of her courage—of the courage it took to handle this type of matter.

"I go back to . . . Plei Me." He had almost forgotten the name of the camp. Where *was* home these days? he wondered, and the thought both troubled and puzzled him—it was the first time such a thing had ever come to him in Vietnam.

"Too far," Koy whispered, using both her hands to clutch one of his. "Too dark."

"But I must go."

"VC will get you. If not VC, then MP." She did not sound worried. Only practical.

"The VC do not scare me . . ."

"They should." Koy could not hold back the grin.

". . . And I do not think the MPs got a good look at my face."

"Tonight . . ." Her hands tightened on his until he gazed down into her dark, beckoning eyes. "You come home with me . . ."

Was it . . . *pain* Brody thought he detected in the razor-thin lines at the edges of her eyes? Or just the fear of rejection? "All right . . ." he said simply, wondering if disappointment came through in his tone: she was surely no cherrygirl after all. A cherrygirl would have nothing to do with him. At least that was the way the custom went, wasn't it?

"It is not far from here . . . ." Koy held on tightly to his hand as she led him through the maze of pitch-black back alleys. She was suddenly terrified—what the *hell* had she gotten herself into? Thrill-seeking was one thing, but actually attempting to seduce one of the Americans was

106

suicide—surely it was! Venn's friend had promised Koy the use of her room in the boarding house, but did any of them really believe their little schoolgirl game would be played through to fruition? What if Venn's friend—and the friend's entire family—were still crowded into the room, clustered around the rice cooker? She surely could not take him back to the caves. That would go over well: My Dear VC comrades, meet my new lover, GI Joe! She was taking enough risks as it was, walking through the ville hand-in-hand with a foreigner. The VC had a thousand eyes. Someone would tell, and this was not a 'mission' cleared with her cell leader. Before the sun rose, she might find herself buried alive in a shallow grave beyond Bien Hoa.

Koy's goals for the evening changed radically as all these thoughts went through her head. Making romance to one of the Americans might, at one time, have been a challenge. Now it seemed a curse.

There was only one thing left to do. She would lure him down into the Cong-controlled edge of the ville. And there she would kill him.

CHAPTER 10

". . . *When your grandmother's grandmother was eighteen, War Chief Peta Nacona took her as his bride. Chief Nocona was held in high regard by our people because he often told the new hunters life would be harsh and unforgiving to them if they continued taking Comanche warriors as slaves and Comanche women and children as servants and barter. Many of our camps were destroyed by the new hunters, and we, in turn, burned many of their homesteads to the ground . . .*

"*The new hunters promoted the caging of the Plains. Fences rose everywhere. Our people, who are nomadic . . . who hold little interest in personal belongings and land ownership, only wanted freedom to hunt our plains unhindered, give your children names of the great animals of the wilds, and worship the sun and the other gods of nature.* . . .

"*The new hunters, they brought in missionaries—servants of their lone god—who tried to influence our ways and our thinking, but Chief Nocona told them, Preach your religion to the white men instead and we will see if they stop cheating the Comanche. . . .*"

His father's words lingered in Broken Arrow's ears like echoes of wind through deep, river-carved canyons when he woke from the opium-induced sleep.

The Vietnamese woman who'd spent the last twelve hours curled up over his lap in the fetal position was gone.

He rose, stumbled out of the bed, and made his way down the narrow corridor to a filthy, open-air cafe of sorts. The lingering heat and humidity made it feel like afternoon—a time when it was customary for indigenous types to skip work for a two-hour siesta—but black candles below one umbrellaed table proved it was night. Darkness lent credible evidence to the assumption. Light from the flickering candles illuminated the faces of Nervous Rex, Stormin' Norman, and two topheavy bargirls. The tabletop was cluttered with empty brown bottles of "33" beer, their red and gold labels visible even from this distance.

"Black candles?" He dropped to his knees behind Nervous Rex and his 'guest,' bracing his forearms on a high and low shoulder. The woman protested with a groan and scooted away. Broken Arrow toppled onto his side and spent a full minute groaning beneath the table.

"Arvin cut the power to this neighborhood," Ritter announced.

"I heard chatter they're making a sweep for VC on the southern edge of Plei Me." Stormin' Norman placed a fresh bottlecap between his teeth, twisted it off, and grinned triumphantly when his 'date" squealed in awe. Stormin' Norman's tongue rubbed blood from the insides of his lips for the next ten minutes, but the bargirl never seemed to taste it during their frequent kisses between the formaldehyde-laced booze.

"Pull of a chair, Comanche-man." Ritter excused his woman with a scowl, and Two-Step climbed aboard.

Stormin' Norman pushed a bottle in front of Broken Arrow, then continued talking as if there had never been any interruption. "But it must really make you feel . . . *powerful* inside," he said.

"I feel no different than before," Nervous Rex lied, sounding tense and irritated.

"But . . . but killing more than thirty of the enemy in . . . in hand-to-hand combat—and in less than a year. *Jesus!*"

110

"Cut me some slack, okay, Stormin'?" Ritter downed half a bottle of "*33*" and glanced over at Broken Arrow, allowing the stare to linger, as if appraising the soldier's condition.

"Don't be modest, sarge . . ."

"And don't call me 'sarge'!"

"Okay! Christ . . ."

The girl hiding beneath Stormin' Norman's massive arm peeked out at Ritter and blew him a sloppy kiss. Broken Arrow watched the spittle fly across the table. "You veddy brave, Joe! *Fini bookoo* VC, no? *Coka-dau* bookoo comn-'nists!"

"I'm gonna *fini* you, woman, if ya don't go back to suckin' on apeman's tit!"

Broken Arrow might have expected the bargirl to cower back under Stormin' Norman's protective wrist, but she merely giggled, and the birdlike laugh started Two-Step to chuckling too. Before long, Stormin' Norman was bellowing louder than them all, and the entire backalley cafe was clacking away, though half the Vietnamese were not sure what they were laughing about.

Nervous Rex glanced around, expecting to see several disapproving stares—at least a few pair of hostile eyes from Arvins in the crowd—but there were none, and, to Nervous Rex, that was a bad sign. There wasn't really that much of a crowd, either, since it was fast approaching curfew, and perhaps that was a good sign. But Nervous Rex remained uneasy nonetheless.

"It does . . . *change* you," he said finally, and the place went deadly quiet.

"How so?" Stormin' Norman spilled a quarter bottle of beer down the front of his shirt without noticing.

"You begin to feel . . . inhuman." He leaned closer to his fellow Green Beret. At the same time, Broken Arrow leaned back in his chair, feeling suddenly sober. Sober and entertained.

"Inhuman?" Stormin' Norman's eyes were fast growing large as chicken eggs, and his whore resumed her giggling routine.

"Well . . . not inhuman, maybe . . . but . . ."

"'Above it,'" Broken Arrow volunteered calmly. "You feel 'above it all.' As if you're gliding down into Void Vicious, prowling for prey . . ."

"*Yah!*" Nervous Rex was nodding energetically. "You're right, Comanche-man. *That's* what I meant. *That's exactly* what I meant!"

"You're in control," Broken Arrow continued. "You feel almost . . . invincible . . . . Like, no matter what the odds, you're gonna come out of it victorious . . ."

"*Yeah!*"

"With a half dozen more Cong heads hanging on your web belt . . ."

"By George he's *got it!*" Ritter pounded the tabletop, and a beer bottle rolled off, crashing on the ground.

"Say, you're pretty good with this." Stormin' Norman pushed another bottle in front of Two-Step. "I take it you've ripped off a coupla Charlie's ears yourself."

Broken Arrow swallowed hard, but none of them seemed to notice. The bargirl's smile faltered, and *she* might have noticed—might have read it in his eyes—but he didn't think Nervous Rex or Stormin' Norman did. "Naw . . . No, just a couple. Back when the jungle was teeming with 'em. You know, when it was easy pickin's, and. . . ."

"Yeah, I know." Ritter glanced up at one of the slowly revolving ceiling fans above the bar counter, a dreamy look in his eyes, then he leaned back from under their table's umbrella to inspect the night sky. "Christ, you can't see the friggin' stars anymore for all the flares!"

"How many VC *you* kill?" The bargirl pointed her chin at Stormin' Norman both accusingly and as a challenge.

"Me, honey?" Stormin' Norman hugged the woman and nipped at her ear. "Hell, I ain't *cocka-dau'd* a single Victor Charlie, baby! Stormin' Norman's a lover, not a fighter. . . ."

Nervous Rex listened to the mandatory giggle, then turned to face Broken Arrow again. He lowered his voice, so that only those at his table could hear. "Do you . . . sometimes . . . feel almost . . . godlike? I mean . . ."

112

"I think you've got me wrong, Sgt. Ritter. I ain't no member of the Dirty Thirty . . . that's for fuckin' sure. *You're* the only one in-country, ain't that so? I was just talkin' . . . ."

"Well then, let me re-phrase it, my friend . . ." When Ritter spoke this time, his eyes seemed almost to glow slightly, but Broken Arrow knew it was only an optical illusion caused by the collage of candles on so many tabletops. "After about my fortieth kill, I began to have dreams. Strange dreams and even stranger thoughts. . . ."

"You mean like . . . like you'd been elevated? Elevated to a position equal to, or maybe just below God?" Broken Arrow answered with a knowing grin, but it was a tight grin and Ritter surprised him with his reply.

"I felt like I had *become* god. . . ."

Broken Arrow frowned. He was not a religious man. Compassion for the animals and a respect for the land was his idea of faith. He did not attend any church. And Nervous Rex's brand of talk—or was it just a variation of the usual old Green Beret been-in-the-jungle-too-long humor?—was making him feel uneasy.

". . . I often felt . . . in*VIN*cible." He sat up straight in his chair and took in a deep breath of air, expanding his chest. "I was in total control. I *had* created the jungle, therefore it would not harm me. . . ."

"You talk *dinky-dau*." The bargirl's smile became insincere, and she began drinking from Stormin' Norman's bottle. Ritter ignored her.

". . . The animals . . . even panthers, tigers . . . you name it . . . even them crazy rougue elephants did not concern me. Only Charlie . . . Only riding my domain of Victor Charlie."

"And you weren't worried maybe ol' Charlie'd get a lucky one in and cancel your ticket, sport?" Stormin' Norman opened another beer.

Ritter laughed. It was the laugh Stormin' Norman was sure would greet him at the gates of hell. "Shit, I've had a hundred AK rounds comin' at me before—all at once—and I'm still here jawin' with you, ain't I? I've walked into the

113

middle of snakenests full o' commies in the past, and came out smellin' like a rose. Now you tell me," Nervous Rex began his own challenge, but the bargirl interrupted him.

"True God would not talk 'dis way," she said, moving slightly away from Stormin' Norman's protective cuddle, then immediately backing against him again when she saw the look in Ritter's eyes.

"Oh, *REALLY*?" The Green Beret sergeant leaned across the table until his nose was only inches away from the woman's. "And what might your name be, my little sweetie . . ."

"Janet!" The last traces of her smile disappeared completely.

"Ahhh . . . Janet. *American* name!'

"Yes," Janet swallowed loudly. She sounded guilty when she said, "American name."

"Well let me tell you something about your 'God,' Janet, my dear. Are you Buddhist? Or Christian, perhaps?"

She just stared back at him with blank, watery eyes.

"Makes no difference. Let me start off by asking you this: did you happen to hear about the massacre last year? The one in Binh Dinh Province? The one where the VC executed hundreds of civilians and dumped their bodies into a mass grave?"

Janet's lips did not part. Her expression did not change.

"Sure you did. It only happened last year, and you're older than a year, am I right? You don't walk around Vietnam with blinders on, do you, honey? You may not be able to read, but you can see photos on the newsstands, right? You hear the people gossiping, don't you?" Nervous Rex paused to empty a beer bottle and, as if they'd practiced the routine on countless past occasions, Stormin' Norman supplied him with a replacement.

"I read Vietnamese and French. I am study Chinese nighttime. . . ."

"Obviously not *TO*night, right?" Ritter grinned across the table at her. He wanted to belch in her face, but his stomach would not cooperate.

"I speak more languages than *you*!"

114

"*Touché*!" Ritter's right hand flew up over his head as if there was a sword in it.

"So no call me stupid."

Nervous Rex's grin abandoned him. "I no *call* you stupid, woman. I say you 'may not be able to read.' Nobody said anything about your intelligence. I'm sure you're gifted with some very skillful talents, as Stormin' Norman will attest to." When she glanced up into Stormin' Norman's eyes, Ritter leaned his head back for Two-Step's benefit and began stroking an invisible erection.

"What mean 'intelligence'?" Janet asked Stormin' Norman. Broken Arrow broke out laughing and nearly tipped over backwards in his chair. When Stormin' Norman did not immediately answer, Janet punched him in the arm roughly.

Rubbing the spot, he still refused to acknowledge her presence. Instead, he asked Nervous Rex, "Just what, exactly, is your point, honorable sergeant-sir?"

"Okay, let's take that plane crash last year near Tokyo. Remember? During the summer Olympics. How many died. Couple hundred, maybe? Sure, couple hundred, *minimum*."

"So?"

"*So*? Was it weather-related? Or engine failure, maybe? It surely wasn't a bomb. . . ."

"They never solved that one . . ." Stormin' Norman was perplexed, to say the least.

"Then it was . . . heaven forbid: an act of God?" Nervous Rex threw his arms up dramatically.

"Well. . . ."

"Okay, take that little ol' innocent housewife that was diddy-boppin' down Wall Street last month—I read about this one in the *Stars & Stripes*—the one who was pregnant with twins. Remember her?"

Stormin' Norman nodded even though he didn't read the newspapers and had not heard the story about the pregnant woman.

"Well, chunk o' ice fell off an airliner passing over the Statue of Liberty and smacked her right on top o' the head.

115

Pounded her noggin' right down between her shoulderblades and left it sittin' in her pelvic cavity. Just about. Remember that one? The twins were D.O.A., dude. . . ."

Janet glanced up at Stormin' Norman again, and when he muttered, "Dead On Arrival," it was obvious she still didn't know what they were talking about.

"Now what are ya gonna call *that* one? Negligence on the part of the airlines for lettin' frozen piss fall out the bottoms of their jetplane toilets?"

"That's a start," Broken Arrow entered the 'conversation,' but Ritter ignored him.

"Or maybe ya wanna call it premeditated murder? Some goblin was up there ridin' the plane's belly, chippin' away at them big, blue icecubes and aimin' 'em for nice ol' never-done-nothin'-to-nobody ladies pregnant with twins. Or would you rather call it a terrorist bombing?"

Stormin' Norman frowned, searching his brain for a witty rebuke.

Ritter erupted into uneasy laughter. "I got ya by the balls, Stormin.' And now I'm gonna twist: okay, so ya combine all them alledged 'acts o' God' with all the so-called natural disasters . . . you know, drought, famine, fire and floods, car accidents. . . ."

"The black syph." Nervous Rex nodded, his eyes falling to the ample swell of dark flesh against Janet's lowcut blouse. "Now ya take all them and combine 'em, and you tally up all the lives lost—and you still have the gall to tell me there's a God?"

"You must believe!" Janet waved her finger at him again after covering up her cleavage with a scarf. "God test you! You need *faith*!"

"Fine . . . *fine*!" Ritter's hands came up again. "But you know what, Janet?" He leaned across the table again, until they were nose-to-nose. "Every time I *fini* another handful of Viet Cong guerilas, *I* become closer to God. *I* become godlike, don't you see?

"When it happens, it's always just me and them and the jungle—just the three of us . . . out in the middle of

116

nowhere. The way it was meant to be. Far away from civilization. In the heart of the rain forest. . . ."

"You crazy man." Janet moved about on her chair as if she'd tired of the game and wanted to leave these three animals.

Broken Arrow stared at Ritter quietly for some time, gauging his facial expression as he spoke. Green Berets were notorious for telling tall tales, outrageous war stories, and generally exaggerating. Two-Step wanted to know if all this was an act, or if Nervous Rex Ritter was serious. Two-Step wanted to know this because he'd had similar feelings in the past. Gut feelings, perhaps . . . things he thought about late at night, when he was all alone, long after his team had been extracted from the rain forest. But emotions nonetheless . . . emotions that sometimes forced him to question his own sanity.

"You *dinky-dau*," Janet repeated, as she rose from her chair finally. "Bookoo *dinky-dau*." She gave Stormin' Norman a look that demanded to know if he was coming or not.

"Well, gentlemen." Stormin' Norman glanced over his shoulder at the short-time stalls down one corridor, and the more permanently constructed all-nighter rooms on the other side. "I guess it's about time we butt out and . . . sing a song for freedom!" He patted Janet's well-founded bottom. "Time for some *boom-boom*, my friends! I'm sure you understand . . ."

"Just remember what I told you, Janet!" Nervous Rex called across the room to the prostitute. "The more men you off, the closer you get to *nirvana*, dear!

"And watch out for Stormin' Norman, honey. He's not the gently giant you think he is. Stormin' Norman likes it from behind!" Stormin' Norman was furiously trying to wave Ritter silent. "He likes to mount his mares from behind, baby—the easier it is for him to snap their necks! You ever heard of the term 'double vet'?"

But Janet was ignoring him, much to Stormin' Norman's relief, though Stormin' Norman didn't have anything dastardly planned for the whore. But he didn't want to sleep with a woman who kept a switchblade between her thighs, either.

"And what the flyin' fuck are *you* starin' at, Comanche-man?" Ritter turned around to find Two-Step unable to take his eyes off the Green Beret. "You ain't one o' those queer kinda fairies, are ya, boy?"

Broken Arrow could not speak. It took every bit of concentration at his disposal to break the spell created by Ritter's speech and nod his head from side to side.

"Well then just what the hell *is* your major malfunction, *pal*?" Nervous Rex was getting nervous. Homosexuals made him nauseous. Nauseous and nervous. And this Indian character was giving him 'that look.'

"It's not what you think, sarge," Two-Step finally said.

"It better not be." Roughly, Ritter slid a bottle of beer across the table at him. The trance broken, Two-Step caught the bottle easily and began drinking from it.

He wanted to explain to Sgt. Ritter what he was feeling, but he couldn't bring himself to talk about it. Not just yet

. . .

Chance 'Two-Step' Broken Arrow was a quiet soldier. He didn't boast about the firefights he'd survived, or the men he'd killed. To him, stalking soldiers through the jungle with his crossbow was a challenge—a throwback to the days his ancestors hunted white men on the Comanche frontier. The Vietnamese became Texas Rangers and white settlers—the whites in his squad, and the blacks and Mexicans became red, like himself. Indian. Broken Arrow had been killing VC and enjoying it for nearly three years now. He'd moved to seven different duty stations, and, each time, neglected to tell anyone how many Cong he'd termi-nated. Because the number was well over thirty. Over thirty done away with in hand-to-hand.

Broken Arrow was not skeptical about the curse attached to The Nam's Dirty Thirty fraternity. He'd seen it happen to a dozen men. Buddies. Fellow Indians, with white and black and brown skin. But they were men who boasted. Soldiers who kept score. Therefore, others felt required to maintain their own tally. And legends were born. Only to die.

Broken Arrow was convinced that he would long out live whatever fate befell Vietnam. He was positive he would survive this thing called Dirty Thirty, and live to tell about . . . on some future evening . . . on distant ground . . . beside the campfire, to his grandchildren . . . on the reservation . . . So long as he told no one about the notches on his crossbow.

So long as he did not boast about it and bring the attention of the evil forces in the rain forest down on himself.

Broken Arrow wanted to explain to Sgt. Ritter that he understood the Green Beret was telling Janet all about. He *knew* what Nervous Rex knew. But he wasn't sure if the man could keep a secret.

And when he decided to find out, well, that was when the squad of black-pajama-clad communists burst into the open-air cafe, bayonets bristling on the barrels of their AK-47 assault rifles.

CHAPTER 11

Koy was trembling. She hoped this man named Treat could not tell, but she was trembling violently inside. It did not really matter, though. During the long walk to the dwelling of Venn's friend, she had formulated her plan: she would pretend to have trouble with the latch, and when the American opened the door, she would jump on his back and plunge her knife down into his throat, in front of them all. Blood would shower onto the lot of them . . . onto their rice cooker and across their sleeping mats, and they would see that Koy was a good communist. She would prove where her loyalties truly lay!

The dwelling was empty. Dark and empty, just as Venn had promised.

Before following Brody inside, she glanced around, up and down the dark alleyway, but it appeared they were alone. And she did not sense the thousand eyes watching her from afar like before.

Koy felt her resolve melt when Brody closed the door gently, swiftly, without sound, and swept her up in his arms. His lips came down on hers, roughly at first, then instantly as gentle as clouds . . . clouds she had climbed up to and sang for and whistled into when she was but a child, scavenging for evening flowers atop the Chu Pong massif.

"You still taste like ice cream." He smiled down at her.

121

"*Vietnamese* ice cream." Koy felt her revolutionary fervor abandon her. She no longer wanted to kill this man. She wanted to love him.

"You mean there's a difference?" Brody couldn't help but feel he'd seen her face before. But he just couldn't place it. They didn't have that much contact with civilians in An Khe—especially women. So where could it have been?

"Of *course* there's a difference. Some night I will show you. You never want any other kind again."

"I've heard it is very sweet . . ." Perhaps he had seen her in his dreams . . . while he was out on a lonely twelve-hour LP somewhere, thinking about the *ao-dai*-clad lasses gliding along on the breeze down in Saigon. "Maybe *too* sweet."

"Sweet like me?" Koy blinked her eyes seductively. She could not believe she was saying these things—that the words were coming to her so easily.

Brody lowered his face again and gently kissed her nose. "Yes, Koy. Sweet, like you."

He kissed her on the nose again, letting his lips linger.

"You like Vietnamese woman?" Her eyes grew large, her mouth sad.

"I . . . I think so . . . yes, I like Vietnamese women." He smiled and tried to kiss her again, but she darted out from under him, over to the window overlooking the edge of the ville.

Koy touched her nose for his benefit. "You no think Vietnamese woman nose too flat?"

"I . . . well . . . I never really thought about it, Koy. You have a very pretty nose . . . a very beautiful face . . . ." He floated up behind her and rested his hands against her arms, just above the elbows. His own nose brushed against her long, dark hair. "Vietnamese woman smell very good."

"You like?" Her eyes remained on flares descending slowly in the distance.

"Yes, I like."

Koy slowly drew the wooden shutters tight. She unfastened the top buttons on her blouse and fanned herself with the cloth, as if trying to cool down. Then, confident she'd given Treat an eyeful, she turned around in his arms, eyes closed, and raised pursed lips to him.

Sporadic rifle fire in the distance crackled when Brody kissed her. It was near enough to make him tense up, but Koy began working her lips against his, as if the sound were an everynight occurence, and he relaxed.

His hands held to her hips as her arms wrapped around his neck, and he brought her closer to him. Their chests rubbed, and he found himself lifting her by the haunches to her tiptoes as the kiss heated up.

Koy groaned lightly—a deep, throaty invitation to proceed—and his right hand slid up to cup the breast over her pounding heart. He unfastened the rest of the buttons on her blouse with his free hand, and the shirt soon fluttered to the floor. The skin along her throat taut as she dropped her head back, Brody's lips slid down across her chin and along her neck and her moans grew louder.

His tongue circled her nipple after licking the slope between breasts, tasting her, feeling her heart race. Her perfume was making him light-headed, and the natural fragrance of her flesh . . . her scent was whipping his lust into a frenzy . . . screaming at him in silence . . . shouting at him to devour her and be done with it, when what he wanted to do was take it one step at a time . . . slow . . . go ever so slowly. . . .

Another burst of bullets a mile away reached his ears as her nipples grew rigid and he brought his lips over one, sucking Koy up . . . engulfing her. . . . He wanted to drop to the floor and ravish her, and Koy sensed this.

"Not here . . ." she whispered. "Not . . . like . . . this . . ."

"I think I could live on a three-course meal of nothing but 'Koy,'" he whispered back, "day after day after . . ."

She silenced him by pressing her breast as flat as she could with his mouth. "You find Koy attractive?" She sounded like she already knew the answer. Or hoped she did.

"I've been under your spell, my queen, since the first time I saw you on the street back there . . ."

"Under my spell?"

"Yes."

"You have eyes for no other? You would not butterfly on Koy if Koy allow you into her life?" It seemed the beginning of a game. *Some kinky little Oriental striptease*, Brody grinned.

"Butterfly?" He hoped he did not sound too stupid.

"You see butterfly go from flower to flower, from place to place . . . never come back. . . . You do like butterfly? Go from girl to girl . . . never come back to me? You think you might cheat on Koy?"

"Me? Cheat? No, no . . . nebbah happen, honey! Not Treat the Whore-uh, I mean . . . not me, babes!"

"If you butterfly on Koy, I find you, *mianoi*. I sneak up on you and you no can butterfly again. Never! You no can afford to—"

"But I thought . . . I thought butterflies were free." He grinned sheepishly.

"I find you . . . and *em cat chim anh!*"

Brody swallowed hard. He'd heard the expression before. Down in Saigon. It meant 'cut off your bird.' "That would definitely be the ultimate million-dollar wound."

"Million-doll' wound?"

"Yah. . . . Ticket home, honey. Guaranteed. But I'm not sure it would be worth it." Her hand fluttered in front of his crotch briefly, and he could no longer control his desires. Brody began dragging her down onto the teakwood.

"No. . . ." she whispered. "Over there . . ." And she led him to the single-room dwelling's only bed.

Koy was wearing a skirt that dropped a few inches below her knees. The blouse had been a longsleeved affair, in blue-and-white stripes, with the collar buttoned against her throat. She had been the only girl earlier not wearing the traditional *ao dai* gown.

As she sat on the edge of the bed to unbuckle her shoes, Brody dropped to his knees beside her. He kissed her leg, above the knee, expecting to feel the harsh texture of nylons, but was surprised to find Koy was wearing no stockings at all. *These Viet babes*, his mind smiled as she

124

unsnapped the three diagonal buttons holding the skirt in place. *Legs so dark and smooth . . .* He was in heaven. Snakeman's words from one long-forgotten get-together swirled about in his head, *Dem Viet chicks got no hair on their legs, Treat, ol' boy . . . 'least not much . . .'course the bad news is that they got none on their snatch, either . . . most of 'em, anyways . . . which ain't all that bad, dependin' on how ya look at it: you won't get no stubble burns on your cheeks, and it's doubtful you'll come away with any pubic-type curls between your teeth, dude!*

Koy unwrapped her skirt and then, sliding away from the edge of the bed, her legs. Biting her lower lip—he could not see this in the dim glow from the moon standing guard outside—she reached out to him.

Brody was a pro at this. He had his shirt and trousers off on his way to her arms.

"Make romance to me," she whispered in his ear, trembling as they embraced and she felt him against her, hard warm and hungry. Aching to devour her . . . to engulf her. To fill her with himself until she was no longer Koy, but a reflection . . . a mirror image of Brody . . . all his thoughts and emotions and needs . . . everything he stood for . . . Everything he wanted . . .

"Make . . . romance . . . to . . . me . . . ." It was a low, supressed, animal sound she made as she nibbled at his ear.

They kissed for several long, drawn-out minutes, Brody feeling fully in control, exploring her at his leisure . . . taking his time. Spreading her knees with his own finally, he felt her grow rigid in anticipation.

His hand slid from beneath her haunches as he centered his weight on an elbow, lowering himself beside her for a moment while his fingers massaged the coarse mound of hair where Koy's thighs flared, coming together.

She gasped, sounding startled, as Brody probed, opening her up slightly. His mouth moved back and forth across her breasts, and Koy began twitching slightly with the diversion . . . the pleasure.

Feeling her grow moist, his hands both came up, clasping hers, and their fingers intertwined as he hovered over

125

her *almost like a helicopter*, the voice in his head laughed. *Thump-thump-thump!* He saw himself and Snakeman and Doc Delgado, cruising above the void aboard *Pegasus* as he raised Koy's hands above her head, slowly lowering his groin against hers. *Whop*-whop-whop! He wanted her to cry out. Hovering like a helicopter . . .

Brody found it difficult to enter her.

Koy raised her legs above his hips, locking her ankles over his back, as if by instinct, but Brody sensed trouble. Something was wrong here. She was refusing to open up to him.

And now there were tears streaming down from her eyes. Koy was crying.

Feeling all passion desert him instantly, Brody slowed the movement of his hips. Koy unwrapped her legs, and Treat rolled gently to the side. He cupped her breast with his fingers and kissed it. "Koy, you're crying. What is it? What's wrong?"

Hiding her face in her hands, she rolled over onto her side, turning her back on him. Uncontrolled sobs wracked her body.

"*Koy*. Are you ill?" Bewildered, Brody glanced down at himself, fighting the smile that was trying to get out. It's not *that* large, he joked with himself.

Koy refused to explain. He rubbed her shoulder, kissing the back of her neck, but she would not face him. The sobs only grew worse. "Koy, please talk to me . . . please *look* at me. I'm sorry if I got a little rough . . . Tell me if I . . ." His voice trailed off. And then it struck him.

Brody glanced down at his penis again, rolling backward slightly so moonbeams filtering through cracks in the shutters bathed it in weak silver light.

It was Brody who gasped this time. But it was an inward gasp—one he did not think Koy heard or felt: there was a trace of something dark across the shaft of flesh.

Blood.

He saw himself jumping up and down on the bed, rejoicing, victorious over this conquered maiden but, in reality, Treat felt queasy to the root of his gut

126

"Koy. . . . His lips brushed against her ear. "This is . . . your . . . your first time. This is. . . ." He found himself praying she was only on her period . . . that she was embarrassed her cycle had started early . . . or something. Anything. "This . . . tonight is . . . you're a virgin. . . ."

"Yes. . . ." The cracking of her voice as she slowly turned to face him confirmed the Whoremonger's worst fears: Koy was a cherrygirl.

Brody didn't know what to do. Oh, sure his big boast was that this number one goal in life was to bed down a virgin in every country of Asia, but the truth of the matter was, Spec-4 Treat Brody had only had whores. Whores and a promiscuous nurse now and then, but never an honest-to-God, unspoiled maiden! His first lover had been one of his high school teachers—and she was ten years his senior!

"Please do not be angry with me." Koy allowed him to wipe the tears from her cheeks.

"Angry?" A tight laugh escaped him "Why would I be angry? I'm . . . I'm honored!"

Sniffling now, and eyes blinking wildly as the tears refused to stop, she asked, "Honor? I *honor* you by embarrassing you?"

"You don't understand . . . ." Brody couldn't get rid of the smile. He sat up, and moved to the edge of the bed. In his mind, he saw himself jumping on top of her again, forcing himself into her, staring into her eyes as he did it, smothering her lips with his own as she cried out . . . memorizing the reflection in the *depths* of those eyes when he finally broke through . . . then she surrendered, drawing him in . . . transferring the power of her virginity through him . . . into him. . . .

"I want you to make love to me." Koy reached over and draped her hand across his thigh.

Brody took hold of it gently, seeing, in his mind again, the fingers being bent backwards until they cracked, breaking. . . . "Koy," he began slowly, "I do not think I am deserving of you. . . ."

"Do not talk like noble man." She sat up beside him. "You are soldier. Lonely soldier. I am woman with no man.

127

Now I want man. I want you. I want Treat Brody to make romance to Koy. . . ." She wrapped her arms around him and pulled him down onto the bed again.

They embraced, and kissed for several minutes, but when she rolled beneath and took hold of it . . . thighs wide, beckoning him . . . and when she tried to guide it in, Brody felt himself begin to shrink, and he just lay atop her, holding her tightly, refusing to move.

Koy's legs came down again. "I no longer excite you, Treat Brody?"

"It's not that." The words came out almost as a whimper.

"It must be."

Brody wanted to yell at the ceiling. He was so angry with himself—for surrendering to chivalry when his nature demanded *Attack!*—he wanted to slam his fist against the headboard, which would have left him with only the wall to assault, and he'd seen what taking one's frustrations out on cement could do to knuckles before. Instead, he simply sighed. "You don't deserve me, Koy, and I . . . don't . . . deserve . . . you. . . ."

Koy sighed back. It was an I-just-knew-it sigh. "You would rather have round-eyed girl. After all."

"No . . . no." Brody kissed her eyes softly. "I do not deserve a . . . a woman so . . . so innocent . . . I have had many. . . . I have done many . . . many bad things of which I'm not proud, and. . . ."

"You have had many women before me, no?" Her voice took on an almost French accent.

"No. I mean, yes. *Yes*! I am a soldier. A soldier who suffers from . . . from a less than respectable background as far as . . . I mean . . . I've been around, Koy. I've slept with a lot of . . . a lot of women of rather questionable virtue . . ."

"Virtrue?"

"I've . . . I've spent bookoo nights with some real lowlife kinda tramps, which is something I'm not proud of, but. . . ."

"One waits for you back home tonight?" There was a twinkle of mischief in Koy's eyes now.

128

"No . . . no, of course not . . . but—"

"Then what is the problem, Treat Brody?" Her hand drifted to his crotch again, and he removed it.

He leaned over, to kiss her nipples . . . to be close, and to explain. "The problem is that. . . ." But he could not find the right words.

"You think that my first . . . 'night' should be spend with a . . . a 'cherryboy,' " she said matter-of-factly.

"Something like that."

"I am not born of royalty. I am not from Hue, or a rich family in Saigon. I'm not—"

"That's not what I meant. You misunderstand me, Koy." He watched her whip her long black hair over one shoulder, leaving breasts that were firm and inviting (*You've hardly touched your meal*! he heard Snakeman in the back of his head, shaking a finger in mock reprimand) in full view.

"In Vietnam, it is common for the man to have several wives. For husbands like these, we cannot always be their first. . . ."

Brody was finding himself puzzled. It was like back during that last year in high school, when he was cramming for finals, and his brain was rejecting superfluous data. Nothing, or very little Koy said, was registering. He leaned back and rubbed at his temples. "Damn, could I use a *blow-job* right now!" He stretched his arms out, took in a deep breath, and let it out loudly. "A real, genuine ball-buster!"

Koy cocked her head to one side, appraising the man in her bed. "What . . . is . . . 'blow-job'?" she asked a little too innocently, and Brody quickly sat upright. He swung his legs over the edge of the bed and started to get up.

This time, Koy did not stop him.

She watched him pull in his trousers, and after he slipped on his boots and began lacing them up, she too rose, stepping back onto the pile of clothing beside the bed. "I think I love you, Treat Brody," she said softly, after he tucked his shirt in and lingered at the door, waiting for her. Koy slowly fastened the buttons of her blouse. "I truly

129

think I have fall love for you."

"It's not love, beautiful lady," he sighed, unhappy there were no flares to watch through the shutters.

"It is not?"

"It's lust."

"Lust?" she joined Brody, taking a position by his side, and then one of them sought out the moon only to spot a falling star together.

Brody pointed at it as the golden flash disappeared over the horizon. "Yes. You have heard the word?"

"I know it. It is all my girlfriends talk about: *duc tinh*."

"I see. . . ."

"Come back to me, Treat Brody." She made him face her. "I will wait here for you. Until you are ready. . . ."

"Until *I* am ready?" He placed his forefinger against his sternum.

"I will wait for you in this very room." She clasped his hand, brought it to her lips, and kissed his knuckles, "It has become a . . . very special room . . ."

"I don't think so, Koy . . ." His hand dropped to the doorlatch, and then the knob.

"You. . . . you 'dump' Koy?" A tear raced down the left side of her face. Several more followed, and Brody watched them drip down onto her blouse until the outline of one breast became very clear, its nipple taut against the wet fabric. "You can go out tonight," she decided. "Bookoo VC, Treat Brody. Bookoo VC wait for Americans in the night."

"I know . . ."

"Stay with Koy until morning."

Brody ran his finger along the moist nipple. "I'll take my changes with Charlie." He smiled down at her. "If I stayed, I'm not sure I could guarantee your . . . 'safety,' my dear sweet thing." His lips dropped to the swell of flesh beneath her throat.

"It is not guarantees I ask for," she whispered in his ear as he nibbled at her breast.

"Goodbye, Koy." Brody kissed her lips, and then her forehead, and quickly opened the door. "I want you to save

130

yourself, you hear? Save yourself for . . . *for a gentleman.
. . .*"

"I'll wait for you to come back to me, Treat Brody. . . ."

He closed the door softly behind him, and Koy twirled
around, braced her back against it, and clasped her hands
to her heart. A chill went through Koy—the chill of love
escaping through her fingers but love nonetheless, or the
brief experience of it—and, though she felt instantly sad,
she could not stop smiling, for tonight she had met the
strangest man. One who had not just tried to take, but who
loved back . . . who cared. Koy knew that, even if this
really were the last time she ever saw him again, she would
never forget Treat Brody.

The Whoremonger chose his most bawdy bar-room
ballad to whistle as he wandered down the back alleys of
that lonely, deserted ville, trying to find his way back to
Plei Me.

A half block from where he kissed Koy's forehead, and
her lips, and a set of rigid nipples the sight of which he
would never forget, Venn and four of her girlfriends
confronted the First Cavalry doorgunner.

That was when the big Chinaman hit him on the back of
the head with a crowbar.

CHAPTER 12

"Your grandmother's grandmother had many opportunities to escape from the Comanche, but she chose to stay. She was a good woman. She adopted our religion and language. She dressed like a Comanche. She lived the Comanche customs and traditions. . . .

"Her son by Chief Nocona was Quanah, your grandfather's father, and he became a very important leader of the plains Comanche. . . ."

He was one-*half* white. That was what she had not said. Quanah was one-half white. So don't feel bad, poor Chance. *You're* only an eighth caucasian . . . You can live with that now, can't you, son?

"No, mother . . . no I can't . . ." He heard all his thoughts clearly, as if they'd been spoken, and not simply thoughts at all. His mother's words came to him the same instant Stormin' Norman knocked him aside, out of the way, as several guerrillas charged into the courtyard. The rifles began blazing as soon as the two Green Berets made for an exit in line with the ground-floor bordello, and all Two-Step could really remember was striking his head on a table corner. Table corners and bayonets.

And his mother's blur of a face, down by the river. Broken Arrow had no weapon. He barely had control of his senses as effects of the opium lingered in his system. Crawling for better cover, he promised his dead Comanche ancestors in nameless graves across the Texas plains, and he promised his mother and himself that he'd just experimented with his first and last drug. Not including mushrooms, of course. But opium was out. It left him with no control over his actions . . . his decision-making processes were *all* disoriented, and he didn't like the idea of leaving his destiny in the hands of some doped-up sapper with a brain fried worse than his own.

One guerrilla was rushing toward Nervous Rex—Ritter was fighting two of the communists—and Broken Arrow stuck his boot out, tripping him. Stormin' Norman, who was on the bottom of a pile of half a dozen VC, managed to stick out his pistol and fire two shots at the guerrilla as he, sliding across the floor on his elbows, managed to point his AK at Ritter.

Both rounds missed, and it seemed left up to Two-Step. Taking a deep breath—well aware it might be his last—Broken Arrow started rising from beneath the card table.

That was when the Viet Cong standing behind him placed the steel point of a bayonet at the base of Broken Arrow's skull. The Comanche didn't even bother raising his hands. He was convinced he would be executed any second—that before he could inhale again, his thoughts and emotions and goals and dreams would be splattered across the reflection of himself twenty feet away.

Broken Arrow was staring at a reflection of himself because along one entire wall of the open-air cafe there was a long, unobstructed mirror. A mirror more commonly found behind fancy bar counters, or in nightclubs—and this joint may have, in fact, been such a place, during better times . . . perhaps when the French were buying Saigon tea for the 'hostesses,' instead of Americans.

Broken Arrow was trying to get a good look at the VC

134

standing behind him when the long, semi-frosted mirror disintegrated. It shattered and began collapsing because dozens of bullets were flying over Two-Step's head and impacting across its center, from left to right.

In one of the falling shards, he saw the reflection of a face. A grimy, unshaven face on a monster of a man, and the sight gave Broken Arrow hope. God or Buddha or Manitou or whoever was in charge upstairs had seen fit to smile down on Two-Step this evening. The Creator had delivered unto Chance Broken Arrow a miracle. A rescuer in the form of the biggest, meanest, most courageous doorgunner to ever ride a First Air Division gunship into the fiery hell of battle. . . .

The Cavalry had arrived! And it stood atop two size-13 jungle boots, rising all the way to the ceiling. The Cavalry had to crouch.

"DON WICKMAN!" the soldier with the bayonet against the base of his skull yelled, then dropped flat across the floor, well aware what would follow.

Wickman promptly sprayed the area where Broken Arrow had just been standing, as instinct dictated, and the Cong with the bayonet watched a string of glowing green tracers erupt out of the front of his belly, strewing his last meal of rice and fish heads across the empty mirror frame.

Lowering the smoking M-60, Wickam started toward Stormin' Norman. The stub of a cigar balanced precariously on the edge of his lower lip, 'The Brick'—as Wickam was known within circles of the Airmobile Forces—twirled the heavy machinegun end over end until he was grasping it like a baseball bat.

The Brick was the biggest they come: somewhere between six-foot-two and six-foot-six (he hadn't let supply sergeants touch him with a measuring tape) and two twenty-five to two-fifty. But they were all well-proportioned pounds—the soldier's muscles were so symmetrically shaped it was difficult to appreciate his huge size unless he stood amongst normal men. Though his skin was the hue of polished copper from spending

135

most of his life in the tropics, the Asian sun had not bleached his hair as it did many Americans'—The Brick's locks remained dark. Equally swarthy was the perpetual Death's head grin beneath Wickam's thick mustache. It was a Hollywood mustache—the kind all the heroes in Broken Arrow's favorite war movies wore. And he just knew in his gut if they ever made a film about The Nam, his buddy The Brick could be its only star.

Yes, The Brick was the biggest they come, and the VC piled atop Stormin' Norman didn't have to be persuaded to bow out of their current engagement: Vietnamese began running in all directions. Tracers stitched back and forth across the ceiling, and more sappers began *flying* as The Brick's 'bat' went to work—Wickman wasn't in the mood for any encores.

A gut-twitching *snap!* reached Two-Step's ears as he struggled back to his feet again. He turned to see Stormin' Norman still on the floor slick floor, grooping a stocky guerilla in a chokehold.

But Stormin' Norman was not choking the sapper. "That's *it*!" Stormin' Norman yelled. "Finally! Well awwrrright!" He jumped to his feet and began waving his fists victoriously in the air, ignoring the enemy riflemen racing for the exits. Stormin' Norman had not choked out the sapper. He broke the man's neck. In hand-to-hand combat.

Stormin' Norman was as proud as a first-time father: he'd finally achieved the ultimate dream of his military career—he'd ascended into the ranks of the Dirty Thirty.

Wickman was in the front doorway to the open-air cafe now, spraying the street and shadows darting down it with sustained burst from the M-60. When the machinegun's barrel began to glow, he lowered the weapon. "*WELCOME TO DONALD WICKMAN'S WORLD, ASSHOLES*!" the Brick called after them, delighting in the faint echo of distant groans and screams—hot lead from his Hog-60 had found its mark more than a couple of times.

"Hey, it's The Brick!" Broken Arrow slid up behind Wickman and slapped him on the shoulder. "How's it going . . . Buddy?" Two-Step never knew how to address the big man. No one was quite sure if he was a sergeant or a warrant officer or an officer. He wore no rank whatsoever, and Neil Nazi was forever sending him out on clandestine 'details' beyond the bamboo wall . . . Missions he never talked about when he got back. The Brick ate Cong bone marrow for breakfast, but Two-Step felt he was an intelligent, likeable guy when you got to know him.

"The . . . Brick . . . is . . . crushed. . . ." was Wickman's only reply as he stood in the bullet-riddled doorway, sniffing at the gunsmoke and petting his machinegun.

"Uh . . . pardon me, Don ol' boy?" Broken Arrow didn't want to get his head broken. Wickman was talking almost in slow motion, like some laboratory creation whose energy packs had run down, but Two-Step felt safe in assuming it was probably an act—he'd heard the man talk non-stop in five- and six-syllable words before.

"I come into this dive to kill a commie for mommy," he turned slowly and stared down at Two-Step, "and what do I have to show for it?" He waved a meaty hand in the direction of the deserted street.

"*I* think you did some pretty fanfuckintastic shootin', bud! I really do!"

Wickman's eyes shifted to the belt of bullets draped across his left forearm. "A hundred lousy rounds. . . ." he ground his teeth back and forth, "and what do I have to show for it? Stormin' fuckin' Norman in there's got more of a body count than *me*!"

"No sweat!" Broken Arrow ushered The Brick back into the establishment. He felt they were too tempting a target in the cafe's doorway. "*No problem* . . . . We'll round up a couple guys or somethin' and beat feet out there to tally skulls for ya!"

137

"Fuck it," The Brick mumbled, switching ammo belts before sitting at a blood-caked dining table. "Don' mean nothin' anyway. . . ."

"Huh?"

"I'm . . . considerin' . . . retiring. . . ."

"You?" Boken Arrow was aghast. "The Brick? *Retiring?*"

"Don't worry, pal." Two-Step glanced over at a jubilant Stormin' Norman as he slapped The Brick on the shoulder. "*You'll* make it into the Dirty Thirty too! Sooner than you thin—"

"Dirty *Thirty*?" Wickman erupted with laughter for the first time. "Shit, Two-Step! You know me better than that. I don't give a righteous fart about such a proliferation of unadulterated hippopotamus crap!"

"Oh. . . ."

"I don't dwell on matters of astronomical insignificance unless we're discussin' the body count. Hand-to-hand is all fine and dandy, but with me, snappin' Cong neckbones doesn't prove a thing—except that I'm big and bad, right? And we all already knew that, do you agree?"

"Uh, *right*, Don!"

"Fucking fine." Wickman set down his M-60 beside the closest table and pulled up a chair that looked ridiculously small beneath him.

"But . . . uh, then just what exactly is . . . uh, *buggin'* you, Don ol' Boy?"

"What's BUGGIN' me!?" The Brick stood up twice as fast as he'd sat down, picked up the table in one hand, and slammed it against the nearest wall. Broken Arrow scampered backwards, but the shower of splinters still reached him. Shielding his face, he contemplated fielding any more questions until The Brick had been 'anesthesized' with a case of *ba-muoi-ba*. "I'll tell you what's buggin' me." Wickman glanced around, a confused look suddenly glazing his eyes.

"Hey!" he changed the subject.

"Hey, *what*?" Broken Arrow had been returning in

138

an attempt to settle the wonder warrier down, but now he kept his distance.

"This ain't fucking Saigon!"

"Uh . . . no, it ain't Brick." Two-Step swept the splinters out of his hair.

"And you. . . ." He levelled a huge forefinger at the Indian, and Two-Step added several backwards paces to his caution. "You're Corporal Straight Arrow!"

"Uh . . . *Broken* Arrow, Brick."

"Correct! You're a doorgunner with my outfit!" Wickman was sounding drunk on adrenaline.

"There you go, bud . . . ya remembers me!"

"But you're supposed to be in Plei Me, *bud*." Wickman cocked a suspicious eyebrow Two-Step's direction.

"We *are* in Plei Me, amigo. The outskirts of it, anyway. . . ."

"Why, them cocksuckers." Wickman scratched at the whiskers on his chin.

"Them?"

"Those pussy-pads were supposed to be takin' me from An Khe down to Saigon, for my R&R."

"You accepted an in-country R&R?" Broken Arrow was incredulous.

"I happen to like Saigon."

"Oh. . . ."

"I'm gonna *KILL* those sons o'. bitches!" The word 'kill' bounced back and forth off the walls of the open air cafe.

"I'd say they did that on purpose . . . droppin' you off out in the sticks like this, I mean. . . ."

"I *know* they did it on purpose. *Now* I know why that goofy-fuck of a crew chief was grinnin' the whole time since we left An Khe. . . ."

"Zack?"

"Naw. . . . The Black Buddha wouldn't pull that kinda crap on The Brick. It was that fart in the wind, Roscoe!" Broken Arrow let out a laugh but abruptly silenced himself. The outburst didn't seem to irritate

Wickman. "It was partially my fault, I guess . . . now that I think back on it. . . ."

"Was Lawless behind the boner stick?"

"Naw . . ."

"Gunslinger Gabriel?"

"That wingnut The Stork set me up!" Wickman proclaimed. "Him and his nonstop pacifist propanganda clackin' away like one of them little singsong secretaries they got plays the skinflute all day long as Disneyland East. . . .

"Was Snakeman aboard?" Try as he would, Two-Step could not get rid of his smile. "Snakeman and the Professor?"

"What do *you* think?" The Brick's eyeballs rolled in Broken Arrow's direction, then wandered about the ripped-apart room, coming to rest on a bargirl who was bending over about ten yards away, sweeping up broken glass with a short, Asian-style broom.

Oh, shit. . . .

"Yeah, they had me comin' and goin' . . . never had a chance to get myself fucking oriented, you know? If I coulda looked down just once, I woulda seen there were no lights spreadin' out down there as far as the eye could see. . . . No Saigon neon . . . no Tu Do glow. . . ."

"Right. But Snakeman and Larson had you *alll* distracted! What the hell kinda tricks did Fletcher have up his sleeve to capture your attention like that?"

For the first time, Wickman's usual scheming sparkle returned to his eyes. It was the kind of gleam that announced a million-dollar project was in the works and investors would reap a tenfold profit. There were dollar signs in his eyes. But Snakeman's latest caper did not involve money. "That goofy, no-account Fletcher brought his goddanmned snakes aboard. . . ."

"He's never without 'em." Broken Arrow nodded as the cafe's swinging front doors parted for a squad of QC helmets. "Oh-oh . . . here comes the goon platoon."

Using his thick arm to encompass the entire cafe, Wickman motioned for the Vietnamese MPs to come in. "Enter, honorable law-enforcers of the illustrious A.R.V.N.!" He turned to Two-Step and, shielding his mouth with an open hand, said, "When you hear the pitter-patter of little feet, it's the Arvin Army in full retreat!"

The local contingent of military policemen were not smiling back. They all wore business-like expressions, and had automatic rifles poised for action resting against their hips from shoulder slings as they surveyed the carnage all around: the only table left standing was the one between Wickam and Two-Step.

The Brick engaged in a brief stare-down contest with the ranking QC, but then the Vietnamese shifted his glare to the dead bodies. Pointing with his finger, he began counting mentally. His lips moved as the tally rose.

"You like?" Wickman forced a diplomatic grin.

"Numba One." The leader of the QCs flipped the two Americans the thumbs-up. Number One was Saigon slang for "The Best," whereas Number Ten stood for "The Worst."

The Brick patted his M-60 affectionately. "Use same-same baseball bat," he explained, using hand motions without picking up the weapon, "*fini* bookoo VC *rikky-tik*!"

Broken Arrow had to laugh silently to himself. Wickman was talking the way all the cao bois spoke to the Indians in every western he had ever seen. And yet these Orientals understood him.

"Ahhh, Numba-*fucking*-One," the QC sergeant ammended his earlier observation. Then the Vietnamese military policemen slowly backed out of the cafe, never lowering their rifles, electing not to bother further with the bodies—these Americans with First Air Cav patches on their shoulders, and the two Green Berets, seemed to have the situation under control.

Sporadic shooting had erupted up the street while

Wickman was doing his Babe Ruth imitation, and the QCs jumped into their jeep and were off.

"So anyway," Broken Arrow spoke as if they'd been interrupted by a mere cloud of marauding mosquitos, "you were about to tell me what got you so upset, Don . . ."

"Yes, I was, wasn't I?" Wickman struck the tabletop one time with his fist to get the attention of any evil spirits prowling the building. "Well, I'll tell you, Straight Arrow . . ." Two-Step did not bother correcting him this time but was still every bit attentive. ". . . I was havin' a field day last week, for instance. Bagged me fifty-four Charlie Congs, and it friggin' *rained* five of the seven days!"

"Yeah, I remem . . . *fifty-four!?*"

"Which ain't half bad. No, it ain't bad at all. But you know The Brick's gettin' short, my friend. . . ."

"That's what I heard." Using an empty hand, Broken Arrow finally made eye contact with one of the host esses. He motioned for a couple beers, but she ignored him and resumed soaking up the blood on the floor with multi-colored dish towels.

"And wouldn't you know it: The Brick gets short as a single-digit midget, and he's ten VC skulls away from the Big Thousand and—"

"The Big Thousand?" Broken Arrow rose up off his chair slightly.

"Sure. You didn't know The Brick chalked up his nine hundred and fucking eighty-ninth kill the last week o' June?" His eyes grew in mock pain.

"Uh . . . no, I didn't. I mean . . ."

"Nine hundred and fucking eighty nine VC hearts, and that bastard Buchanan pulls me outta the rain forest and takes away my sniper rifle and insists I need a rest. *I* need a rest. *Ha!*" Wickman curled a hand under his armpit and imitated the passing of gas. Loudly. "That shows you what I think of Neil Nazi's opinion.

"A week left in The Nam, and they got the gall to tell me I'm gettin' a belated R&R, and that when I get back

142

from Sin City, my walkin' papers and a ticket for the freedom bird'll be waitin' in my hooch! Can you fuckin' *believe* that? Shit, that Major Cum-for-brains just doesn't want to see me punch the big scorecard—the brown-nosin,' ass-kissin,' limp-wristed sonofabitch!"

"I feel for ya, Brick." Broken Arrow frowned, thinking that was a poor choice of words.

"All this Dirty Thirty business you guys are always harpin' on is fine," Wickman added, wiping the gunpowder residue off his machinegun's barrel now. "But me? I outweigh these little zips by three, maybe four to one, okay? Now what kinda challenge is that, I'm askin' ya?

"For me," he continued, "the challenge involves crosshairs and cold steel. My talent is revealed through the muzzle of a 30.06—if you get my drift. . . . And I'm not leavin' The Nam until I'm wearin' the molars from Numba One *Thousand* around my neck!"

"I'm behind you one hundred percent on this one, Don." Broken Arrow was not sure how much longer he could keep from laughing.

Wickman walked over to the doorway and surveyed the narrow street outside. He rubbed his palms together as if suddenly excited—rejuvenated. "But Neil Nazi done fucked up," he told Two-Step. "Him and his boys screwed the goose and dropped ol' Wickman in Plei Me." He turned to face the Comanche. "And we all *knooowww* the huntin' good in Plei Me!

"Speakin' of 'his boy,'" Broken Arrow said, "what exactly was Fletcher doin' with those snakes o' his that you were so absorbed in . . . You never did tell me—"

"Snakeman wasn't doin' *anything* with those repulsive reptiles," Wickman explained. "It was this scrawny little, two-bit stow-away hooker Larson smuggled on board *Pegasus. She* was doin' all the doin'!"

"Let me guess . . ."

"Right! She had them little slimy garter snakes or whatever they are—just as long as they weren't two-

step krait vipers, right?" He winked over at Broken
Arrow. "Anyway, she had them suckers slitherin' in an'
outta her ying-yang, slicker 'an shit, and—"

"Her . . . ying-yang?"

"Hey! Read my lips, dildo nose: *ying . . . yang.* I
mean to tell ya, she even had knockers the size o'
cantaloupes, with nip's big as silver dollars! But *that*
wasn't what was holdin' my attention, pal. And I'll get
you wanna know just exactly what—"

"I'm all ears." Two-Step was trying to ignore a
commotion taking place in the top floor rooms above
the bordello.

"Well, that goofy fuckwad Hal Krutch—don't get me
wrong, now: he's a hell of a chopperjock, but he's a
malingerer and a discontent, too—anyway, The Stork
somehow coaxed this Evac nurse aboard and—"

"American?"

"You know what? I'm still not sure about that! She
didn't talk too much, though her mouth was sure busy—
don't worry, I'll get to *that* part in a second—but when
she did talk, it was with a . . . a European accent.
Maybe French, now that I think about it. Yeah, a
French pussy, which reminds me o' something else I
want to talk to you about . . . But, this French gal—she
was probably one o' them civilian volunteers from
some international agency—well, she seemed to be on
exceptionally good terms with Stork and the Professor."

"Yeah?"

"And . . . wait 'till you hear this? they were, so they
claim, transportin' an X-ray machine down south to
Saigon . . . *You see*! That's where I shoulda got fucking
suspicious. Anyway, this X-ray machine is one o' them
portable, power-jack jobbers, and they're operatin' the
dam thing while *Pegasus* is airborne—"

"Fletcher and Larson?"

"Yeah! And they're taking friggin' *X-Rays* of each
other, but these aren't your normal everyday broken leg
or chipped collarbone X-rays, my friend. . . ."

"They weren't?"

"These were skulljob specials . . ."

"Are you tellin' me what I *think* you're tellin' me, Brick?" Broken Arrow tried to picture the scene aboard his friend Brody's favorite gunship. He tried to imagine how big the X-ray machine was, and how in the heck could they take boner shots of some sodomy-in-progress—and at five hundred feet, no less.

"I don't think the Professor got his rocks off or nothing, but they had him sittin' sideways on the machine with Miss Paris's ruby-red lips in a compromising position. . . ."

"And it came out?" Two-Step couldn't believe it.

"Damn right it came out." Wickman started laughing at the memory. "I mean, here's this side view of a skull, jaws slightly apart, you know? With the nose bone smack dab up against someone's pelvic bones."

"Too bad hard-ons don't show up on X-rays." Broken Arrow was laughing now too.

"Yeah! *Hey-hey*! It was a gas, brother!"

"Too bad you didn't get a souvenir. . . ."

Wickman's eyes lit up. "Ahh, but I *did*!" And he pulled the folded and rolled-up memento out of a thigh pocket. "They took a half dozen—one for the whole crew."

"Larson's gonna get cancer of the—"

"That's what *I* told him, but he said if he was worried about his pecker fallin' off, he wouldn't be flyin' gunships in and out o' Void Vicious . . ."

"Yeah. . . ."

"Fuck it."

"Yeah. So *that's* why you were so preoccupied . . . that's why you ended up in Plei Me instead of Saigon . . ."

Wickman's smile faded somewhat. He appeared on the verge of replying when a commotion on the veranda overlooking the courtyard prevented it. Nervous Rex and Stormin' Norman were fighting over a captured guerrilla—Ritter had the Vietnamese in a crushing headlock, and Stormin' Norman was trying to pull him free. So he could kill him.

"We chased the little bastard up here!" Nervous Rex's grip held the sapper several inches off his feet.

"Any more of 'em runnin' around?" Broken Arrow rose from his seat and pulled a slender commando knife from a sheath strapped to his boot. "I been havin' some Numba Ten dreams lately, but I think me," he kissed the blade's sharp edge gently, "and Miss 'Cold Steel' can come up with a remedy."

"Bank on it, bwana-san." Nervous Rex slammed his prisoner against the edge of the wall to show encouragement.

"I already have." Broken Arrow began running up the steps. "I . . . .already . . . have . . ."

146

CHAPTER 13

The priest's sermon had been devoted to political rhetoric for something near a half hour now.

Treat Brody, going on thirteen years old, was not quite sure what all the concern was about, but for the last few weeks, he had listened to his parents discuss a surge of political unrest and dissent in the Catholic church—a surge that had been seeping into the sermons of the younger priests. It was a surge Treat's father found disturbing. . . .

Nineteen-year-old First Cav doorgunner Treat Brody turned his head to face a dim shaft of light falling through the bamboo window shutters, and he was slapped hard by the Vietnamese woman again. The blow sent his mind drifting back to the dream again . . . the memories of his parents, and their disenchantment with changes in the church when he was a boy. But Brody shook the hazy pictures from his mind—the scenes flashed in front of him like damaged film footage flickering in a smoke-filled porno theater. He was tied down to a table—he could feel the twine against his wrists and ankles now. But he just couldn't remember why he was here. And then the memories from his youth returned to haunt him again . . .

All the attention had been focused on some tiny,

insignificant, no-name country down in Central America. The priests, who ran a mission south of the border, had run into some technical problems with Latin government officials over allegations the clerics were smuggling refugees north, into Mexico and the United States. It was the usual cycle of liberal philosophy and sanctuary movements the Press Corps loved to latch onto every other decade or so, but this time the news media could not be blamed for all the attention being focused on the Catholics: a radical priest had taken sides with left-wing, pro-communist rebels in some godforsaken jungle north of Panama, and, with his crucifix in every photo, was soliciting contributions from his old parishioners. Which the Vatican didn't take kindly to.

The only way the oppressed masses will ever be free of poverty, the priest told his riverbank audiences, and the only way to rid our people of the government death squads, is to *overthrow* the government. I am not a communist sympathizer, he claimed for the benefit of the camera teams in their TV-safari suits. "But have you ever heard of Socialism?"

And that was why Treat Brody's father broke with the Catholic church. When the sermons turned increasingly from God-and-family subjects to speeches on support for the insurgents across Latin America, Brody's father decided he had had enough. He stopped attending church, encouraged his wife to do the same, and told her Treat was old enough to make his own decision.

Well, naturally, Treat Brody—who could not have cared less about revolts in Latin America and revolution in general—sided with his father. That left Sundays open for more baseball with the guys. Baseball and girls, who could be a royal pain when they opened their mouths, but who were also becoming increasingly attractive from the neck down, where interesting developments were taking place. Developments Treat and his friends had never really paid much attention to the year

148

before they became teenagers.

That was why Spec-4 Treat Brody, gunship doorgunner extraordinaire, did not now have a god to turn to in his hour of need . . .

The woman's fist came down hard on Treat Brody's face again, but the young soldier did not feel it. They had been beating him for over an hour now, and all he felt was a numbness in his extremities and throbbing pain throughout the rest of his body. The Whoremonger was definitely all alone in his private little world of hurt.

"I asked you your unit's mission!" the woman screamed into his ear.

Brody still wore his fatigue uniform, and as he choked on the blood draining back through his nose, he heard one of the other women—in a rapid torrent of some strange dialect he'd never heard before—mention something about the First Cavalry patch on his shoulder. Which only served to infuriate the apparent ringleader, for she hit him with her dainty fist again. But it was a fist that really packed a punch, and Brody felt himself falling deeper into the pit. "Why does helicopter soldier come Plei Me!?" she demanded. "What do Americans have planned for Plei Me that they need Hueys and send spy for first?"

He realized it was not a dream when the woman's reaction to his silence was to place a shiny dagger against his Adam's apple, and for the first time in hours he felt something. The sensation of the blade's point against his throat was overpowering.

Brody had always faced death with a carefree attitude. He did not live simply "day to day," as many of his soldier buddies professed to. And yet he still, after all these years of "research" and participation in various religious "experiences," had come no closer to the Creator, he felt, than that year he spend as an alter boy, lighting candles, preparing the priest's robes, and siping a swallow of communion wine now and then. His time in-country with the First Cav had pitted him against death and violence so many times that he became to believe in "the power of the jungle"—for Void Vicious was where he witnessed all the killing and destruction. The rain forest became one great, all-encompassing evil force each time Brody's people set down in their landing zones to take a body count. That oppressive, almost menacing swirl of emotions and energy and hate that always fell over the LZ's when the giant trees seemed to press in for a closer look and the triple canopy above became a suffocating death shroud, became Brody's "religion." Like many who had challenged the jungle and escaped her . . . like those rare few who had made it into the Dirty Thirty, he felt a god devised by mere mortals—so many gods from so many different lands—could never compete with the power of the jungle, be it a good force or all that was evil. "You have never lived until you have almost died . . . and for those who fight for it, life has a flavor the protected will never know . . ." Brody knew how accurate that motto was. Having survived a hundred Hot-LZ's had severely changed his attitude and outlook on life. And death. He relished every rain forest contact with the enemy, convinced the jungle was the only honorable place to die . . . the only place where he really stood a chance of meeting whoever or whatever created Treat Brody and Vietnam. And, having proved himself in combat, the Whoremonger would become one with whatever power it was that swirled through the forests of Void Vicious. Immortality would be this: death in the void—an honorable death, with blue bullets flying and gunsmoke mingling with the mist—would guarantee him a bottom-level canopy seat over his favorite warrior's arena forever!

At least that was Brody's way of thinking before the woman placed the knife against his throat and it appeared death was imminent. Now his belief in the supernatural power of the jungle abandoned him.

He found himself calling silently to the God of his

youth—the Lord he had been raised to worship and pray to when times got hard. And when that uncaring voice in his head taunted Treat about his hypocritical beliefs and lack of faith—faith in the power of life and death and survival in the jungle—he forgot about the blade at his throat, and drifted back to those other experiments with religion after he'd turned his back on Catholicism.

. . .

"Cut one of his balls off first!"

Spec-4 Brody was relieved when the woman took the knife away from his Adam's apple. The smile almost returned when his trousers were pulled down to his knees and the female insurgents—or whatever they were—made two discoveries: the Whoremonger was wearing no undershorts—which was normal in The Nam, since most vets in the jungle quickly learned such garments only encouraged crotch rot. And secondly, Brody was already missing a testicle.

A firearms accident shortly after the loss of his best friend was the culprit, but if the discovery served to lighten their mood, it didn't last long: the ringleader of this little band of Indochinese amazons slammed the knife handle against his temple. "I ask you this last time." She sounded as exhausted as Brody. "What mission brings you the First Cav Hueys to Plei Me?"

"You know the rules of the Geneva Convention, baby," he replied slowly, resigned to the probability he was taking his last series of breaths. "You can ask me anything you want, but I only have to give you my name, rank, serial number and—"

The woman reached down and grabbed the head of his penis and pulled. She pulled hard until Brody groaned in pain. Brandishing the long knife in front of his face, she screamed, "Meet Miss Geneva!" and roughly placed the blade's edge against what remained of his scrotum.

Brody felt the fear again. Not the fear of death so much—he knew he was going to die and there was nothing he could do about it. But it is natural to plead for help from a higher source—if only in hopes that supreme being will make the passage through purgatory, or whatever other limbo of lost souls awaits man on his journey to the hereafter.

He kept hearing the same words over and over again. "Thou shalt not worship false gods," and he remembered every catechism class where the nuns with sharp-edged rulers taught about gold idols that doomed whole peoples, and primitive lands where heathens prayed to three spirits, and the sins and sacrilege that led to the fiery deaths of Sodom and Gomorrah . . .

"Cut off his nose first!"

The short one . . . the short Vietnamese woman with the Jane Fonda hairstyle was beginning to get on Spec-4 Brody's nerves: always coming up with suggestions . . . slice off this, hack off that, burn away both of those . . . .

"I want one of the foreigners' long noses. I want to keep it for souvenir, and I want to see inside his head."

"Cut off his ears too!" someone else requested. "Same-same the way they cut off the ears of VC!"

Brody didn't have the energy to argue. He didn't have the strength to remind these people the communists were the first to disfigure enemy corpses . . . that the Viet Cong were ripping off American ears and stuffing castrated penises into the mouths of the dead and sometimes not-so-dead soldiers long before the Western news media exploited U.S. imitations.

The single light in the room went out. One woman gasped, and two others stumbled over each other in their haste to arm themselves. Brody thought for an instant that perhaps he was being rescued . . . that his First Cav buddies or shock troops wearing black helmets with glowing white "MP" letters across the front of them might tear down the door and storm the joint. But it soon became evident that another untimely power outage had struck Plei Me—or wherever they had him strapped down.

The leader of the Vietnamese amazons brought out a

152

large box of kitchen stick matches, and, at first, Brody feared they were going to start burning his hair away. Or using his flesh to put out cigarettes—that was an old P.O.W. camp favorite. He'd read somewhere that Orientals were particularly fond of peeling a prisoner's skin away, in long strips. Starting with the face.

When it became apparent the matches were only going to be used to light candles, Brody felt a sense of overwhelming relief, but the skin along his chest remained tight and he held in his breath for a long time without knowing it: dancing shadows on the wall, created by the flickering flames, reminded him of Dawn. Not dawn, the sunrise, but Dawn, the only witch he ever met who didn't eat newt eyeballs and lizard tails and vampire bat balls for breakfast. . . .

Her knife was against his penis again.

Treat Brody, notorious Whoremonger and legendary gunship commando, was at a loss for words as her knuckles bounced off his temple. He was in desperate need from the Almighty, whoever he—or she—was. But he also, in the pit of his gut, feared the Supreme Being—be he Buddha or Christ, Mother Nature or the werewolf of London—was no schmuck. Any Creator worth his salt would be well aware of the young soldier's past misdeeds and mortal sins, and wouldn't waste the blink of an eye on Treat's behalf.

"Just answer my question," the female guerrilla whispered into his ear almost seductively, "and I will spare you more pain. . . ."

"You will kill me quickly." A chuckle rose through the bubbles of bile in his throat.

"Correct."

"You will execute me without so much as a war zone tribunal. . . ,"

"No shit."

"What?" Her tone became arrogant. How dare he address her so? Considering his present condition and position.

"You know what you need, bitch?"

153

"What!?" The word was spoken not with curiosity, but uncertainty over what he had actually said.

Brody was well aware he was going to die. So what did he have to lose? "I said, 'Do you know what you need?'"

"I heard what you said!" She struck him again. "The question becomes: 'why did you—'"

"You're nothing but a frigid, insufferable cunt. . . ."

"What!?" She glanced around to gauge the reaction on the faces of the women standing behind her and promptly brought her fist down on Brody's mouth again.

"What you need to settle you down and put you in your place," Brody mentally said goodbye to himself, "is for some GI to wrap your lips around his whanger so he can shoot his wad in your mouth and—"

She whirled around, bewildered by all the slang. "What say?" she asked one of her friends, who responded in rapid-fire Vietnamese with an informal translation.

The woman stretched his penis out again, as far as was possible without ripping it out by the root. "Maybe I make you choke to death on your 'whanger,' GI! That is if you don't bleed to death first . . ."

154

CHAPTER 14

Nervous Rex had the prisoner by the ankles. Stormin' Norman had him by the neck. Both Green Berets were trying to tear the captured sapper in half when attractive little Koy, by far the prettiest female in the establishment, rushed through the swinging front doors, crying for help from the Americans.

"He needs you! Treat needs you badly, and he needs you now!"

"Where, little lady?" Both Nervous Rex and Stormin' Norman dropped the unconscious insurgent, and Ritter rushed over. He grasped Koy gently by the shoulders. "Where exactly is he?"

"What's the Whoremonger gotten himself into now?" Stormin' Norman asked. They'd tried to find Brody after the run-in with the MPs, but to no avail, and after the ville was saturated with military police reinforcements, they had hidden out down in this underworld open-air cafe, waiting for the situation to cool down.

"VC!" Koy shouted, suddenly aware of the dangerous position she was putting herself in. But she had also fallen in love—there was no denying that. "*Women!* Bookoo women VC!"

Noticing Wickman and Two-Step for the first time, Nervous Rex motioned them toward the doorway. "Join

155

in on the fun, gents." He winked mischievously. "Female terrs! I got dibs on interrogations!"

"Show us the way, my dear." Stormin' Norman led Koy outside by the wrist.

Koy could not help but overhear all the commotion outside after Treat left the dwelling where they had lain together beneath the flares. Though well aware it meant her own death if she were caught following her girl friends through shadows, Koy did just that. She knew they would kill him. That had been the plan from the first, really. But Venn wanted Koy to have some fun with the foreigner first. To find pleasure with him. To satisfy her own desires and fantasies in what short time the American had left.

Koy took Nervous Rex and his three friends the long way around through the back alleys. After she pointed out the small crackerjack box of a structure down the middle of a dead end block, Koy vanished. Stormin' Norman had the others so charged up they never even noticed her silent exit. As the Green Berets and First Cav troopers buttoned up their flak-jackets, expecting the worst in resistance, Koy climbed to the roof of a building across the street. Rats scurried from one end to the other as she reached the top, but Wickman dismissed the weird sound as that of doves or pigeons taking flight. The birds sensed their approach, and anticipated trouble, he felt.

"On 'three,'" Nervous Rex whispered after they had moved slowly up to the only door visible in the structure and detected no movement inside. "One . . . two. . . ."

Stormin' Norman crashed through the flimsy plywood door with his shoulder on 'two.' Still on the run, he passed through a dark and deserted front room, guiding on a dim light beyond a rear partition.

A burst from his rifle lit the place up when a woman holding an AK-47 appeared silhouetted in the distance. Three red tracers split her chest open, lifted her off her feet, and catapulted her backwards as her weapon

156

clattered across the teakwood floor.

A second woman—one with an almost out-of-place, uncomprehending look on her face—replaced the first. She too was holding an automatic rifle—one she had obviously never killed with before. Stormin' Norman took this one out with a single shot to the face—which was no small feat, considering he was still running and fired from the hip.

From the corner of his eye, he watched the slug split her nose down the middle. The bullet must have fractured somewhere inside the skullcap, for her left ear slammed against the partition as a shower of blood sprayed the wall behind her.

Stormin' Norman knew his luck was running low. He sensed more people in the next room, and they all couldn't be such novices with firearms. There had to be a leader in there. He dove to the right out of instinct, and sent a five-round burst stitching across the ceiling, hoping to disorient and frighten Brody's captors.

The leap didn't come an instant too soon. Venn herself appeared in the doorway, and she didn't pause to assess the situation: she already knew Death did not knock, and it was amongst them now. Bullets were flying in a steady stream the moment she appeared.

Nervous Rex and The Brick scattered in opposite directions, rolling out of the line of fire. They did not see the single slug strike Broken Arrow over his right breast, knocking him off his feet.

Venn dropped too. She hit the floor and proned out, ejected the spent banana clip in her Soviet-made Kalisnnakov, and rammed a fresh magazine home. She fired a sustained, thirty-round burst as she rolled back behind cover while wounded women screamed in back of the partition.

Don Wickman charged as soon as Venn began reloading. He dove against the partition, using his good shoulder as a battering ram, and the wall collapsed inward, covering a man tied down on a table in the back room.

157

Using his M-60 like a baseball bat again, The Brick began swinging, World Series homeruns in his eyes, the heads of two more women the projectiles. Then he pivoted as he sensed Death sneaking up behind him.

Venn was not moving at all, really—except to bring up her AK. Wickman pulled the Hog's trigger for the space of a second or two, and the *chug-chug-chug* of heavy discharges pounded the VC girl into the wall behind her. Her stomach had taken nearly a dozen of the huge machinegun rounds, and she stared up at Wickman in disbelief, though her eyes were already lifeless.

A shadow flew toward him in his peripheral vision, and The Brick brought up an elbow, catching the last woman in the jaw before she could stab him with the machete. Unconscious, she dropped like a cinderblock, and The Brick booted her limp form backwards, over the flap of plywood, against the opposite wall. Glass from somewhere shattered, and the floor was quickly covered with a foul-smelling amber liquid.

As he stepped back gingerly, attempting to avoid the substance, Wickman saw the thing for the first time. It was sliding across the floor, on a ripple of the disgusting liquid, beneath the table in the center of the room. Wickman glanced up at the bare feet sticking out from the downed wall of plywood—Brody's feet, he was sure—and then, nausea building in the pit of his gut, The Brick stared down at the shriveled object sliding across the planks of polished teakwood.

A severed penis came to rest in front of his jungle boots.

"The son of your grandmother's grandmother became an expert with bow and arrow. He became a legendary horseman, and led many of the raids against the new hunters. Cavalry troops known as Texas Rangers came to the Staked plains in large numbers to defend the new hungers, and Quanah fought gloriously against them. . . ."

158

On a windy October day in the year 1860, the Texas Rangers ambushed the camp of Quanah and his father, Chief Peta Nocona. Dozens of Comanche braves were slaughtered, Chief Nocona among them. The Texas Rangers, thinking perhaps she was being held captive, carried off Cynthia Ann Parker, your grandmother's grandmother. . . .

"Quanah was only fifteen years old on that fateful day a hundred years ago, when he lost both his mother and his father. Hate in his heart and scars across his soul, he vowed vengeance against all whites from that day forth. . . ."

Chance Broken Arrow sat up, expecting to see his long-dead great, great grandmother, home with her Comanche warriors, riding the storm clouds above the Staked plains of Texas, in search of their happy hunting grounds. In short, Two-Step was sure he was dead. He did not open his eyes to Cynthia Ann Parker, however.

"You okay, ya crazy-fuck of an Indian?" Don Wickman slapped him lightly again. "Hey! Two-Step! Snap out of it. . . ."

Broken Arrow's nostrils curled slightly—the stench of cordite and . . . and something else was heavy in the room. Beyond the pall of settling gunsmoke, he saw the bodies of several young Vietnamese women sprawled across the floor in varying degrees of sudden death, their blood mingling with a sickly yellow liquid from three large pickle jars that had been broken in all the commotion.

Sitting bolt upright, Broken Arrow's hands began groping along on his chest.

"Hey-*hey!*" Wickman slapped Two-Step on the chest, knocking him back down. "Another undeserving GI saved by forty-nine dollars worth of rotting body armor!"

Broken Arrow gasped when The Brick struck him. Though it was a playful thump, it landed directly over the growing bruise across his right chest, where one of

159

the first bullets fired struck his flak jacket and was, apparently, deflected.

Rising again slowly, Brody glanced into the connecting room as Nervous Rex and Stormin' Norman began pulling the panels of plywood off the body strapped across a table. The blink of an eye later, Wickman jumped up, his machine gun poised for action: the dwelling's front door was opening.

A heavyset woman in her late forties or early fifties rushed into the building. Dressed in Chinese *chongsam*, black high heels, and a bright red scarf, her once-flawless face was now coated with an inch or two of make-up, it seemed. The manner in which she applied eyeliner had turned her into an underworld fiend straight out of some Fu Manchu thriller.

"What are you *doing* in here?" She click-clacked right up face-to-face with Don Wickman, grabbing the front of his shirt. She either didn't notice the menacing-looking M-60, or didn't care.

"Back OFF, bitch." The Brick jabbed her in the potbelly with the Hog's muzzle. "What are *you* doing here?"

"I am Madame Phuc!" she said indignantly. "I *own* this house, kind sir, and—"

Wickman jabbed her again—she was still too close for his tastes. "Then you take responsibility for the actions of those communist insurgents back there who were using your property as—"

Madame Phuc screamed. She rose up on the toes of her high heels, trying to see over Wickman's shoulder, and screamed again. She glanced around him, and screamed a third time, then tried to rush into the back room.

"I . . . don't . . . think . . . so." The buttplate of Wickman's M-60 flew up, connecting with the retired whore's lower jaw. She flew backwards off her feet and crumpled across the floor, semi-conscious. "You're *fucked*, Madame Phuc." She slowly turned over until she was face down in the sticky yellow substance.

160

The Brick reached down to help Two-Step up. "What kinda name is that, anyway?" he asked in Indian. "Phuc. Don't these people have any class?"

"It's spelled P . . . H . . ." Broken Arrow started to explain.

"I know how it's spelled," Wickman cut him off.

"It's kinda common around here," Two-Step persisted. "Kinda like Smith or Jones back in The World. . . ."

"Oh. . . ." Wickman's face was creased with disgust and irritation. "And we're trying to *help* these people out. . . ."

"What *is* this crap, anyway?" Broken Arrow was wiping his hands on his trousers. He brought his palms to his nose. "Smells like . . . like formaldehyde."

Stormin' Norman heard his question from the connecting room. "They got a whole shelf o' bottles full of the stuff." Broken glass crunched beneath his boots. "And you guys oughta come back here and see what these lowlife cunts were keepin' in 'em!"

"My pecker's killin' me," Brody was moaning. "That bitch has been stretchin' my *ying-yang* like a rubberband for the last three hours."

"We took care of 'em for ya, Whoremonger." Stormin' Norman wore an ear-to-ear smile. "Stitched one right across the boobs, brother. Blew 'er into never-never land for ya!"

"Well, I wish you woulda saved the broad for me," Treat complained, visions of Judy and Dawn and the others still swirling about in his head. "I'd have shown her how to *really* conduct a session of truth or consequences, brother, let me tell ya. . . . My ding-dong is gonna be worthless for a week!"

"At least you've still *got* a ding-dong." Nervous Rex sounded suddenly squeamish as he brought Brody's attentionto the lone remaining pickle jar and then the objects mired in a sticky substance between piles of broken glass.

Brody bolted from the room when he saw the collection of severed penises from a hundred castrated Americans. Clutching his precious crotch, he aimed for the front door, but didn't make it and vomited all over the fiendish Madame Phuc instead.

After he recovered from the shock of his narrow escape, Brody the Whoremonger returned to the open-air cafe with Don Wickman and the others. They downed a case or two of local Vietnamese brew, laughing up a storm over how the QCs booted the plump Madame Phuc into their jail van, and wondered how American CID investigators would react to the grisly collection of body organs in the back room.

"Some o' them whangers just *had* to belong to Frenchies," Stormin' Norman argued. "They couldn't *all* belong to Caucasians—we'd o' heard about it long before now. I mean, how you gonna hide the fact nearly one hundred U.S. soldiers have been castrated by a squad of cunt Cong *pre*verts? Huh? You explain *that* one to me, Ritter, old pal. . . ."

Brody and Broken Arrow were braced forward, elbows on the table, chins in their hands, eager to hear Nervous Rex's explanation. Wickman didn't seem interested as he lit up an expensive cigar. "All I can tell you, Stormin,' is they got this island where they send all these guys. . . ."

"You mean." Stormin" Norman swallowed hard. "The same place they send the guys with . . . the guys with the . . . the black syph?"

Nervous Rex nodded solemnly.

"The guys who leave on a Dustoff . . . the dudes everyone thought got a million-dollar wound . . . an accidental bullet in the foot, or. . . ." His voice trailed off as Ritter slowly nodded up and down again. "Aw, fuck. . . ."

"Really. . . ."

"Them poor guys. . . ."

"Double-fuck," Broken Arrow muttered upon downing another beer.

"It's just not right." Stormin' Norman was talking to

162

himself now.

"That's the way they want it," Nervous Rex replied, referring to the inhabitants of Quarantine Island

"You think the Madame Phuc, or whatever her name is, will get the noose over this?" Brody asked Sgt. Ritter. "I mean, it *was* her house and all."

"She probably never made it to the monkey house," Nervous Rex responded.

"What do ya mean? I'd really love to testify against the bitch. . . ."

"Testify?" Ritter laughed. "Shit, Brody . . . them QC's probably already sentenced the old whore. . . ."

The Brick grunted. "With a bullet in the back of the head." He did not sound as if he thought such an outcome would be a regrettable incident.

"Do you think those cuties were her daughters?" Brody persisted. "I mean, was she a Queen Cong, or what?"

"I think she was runnin' a short-time parlor out of that joint for the local Arvins," Ritter said. "I think, unbeknownst to her, her girls were spreadin' their legs and suckin' cocks up until martial law curfew, then roamin' the rooftops and flyin' VC flags as they sniped down on the same customers between midnight and daybreak. . . ."

"Sounds logical to me." Broken Arrow motioned one of the bargirls over to their table. She was wearing a very short mini-skirt, and the others watched silently as she sat on Two-Step's lap, where his hand was also poised. The woman giggled, licked Broken Arrow's ear, and shifted her bottom about in an attempt to get comfortable while Two-Step re-arranged her panties slightly.

"Now don't go playin' stinky finger on us," Stormin' Norman waved a finger in mock reprimand at Two-Step, "and foulin' up the aroma of beer at our table with the stench of . . . of . . . well, you know 'of what.' Unless, of course, you're gonna share."

"You buy Sally Plei Me tea?" the girl cooed into

163

Two-Step's ear.

"I'd wager he's already playin' with you, honey." Wickman licked his lips loudly.

Treat Brody had had enough of the bar scene. He had something to check out, and started to rise from his seat.

Brody's entire crotch—from his lower belly to upper thighs, in fact—ached from the torture treatment at the hands of Madame Phuc's girls, and he groaned as he straightened out. "Ohh, fuck me till it hurts. . . ." he complained.

"Where's the Whoremonger off to?" Wickman moved his big machinegun aside so Treat could slide out from behind the corner table they'd chosen.

"I got business to attend to, gentlemen. I'll only be a few minutes. Then again, I might be all night. . . ."

"Does business have tits and a box lunch?" Stormin' Norman chuckled as he finished off another beer.

"Wouldn't matter if it did." Nervous Rex laughed. "His whanger's as raw as a sunburned lobster. One hard-on and we'll hear screams in the night: it'll be an eight-point-five on the Ritter scale of pain, my friends . . . an eight-point-fuckin-five. . . ."

"No doubt about it." Stormin' Norman was nodding again.

"Pick a rubber, Whoremonger." Two-Step held out a bright accordion of multi-colored prophylactic packets which unfolded in front of him like a wallet flap full of credit cards.

Looking like he wanted to throw up again, Brody rushed from the bar without a response.

There is a saying among cops and underworld types that 'the streets all look different after dark,' which shouldn't have mattered much to Treat Brody, since he followed Koy home at night, but it still took him over an hour to find the single-room house again.

Holding a pistol The Brick had given him, he kept the automatic against the side of his leg, out of sight, when

164

he knocked.

An old, bent-over papa-san answered the door. He wore glasses thick as ash trays, as well as baggy o.d. green shorts and a white sleeveless t-shirt. The man held a bowl full of rice and chopsticks in one hand. "Yes?" he asked in Vietnamese. His nearly blind eyes watched the flares floating above the American.

Brody stared past him, into the bowels of the small dwelling. Several people sat clustered around a small black-and-white TV set on the floor, in a semi-circle. They too were all eating rice. Some glanced back over shoulders, up at the unexpected visitor. Others buried their faces in the small porcelin bowls. Koy was not among them.

The old man told Brody he had never heard of her.

CHAPTER 15

"*Quanah became a fearless night-raider, expanding his operations to include mining camps, ranches, and trading posts. The Santa Fe Trail was impassable because the area quickly fell under his control. . . .*" The overabundance of beer altered Broken Arrow's hearing somewhat. Instead of the Vietnamese music, drifting in sing-song chords from a sentry's transistor radio, he heard the soothing words of his mother. Jet fighters roaring overhead, above the Plei Me Special Forces camp, became the rapids of the riverbank along which his mother spoke the history of their ancestors to him. Green Berets laughing raucously with The Brick and Treat Brody became the war cries of Comanches attacking a group of Texas Rangers. Distant artillery became thunder along the dark horizons of the Staked plains in Texas. Nothing . . . nothing about Vietnam could pull him from his daydreams about those good times, so long ago, when his mother would tell him the stories, down on the riverbank. . . . "*. . . Quanah became Chief of the Kwahadi band when he was only twenty-two. It was a position he earned through respect from his fellow warriors, not a title he inherited because of Peta Nocona. Quanah did not give orders he himself would not follow. Quanah led every raid against the* *new hunters. . . ."*

Spec-4 Treat Brody sauntered into the beer bunker at the Plei Me CIDG camp, and sat down next to Broken Arrow, but the American Indian did not acknowledge his arrival, other than to nod pleasantly as he gazed off into the drifting clouds of cigarette smoke, a dreamy look in his eyes.

There were five or six Green Berets in the underground bunker, which was the size of four conex containers welded together with the inner walls removed—about twenty feet by thirty. He spotted The Brick quickly enough, and waved at Nervous Rex too, but didn't see Stormin' Norman's alternately amused and shocked countenance.

Brody had been scouring the ville for the past two days, but if the streets all looked different after dark, it was another town entirely when the sun came up.

He had no luck finding Koy—not a single clue, and only hoped she had avoided the QC sweep of the area which followed the gruesome discovery of Madame Phuc's pickle jars.

"How's it holdin', Two-Step?" he asked Chance, and when the Comanche merely nodded again and muttered something in untelligible Indian, Brody moved off to another pile of sandbags.

"I really mean it," Don Wickman was telling another soldier with a First Cavalry combat patch on his shoulder. "You gotta promise me that . . . if that fateful fucking day comes. . . ."

"*Brody*!" The buck sergeant in whom The Brick was confiding spotted Treat before he could *re*treat.

The Whoremonger forced a smile. "Why, hi-ya, Sgt. Delgado. What the hell brings you to Plei Me?"

"As if you didn't know, hog wad. . . ." Delgado was one of Echo Company's medical corpsman. A stocky Chicano in his mid-thirties, he wore his dark hair longer than regulation, and slightly over the ears. Ammo bandoliers crisscrossing his chest were filled with morphine, bandages, and other essential first-aid

168

supplies, not bullets. He carried no rifle today, but wore a .45 on his hip.

Brody's only excuse was a shrug.

"Don't gimme *that*, Whoremonger. You know why I'm here: Neil Nazi wants you clowns back at An Khe *rikky-tik*. First he sends Two-Step after your butt—which we all know was mistake numba one—and now *me*! And I ain't losing these stripes again over the likes of—"

Wickman nudged him, as if the matter was not serious enough to waste words on. "So anyways, Doc . . . we'll take care of Neil Nazi and the war later. First, you gotta promise me you'll do it."

Delgado leaned back and began laughing. "Has he told you his last wish?" The medic locked eyes with Brody.

"I just thought it up this morning." The Brick answered instead. "After I saw them two Phantoms turn that would-be sapper into a crispy critter on the other side of the wire. . . ."

"Was that what all the smoke was about?" Treat asked.

". . . But the second half of my . . . 'last wish' has been floatin' around in the back of my head for some time now. . . ."

"You gotta hear this, Whoremonger. You'll love it. Go over it again, Brick. From the start."

Wickman may have blushed slightly—it was too dark in the bunker to tell for sure—and he may have just been pausing for dramatic effect as he leaned back a little. It surely would have been the first time Brody saw anything embarrass the monster of a man.

"I'm listening," said Brody.

"Okay, here's the plan." Wickman leaned closer to the doorgunner as if the information would bind them together forever. "But once you hear it, you gotta keep a steel pot on the particulars," he instructed calmly. "And if the time ever comes, you *must* go through with it, understand? Or hire someone who will, okay? You guys have to promise me this one thing—I've never asked anything from either of you before, have I?"

"Go through with *what*?" Brody pressed The Brick with bulging eyes.

"Okay," Wickman glanced around, but no one else seemed to be listening other than Brody and Delgado. "When I die, I want you guys to promise and see to it they cremate ol' Don's bones. . . ."

"When you *die*?" Treat couldn't believe his ears. In Vietnam, words had power. You didn't talk about death unless it was defiantly. Brody stared at Doc Delgado. "What the fuck's he talkin' about?"

"Now you know how ol' Don loves the taste of pussy," Wickman continued, as if in the third person. "You know how he loves the smell of spread thighs in the morning. . . ."

"What does that have to do with death and cremation and the number of flagpoles in Washington DC?"

"Just listen," Delgado urged. "You're gonna love this one.

"Now I'm feelin' lucky this week," The Brick went on. "And I got a premonition ol' Don's gonna make it outta The Nam without a scratch, so the war and the First Cav and flyin' gunships into the void don't figure into our little talk here, see?"

"Well, the suspense is *killin' meeeee!*" Brody exploded sarcastically.

"But we all gotta go sometime." Wickman was not affected by Treat's outburst. "And since we all endured our Tour-365's, and more, together, it's only natural we take an oath to watch out for each other back in The World, or wherever our wanderlust takes us, right?" Brody nodded as if his head were going to fall off. "Okay, so say you get a cable from whoever I'm ballin' back on the Bayou, and it says poor ol' Don died of a cardiac while gettin' laid or whatever—those would be the ideal circumstances, of course—but anyway, so you pack up and boogie on down to Louisiana or Alabama or wherever poor ol' Don's body is lyin' in state. And

170

you guys make sure they burn ol' Don up good. . . ."

"REEEal good," Delgado nodded.

"None of this crap where they leave a molar or two and some pieces o' bone in the ashes. . . ."

"Right," Brody rolled his eyes toward the ceiling for Doc Delgado's benefit.

"And don't let whatever chippie I'm shackin' with have the urn, you understand?" Wickman's eyes got real large and serious. His shoulders raised in combination with his brow and large wrinkles appeared below his cheeks, as if he was a half-human vulture, preparing to pounce.

"Don't let her have the ashes?" Brody sounded genuinely disturbed by the instructions.

"*Never*! Under no circumstances! I don't care if they slap you in the face with a court order—not that I'd allow a representative of the female gender with that much intelligence to reside in my roost for any length of time—they slap you in the face with a court order, cancel their ticket with a L.A.W.!" L.A.W. was military terminology for Light Anti-tank Weapon—what was commonly referred to as a bazooka in earlier wars, and had now evolved into a sophisticated shoulder-launched rocket.

"But what if. . . ."

"If she's stubborn?"

"Yeah. . . ."

"If she fails to acquiesce peacefully, then escort her beautiful bod off the premises of my humble abode . . . and off her *ass*!"

Brody was getting tired of arguing over something so ridiculous. "Okay, so what do we do with your . . . uh, ol' Don's ashes once we get our hands on them?"

"Here comes the good part." Doc Delgado smiled broadly, rubbing his hands together.

"You gotta get a job at the Mazzengale Douche Company in New York City," Wickman revealed.

"A *job*?" Brody leaned back against the cool sand-bagged wall.

"Right," The Brick acknowledged matter-of-factly.

"At Mazzengale's . . . at a . . . at one of *those* kinda factories?" He refused to look Wickman in the face and elected to count the two-by-four beams lacing the ceiling instead. Two small beady red eyes were glowing back at him. It was either a rat or a hell of a big lizard. He couldn't tell, and he didn't care.

"Right."

"It gets better," chuckled Delgado.

"Do I look like . . . like . . . a *douche-bag*?" Brody was incredulous.

"So you guys have gotten entry-level positions at Mazzengale's," Wickman continued, "which means they've got you in the vat room. . . ."

"The *vat* room?"

"Yeah. I've already checked this out. They've got these huge ol' vats, just like the beer breweries. And the entry-level dudes spend all their time on planks beside these huge ten foot-tall steel vats just stirrin' away at all that douche formula. They say it makes you real light-headed—the aroma, if you catch my drift. . . ."

A grin creased Brody's features. "Wait a minute," he said. "*I* get it, now. . . . The urn and the ashes . . . the vat at Mazzengale's." Brody laughed for several seconds. "Brick, you'd never get away with it."

Wickman's own smile vanished. "Why not?"

"You . . . you just wouldn't."

"This . . . is . . . my . . . dream . . . ." he said in a melancholy voice, making it clear the Whoremonger's tone had hurt him dearly.

"I'm sorry, pal. It just won't work. There's no way you could do it without anyone seeing—"

"Are there guards there beside the vats?" Delgado sided with Wickman. "Are there even any at the front doors? I doubt it. We're not talkin' thousand-dollar-an-ounce perfume here. We're talking pussy cleaner, dude."

"My mole at Mazzengale's tells me one vat makes

172

200,000 bottles worth of douche." Wickman's expression was now one of a funeral parlor director.

"And there's six vats goin' at all times at the factory in the Big Apple," Delgado said.

"That's over a million doses o' douche." Brody was getting excited and couldn't understand why.

"They sell to an international market," Delgado added. "France, England, Denmark, Sweden, India . . . ."

"India?"

"South Africa . . . Russia . . ."

"They douche in Russia yet?" Brody was being reeled in

"Of course they douche in Russia." Delgado was doing all the talking now. "Can you imagine how business will soar when they expand to China? You're talking 900 million . . . maybe a billion more snatches in need of a squirt or two, Treat ol' buddy."

"You're shittin' me, Doc"

"Hell no, bro! Orgasms is big business."

"My dream is to have my soul live on." The Brick spoke up finally. "I want you, my friends, to take ol' Don's ashes and dump them in those six giant vats of douche formula. . . ."

Brody began laughing so uncontrollably he had to hide his face in his hands.

". . . And I want you to stir 'em up real good, do you understand? So there's no residue. So the quality control inspectors if they have such things at Mazzengale's won't suspect anything."

"A couple million bottles o' douche. . . ." Doc Delgado sighed. "Don 'The Brick' Wickman's remains floatin' around in a couple million bottles o' douche. . . ."

"Not 'remains,'" Wickman corrected him. "It's going to be all that's left of ol' Don on this earth . . . it's going to be his . . . his essence. . . . His final statement about life and love and the . . . the *only* way to 'go'!"

173

"So for who-knows-how-long," Brody's voice rose as a med-evac helicopter landed in the compound with a sudden flapping of rotorblades, "millions of women all over the world are going to be cleaning out their . . . their you-know-what, with . . . with a solution containing ol' Don's ashes. . . ."

"Including what had once been ol' Don's tongue." Delgado winked in a way that told the Whoremonger he wished *he'd* thought of this one.

Ol' Don folded his arms across his chest proudly and beamed. "Won't it just be heaven?"

"Anyone seen Stormin' Norman lately?" Brody asked Nervous Rex in particular as the Dustoff helicopter began ascending a few minutes later, and one of the Green Berets hustled up the sandbagged steps to pull the trap door in place—a whirlwind of dust was approaching the bunker.

With zero expression on his face, Sgt. Ritter pointed up at the medical evacuation chopper. "He's on board that Dustoff."

"The *Dustoff*? What the hell did I miss?" It had to have happened in the last few minutes, unless it was a shuttle coming in for routine dispensary cases—he hadn't heard any weapons discharges at all.

"I didn't see it personally," Nervous Rex frowned, "but word from Rumor Control is that ol' Stormin' Norman accidentally shot himself in the foot."

CHAPTER 16

The Whoremonger's knuckles were bone white as he held onto the M-60 mounted in the Huey's side hatch. He could feel it in the air: this was definitely going to be a hot one!

He could tell by the way the treetops below—the upper canopy of that living, breathing hell most gunnies called Void Vicious—were alive with activity. Gibbons and larger monkeys were racing from branch to branch, despite the danger posed by such maneuvers two hundred feet above the rain forest floor. Parrots and other multi-colored birds were flocking frantically from tree to tree—and they weren't being frightened by the downblast from *Pegasus*. It was as if they were being chased by invisible furies.

A swirling cloud of blue color appeared now and then, only to vanish. Brody knew it was not jungle mist. It was a swarm. A beautiful swarm of hundreds of thousands of azure blue butterflies—a mystical sight Brody only saw a few times before. And always just before disaster struck, it seemed. Always before hell broke loose on them. . . .

175

They had just lifted off from the 'Turkey Farm,' a helicopter camp for the First Air Cavalry Division near the Tea Plantation, where ten thousand tents were home to Airmobile soldiers in the Ia Drang Valley of Vietnam's Central Highlands.

The First Team, as the Cav was known, had been in the Ia Drang for only a couple of weeks now, engaging North Vietnamese troops in full-scale firefights as the NVA retreated toward the Cambodian frontier.

Corporal 'Saint Pat' Patterson had been reunited with The Pack—Brody's clique of buddies—only an hour before Leopold 'Black Buddha' Zack, the stocky Negro NCO and crew chief for *Pegasus*, rounded them all up for a rescue mission: the Green Berets at Plei Me Special Forces camp were calling for help!

Patterson had recently been released from field hospital care following his capture by the Viet Cong after his entire patrol was killed in an ambush. The leader of the guerrillas—a beautiful woman with long black hair, a defiant attitude, and a grisly sense of humor—had tortured Patterson mentally before forcing him to strip and flee through the jungle naked—a VC flag patch nailed to his shoulder blade by the leader herself.

Patterson was a welcome addition to Echo Company, but there were three newbies Brody and the others were not so sure about. First Lieutenant Jacob Vance was a semi-arrogant replacement for Second Lt. Winston, who had kissed Lady Death on the lips his first month in-country. Vance had some obvious hang-ups about rank and military discipline (and Treat suspected he had some even more serious sexual hang-ups, as well), but proved himself fairly well in Ia Drang—following an incident where friendly fire killed an entire American platoon, and he was thought to be at fault for several days until proven otherwise.

Buck Private Aaron Chappell and 'Nasty Nel' Nelson were an altogether different concern. Brody was afraid they were both insane, to say the least. Chappell was an eighteen-year-old cherry-boy who compensated for his

176

rather homely appearance and inability to get girlfriends back stateside by carrying the photos of several different gorgeous women in his wallet. He showed the pictures to all the men, but the trouble was—and this was obvious to everyone who viewed them—they were the mass-produced ones that came with the wallet when it was purchased. Nelson, on the other hand, was a Casanova if there ever was one. He carried a collection of small plastic vials in his rucksack containing samples of pubic hair from all his conquests. Nasty Nel was quite disappointed when Snakeman Fletcher told him Vietnamese women didn't *have* pubic hair, which is only true in certain cases.

Hal Krutch, a warrant officer who went by the handle 'The Stork,' was piloting their gunship—a sleek, new Huey with nose cannon, rocket pods on side struts, M-60 machineguns mounted on swivels in both side hatches, and the likeness of a great winged horse painted across *Pegasus*'s olive drab snout.

The co-pilot, or peter pilot, was a new man Brody had only seen around the Turkey Farm a couple times, but his jungle boots were scuffed and he needed a haircut, so he must be an OK kinda dude, the Whoremonger decided.

Brody worked the right-side Hog-60, and Elliot 'Snakeman' Fletcher the opposite hatch gun—that was the way they always charged into Void Vicious. Fletcher was called Snakeman by the troops because of the numerous serpents slithering about in the helmet hanging from his web belt at any one time.

Master Sgt. Leo Zack had spent time in battlefields before—Korea, in particular—but this was his first helicopter war, and he loved it. The Vietnamese had first taken to calling him 'Black Buddha' because he shaved his head bald, and it quickly caught on with the GIs, though Zack preferred 'Leo The Lionhearted.' Naturally.

The 'cargo' this ride in included Em-ho Lee, the only Asian American ever to gain admittance to Brody's

clique of gunship hotdogs. Lee preferred to be called
Lawrence, which was his given name, but Treat found
out about an incident back in Boot Camp where a drill
sergeant had harrasssed him with the nickname Em-ho.
Em-ho sounded Japanese to Brody and the others if
spoken with considerable tonal inflection, but it was
actually the initials for Early Morning Hard-On. Early
Morning Hard-Ons had plagued Lee throughout Basic
Combat Training, due to the prohibition of women
those long eight weeks—salt peter in the messhall food
hadn't helped the young soldier—and now the nickname
plagued him in Vietnam, though it was an improvement
over the earlier handle Snakeman and the other red-
necks had tagged him with, which was, simple, 'Jap.'

Broken Arrow was the only other vet aboard *Pegasus*.
He and Lee crouched in the center of the cabin,
readying their weapons. Across from them crouched
Chappell and Nelson, who Zack wanted on board his
ship for this mission as he could keep an eye on the
FNG's. FNG is in-country slang for 'Fucking New
Guy.'

"What's the mission, Leo?" Brody yelled above the
roar of rotorblades overhead as he stared down at the
treetops fifty feet below *Pegasus*'s landing skids.

"All I know is we got a Brass Monkey out o' the
CIDG compound at Plei Me!" he called back as he
moved through the chopper, using nets hanging from
the ceiling for support and balance. "And now nobody
is answering. Division isn't sure who called the damn
thing in, but the Green Beanies at Plei Me are definitely the ones who need an assist!'

Brody bit his lower lip: this was definitely going to
be a hot one. Those Special Forces guys didn't waste
time calling for assistance—they just died fighting. The
only reason Treat could think of that they'd put out a
call for help was if they feared the outpost was going to
be over run and they didn't have time to destroy all the
sensitive material there. A 'Brass Monkey' was a
Priority One radio broadcast for help—usually reserved

for aircraft. But it was being used more and more by ground troops lately. The two words definitely got HQ's attention.

A burst of green tracer arced up out of the jungle a few meters off to one side, and Brody unleashed a fifty-round burst at the source, though Krutch didn't circle around for a second shot. Green tracers were usually from the enemy. Even if they were carried by spook-types of Lurps, Americans surely wouldn't shoot up through the canopy at the sound of helicopter rotors!

"Plei Me's still a few klicks out," The Stork advised Brody over the intercom system.

The doorgunner raised his left hand in a thumbs-up without bothering to glance up at the cockpit. "No sweat," he muttered, after clicking into the system. "I dropped enough hot lead on those bastards to barbecue a dozen water buffalos!"

Snakeman was not so engrossed in the killing zone passing by below. He was concentrating on Chappell and Nelson, who had lurched forward noticeably when Brody began firing without warning. "Gonna be a hot one!' he yelled at the two newbies, the classic Death's head demonic grin intact. He leaned out the hatch slightly, tongue extended, but kept his eyes on the privates. "I can *taste* it on the air, gentlemen! Gonna be a hot one in Plei Me tonight! Just check out the stars! The stars—they know! The stars don't lie, gentlemen, let me tell ya: the stars don't fib 'bout business a bit!"

Chappell leaned low to glance up at the night sky, but another gunship blocked his view. There were Hueys on either side of *Pegasus*—less than a hundred feet out, it seemed, their rotor tips almost touching—and more behind them. Four more, in fact. Seven gunships comprised this rescue mission to the Special Forces outpost.

Corky Cordova was manning the hatch-60 on the bird across from Snakeman. He flipped Fletcher the thumbs-up, and Elliot raised a rebel's fist in salute. Lt. Vance was on board Cordova's chopper. Vance and

Mohammed . . . and it looked like Larson. *The poor Professor*, Brody thought to himself, *ridin' shotgun for a newby Lieutenant . . . and a gung-ho hard-ass at that!*

As he taped banana clips together, Broken Arrow watched the doorgunner on the ship outside Brody's hatch. The soldier was urinating down into the blur of treetops, and the scene brought a brief smile to the Indian's features as a lone white tracer rose skyward between his chopper and Two-Step's. The distant doorgunner nearly got his family jewels caught in his zipper.

The inscription on the man's M-60 swivel was what grabbed Broken Arrow's attention, however. Even this far away, he could clearly read it: *IRON MAIDEN*. He was not sure if that was the name of their chopper, or simply the nickname the gunny tagged onto his machinegun, for machineguns became dear as a warm woman in the Arena when AA fire left the ground, trying to snag a ship or two and drag it down into Void Vicious.

Another tracer shot up between the two birds of war, and Broken Arrow watched the doorgunner lean into his Iron Maiden, showering the rain forest below with an endless stream of fire.

"Quanah, son of your grandmother's grandmother, proved his courage under fire many times." Two-Step saw his mother's face, unsmiling as always, drifting beyond the distant helicopter. She was following him into combat, now, and he felt strength fill his veins as her words came to him, crisp and clear, even with the rotorwash filling his ear. . . . *". . . His tribesmen were inspired by Quanah's fearless displays of bravery. They all trusted him because Quanah was known as the Comanche Chief who swore he would never surrender to the new hunters . . . no matter the circumstances. His skill came to play in the event the Comanche were surrounded, and his warriors always managed to escape. . . ."*

180

Broken Arrow moved closer to the hatch and glanced back at the other choppers, loaded down with gunhappy grunts, anxious—and some not so anxious—to be dropped into the jaws of hell: a hot LZ. ". . . *Quanah's band of Kwahadi were fifteen thousand strong! They were the most feared Comanche roaming the Staked plains. . . .*"

"LZ in zero-two," Krutch announced over the intercom. They could hear landmines and satchel charges exploding even above the roar of the downblast. The seven gunships had remained low, hugging the contours of the earth and jungle. Now they dropped even closer to the treetops until Snakeman felt he could spit down into the leaves. "You can bank on it: 'tis definitely gonna be a hot one. . . ."

CHAPTER 17

October 19, 1965: 1900 Hours. . . .

North Vietnamese Army Major Lam Van Minh, who was known by the aliases Nguyen Van Luc and Ho Chi Phuc—he was no relation to the fiendish Madame Phuc—was also known to his troops, who borrowed on American humor and pidgin English now and then, as Hard Luck Lam. The American GIs referred to him as Phuc Head. But Minh was not falling on hard luck tonight. Quite the contrary. The forty-five-year-old Son Tay-born career communist was finally witnessing the culmination of his boldest strategy to date: overrun and capture the CIDG compound at Plei Me, then capture or kill the American Green Berets running the camp.

The Major's plan was two-fold, really, for Minh was a mastermind. If the strike force defenders proved worthy opponents—which he was sure they would, since the Green Berets had fearsome reputations as advisor-fighters—then Minh would shift to his second strategy: engage the Strikers and Green Berets in drawn-out firefights, but do *not* overrun the camp. Allow South Vietnamese troops from Pleiku, thirty miles to the northeast, time to arrive as reinforcements, ambush the ARVN reserves, *then* take the camp at Plei

Me. He would regroup his forces after the Americans were slaughtered or sent north to the prisoner of war camps, then spearhead an assault east, capture the now weakly-defended Pleiku, and mount a surprise drive all the way to the South China Sea, effectively cutting South Vietnam in half. The tactic of ambushing rescuing reinforcements rushing to besieged outposts had worked well throughout the summer of 1965, providing the Viet Cong and North Vietnamese Army with their greatest victories of the Spring Offensive. With South Vietnam severed at Pleiku Province, Minh reasoned, it would be a snap to conquer everything north to the DMZ. Then Uncle Ho could move all his NVA reserves south, and Minh could lead the march toward Saigon.

For his assault on Plei Me, Minh used the 33rd NVA Regiment, augmented by VC Main Force units and local guerillas.

What Major Minh did not count on was that commanders within ARVN were finally becoming wise to his strategy of wiping out rescue convoys in elaborate ambushes. The General at Pleiku knew he did not have enough soldiers to both defend the provincial capital and send a contingent of reinforcements to Plei Me, so he called on the U.S. Army for help.

Orders went out to the First Cavalry Division at An Khe to send a battalion of Airmobile troopers west of the thirty-five or so air miles to Pleiku, so South Vietnamese soldiers could be freed to rush to the aid of the Plei Me defenders. American air support in the form of jet fighters was already en route to the Green Beret camp to fire up the perimeter.

Congressional Medal of Honor winner Colonel Neil 'The Bull' Buchanan was well aware that the time delay involved in shuffling troops around like that to please the priority-happy hierarchy could very well lead to the massacre of every defender at Plei Me. That was why, several hours before receiving orders from Division to mobilize his battalion for a muster to Pleiku, he answered the Brass Monkey and sent a rescue blitz of his

184

seven best gunship crews to Plei Me.

It was the first in a string of lug wrenches thrown into the spokes of Major Minh's plastic-explosives-packed bicycle.

CHAPTER 18

"*PHANTOMS*! I need Phantoms *NOW*! All around the camp! Three hundred and sixty degrees!" the Green Beret sergeant yelled over the radio net as explosions sounded one after another in the background. "Just as close in as you can get!" Phantoms were F-4 jet fighters. The problem was, they were not on station yet. But Brody's people were only an eyeblink out. And they were speeding toward Plei Me so fast that Sgt. Leo Zack hoped a clusterfuck of a crash between seven roaring, eager-for-action gunships was not the end result. "We . . . need . . . that . . . air . . . support . . . NOW!" The sergeant was using a calm approach, hoping that might get a better response from the powers-that-be listening on the other end, but a severely wounded soldier screaming nonstop in the background kept the chopper crews' adrenaline climbing.

"Goin' down," Warrant Officer Krutch announced quietly, without discernible emotion, and it was as if they'd suddenly dropped into Hades itself.

Banking sharply to the left, the Stork brought *Pegasus* around in a tight circle a few dozen meters outside the camp perimeter and less than seventy-five feet off the ground. Three ships followed him in the clockwise pattern, while a single chopper raced a hundred meters above the four, counterclockwise, and in a tighter pattern, showering the strands of sparkling concertina with an endless stream of tracers. The last two Hueys hovered outside the target grid, the length of a football field above the action, slightly beyond the treeline, spotting targets of opportunity for the others.

The guerrillas had launched a surprise attack on the Plei Me Special Forces camp from trenches prepared over the last three or four months without the American advisors' knowledge. The trenches had been strategically located a few dozen feet outside the main perimeter, but within the hastily erected secondary barrier of wire constructed after the guard tower was toppled in July.

Under NVA supervision, the local VC had painstakingly dragged pails of dirt from trenches under construction in heavily wooded areas outside that protective zone where the brush and trees had been cleared away. Now a spiderweb of the things almost completely encircled the SF outpost, and each trench was crowded with communists eager to lead the main charge against the camp.

"We're fucked if they got an underground tunnel system to link up all them goddamned trenches!" Brody clicked-in as they made a second pass over the area and his M-60 barrel began to glow.

"Stay off the system," Krutch ordered. Radio traffic was heavy enough as the chopper pilots coordinated their assault—he didn't have time to monitor on-board chatter.

"Aw, eat it like a man, Whorehumper!" Zack yelled at the perspiration-soaked doorgunner as he leaned over Fletcher and fired an entire magazine full of white tracers down at one of the trenches. Glancing over his shoulder, Snakeman nodded with approval as several black-pajama-clad riflemen crumpled in the muddy trenches and didn't get back up.

"Python-Lead . . . uh, Python-7," one of the spotters called down to Krutch, "appears you got trouble on

188

your whiskey. Repeat: on the whiskey side of the compound. Approx fifty Victor Charlie rushing the wire, over."

"Rodg, Python-7," The Stork acknowledged. "We see 'em, thanks. Python-2, Python-3 . . . guide on me. . . ."

"Python-2, rodger . . ."

"Python-3, copy. . . ."

Pulling pitch, Krutch accelerated, which upset all the doorgunners, for their targets instantly became a blur, but he needed to get over to the west side *rikky-tik*, and didn't want to cut in front of anyone—a million dollars worth of mangled machinery was more than he was willing to risk for a simple rescue flyover.

It looked more like a hundred sappers were rushing the main perimeter when *Pegasus* arrived. The first wave was working in pairs—about twenty of them altogether—and was carrying *bangalor* torpedos: bamboo poles stuffed with explosives. VC carrying crudely constructed, lightweight ladders followed, as well as a dozen or so heavily clothed teenagers—youths who would throw themselves over the rolls of coiled barbed wire so the soldiers behind them could run across their backs, into the compound.

Krutch wanted to flare into a hover off to one side so his doorgunner on the port side—Snakeman—could mow down as many of the sappers as possible. The angle was not right for a rocket attack this close to the defenders, though the Green Berets had acknowledged the First Cav's arrival, and were calling for the gunships to unload everything they had "right on top of the perimeter!" Krutch wanted to flare into a hover, but he knew that would have left him vulnerable to snipers in the treeline, or some of the sappers themselves. *Pegasus* wouldn't last a half minute in a stationary hover—she'd go down in a ball of flames and exploding armament. And he couldn't dazzle the defenders with fancy in-and-out flying—not with three other ships on his tail. Decapitation by broken rotorblades was not his

189

idea of a pleasant death, though it would definitely be over quick.

Snakeman was getting help as Krutch slowed over the western defenses to allow his machinegunner to empty a couple of well-placed belts down onto the enemy. Zack was leaning over one shoulder, blasting away with magazine after magazine, and the two newbies, Chappell and Nelson—per Leo's instructions—were leaning over the other, also shooting their M-16s nonstop. *Maybe we'll use up our ammo this way and won't have to land and get out!* Chappell's mind raced as he fired at moving shapes two hundred feet below, never quite sure if he was hitting anything as tracers from the other three soldiers zinged down, smoking and glowing, ricocheting right through many of the attackers. *Maybe this will be over soon . . . maybe it's too hot down there to land, and we'll fight this whole crazy thing from the air!* Chappell had volunteered for Vietnam, but it was all happening too fast. He'd only arrived at An Khe that afternoon, and already he was in the midst of a blazing firefight! He would be more than eager to defend Old Glory on some godforsaken, numbered hill—but later . . . give him some time to readjust to the heat, and the attitudes he was encountering, and the hostile environment. Chappell wanted someone to take some time with him . . . to brief him on the situation . . . to tell him what to expect and how to handle it—to *walk him through it*! The way he'd been painstakingly walked through every other difficult endeavor in his life up to this point. Why were they throwing him to the lions like this? Thank God he was shoulder to shoulder with two teeth-gnashing veterans who knew what they were doing, anyway—*Thank God for that*!

Nelson on the other hand felt just the opposite. And he was voicing his thoughts out loud. "When do we go in?" he screamed above the downblast into Zack's ear. "When do we land so I can . . . *GET SOME*!" Wasn't that the phrase? "When are we goin' down, sarge?" he yelled between clips. He dropped a magazine, and it

190

flew out the hatch as Krutch brought the chopper around for another pass. "I can't tell if I'm hittin' 'em! You guys are in the way! The doorgunner is in the way! I . . . WANNA . . . KNOW . . . WHEN . . THEY . . . GO . . . DOWN! *I WANNA SEE IT*!"

Seemingly ignoring Nasty Nel, Zack slapped Fletcher hard on the shoulder. "I saw that, Snakeoil! Good shooting!" Fletcher had bowled over nearly a dozen sappers with a single burst—many were taken down by ricochets or bullets passing through their comrades, due to the angle of the shot—but now Elliot's M-60 barrel rose sharply, and a sputter of tracers sailed off into the night sky, began arcing, and disappeared in a wall of low storm clouds.

"It's Snake*man*, sarge!" Fletcher gritted his teeth as Nelson smiled. "Snake*man*, if ya don't fucking mind!'

"Uh, right!" Zack pounded him on the shoulder again, and Brody watched Fletcher wince. "Just keep up the good shootin'!"

The Viet Cong, led by several North Vietnamese cadre wearing similar black uniforms of mixed khaki and calico, were charging the compound on all four sides now. Sappers in the first waves would hurl the bamboo torpedos into the chainlink fenceline, blowing out several sections, only to charge insanely into the diagonally mounted punji sticks that lay between the two circles of drooping concertina. It was a suicidal, last charge for most—many were gunned down by the communists behind them, and those that weren't plucked out of their Ho Chi Minh sandals by the doorgunners, were picked off one by one by the defenders within the compound.

"Did you see that?" Brody listened to Krutch exchange chatter with his co-pilot. "Was that a fucking optical illusion, or *what*?"

"Hard to tell due to darkness," came the dry response. "Hard to be positive, but—"

"But that was a shoulder-to-shoulder mass o' black-fuckin'-pajamas movin' through the treeline. . . ."

"Just like Korea," the peter-pilot muttered, though he was only twenty-five and this was his first war. "'Wave after wave after wave of 'em . . . .'"

"Uh, Python-Lead to all Pythons." Krutch clicked into the main system and spoke ship to ship. "Hold onto your jockstraps, gentlemen, but appears bookoo Victor Charlie massin' along the November and Whiskey sides of the compound . . . gettin' ready to reinforce the body count inside the trenches."

"Couple thousand," the peter pilot added. "Looks like a couple thousand . . . and that's a conservative estimate."

"We've got 'em on the Sierra-Echo, too," another chopper jock responded, his minigun pumping lead as he spoke.

"Identify. . . ." Krutch said simply, his voice commanding though he was usually not in charge of anything, let alone a rescue scramble.

"Python 4, Loud. . . ."

"Roger, Four . . . . Python-3, Python Lead, over . . . ."

Python-3 didn't have time to reply. "Lead, this is Seven. We've got flashlight glow all over the place down there—360 degrees!"

"Specify, Python-7. . . ."

"I said 360 degrees—*all around you!*"

"Where's it worst?"

"The Sierra-Echo side, but it's all a big dim green glow converging on the camp . . . it looks like ten thousand of the bastards, over . . . ."

"And we don't have that kinda ammo reserve onboard," an anonymous pilot reminded The Stork unnecessarily.

Damn! Krutch thought to himself as he brought *Pegasus* around for another low pass on the southeast quadrant of Plei Me's CIDG outpost. *It couldn't be! Military Intelligence would have spotted a troop movement that large!* "Okay . . . okay." His voice was no longer emotionless. "Python-7, Python-6 . . . drop

192

back and kick loose a couple pods on the bastards, Pythons 5 and 3. . . ."

Krutch didn't have time to finish the directives. Two Phantoms, swooping down low, appeared suddenly between *Pegasus* and the choppers in front of her.

The night air filled with the roar of their afterburners, and they began an abrupt climb, steeper than their descent. Krutch and the other pilots had to shield their eyes as the darkness was chased away by dual explosions beneath each fighter: their napalm cannisters disgorged, sheets of flame rolled and billowed across the sea of elephant grass, incinerating dozens of guerrillas. Bones and bamboo turned to ash, floating away on the breeze as endless screams rose from the earth.

"Holy *shi*—" Brody began as two more Phantoms swooped in for their attack. In the glow of secondary explosions, he could clearly see one cannister bounced through the concertina—*right into the compound*! But it kept on bouncing, failed to explode, and disappeared in the jungle on the other side of the camp.

"I've never seen anything like *that* happen before!" Snakeman turned to gauge the reaction in Zack's eyes.

He could only shake his head from side to side as he slammed a fresh banana clip into the M-16 well. "They sure ain't the fuck designed for no basketball game, that's fer sure!" He imitated one of the crew chiefs on another gunship—one of the thirty-year buck sergeants who left a Florida swamp commune without completing junior high—and everyone, even Chappell and Nelson, laughed. Everyone except Two-Step.

Broken Arrow could see the glow. He could see the green glow now that the other chopper pilot had warned Krutch about—and it was vast! It extended as far as he could see along the treetops, and a chill ran down the muscular Comanche's frame.

"That ain't the Cong," he muttered aloud, but too low for anyone to hear him over the rotor downblast. "That ain't the motherfuckin' enemy at all, you guys!" But still, nobody seemed to be listening—they were all watching Snakeman melt the barrel on his Hog-60.

Broken Arrow believed the green glow came from the jungle itself. He truly believed his time as a fightin' member of the illustrious First Air Cavalry Division was coming to a climactic close. The jungle knew. She knew he'd achieved Dirty Thirty status, and the time to pay his dues had come. The rain forest was aglow down there—getting ready to chomp down on him the instant he stepped out the hatch . . . the second his boot touched that skid, it was *slam, bam, thank you ma'am. Fini!*

"I ain't goin' . . ." he muttered, louder this time. "No way." With each word he felt immense self-shame. He felt his face flushing red as an apple despite his natural skin shade. With each word he felt like he was betraying his people and his country, his squad and himself. But he could not help himself. He could not stop the words. They flowed like water from a beaver dam destroyed by trappers. "I'm not leaving this bird, I feel it now. I don't stand a chance out there. . . ."

"What?" Zack whirled around, an evil smile still on his face as he finished off another magazine. The barrel of his M-16 turned with him, though it was pointed at the chopper's olive drab ceiling now.

Broken Arrow stared at the curls of gray smoke floating up from the rifle's flash suppressor. "I said I've had enough. I don't care what you do to me. . . ." He was not even sure *any* of them would make it out of this shitstorm. ". . . But I ain't steppin' one foot off *Pegasus!*"

Void Vicious had caught up with him—of that, Two-Step was convinced. There *was* something to this Dirty Thirty curse after all. The rain forest was converging on this jungled spot, sacrificing all these men—on both sides—just so it could gobble him up. Broken Arrow truly believed that now. There could be no other explanation. No other reason for the way the treetops looked from the air as they were racing toward Plei Me. Evil had always been green to him. *That* was what was glowing in the dark out there. *Evil.* The evil of this wild stretch of angry land had finally taken notice of Broken Arrow. And now he was going to pay.

"*Quanah's band of Kwahadi had taken to striking the new hunters hard.*" Broken Arrow could hear his mother's voice in the staccato roar of dual M-60s on either side of him now as both Brody and Snakeman resumed firing down at the sappers. He could see the reflection of his mother's face in, of all places, Leo Zack's wide questioning eyes. ". . . *In fierce hit-and-run raids, where surprise was essential. They would whirl after the initial onslaught and flee back into the hills, only to attack again at another ranch or settlement miles away. Quanah's bravery under fire was legendary. No man ever questioned his courage.*

"*One time, Quanah witnessed an act of cowardice among one of his braves. The man was killed by Quanah on the spot—an arrow through the throat. As he grew older and, perhaps, more wise, such sins were treated with banishment from the tribe . . . though your grandmother told me of only two other instances over all those years when a Kwahadi warrior backed down from a fight or fled under fire of the Texas Rangers, who became Quanah's biggest nemesis. . . .*"

"You talkin' to *me*, Two-Step?" Zack glided over to Broken Arrow's side of the craft as he spoke. It was as if Chance's mother were floating toward him on the smoke of a morning campfire beside the river in the heart of the Staked plains.

Broken Arrow's jaw jutted forward in response. His lips parted, but he could not speak. He could not tell this big, black, no-nonsense master sergeant that he quit. That he'd given up . . . no longer wanted to fight. He just couldn't do that to Leo.

And he couldn't do it to himself.

"Aw, fuck it." He rose from a low crouch behind Brody and fired down at the confusion of black figures racing toward the concertina from several fingers of treeline.

"That's what I thought you said." Zack grinned as three tracers popped from Broken Arrow's M-16, signaling an empty magazine. But it was a tight, troubled grin as he returned to the opposite hatch to monitor the newbies.

Brody glanced at Two-Step out the corner of an eye as the Indian reloaded swiftly. Brody didn't have to aim much—the ground was a blanket of black uniforms surging toward the CIDG compound, it seemed—so he watched Broken Arrow, and he watched him closely. Brody had overheard Two-Step's grumblings, and, though he thought he understood the soldier's symptoms of burn-out, he also experienced a vision. A vision of the proud Comanche freaking out as he slammed a fresh thirty-pound clip into his rifle. A vision of Two-Step whirling around inside the cabin, spraying everyone with hot lead on rock & roll, popping an M-79 into the cockpit, then bailing out . . . down into the void   down into the pit as *Pegasus* rolled over onto her side and crashed. It was a very disturbing vision, so Brody The Whoremonger kept an eye on Broken Arrow, hoping his instincts were wrong. Because they'd been wrong before.

"Gonna get some, Treat!" Broken Arrow fired off the entire magazine with a Comanche war cry and locked eyes with Brody as he reloaded. "Gonna kill me some zips tonight!" He was singing along with a hard-rock tune that blared now from the transistor radio Snakeman had taped to the side of his helmet. Brody was sure Zack would tell him to turn it off, or simply *knock* it off with the butt of his rifle, but Leo The Lionhearted was too busy *getting some* himself to care about a little Led Zeppelin. "Gonna burn down the night, baby-san!"

Brody glanced over at Chappell—the kid was scared to death; that much was obvious. But he was blasting away with the rest and the best of them, and just trying to keep out of Nelson's line of fire. Nelson—he was going bonkers over the body count. "I knew I shoulda joined this man's Green Machine earlier!" he screamed above the roar of Snakeman's M-60. "I coulda enlisted right outta high school, but I waited seven months, you know!? Wanted to cruise Main Street USA a while in my jalopy before goin' to war and givin' up Pepsi-Cola, you know!?"

"What!?" Snakeman paused to slip in a new ammo belt. His fingers worked automatically as he glanced up at Nelson.

"I said this is great!" Nelson leaned closer as he fought with a jam. "I love killin' dink motherfuckers! I can't believe the goddamned job satisfaction!" *Pegasus* lurched to the right but Nelson kept his footing without reaching for support, as Chappell had to, and that added to his surge of pride and self-esteem. "All my buddies are flippin' hamburgers and greasin' themselves with French fries burns in some nowhere dive back in The World, and *I'm* GREASIN' commies for mommy in a fucking war zone! Can you believe THAT?"

"At least they're *back* in The World." Fletcher was irritated he would defend beach bums he didn't even know, but as gunsmoke filled his nostrils, and they began slipping around on the growing piles of empty brass, it seemed the only natural thing to say.

"Fuck that," Nelson replied.

"What's that?" Snakeman didn't look up this time, but concentrated on a group of insurgents rushing toward the fenceline, carrying a long bamboo ladder.

"I ain't *never* goin' back! Can you believe they're actually payin' us to do this—to waste these zipperhead motherfuckers! And Uncle Sammy's taggin' on bonus pay to boot!"

"It's called *combat* pay, doofus!" Brody overheard him and called across the cabin.

"Well whatever it's fucking called, I'd pay *the government* to be here!" Nelson flashed Treat the thumbs-up while, with his other hand, he resumed firing down at the ground, using the M-16's pistolgrip revolver-style, on semi-automatic.

"*Hi, Luv!*" a sexy, smoky, feminine voice filled the cabin as empty brass flew about and the ear-splitting clamor of discharges was beat back by rotor blades vibrating overhead. Brody and the others automatically matched the AFVN radio disc jockey's routine, word for word. "It's Chris Noel! and it's time for 'A Date with Chris.' *Good Morning, Vietnam!*"

Brody tried to orient himself as *Pegasus* bucked to the left and right like a bronc at some rodeo, dipped, climbed, shuddered and dipped against turbulence from the multiple explosions outside again. He tried to figure out which direction was east, but everywhere he looked, there was only darkness. Darkness and the flash of bomb blasts lighting up the night. It was late, but there was no false dawn illuminating the horizon with a dull glow—only the sizzle of red, green, and white tracers as they arced out over Plei Me and the surrounding jungle.

Good Morning, Vietnam! Beautiful Chris Noel's back-home voice echoed in his ears. But it was far from morning. AFVN—Armed Forces Vietnam Network—was obviously playing taped programs again. Programs that were flown up to Pleiku from Saigon and retransmitted because much of Ia Drang was a dead zone, and a special relay at Duc Co had to be used if the troops in parts of II Corps were to be able to hear the Voice of America broadcasts.

Chris Noel. . . . She had actually flown out to meet the guys one time a couple months ago. Landed in one of those monstrous Chinooks—Jolly Green Giants—on a firebase out in the middle of nowhere. There were snipers everywhere, but if they were lucky enough to have scoped rifles, they were using them for other purposes: Miss Noel stepped from the helicopter wearing her trademark: tall white boots, a mini-skirt, and long blond hair. She sang for the men, danced with them to slow country-and-western music, and even signed autographs. She brought a duffelbag full of mail

198

with her, and spent several hours at an aid station, reading letters from home to GIs who were too banged up to read the things themselves. One poor guy even got a Dear John, and she held his hand from smile to frown, to a trembling phase—where Treat was sure the young man was going to bust out in tears—then, strangely enough, back to a mischievous grin: "She was never very important to me, anyway," he flushed. How could she be, now that he was holding Chris Noel's hand?

Before she left the firebase, Miss Noel promised the GIs that, if they would drop her a line, down in Saigon, she would play requests for them over her 'A Date With Chris' program. Any men sending a group photo would receive, in return, an autographed picture of Chris.

Brody had sent her a brief note a few weeks later, thanking her for her kind words and thoughtfulness— and all the risks she took to fly out to an outpost in the middle of a free fire zone in the first place. He had included a small snapshot of *Pegasus*, and all the guys—Snakeman, the Professor, Krutch, Two-Step, Zack and himself—hanging out the hatch, boots dangling in this air, rifles balanced over their thighs (the picture had been taken by a second gunship, cruising above the treetops beside them, somehwere over the heart of Void Vicious), and, though he had never really expected a response, a petite little envelope arrived only a few days later. Chris Noel had delivered her promise, and included a personalized perfumed note of thanks to boot.

"There's definitely nothing phony about that lady," he told all the guys afterwards, allowing them to touch the photo and smell the envelope for only a few seconds each. Before coming to The Nam, Brody was lucky enough to see the movies "Soldier In The Rain," in which Chris starred with Steve McQueen and Jackie Gleason, and "Girl Happy," in which Elvis Presley was the main attraction. But ever since she began coming to Southeast Asia to entertain the troops, Hollywood was giving Chris the cold shoulder, and Brody took it personally. She was already practically a legend among the American soldiers—the VC too, apparently, since they'd placed quite a bounty on her head, deciding she was too much of a morale booster—and Treat envisioned the day when Tinsel Town would get its act together and do a movie about the woman. He hoped they let Chris pick the title herself, and he kept his fingers crossed that she'd call it "Good Morning, Vietnam!"

"I'd like to dedicate this next song to you guys in the First Air Cav up in An Khe!" Chris Noel's voice rose between bursts from Snakeman's M-60 like a sound rollercoaster. "It's a special, never-been-played-before *preview* selection by The Animals: 'We Gotta Get Outta This Place!' And a special 'Hi!' to you fellas up in Plei Me—*hang tough*! I just looooove Green Berets!"

"She just looooves Green Berets!" Fletcher imitated Noel as he turned the radio up to full volume and resumed leaning into his smoking machinegun.

A bright series of flashes blinded everyone just then, and *Pegasus* lurched to one side, dropped several meters as the turbine seemed to cough and sputter, then coasted sideways only a few feet above the treetops as Krutch fought to get her back under control.

"Hold onto your hanches," the peter pilot clicked-in. "Looks like we've taken some No-Doz in the tailboom."

"You dudes all right back there?" The Stork glanced back over a shoulder and Zack responded with a thumbs-up.

"Python-2, this is Python-Lead, we're down and dirty *rikky-tik*. Gonna have to ask ya to take the reins for a while, over."

"Rodg your last, Lead. Any way you can make it back to friendly territory?"

"Python-2, Python-Lead . . . negative, Holy Man." Alarm bells all over the console were screaming at Krutch for attention. His eyes darted about, selecting priorities. "But I'm not droppin' ol' Peg down into the

200

void, either."

"What about. . . ."

"I'm pretty sure I can set 'er down inside the compound itself. . . . I thought I saw a bunker big enough on the Sierra side, over. . . ."

"Rodg, Stork . . . the November-Sierra side. Looks like a messhall or maybe storage or something, over. . . ."

"Rodg. . . ."

"That was 'We Gotta Get Outta This Place,' by The Animals." Chris Noel's voice competed with the grating whir of out-of-sync rotors as *Pegasus* descended in a tight circle toward the CIDG compound, smoke belching from melted fiberglass and magnesium near the fuel cells. "It's goin' out this morning by special request to a Lt. Winston up at the Golf Course—that's gunny slang for First Cav territory in An Khe, for all you gorgeous guys unfamiliar with the term. . . ."

Every man aboard Pegasus was firing his weapon on full-auto as she grew closer to the ground and the black-clad shapes got larger—much larger! Some of the shapes began shooting back.

"But first, MACV wants me to read this directive regarding displays of open affection in public between American personnel and indigenous. . . ." Miss Noel's announcement was interrupted by the claymore antipersonnel mine going off below their craft.

None of the crew reacted to mention of Lt. Winston's name over the radio but they were all thinking the same thing: the Lieutenant hadn't lived long enough to hear his request played on the air.

A sniper had put him on the K.I.A. list only a few days ago.

CHAPTER 19

That they did not crash and burn was something akin to a miracle—if such things exist in the jungle.

"Out!" Master Sgt. Zack was yelling at the top of his lungs. "Everyone out!" Which was an unnecessary exclamation, for Brody and the others were all leaping down over the angled-up skids even as *Pegasus* was still ten feet off the ground.

It looked like she might strike the earth tail-first — the rear verticle rotor was only a few inches off the ground, while the nose cannon kept rising—but Krutch The Stork managed to drop the winged horse mural as the troops dismounted, and Peg was saved.

Pranging backwards across empty crates and bundles of tarmac sheets, the Huey came to rest only ten or fifteen feet away from a stretch of fenceline being toppled by a screaming, shouting human wave of enemy sappers.

"Welcome to Plei Me, you worthless cocksucker!" A tall Green Beret rushed from a swirling blanket of gunsmoke on the other side of *Pegasus* and dove to the ground beside Brody.

"Nervous Rex!" The Whoremonger felt instantly graced and infinitely more indestructible now that Zack's crew was complemented with his old friend

203

from an earlier stint in the region.

Zack and Larson glanced over at Brody as they dropped behind sand-filled oil drums nearby. "Nervous Wrecks?" Leo The Lionhearted called across the solitary tracer dividing them. He pulled a frag from his web belt and heaved it toward the fenceline, and they all covered their heads, flattening out against the clay as much as was humanly possible.

Brody didn't bother explaining to Zack—they could all visit around the same bar counter down in the ville, later. But for now, there were a few other things to take care of first.

"Fuckin'-A! Great to see ya, Whoremonger!" Nervous Rex slapped a double banana clip into his combination M-16/Thumper. Thumpers were capable of flinging M-79 grenades at Charlie. "And glad to see all the heavy hardware!" Brody sensed the Green Beret was just about to rise up and unload on the enemy when two more Phantoms passed overhead—less than a hundred feet above! As if in slow motion, five-hundred pound high explosive bombs twirled from their bellies and impacted on the other side of the perimeter with a terrific *whooOOOsh*! that lit up the edge of the jungle and sucked the oxygen from the battlefield.

"Jesus!" Brody crowded against a lone sandbag again as the shock wave passed over the Americans. "*JESUS*!" Something had struck him in the back of the head—and hit him hard!

The severed arm came to rest beside Treat Brody, and a startled yell escaped him when he realized what it was.

He glanced over quickly at Sgt. Ritter to see whether the Green Beret heard the moment of weakness, but Nervous Rex was beneath a big black bundle of rags. Rags laced with crimson and shreds of flesh. The rest of the dead Viet Cong had landed across him!

"Lighten up, DUUUDE!" A huge shadow beneath the floating flares fell across the patch of red clay where Brody had last seen Ritter, and then two giant

204

hands dropped into his frozen field of view. He recognized the voice, but his reflexes still had him stunned. *And it couldn't be*!

"Stormin' Norman!" Brody called out. "But, I thought—"

"How's it hangin', Trick-Or-Treat?" Stormin' Norman didn't pause to exchange pleasantries—he was too concerned about his best friend, and was busy lifting the hefty VC corpse off Ritter as bullets zinged in all around the Americans.

"Get this stinkin' bundle o' rags off me!" Nervous Rex began protesting finally, and it was not clear to Brody if he had also been dazed by the blasts or was just running out of patience with his partner.

Something plopped down next to Treat and, expecting to find another airborne body, he was pleased to discover Broken Arrow diving in next to him instead. "Welcome to the party!" Brody nodded as he lifted his rifle above the sandbag and fired off a long burst without taking aim. Screams from several different VC was the satisfying response.

"We're fucked," Two-Step muttered as he took aim on several sappers breeching the wire and began picking them off one at a time, using semi-automatic.

"Huh?"

"And *you're* definitely screwed, buddy." The Comanche motioned toward the single bandolier drooping from Brody's right shoulder, "if you keep wastin' ammo like that!"

Brody glanced down at the cloth magazine holder. There were only three or four clips left. He had burned up two and a half bandoliers from the air, and lost a fourth sometime during the crash landing. Brody stared back at *Pegasus*—Krutch was just now climbing down out of the cockpit, trying to bring as little attention to himself and his crippled bird as possible. "Hey, Stork!" Brody yelled as the Warrant Officer crawled around to the tail section to inspect the damage. "We need some ammo over here! *ASAP*!"

"Stormin' Norman!" Two-Step called out upon recognizing the supposedly quarantined Special Forces commando. "What the fuck are *you* doin' here? We thought you kiped a one-way ticket to the island!"

"The island?" Stormin' Norman asked without looking over at Broken Arrow—he was too busy knocking VC down from the strands of concertina wire.

"Yeah! You know—Black Syph Island or whatever it's called?" The first mortar of the night landed fifty feet away, and everyone buried their face in the dust.

Everyone except Stormin' Norman. He was staring at Nervous Rex when Ritter's head came up to fire again.

"Is *that* what you told everybody?" he asked, both insult and relief mixed into his tone.

"I ain't got fuckin' time to explain." Sgt. Ritter killed three VC with two lucky shots before glancing over at Brody and Broken Arrow. "But they looked like they needed a good laugh *at* the time." He winked as a string of ricochets kicked dirtclods in his face.

"Well I was on an ash 'n trash flight over to the field hospital!" Stormin' yelled above the clatter of a Soviet-made submachinegun rushing toward the perimeter, ". . . To pick up medical supplies for the adopt-a-Yarde-brat visits guys like you and Delgado are so fond of!" Stormin' Norman waved a fist at Ritter then felled the SMG-toting guerilla with one head shot. "I *got* no problems with *my* pecker! You can check!"

"Pull it out and prop it up!" Nervous Rex dared.

"Yeah!" Broken Arrow laughed for the first time since *Pegasus* touched down inside the compound. "Prove it!"

"Aw, fuck you clowns and the horse the five o' you rode in on!" Stormin' Norman responded without enthusiasm.

"We 'rode in on' *Pegasus*, hairball!" Brody was only half kidding. "So show some respect!" He spoke with a Rodney Dangerfield accent now—his favorite nightclub comedian.

"Yeah!" Broken Arrow slid an ammunition clip

across the clay to Brody. "She's got wings, scrotebag!"

"Hairball?" Stormin' Norman concentrated on improving his marksmanship skills as more and more targets presented themselves atop the sagging loops of concertina. "Scrotebag? Is Stormin' Fuckin' Norman bein' complimented, or what?"

"Ohhhh, *FUCK!*" Krutch had just made his grand appearance by ending a running dive between Brody and Broken Arrow, but now he was rising to his feet again. Several of the extra ammo bandoliers he had slung over both shoulders dropped into the dirt. The Stork drew the .45 from his shoulder holster and began firing wildly at a point in the perimeter where several sappers had formed a human chain—using dead bodies—to get over the concertina. Three of the VC had sacrificed their lives to charge the punji stick field with explosives strapped to their torsos, and now a path had finally been blown through the perimeter of sharpened stakes.

Guerillas clad in black 'pajamas' were streaming through the bamboo maze by the dozens, firing AK-47s and SKS rifles from the hip.

"This is it!" Broken Arrow stood up too and began firing from the shoulder as he moved forward slowly.

"Shit." Brody started to stand and was immediately struck in the knee by a splinter of ricocheting lead. The leg gave out on him and he collapsed, jerking a three-round burst of bullets up into the night sky.

"You, okay, Whoremonger?" Nervous Rex started toward him, but Brody waved the Green Beret off.

"I'll be fine!" He forced himself back on his feet. Glancing down and expected to see the leg covered in blood, he was surprised to find only a small entry hole in his trousers and a trickle of crimson—but the flesh wound burned like hell!

Nodding, Nervous Rex joined Stormin' Norman, and the two NCOs—Stormin' had obviously just been recently promoted—began running toward the fenceline, hoping to plug the hole.

Brody's jungle boots were kicking up clods too, and he fired the last round of a magazine at the nearest cluster of sappers. All five men went down screaming—their arms and legs jerking spasmodically afterwards as Brody jumped over them, behind Ritter and the others.

He was reloading on the run when a Viet Cong flew from the darkness—out of nowhere, it seemed—and tackled him. His M-16 knocked from his hands, Brody rolled with the impact, allowed the VC soldier to hold onto him as they tumbled down an embankment near a series of bunkers, then dug a bootheel into the reeds and pivoted, coming out on top.

With both fists clenched together, Brody smashed the Vietnamese sapper's nose, trying to force the nasal bones up into his brain, but somebody else rammed into his side, head first, and the Whoremonger was rolling again.

He came up with fists swinging, and was jumped by three more guerrillas who promptly flattened him against the red clay of Plei Me again. "Mother*fuck*!" he yelled, feeling the knife blade against the base of his skull—all the bastard had to do was ram it in, scramble his brains the way Treat had tried to do with his comrade twenty feet away, and it would be over.

But then the blade was withdrawn. The blade and its handler—Stormin' Norman was tossing Asians over his shoulder, one after the other.

"Thanks, Stormin'!" Brody called out, stumbling several feet as he struggled to his feet. A flurry of point-blank shots sent both Americans to the ground again, and Brody rolled away from the sound of the discharges—he had seen no one, not even the powderflash. But he knew the gunman was close because, even though his ears had been aching ever since the first hatch-60 was fired aboard *Pegasus*, now a sharp pain corkscrewed through them, and a vicious headache throbbed between his temples.

The moment he had regained his balance, another

208

Viet Cong was confronting him. Brody's right boot came up, out of automatic reflex, and the sapper with glazed eyes flopped over as his crotch was crushed. On the way down, Brody kicked the man across the top of the head too, and, shifting to the side, brought his boot back one final time for a final blow to the temple, when he was tackled again.

Before the two soldiers—American and Vietnamese—stopped rolling, the communist was dead from a broken neck as Brody twisted as hard as he could, waiting for the snapping sound, but hearing nothing due to the ordnance exploding all around.

He jumped to his feet, suddenly exhilarated in the knowledge he'd just earned that thirtieth notch on his Cav dagger, and began running straight for a group of charging sappers. This time Brody did the tackling—shocking the Vietnamese . . . catching them off guard by so bold and insane a move. He bowled a half dozen over.

One VC stabbed at his feet with a survival knife, but the anti-boobytrap steel plate running between the sole of the boot and the bottom of his foot saved him, and Brody kicked the man unconscious, took his blade away from him as the other Vietnamese scrambled for their weapons, and slit his throat from ear to ear.

That should have been it. That should have been Treat Brody's last firefight—the VC and their NVA sergeant were scooping up their rifles and pistols and machetes, and soon the Whoremonger would be just another slab of sliced meat at the floating market. Brody should have been saying his prayers, or running after his life—*but . . . all . . . he . . . could . . . think . . . about . . . was . . . the . . . kill . . . that . . . put . . . him . . . over . . . the . . . top . . . .* Into the Dirty Thirty. He wanted to tell Stormin' Norman so bad.

He wanted to say "Welcome me, brother! Welcome me into the ultimate fraternity! I paid my dues—Oh Lordy, have I paid my dues!" The Brick ran past his field of vision—Don Wickman, with his monstrous physique accented by that huge M-60 he carried like a squirtgun—and he focused on the patch across the back of the man's flak vest: *I'M SURE TO GO TO HEAVEN 'CAUSE' I'VE SPENT MY TIME IN HELL*!

Brody's gut instincts screamed *Survive*! But all he could think about now, as he picked a machete up out of the dust and flung it at the nearest guerrilla, leaving a gaping, bloody crevice where his left eye used to be, was that thirtieth kill. Three carbines were pointing at him now, and a discharge flash—now two discharges— lit up his night. Bullets missed him by inches, raising puffs of dust on either side of his feet, and he commanded those feet to run. Run back to the thirtieth kill . . . look at his face . . . memorize his features . . . pry his eyelids open and stare into his soul! *Feet, do your thing*! But Brody's jungle boots would not respond.

And he knew.

His mind was screaming *Wish I had a camera! Wish I had a camera*! yet the whole time he knew he was about to die. . . .

The downblast from a gunship only twenty feet above the battlefield sent the VC into a dustbowl frenzy. Several cupped their eyes with open palms, blinded. Two dropped to their knees. All lost their weapons. And The Brick ran from Vietnamese to Vietnamese, bashing their brains out with the buttplate of his M-60 from behind.

"They're retreating! They're retreating!" A Green Beret Brody had never met raced between them and Wickman as Lt. Vance's gunship landed on the squad of guerrillas, crushing those that weren't already dead.

"Bullshit!" he heard Sgt. Ritter yelling in reply. "They're just regrouping for another assault. Round up Stryker and the others, and start checking all the posts—get me a stat repo on the yardes. *Double time*!"

"Stormin' Norman!" Brody willed the rubbery legs away and skidded up nose-to-nose with Nervous Rex. "Have you seen Stormin' Norman, sarge? I gotta tell him something! Something really important!"

"I saw." Ritter sounded emotionally exhausted. "You're over the top." His fist did not come up for a handshake like Treat expected, but he muttered, "Congratulations."

"Yeah, thanks!" Brody was nearly hopping around, refusing to let a sergeant's understandable concern for the grave situation and his missing men bring him down off his high horse. "But I gotta find Stormin' Norman! We talked about this before!" He picked up two AKs lying in the blood-red clay and slung one over his shoulder. "I wanna tell him how I feel!"

Sgt. Ritter motioned over a shoulder using a thumbs-down without looking back. "That's Stormin' Norman right there, troop," he said matter-of-factly.

Brody froze. His face went blank, all excitement drained from his eyes. Like a zombie he started toward the body lying between two urine-soaked punji sticks. Halfway there, he began running, tears streaming down his face. Blades from three machetes protruded from tiger-stripe fatigues stretched across a broad back.

The Whoremonger dropped to his knees beside the big Green Beret, hope in his sobs—blood still trickled in small spurts from the knife wounds, as if the heart was still pumping life.

"It's not like you said it would be." Brody's throat cracked from dust and adrenaline as he turned the twitching body over, only to find it had no head.

Stormin' Norman was dead as they come.

CHAPTER 20

"Come on, Specialist Brody!" Vance, the new lieutenant, was slipping his hands beneath Treat's underarms and lifting him to his feet, away from Stormin' Norman's decapitated corpse. "We gotta boogy on back out into the sticks! Got some—"

"But his head." Brody was speaking as if from a mist-enshrouded dream—a dream-turned-nightmare, where he could see no one or nothing but the blades . . . the blades from three machetes protruding from Stormin' Norman's back. "We gotta find his head, sir!"

"We got some SF-types on the other side of the wire callin' for help!" Vance almost slapped the Whoremonger, but he held back, deciding they only do that in the movies.

"You can't do this to Stormin'!" Brody whirled around, eyes wide—a wild look in them.

"You're suffering from . . . from shellshock, soldier." Those were the only words Vance could come up with.

"Do you know what happens to a man if he loses his head in The Nam, sir?" Brody brushed his nose against the lieutenant's. "Do you fucking KNOW?" Vance could tell by the way the Spec-4 was bobbing about on the heels of his feet that his fists were clenched.

"It appears to me as if *you* are losing your head, soldier. Now why don't we get our act together and—"

"It's even worse if you're in the rainforest . . . out in the jungle   in the boonies like this." Brody waved his arms to encompass the sparkling perimeter wire.

"I know . . . I know." Vance wrapped a wrist around him.

But Brody pushed him away. "If you lose your head out here in the jungle, sir, the Viets say your soul . . . your spirit is destined to race around in circles at the scene of your death, for all eternity, sir! For all fucking eternity!"

"I know, soldier . . . I know. . . ."

"Destined to chase your butt around in circles for the rest of time, searching for your head!"

"We'll find his head, soldier. . . ."

"Then let's start looking." Brody stomped off in the direction of a pile of bodies, but Vance stopped him.

"After we fly balls-to-the wind and help out those Green Berets, okay, Specialist?"

"How can you do that to Stormin' Norman?" Brody cried. "If we don't look for it now, we'll *never* find it, Lieutenant!"

"What about them Green Berets!?" Vance was losing his own temper now, and the jutting jaw slowed Brody. "Huh?"

"How would you *fucking* feel if one or two of *them* lost their heads out there?" Vance showed the Spec-4 he could curse too. "And because you're pussy-footing around back here in the rear, over a dead man that—and you and I, as Occidentals know this for a fact—don't give a healthy shit about his goddamned head!"

"But. . . ."

Vance grabbed Brody's wrist again and hurled him toward *Pegasus*! "No more buts, soldier! Just get aboard that gunship and do your job! Quit feeling sorry for yourself, okay? That's all I ask! That's all *any* of us ask from you. . . ."

"But—"

214

"*Brody*!"

"Sir! Peg's deadlined, goddamnit! We were *shot down*!"

"She's patched up good as new!" Hal Krutch was running around beneath her tailboom. "A couple of fuel cells got a free vasectomy, and Peg's ass is now airconditioned—I had to bend a couple things back into shape, too," he added as an afterthought, "but she's ready to rock-'n-roll otherwise! Just name the cords, Lou! Anything within three or four klicks radius of Plei Me. Farther out than that and I gotta wait for parts, and I don't think you'll find a supply sergeant in R V N willing to make a trip out here right now, if ya catch my meaning. . . ."

As if to accent his statement, a shrill whistle punctuated the eerie calm. The Americans sprinted away from *Pegasus* as the mortar descended. Several screaming projectiles followed the first, but they all detonated against sandbags, falling on the other side of the camp.

Krutch was the only one to run *toward* Peg.

He had the overhead rotors twirling lazily before the rest of Echo Company was lifting their faces up out of the red clay and dust.

Three heavily-armed Green Berets also boarded *Pegasus*. As Brody climbed up over the skids, into the hatch, he glanced back toward Stormin' Norman's body one last time. No secondary ground assault followed the short barrage of mortars, so Strikers and a few Special Forces NCOs rushed about, dragging American and Montagnarde bodies back away from the wire.

Stormin' Norman's decapitated corpse was being taken over to a growing pile of mangled and mutilated flesh beside the CP bunker, and as Brody was about to close his eyes in sorrow and pain, he noticed something. Something in a stretch of bamboo a few meters beyond the wire. Movement. A swirl of ghostly shadows—but the shadows seemed white. And they had shape! It looked like a squad of Caucasians gliding through the bamboo—Americans wearing tiger stripe

215

fatigues and carrying M-16s, but with faces white as death itself. White as death, but streaked with green and black camou paint. The figures meshed, and as the helicopter pulled pitch, bucking slightly, the distant scene became a blur.

Brody sat up straighter, and the phantom patrol vanished altogether in a swirl of mist.

"Hold up!" he heard Vance saying. Two more soldiers were running toward the chopper from the CP. Both were heavily laden-down with extra bandoliers of ammunition. Broken Arrow and one of the newbies—Chappell.

When Brody glanced back over at the smoking fenceline, he gasped. It was a silent gasp—one no one aboard *Pegasus* heard because of the *whomp-whomp-whomp!* of rotors overhead. Scrambling over rucks and through piles of empty brass, he moved closer to the hatch, and saw the hunched-over figure again.

Stormin' Norman was squatting inside the wall of bamboo, a strange, bewildered look on his ashen features. He was staring straight at Brody, it seemed, but he was pointing toward a distant stretch of barbed fenceline. In the middle of the stretch of concertina, a couple feet off the ground, something was hanging in the razorsharp strands. From this distance, Brody couldn't tell for sure. . . . But the mishapen object looked like a head.

"I'll get it!" Brody seemed to see himself scream from afar. And then he was clawing past a startled Two-Step, leaping from *Pegasus* as she trembled before a false ascent. "I see it, Stormin' Norman! I'll get it!"

Broken Arrow was groaning—had his heel crushed the Comanche's ankle as Brody sought leverage underfoot for the jump?

"Brody, you son OF A BITCH!" The Lieutenant was yelling after him now. "Get your ass back onboard this ship! What the hell are you doing!?"

"I'll get it for you, Stormin'!" Brody was sprinting as hard as he could now, but the fenceline seemed to

216

remain out of reach . . . falling back—each sharpened barb sparkling like cats' eyes. And then he was right up next to it, sliding to avoid impaling himself in his excitement!

It was Stormin' Norman's head all right. Hanging from the small, hatchet-like barbs—one ear torn away, the lower jaw a pulpy mess, both eyes bulging, yet drained of life.

Brody took hold of the sticky, crimson-slick strands of hair along the back, but he could not pull the severed head from the wire. Trying to be gentle at first, he tugged harder now. . . . And suddenly huge hands were around his own—on the other side of the fenceline!

Stormin' Norman was trying to wrestle the head form him!

"No!" Brody screamed, refusing to let go. The ghoul on the other side of the concertina already had a head! he had Stormin' Norman's features, and Stormin' Norman's glare—even Stormin' Norman's shit-eatin' grin. But it wasn't Stormin' Norman over there, trying to drag his prize back into the bamboo and deep into the sea of shimmering elephant grass. It couldn't be!

"No!" Brody's fingers slipped from under the other man's, but he held onto the head's nose and ear, refusing to let go.

"Let go!" the ghoul with Stormin' Norman's face and voice screamed like a thousand souls echoing in a crypt.

"*NO!*" Brody pulled with all his might.

"Let the fuck GO, Whoremonger!" Stormin' Norman's double let out a demonic shriek.

Recoiling in horror as the ghoul's jaws parted and snapped at him like an attack dog's, Brody felt his heart stop.

"Brody!" He could hear Lt. Vance's voice calling to him from a hundred meters away as *Pegasus* remained in place, hovering but restless. "Get your ass back onboard this chopper!" *Get my ass back on board the chopper*? Why weren't they charging over here to help

217

him?

"Let fucking *GO!*" he screamed again, and the face on the other side of the fenceline was forcing the barbs into his cheeks as its nose brushed against Brody's.

"*You* let fucking go! It's *MY HEAD!*" The odor was revolting, but Brody held on for dear life.

And then he whirled around with all his might suddenly, breaking free, Stormin' Norman's head in his hands! Losing his balance, he tumbled across a carpet of mortar fins imbedded in the clay.

The ghoul was several feet off the ground now, hanging onto the sagging coil of concertina atop the fenceline, shaking it back and forth in a screaming, enraged fury, trying to get over.

Brody got to his feet and ran toward *Pegasus*, clutching Stormin' Norman's head against his belly protectively. His rucksack—one strap broken and whipping against his leg like a bee stinging him over and over—seemed to be calling up to him, and halfway to the gunship, he placed Stormin' Norman's head inside the pack and sealed it tightly shut.

Vance, a preoccupied look creasing his features, grabbed Brody by the front of his shirt as he scrambled over the skids, and helped pull him into the chopper as it quickly rose from a hover, nose low.

He stared up at the Lieutenant, the look on his face a question mark: Why didn't any of you guys come out there and help me? But Vance, strangely enough, was avoiding his eyes as Peg roared across the fenceline, barely clearing the treetops.

Brody could not remember rushing over to his spot in the cabin, but suddenly he was there, leaning against his M-60, feeling the warm downblast swirling through the hatch against his face.

He glanced back at Broken Arrow, but the Indian was rubbing oil into the dustcover of his rifle when he should have been rubbing his ankle. Vance should have been staring at him, giving Brody the evil eye that promised trouble and a court martial when this was all

218

over, but he was jabbering with Zack about the heat or the price of pussy in Plei Me or some such irrelevant crap.

Don't mean shit! Brody chuckled to himself.

"D'you say something, Whoremonger?" Two-Step looked up from his weapon, but Trick-Or-Treat just giggled again.

It was mindfuck to the max, he realized now as he leaned out the hatch to catch the humid, sticky breeze in his hair and a better look at the perimeter wire disappearing below. He saw no movement down there. No spirits gliding around in circles. Not even Charlie, massing for another attack. *Don't mean nothin'*, he reached down and patted the rucksack. *So long as I got. . . .*

The pack was still sealed tight, but it felt different now. It felt like a ruck full of ammo magazines instead of . . . .

Allowing the barrel of his Hog-60 to rise and strike the hatch with a dull *twang*!, Brody dropped into a squat beside the Infantryman's pack and worked furiously at unlacing the straps.

A few members of the crew glanced his way, but dismissed his actions as routine nervousness before a dangerous rescue mission. "Need some help, Brody?" Two-Step carefully laid down his rifle and moved across the cabin floor on strong ankles, always the lithe and agile Staked plains warrior, loyal to his brother braves.

Brody didn't reply, but kept fumbling with the straps until he had the top flap open and banana clips of soft-nosed five-point-fifty-six slugs sliding out, onto the floor at his feet.

A pile of shiny magazines rose in front of the Whoremonger, but Stormin' Norman's head was no-where to be found.

CHAPTER 21

A limb dangling in the treetops was how The Stork found them. The Green Berets. The nation's finest jungle experts who were used to fending for themselves under difficult circumstances and hostile fire, but were never trained to survive a counter-ambush when they were outnumbered a hundred to one.

That was just about how bad it seemed, anyway—to those twelve soldiers caught outside the wire when Victor Charlie launched his surprise attack. And Minh the Mastermind had shock troops waiting for the Green Berets when they completed their long-range reconnaissance patrol across the border into Cambodia, a scat ten or so klicks away. 'Klicks' is GI jargon for kilometers, which is local lingo for just under a mile in distance—the Viets like to say 'kilo,' which everyone else mistakes for controlled substances of the Thai stick persuasion.

But the ripped-away boot was what caught gunship pilot Hal Krutch's eye.

Despite the triple canopy concealing the jungle floor beneath, Charlie was lobbing mortars at the Green Berets. Either that, or one of the sapper squads had an NVA cadre with them who was armed with a blooper. Some GIs call bloopers elephant guns, or thumpers, all names for M-79 grenade launchers. M-79 grenade launchers look like sawed-off shotguns with a single, oversized barrel, which also breaks down much like a shotgun.

The Green Berets happened upon an old anti-tank trench, complete with iron girders, only a few hundred meters after they were first intercepted by the Cong, and this enabled them to set up some fairly inpenetrable defenses. But it was only a matter of time before the communists tightened the noose they were forming around the American's position.

One of the Minh's favorite spies, a pretty young thing named Koy, had obtained information regarding the SF troop movements, especially the Lurp patrols and F.O.B.'s. She saw no trouble in spending long nights in bug-infested treetops watching the activities in and out of Plei Me's CIDG compound. Koy was one of his few literate agents, and she took copious notes about everything she observed. That included the times of LRRP deployments and extractions, which were never supposed to take place routinely but seldom varied from three periods of duration. Thus, it was easy to estimate when this latest patrol would return from the Khmer frontier—and Minh took no chances: he posted ambush teams at seven different probable re-entry zones and covered all three time factors. Which is how the Green Berets were intercepted during the third and final predicted hour of return.

They managed to get to within a mile of the compound itself, so Krutch had been airborne less than a minute when he made the gruesome discovery. He just hoped he had the right victims.

The Green Berets took to blasting trees out of the way with C-4 charges as soon as they heard rotors flapping overhead. Krutch took *Pegasus* around low on the first pass, allowing the crew to unload on the enemy as a small clearing slowly formed where the trunks of mahogany and rosewood and ebony teak were falling. Green tracers arced up wildly from several different sources in reply.

"I think we got room now to lower a ladder, Stork!" Brody called up to the cockpit without clicking-in. He began pulling coiled rope from a compartment marked, in bright red, RESCUE.

Krutch did not answer the Whoremonger verbally, but flared into a dangerous hover directly over the clearing as both his doorgunners and the men standing behind them unloaded on the enemy with everything they had.

Sparks showered down from above as a string of white tracers struck the undersides of the rotors and ricocheted off, creating a sort of glowing white halo for a few minutes.

Krutch was bringing *Pegasus* down, a foot at a time, the ballast rims on her blade ends missing several tree trucks by only inches while shaving away smaller limbs like a giant fan. Zack was leaning out the hatch, his headphone on, helping guide The Stork in as Peg slowly descended. The clearing was becoming a crackling hell as flames raced up several crisp and brittle fingers of gnarled Japanese pine. The Green Berets set off another claymore, and the concussion rose swiftly, rocking the ship wildly, but Krutch managed to keep it under control.

"Jesus, Zack! Get on the horn and tell them guys to cool it—just for a minute!"

"Out of the question!" the master sergeant yelled back. "And I think you better abort, Mista Krutch! Pull this bird up! Victor Charlie's makin' his move—I got black pajamas swoopin' in on two sides!"

"Fuck," Krutch muttered into his mike, pouring power into the screaming blades.

Before *Pegasus* could rise, however, the blanket of heat smothering that clearing parted for two sleek, metallic predators. "Lawless!" Brody cried as the two prototype Cobra gunships dropped from the skies and turned night into day with dual barrages of rockets.

"Hey! *Hey!*" Warrant Officer Lance Warlokk spoke bird-to-bird over the radio net. "Sorry we're so late,

Stork, but m' mate got his jockstrap caught in a. . . ." The rest of the remark was lost in the rapidfire string of explosions that followed as both gunships, their snouts decorated with evil-looking sharks' teeth, darted about, slaughtering Vietnamese on the ground at will.

"We're *fini* in zero-five!" Krutch responded, dropping slowly again, both hands and feet working Peg's controls.

"Python-Lead, Snake-One . . . rodg your last. . . ."

"Hold it right there, Mista Krutch!" Zack was almost screaming—he nearly missed a splinter of bamboo rising up through the gunsmoke and collage of dancing shadows. "You can't make it down any further!"

"We're only about ten feet off the ground!" Brody was halfway out the hatch already. "We can jump it and lift the casualties up to—"

"That's what I was just about to suggest—"

But a face streaked with blood was already rising up over the skids. A semi-conscious form was being propped up from below, and Brody took hold of the gut-shot soldier as the Green Berets on the ground performed a sort of evacuation triage on the spot.

"Get down there and help 'em!" Zack took Brody's place, and the Whoremonger jumped into the unknown, feeling like a true paratrooper again.

Broken Arrow assisted Zack with wide eyes and numb hands. They only had two casualties in the cabin, and already the floor was soaked with blood. He was positive one of the men was dead, but didn't say anything—he didn't want to have to be the one to make a decision when they reached their payload capacity and had to start either tossing the lifeless back into death's jaws or ascend with men left on the ground.

Between bodies, he leaned out over the hatch, expecting to see wild, terrified faces down there—the VC had bounties out on the heads of every Special Forces soldier in II Corps, if not all of Vietnam—but instead there were simply grim, unworried looks on the Green Berets as they hurried to get the job down in the time

224

allotted.

"What's the count?" Zack was calling down to an E-8 with crimson-soaked bandages across several different parts of his body.

"Seven K.I.A.!" came the answer like a lightning bolt, and as explosions and discharges began going off all around again, the voices of men working to save others and the groans from the wounded merged until the only thing audible was a roar.

Brody stumbled on what may have been a torso when he landed on the ground. The communists had fired RPG's into the position from all four sides prior to the arrival of *Pegasus*, and limbs were everywhere—hanging from vines and branches, strewn across the blue and silver carpet of mushrooms. Brody flipped the mutilated body over. Both legs and an arm were gone. He could not tell by looking at the face whether the man had been a man, let alone black, brown, or white. Bone white, his ribcage protruded from a split-open chest cavity in shattered splinters.

"Leave him!" someone behind Brody was yelling. When he didn't respond, the SF soldier grabbed him by the elbow. "That's it—let's go!" It was hard to hear anymore due to the constant din of explosions, and Brody just turned and stared. The sergeant shouted, "Thanks, buddy! Now move it or lose it!" and he grasped the Whoremonger's wrist in an Indian-style handshake and heaved him up through the hatch.

Brody crashed down on top of Broken Arrow, and Two-Step nearly rolled out the opposite hatch, groaning. "*Jesus*, Treat!" He was clutching his calf. "You nearly broke my ankle, asshole!"

The last thing Brody saw before *Pegasus* ascended up out of that fiery hell hole was the Green Beret master sergeant clambering aboard, several sets of dogtags chains in one bruised and bloody fist.

It was as if time began moving backwards after that.

Lt. Vance was making the same facial expressions he'd made before the mission—*exactly* the same. Zack laughed in the identical sequence—but in reverse.

Brody shook his head violently, clutching his three rifles to his chest. "Motherfucking *déjà-vu*!" he muttered. That's what it had to be—there was no other plausible explanation.

That he learned about the phenomenon a few months back didn't help any. The article in *Overseas Weekly* had mentioned something about mindfuck. Not in those words exactly, but close enough for Brody. The brain plays games on us now and then, the story claimed, taking something just seen or experienced and flinging it back in our memory so that we think we're someplace we've been before, or doing something out of the ordinary identical to a way it was done in the past— when, in reality, that scene we think is being resurrected from the depths of our memory actually transpired only a few seconds earlier after all.

Something was gnawing at Brody, though. It was scratching his gut, trying to eat its way through, into his instincts—and it told him this was not *déjà-vu*, but something else altogether. This was evil, and it was spawned by something happening in the jungle . . . a disease festering in the rain forest. Void Vicious was behind all this, he was convinced—somehow. It was all coming together . . . the Dirty Thirty, Stormin' Norman's demise, the attack on Plei Me, the blanket of blood and mushrooms below . . . even Two-Step's twisted ankle. . . .

"My God! Will you look at that!"

They were approaching the CIDG outpost now— *Pegasus* was a couple hundred meters outside the main gate, staying low above the contours of the land.

"Jesus. . . ."

Rising from the outer perimeter of concertina—the same circle of silver where he'd spotted the naked female sapper over three months ago—were three bamboo poles, about fifteen feet tall, and three of four feet between them. Mounted atop each pole was the decapitated head of an American soldier.

Brody was the first one off the chopper when it landed inside the compound.

"You can't go any farther!" Someone was trying to grab his wrist, trying to pull him down prone, spread-eagle against the earth, but he managed to break loose. "Charlie's still out there, you idiot! You're fixin' to get your brains blown out!"

Nervous Rex followed him through the minefield and punji sticks. Broken Arrow was right behind the Green Beret sergeant.

"It's not him!" Brody finally proclaimed, after they'd lowcrawled the last fifty yards through razor-sharp reeds and leech-infested elephant grass. It's not—"

"No, it's not Stormin' Norman." Ritter was beside Brody now. He spoke as if it was a new discovery for him too, but one he had expected.

"Can we get outta here then?" Broken Arrow plopped down in the muck beside Nervous Rex, wondering why he even risked his life for these two maniacs.

Several flares were drifting down through the area. As they swung from side to side beneath their silk parachutes, leaving smoke trails crisscrossing against the night sky, they threw flickering shardes of golden light down across the faces on the severed heads.

"Do you know any of 'em?" Brody asked Ritter.

"They're not with Special Forces." Nervous Rex was glancing around at the enemy positions nearby and paying little attention to the bamboo poles or the blood dripping down them.

"But, they're *Americans*," Broken Arrow decided.

"Probably State Department," Ritter mumbled, testing the seal on his M-16's clip.

"State Department?"

"C.I.A."

"Oh. . . ."

One flare was all that floated overhead now, and when it broke free of its 'chute, plummeting to earth like a falling star, Brody rose and began running back across the free fire zone.

"Brody!" Ritter called after him, a loud *swoooOOOSH*! in the distance announcing someone on Charlie's side had launched another flare. "Prone out, you fucking fool! *Prone out*!"

When the flare popped directly over the Whoremonger, he was still sprinting toward that section of fencing where he'd confronted . . . or, where he *thought* he'd confronted the ghost of Stormin' Norman—before the flashbacks, and the mindfuck, and the self-doubts, and the guilt. Before he was flooded with sorrow and the irresistible urge to end it all with suicide—a flash of glory. That was it! He would die, not like a candle in the night—but that meteor burning bright! That meteor some nameless wrote about—the only poem Brody ever read in his life, but it stuck with him through all these years.

With hot lead and sizzling tracers bouncing about at his heels, Brody ran faster than he'd ever run before. Somehow, he made it back to the primary fenceline without getting shot. And it was there. Right where he knew it would be. Right where the tiger-striped ghost had pointed.

A couple of feet off the ground, tangled in the strands of barbed wire and razor-sharp concertina, was what remained of Stormin' Norman's head.

CHAPTER 22

Koy the Cambodian-trained guerrilla girl raised the AK's front sights to compensate for range, but she could not bring herself to shoot Treat Brody in the back. The thirty bullets, fired in four-and five-round bursts, kicked up dirt clods and sparks at the American's heels, but did little more harm. Tears were streaming down Koy's face as she fired at the only man she had ever really loved.

She was alone—the others were in a trench on the other side of the rise—so she could cry freely here. Koy felt abandoned by both sides. She had not seen Venn since the night of the shooting. And now, there was no way she could attempt to arrange a rendezvous with Treat—he would blame her for whatever had gone wrong that evening. Koy was just grateful her gods had seen fit to spare the young soldier his life.

When Brody and his two friends reached cover, another lull in the fighting followed, and Koy used the time to check over her firearms and reflect. . . .

She had suffered a change of heart after warning Ritter and Wickman and the others that Treat was in trouble. As soon as the Americans charged down the block, Koy dashed to her cell leader's home, up the street in the opposite direction. She told the hunter she'd spotted some GIs sneaking around the safehouse where they kept the pickle jars.

She had protested when the hunter told her to wait in his house until he came, but there was little else she could do—disobedience easily led to death, in Plei Me.

She clearly heard the shooting that ensued shortly thereafter—long before he could have had time to get together any of the men. And from the hunter's residence, she did not have a clear view of the safehouse. He told her later that the Americans had escaped, and that Venn and the others had been rounded up by the QCs and taken away to jail. She knew in her heart she would never hear the true, complete story.

The pain in her soul was intense—Koy's guilt over choosing her lover over Venn then flip-flopping and hurting *every*one left her feeling like a traitor to her own people.

She could not sleep for weeks after Venn's disappearance, and spent nearly twenty hours every day, readying the trenches outside the Special Forces camp. Tonight was the first she had seen Treat again since that evening they lay naked in each other's arms beneath the floating flares.

When the hunter returned after the shoot-out, it happened. His wife, for the first time since Koy could remember, was away from him—on Pleiku, nursing a sick relative.

That was when he laid the first guilt trip on Koy. "Venn was captured because you were not quick enough in alerting me," he accused, thinking he might tell her later most of them were all dead—after he received what he wanted, soothed her pain and sorrow, then snatched away some more of her innocence.

"You have never . . . 'been' with a man, have you?" He was slowly pushing her backwards, guiding her through the dark corridor, into the room where sleeping mats were unrolled at night, and bombs were made by day.

230

"Please. . . ." She could hear her own voice still . . . even after all these weeks. "Do not do this to me."

Already he was slipping her blouse down over her shoulders and fondling her breasts. "Your time has come," had been his only reply.

"It is my time to leave, sir." She had tried desperately to flee gracefully, but he was grabbing her between the legs, dragging her into the room, flinging her down on the packed-earth floor.

"It is your time to remove that sarong!" came the demand, and all Koy could think about was what Treat had told her. He had wanted her to save herself for someone more worthy. Someone . . . some young man who was not as evil as he. . . . Not as soiled and black-hearted as Treat Brody the Whoremonger. And now look how it was happening. . . .

"*Please!*" She had considered clawing his eyes, or kicking him in the groin and fleeing. But where would she go? What would she do? What *could* she do? The insurgency was her entire life. Building bombs and repairing rifles and digging tunnels was all she knew how to do.

He slapped her, and Koy collapsed against the clothes cabinet, bringing it down on top of her. Expensive, made-in-Saigon *ao dais*—his wife's traditional Viet-namese gowns, though she was Cambodian—scattered across the floor, and that was where he forced her thighs apart: on top of them.

The pain was less than she had feared it would be—she told herself the episode with Treat Brody had been more . . . much more than either of them remembered, and perhaps that was why—but the same she felt afterwards nearly killed Koy. She ran off naked, into the jungle, as soon as the hunter finished the third time, rolling off into exhaustion and dreams, and Koy told herself over and over again that Treat Brody had been her first man. Treat Brody, and not this animal, the hunter.

For weeks afterward, her every thought went into

231

plotting. Plotting to execute the hunter . . . kill him from behind . . . one shot to the back of the skull. But Koy could not bring herself to do it. Without the hunter, there would be no organization to her life. No purpose. No timetables, duties and responsibilities.

Koy rarely thought about goals in her own personal life. Oh, when she was alone on guard or look-out duty, late at night—the stars and moon birds only companions—she thought about the future, wondering how much longer she would participate in the military scheme of things . . . what would happen to her after the liberation, when the two Vietnams were once again reunited. . . .

She never thought of children. True, large families of many children were looked highly upon by most Vietnamese—spinsters who never married considered a disgrace—but Koy could not see bringing a child into a world at war. She had no money . . . no resources to take care of it—such an event was not for her. It just did not seem right.

The farthest her thoughts roamed was when she gazed at the night sky, seeking out the crescent moon riding low on the horizon at pre-dawn, and saw the ever-present flares instead. The flares were always in Koy's world, but now each time she saw the flares, she thought not of the battles raging beneath them, but a tiny, little shack in Plei Me . . . where she had lain for a few precious minutes with an American she was sworn to kill. . . .

The hour upon hour of shooting that erupted when her cell leader began the surprise attack on the Green Beret outpost had terrified Koy. Up until now, the extend of her experience with death and killing had involved hit-and-run, one-sided raids where the opponent was usually sleeping; elaborate ambushes where so much C-4 or claymores were used that firefights after the blasts rarely followed; and 'safe snipings' from afar, where she always had a clear field of vision yet her targets never saw her face. Now the enemy was fighting back in force, comrades were dying all around, and her ears hurt.

Her ears hurt from the never-ending rattle of rifle-fire, and her eyes ached from constant explosions against the night, bits of willie-peter from a white phosphorous grenade had burned down into her back and shoulders, and her head throbbed from the slightest movement in any direction. Only now did the comrades allow her time to rest. Finally, after hours of dragging corpses back from the killing zone, to trails hidden in the bamboo.

Koy was high in a tree tonight. She had strapped herself to a think branch, so she wouldn't fall in case she dozed off. She was far above the cloud of drifting gunsmoke, polishing the Kalashnikov she had just fired down at Brody, and trying to recreate that special night in her mind, the evening Treat Brody held her to his chest and treated Koy like she was *some*body.

CHAPTER 23

Fog creeping in from the jungle rose to the Chaplain's ankles as he greeted the rising sun with both sorrow and optimism. Several M-16 rifles rose vertically in front of him, their bayonets deep in the red clay of Plei Me, camoucovered helmets—some bullet-riddled—balanced over the buttplates. A cluster of soldiers crouched in a semi-circle before the military priest, heads bowed but rifles ever ready.

This was not a graveside service. The bodybags which had been filled during the last few hours were stacked beside the helipad, waiting for the fog to lift so slicks could transport them south to G.R. Graves Registration, Saigon.

Dozens of other soldiers listened to the Chaplain's brief sermon and farewell to the brave men who had died defending the CIDG outpost from Major Minh's suicidal sappers. But they listened with their backs to the service and their eyes and rifle sights on the perimeter wire, prepared for another attack.

Fierce fighting had raged through the night—for eight or nine hours after Treat Brody had recovered Stormin' Norman's head from the strands of concertina—but the VC and North Vietnamese had pulled back during the predawn hours. Except for a lone sniper now and then, keeping the Americans pinned down and in place for the most part, the area remained tense but relatively quiet.

The memorial for their fallen brothers was traditional. When he was through reading about soldiers of Christ and the ways of warfare, the chaplain would go from guardpost to post, consoling the men, reassuring them if that was what he felt they needed, sharing brew with the vets who only needed a smoke or a joke, and sharing a box of ammo if he was caught out on the line when shooting erupted again.

Brody could not really hear the army priest's voice as he watched the informal service from a bunker two hundred meters away, but the helmets resting atop M-16s bayoneted into mother earth took him back several months. The fog especially. The silver fog became a deathshroud that reminded him of a dozen funeral veils. Pagoda Pete had more than twelve broken-hearted women kissing his casket goodbye. It had been a closed-coffin funeral, because Pagoda Pete had lost both arms and half his face storming a Buddhist temple in the Mekong Delta, down Mytho way six months ago. and, though everyone had been told it would be a closed-coffin affair, the entire hamlet of Greenfields, Georgia, turned out for Pagoda Pete's homecoming, and that included his dozen or so old flames.

Brody the Whoremonger had accompanied Pagoda Pete and Nervous Rex on that midnight raid back in April. A Staff-Sergeant who went by the nickname Crazy Craig led the sterile assault. It was a 'sterile' assault because the participants wore black uniforms with no markings, and carried weapons of East-bloc manufacture which could not be traced back to any country on friendly terms with the United States.

An Intelligence unit within the Saigon government had learned an East German military advisor was posing as an American in the village of Cho Gao, a klick or two outside Mytho. He was living with a Vietnamese woman, and ferrying information about troop movements in the Delta to Hanoi via a radio transmitter hidden in a small, out-of-the-way temple in the heart of Mytho.

The East German's whore happened to be a double agent,

236

though, and she was learned about Pagoda Pete's mission the night before it was scheduled to take place.

When Brody, Nervous Rex, Crazy Craig, and the others stormed the temple, the East German was waiting for them. Hoping to lure the entire squad into the place of worship then blow them to kingdom-come with a monster, his plan went awry when two members of the team intercepted him at the back exit.

Before he was gunned down, the East German managed to detonate the jury-rigged boobytrap of one dozen claymores. Only Pagoda Pete had made it into the temple when the thing went off, however. He was killed instantly, and Brody and the others were blown back by the rolling concussion, out into the street.

A vicious firefight between the Americans and followers of the East German ensued, lasting over an hour, and it was during the running gun battle that Crazy Craig and Nervous Rex became members of the Dirty Thirty. Which made them understandably paranoid: Pagoda Pete had killed *his* thirtieth communist in hand-to-hand combat only two days before the temple shoot-out.

After a stationhouse-full of VNP *canh-sats* arrived to mop up, Nervous Rex and his crew melted back into the lacquer-woodwork, carrying Pagoda Pete's remains with them.

Pagoda Pete's C.O. awarded the fallen hero a posthumous Silver Star and Purple Heart, and Nervous Rex and Crazy Craig divided up his war trinkets among themselves—for added good luck. The trinkets included a heavy necklace resembling a bicycle chain, fashioned from Montagnarde copper, and a dogtags chain strung with VC molars and three AK slugs which had been taken out of Pagoda Pete's own back.

When soldiers die in combat, it is tradition to allow the dead man's best friend to escort his body back to The World. Nervous Rex had always been close to Pagoda Pete, but Ritter declined to return stateside. He was scheduled to attend Special Forces training in Thailand for an M.O.S. switch, and couldn't bring himself to watch strangers

237

shovel dirt down onto Pagoda Pete. Ritter loved combat and rain forests and The Nam, but he hated civilians and particularly disliked returning to the continental U.S., which was literally quite strange, since Nervous Rex was more than willing to give his life for his country. But that was one of many things Ritter preferred not to think about.

So Crazy Craig, who had just attained Dirty Thirty status and was feeling rather invincible, to say the least, volunteered to take Pagoda Pete home, which was not only unexpected but suspicious, for Crazy Craig hated civilians and the mainland even more than Nervous Rex.

Brody sweet-talked his way into the duty, too. 'Sweet-talk' was his term, but the final result could have been interpreted different ways, since one of the 'conditions' set down by Neil Nazi Buchanan involved a six-month extension. The Whoremonger would have to remain an additional 180 days in The Nam after his normal Tour 365 was completed. Which would have made nine out of ten soldiers serving in Southeast Asia gag and possibly barf up a lung, but the consequences of his 'free' trip to the States and back did not traumatize Treat's outlook on life: he loved Vietnam. Not the country itself, so much, nor particularly the Vietnamese people, either, but Spec-4 Brody, doorgunner extraordinaire, lived for the hot-LZ missions. He prayed for an F.O.B. or rescue muster aboard the gunships every hour of the day and night, and when the scramble sirens *did* go off, he couldn't get *enough* of hatch duty aboard *Pegasus*, his favorite ship. Brody was funny that way. He kept the guys laughing for a month when they found out from the company clerk Treat had insisted the C.O. put the extension orders in writing: he didn't want to receive inadvertent transfer papers sending him to Bumfuck, Egypt—or worse: Germany—a couple months down the line.

Brody spent those first forty-eight hours in Greenfields, Georgia, mourning Pagoda Pete, consoling his friends and relatives—those who would speak to a man in uniform, which were many, since this was the deep South, and not Berkeley, California. Crazy Craig had to return to South

238

Vietnam within five days of the funeral, and Brody spent the following seventy-two hours trying to talk the man out of going AWOL on him, the First Cav, Uncle Sammy, God, and country.

Crazy Craig would have none of it. "You saw what happened to Pete," he complained.

"A fluke," Brody countered.

"He didn't have a chance."

"We should have handled it differently."

"If we'd of handled it *any* differently, they'd be buryin' Pete, *and* Tex Ritter, *and* you and yours truly!"

"What I meant was—"

"I know exactly what you meant, Treat: a little more coordination . . . a little heavier firepower . . . a bit faster on the response end. Shit, that would only have sealed *all* our caskets, brother. There's no way you can outrun a monster, my friend! No fucking way . . . ."

"But what are the chances of something like that happening again? I mean, that type of operation, under those conditions..and involving some sly sonofabitch from East Berlin?"

"Who the hell can say, bud? Who the *hell* can say?"

"I mean, word from rumor control—"

"The wait-a-minute grapevine has been wrong ever since I arrived in-country, Treat . . . ."

"Hold on. Just hear me out, okay?" They were sitting in a small coffeeshop at a truckstop on Interstate 20, just outside North Augusta, South Carolina, and Brody glanced around to make sure none of the half dozen or so truck-drivers at the coffee counter behind them were listening.

"You've got the floor, *General* . . . ."

"Fucking fine, smart ass. Now listen up: I heared it from Crum's own lips that on or around—"

"Crump? *Clarence* Crump The Thievin' Third?" Crazy Craig threw his hands up in the air. "*Our* Clarence Crump—the black radical whose only goal in life is to take over the Saigon blackmarket so he can, in his own words, raise enough *scrip* to arm the bloods back in The World so they can off whitey and The Man? *That* Clarence Crump

239

III?"

"Okay, forget Mohammed . . . ."

"Yah, *Mohammed* My Ass."

"I've heard it from Lt. Winston, too. The scoop is that our unit . . . hell, all the Infantry units workin' the Mekong Delta are going to be absorbed into the First Cav, real official-like."

"What?" Crazy Craig sipped at his coffee as Brody watched a carload of college students skip into the parking lot and knock over a newspaper stand.

"Yah. We're gonna become a bonafide airmobile unit. big time. No more catch-all missions. No more MI-assists, like the one that got Pete killed and gave the rest of us haircuts we didn't need."

"But . . . ."

"No buts, Craig. ALL we're gonna be doin' from now on is humpin' the boonies, runnin' Lurps through the bamboo—all that good shit. I heard we might even rate some skate duty up in II-Corps."

"The Central Highlands?" Crazy Craig turned to see what all the commotion was as the first student through the cafe's door nearly shattered the glass.

"Right. Pleiku, Kontum. You ever seen a Montagnarde woman up close, Craig?"

"Nothin' could beat a Delta dame, hotdog." Craig lit up a cigarette and set his HOG HEAVEN-inscribed Zippo Lighter on the table.

"Stryker told me—"

"Stryker the Green Beret?"

"Rodg. He told me them hill people . . . their tribeswomen raise goats or something and got tits like watermelons from drinkin' all the milk. Stryker says some of the tribes, like around Duc Co or Phuc Do or whatever he told me . . . anyway, around them villes, the broads live on *tiger's* milk! Imagine that? He claims it makes 'em real wild in the sack and—"

"I heard Yarde women file their front teeth down to near nothing." Crazy Craig's eyes said 'checkmate!' "They think it makes them look beautiful or something . . . ."

240

"Yah, well I heard that crap too, smartass, and it just so happens I fucking *asked* Sam about that, and you know what he told me?" Brody threw his chin out victoriously. "He told me only a *few* chicks in a *few* villages still cling to old customs like that."

"Just the thought of it makes my skin crawl," Crazy Craig said, shuddering as he drank some more coffee. "Filin' down your teeth to the gums or whatever they do has gotta be worse than scraping a blackboard with long fingernails."

"But do you see my point?" Brody asked as he watched the college students ignore a waitress who was trying to seat them on the other side of the restaurant. The 'Leader' of the group, clad in bellbottom jeans and a psychedelic t-shirt, spotted their uniforms down at the corner table and, like a Cavalry soldier waving the troops onward, started toward Brody The Whoremonger and Crazy Craig. The college student, in his mid-twenties at the most, wore a long beard, light brown hair to his waist, and wire-rim glasses. He gave Brody a dirty look as his four male friends and two girls squeezed into the tiny cubicle.

"A *soldier boy*!" The young woman closest to Brody make her voice sound like an excited Marilyn Monroe. She had the chest for the part—barely restrained, Treat observed, by a bulging halter-top—and blonde hair that fell to her shoulders only to curl upward again.

"Mornin,' Ma'am . . . ." Brody brought two fingers to his brow in a casual half-salute.

The blonde turned to the other girl, who wore the same mask of hate as the group's leader. "Aren't they so cute in uniform?" Crazy Craig couldn't help but think she sounded like she was browsing through a pet shop, looking for the right color canary.

"Ma'am?" The youth with the glasses stood up. "What the hell is *that* supposed to mean?"

Eyes narrowing in surprise, Crazy Craig turned around and locked eyes with the campus activist. "Were you talking to us?" he asked softly, shifting in his seat just enough to flaunt the four rows of ribbons on his Class-A greens.

"Sit down, junior," Brody suggested calmly, paying more attention now to refilling his coffee mug than monitoring the college student.

"Sit down, Graham . . . ." Two of the boys already seated looked like they didn't want any trouble either. Yet.

'Graham' ground his teeth impressively, moved his chin up and down and back and forth, snarling without making another sound, and sat down beside the blonde girl.

"Why don't *you* guys join up or something?" the blonde asked Graham loudly. "They look so . . . handsome in uniform and—"

"Shut *up*, Patty!" the other young woman snapped.

"But they do!" 'Patty' persisted, turning to face Graham again. "It's about time you go out and . . . *do something* with your lives! Are you going to stay in school the rest of you—"

"There's a *war* on right now, Bimbo," Graham muttered under his breath.

Patty turned around in the booth and ran a slender, manicured forefinger along the colorful black and white combat patch on Crazy Craig's right shoulder. "A birdee!" she all but chirped. "Does it have anything to do with your . . . with your. . . outfit?" she asked cheerfully.

"It's an eagle," Brody said proudly, answering for Crazy Craig so he wouldn't have to turn around in his seat again.

"A *bald* eagle?" Graham asked sarcastically, running his fingers through his long hair as his eyes scanned the two soldiers' crew-cuts disapprovingly. The other boys seated at his table laughed along right on cue.

"A . . . screaming . . . eagle." Crazy Craig turned slowly, focusing his most intimidating stare onto Graham. The youth was broadchested—Brody thought he probably lifted weights between his social science and political theory classes—but he frowned and glanced down at his menu.

"Anyway," Brody continued their earlier conversation. "Now you've got a good reason to stay in. You and me, Craig—we could make a great team! No more of that

242

clandestine crap, takin' chances on behalf of The Agency or Air America. From now on, it'll soon be strictly Hueys, Void Vicious, Charlie and us—you couldn't ask for a better combination."

"Okay." Crazy Craig leaned across the table, lowering his voice. "I fucking listened to you, now you fucking listen to me . . . ."

"You've got my undivided fucking attention." Brody rolled his head back and forth on his shoulders like Jackie Gleason doing a Honeymooner's routine, but Crazy Craig did not laugh. He did not even smile. Crazy Craig made a strange sound that was not unlike a caged panther prowling back and forth behind its bars, waiting for the zookeeper to bring the daily pail of raw meat.

"I'm not going back to Vietnam."

Brody glanced over his friend's shoulder, but none of the college students seemed to be listening. "But—"

"And that's final."

"Desertion in time of war can carry a death penalty, pal. Have you thought about—"

"Of *course* I thought about that! But what you fail to understand is that if I *did* return, it'd be no different than a death sentence anyway, Treat."

"How so?" Brody produced his most skeptical expression then allowed his eyes to follow a topheavy waitress as she walked by with a tray full of steak-and-eggs breakfasts. Her shapely legs stopped beside a table full of truckdrivers, and Brody shifted his gaze when one of the big men winked at him.

"You ever heard of the Dirty Thirty?"

Brody swallowed hard and began spreading strawberry jam across a slice of toast he hadn't planned to eat. "Uh . . . yah, seems I heard something about it . . . ." In fact, attaining Dirty Thirty status had always been at the top of The Whoremonger's dreamsheet, but he felt he didn't have a chance, being in a detachment of the 101st Airborne that blew a lot of VC sampans out of the Mekong River but didn't meet a whole lot of hardcore Cong up close. The Green Berets and Marine Lurps and Navy Seals were the super troopers who got in all the hand-to-hand escapades.

"Well, I snapped my thirtieth Victor Charlie neckbone during that fracas where Pagoda Pete got his ticket cancelled . . . ."

"You *did!*?" Brody sat up ramrod straight in his seat, pretending he didn't already know.

"Yah . . . but shut up a second—that's not the kicker. Pagoda Pete got his Dirty Thirty 'pin' a short time *before* all hell broke loose at that Buddhst temple."

"Meaning you think—"

"Meaning I *know* my number's comin' up next. It always works that way—don't ask me why: I don't fucking know. If I did, I'd make a million grantin' an interview to the National—"

"You're letting your imagination . . . no, make that your superstitions run away with—"

"Listen-up, *pal.*" Crazy Craig suddenly got a frightening sparkle in his eyes. "Just look at the stats."

The stats?

"Five guys in our unit—five guys that I *know* about, got themselves K.I.A. within a couple weeks of fightin' over the top."

"A lot of other men have gone in bodybags too. You can't just lump together everyone who—"

"It's either me next . . . or Ritter . . . ."

"I mean, if you had some kind of . . . uh, scien*tific* survey to show me, or . . . *Ritter?* Whatta ya mean it's either 'you or Ritter'?"

"Nervous Rex rolled over the top the same day I did," Crazy Craig revealed.

"You're shittin' me . . . ."

"Nope," Craig said simply.

"Aw, fuck me 'till it hurts . . . ."

"That's why I ain't goin' back."

"But . . . ."

"No buts, amigo." Crazy Craig finished his fourth refill. "I've looked at it from all the angles, and I stand a better chance of survivin' twelve hours blindfolded in a subway tunnel than if I step foot back in The Nam."

244

"That's a weird way o' looking at it."

"My whole world has turned *weird* on me, Treat. I shit you not, brother. Ever since the . . . the 'event' at the temple, I haven't been the same. I haven't been able to sleep at night . . . mostly, anyway . . . .And when I have, it's been nightmare after nightmare."

"Nightmares? what kind of nghtmares?"

"Well, just bad dreams really." Crazy Craig sounded like he had decided at the last second to hide something from Brody. "I mean, I relive that explosion over and over . . . you know: Pagoda Pete's face and arms flyin' past me while his upper torso is squirtin' blood and his legs just kinda sway back and forth there for an eternity before finally toppling over . . . ."

"Christ."

"Yeah . . . and I see myself chasin' one o' them bad guys in and out of a maze of dark alleys, going around and around in circles until we're back at the temple and we dash inside and there he is . . . ."

"He?" Brody thought he would say Pagoda Pete. Or the East German.

"Buddha."

"Buddha?"

"Buddha's in there, Treat. Alive. Walkin' around tryin' to plug up the bullet holes in the walls with his fingers as we shoot the place up. He's walkin' around kinda calm like, 'cause even though we're blastin' away on rock-'n-roll, Buddha's got a thousand arms and a thousand feet, and he's in no hurry—he's got no place to go, but he's awful damn upset with us, Treat, 'cause his temple's bleedin' and he's runnin' out of fingers to plug up all the bulletholes . . . ."

Crazy Craig snuffed out his cigarette and rested his face in his hands, sighing heavily. It was as if telling the story to someone close only reminded him night would fall again, eventually, and he would have to go through the same whole thing once more, over and over . . . ."Jesus, Craig . . . I really didn't realize . . . ."

"That ain't the worst of it." The soldier with bloodshot eyes sitting across the table from Brody glanced up finally and seemed to stare right through The Whoremonger. "I see all their faces. The motherfuckers offed." There was no remorse in his tone. No guilt. "They follow me everywhere . . . .But especially after dark . . . ."

"Do they . . . have they . . . 'appeared' since we've been stateside?" Brody had been spreadng layer upon layer of jam on the same piece of toast for the last five minutes without realizing it.

Crazy Craig pointed at his eyes with both forefingers. "The eyedrops can't even get the red out anymore," he said seriously. "Not when there's no white left to . . . .White's for virgins, amigo. Virgins and innocence and all that crap."

"I never knew anyone before . . . who was being . . . haunted . . . ." Brody was not making fun of Crazy Craig.

"They laugh at me," he revealed. "They taunt me, saying it's only a matter of time before their buddies hunt my white ass down and lay me to rest beside all the guys in the Duty Thirty Fraternity . . . .But you know the really strange thing? The assholes are talkin' a mile a minute, rippin' me a new *yingyang* in the rapidfire Vietnamese— but I understand what they're saying, Treat. I understand every word they're speaking . . . *fluently.* My own *thoughts* are in Vietnamese!"

"Definitely creepy." Brody felt a chill run down his spine. Crazy Craig had bright green eyes that reminded him of the jungle, and he searched their depths as both men sat staring at each other, unblinking. He searched their depths, unsure what he was looking for—VC charging through the reeds, or dead GIs swinging from tamarind branches . . . .—but saw only the reflection of the truck drivers sitting at the table behind them.

Crazy Craig reached for his glass of ice water for the first time, hoping to dilute some of the caffeine in his gut, but all the icecubes were suddenly in his lap.

"Oh, excuse me!" Graham had picked that moment to walk by and 'bump' the soldier's elbow in the process.

Brody's eyeballs rolled toward the ceiling as Crazy Craig quckly brushed himself off with a napkin and Graham

246

paused, waiting for his reaction. Brody slowly shook his head from side to side, thinking, *Here we go . . . .*

"Is it my imagination." Crazy Craig stood up. He towered a full foot above Graham-with-the-college deferment. ". . . Or are you trying to tell this naive soldier-boy something?"

Graham was ignoring him now, though, and staring down at Brody's uniform. He ran a grimy fingernail over The Whoremonger's blue and silvery-white Combat Infantryman's Badge. "That's a *musket.* From the Civil War. Did you get it out of a Cracker Jacks box?" His finger flipped at it, but the C.I.B. refused to loosen.

"I'd say those qualify as 'fightin' words," Crazy Craig grabbed Graham by the scruff of his t-shirt and slowly lifted him off his feet.

Before anyone could react further, a sharp crack sounded from the counter. Brody and his friend glanced that direction to find a middle-aged black man wearing a bone-white apron and carrying a 12-gauge shotgun. The manager of the cafe weighed close to three hundred pounds, Brody decided. Maybe three-fifty. "We don' use paper plates here," he growled. "And my property damage insurance done run out. You two young 'uns wanna beat up on each other, take it outside!"

"I don't believe that'll be necessary." Crazy Craig produced an uncharacteristically mellow expression and slowly lowered Graham back to the ground.

"I was just fixin' to use your rest room . . . blood," Graham raised his fist in the air, imitaging a black power salute, and the manager frowned. He returned the 12-gauge to its place beneath the counter. "Fucking baby killers," Graham muttered loudly as he disappeared through a swinging door.

"That's it." Crazy Craig started after the student, but Brody grabbed his arm.

"Don't sweat it," he said firmly. "The punk isn't worth the fart bubbles in your bath tub."

His jaw locked, Crazy Craig's countenance softened and he slowly looked down at The Whoremonger. "The fart

247

bubbles in my bath tub?" He broke out laughing and sat back down.

"Come on." Brody motioned toward the cash register.

"I saw a topless joint back down the road a couple miles with some Fort Benning bumperstickers parked out front. It's time we got back to our own kind, Crazy Craig . . . ."

"Yeah." The bigger man stood up again and nodded as he pulled out his product-of-Viet-Nam imitation leather wallet. "I *need* a couple cool nipples against my eyeballs, slick."

As they passed the table full of students, Crazy Craig stopped, placed his huge hands on the edge of the table, and leaned down close to the blonde until he could smell her perfume. "I'm proud of it," he said innocently.

Excited by the unexpected attention, the girl wiggled her bare shoulders back and forth—which caused her breasts to sway from side to side heavily, getting *Crazy Craig's* attention—and giggled. "Proud of *what?* " Her voice rose higher with each word and her eyes grew wide.

"Proud of being a babykiller." Crazy Craig's was a straight face. "In Nam, the babies all run around lobbing grenades. Sometimes their mother and father strap them all up with satchel charges or tape C-4 under their clothing, then send them out to run up to the GIs . . . ."

"Oh . . . ." The blonde's smile faded and she glanced over at the woman sitting beside her.

"Do you know what C-4 is, honey?" Crazy Craig flashed his big, bright teeth in a friendly way, but the blonde could not force any words out. Her head shook slowly from side to side.

"But I bet you're going to tell us." The other college girl sipped a soda straw in her mouth and turned to look out the window as if she were becoming extremely bored.

"C-4 is plastic explosives," Craig said proudly. "A little chunk no bigger than your . . . ." The stress was making blondie's nipples rigid beneath her tight blouse and Crazy Craig could not take his eyes off them, ". . . than your pinky finger . . . would blow this whole restaurant to Birmingham and back," he exaggerated slightly.

"Where?" Blondie finally found the resolve to speak again.

"We're from Chicago," the boy sitting across from her 'explained,' chest expanding importantly. "On Spring break. Just tryin' to see some of the country . . . ."

"Just tryin' to see some of the good ol U.S. of A., eh?" Crazy Craig mimicked him.

"Uh, Ten-4, GI Joe."

"In the MIL-I-TAR-Y," Crazy Craig jerked the youth out from behind his table and twisted his arm around behind his back, "we say 'roger.'"

"Fine, fine . . . okay, OKAY!" College boy squirmed.

"Hey!" The cafe manager slammed hs fist down on the counter. "What did I tell you guys?"

Crazy Craig dragged his prize over to the exit, sat him down in a chair roughly, then pulled out his wallet and flipped through the photosection until he found a small card. He pulled it out and held it in front of the kid's face. "Do you know what this is?" Crazy Craig said dramatically.

College boy swallowed hard as he rubbed at his arm, and he was not acting. "It looks like a fraternity card."

"Look *closer*," the Airborne trooper ordered.

"It says you have a Ph.D. in International Politics and—"

"Well fucking-A!" Crazy Craig slapped the college boy on the back. "The flunky can read! 'Cept you've got one word wrong, son. That's International *Affairs*. Not politics. Politicians are puss, son, pure and simple. It's politicians who are gonna fuck it all up in Nam, you just wait and see."

"Now, you go on back to your healthy young fillies over there, and me and Whoremonger here . . . well, we'll just go out and find us some whores who understand a soldier's mentality. Now what do you say about that, doofus?"

College boy was stil rubbing his arm. He handed Crazy Craig his fraternity card back. "I got no problèm with that."

"Good." Crazy Craig stared at the card for a moment, then said, "Which reminds me why I lugged ths ol' relic

249

out in the first place." He reached out and grabbed college boy's wrist before he could get away, and threw him into the chair again. "Next time you and your cohorts over there go chargin' into a respectable place of business like this, and you see some soldiers sittin' at a table, or maybe you come across as GI all by his lonesome at the bar . . . ."

"Yeah?"

"I want you to stop by and say a couple kind words . . . maybe buy the guy a cup o' brew. Because, whether you wanna face up to it or not, the reason punks like you are free to raise Cain is because men like us are on the other side of 'the pond,' preservin' your freedom to act like an asshole. And another thing I want you to remember about our little . . . 'chat.'" Crazy Craig slipped the cracked and yellowing card back into his wallet. "No matter how hot you think you are, kid . . . .No matter how high you advance up the . . . 'corporate ladder' or whatever, keep an open mind when you see . . .' blue collar types' like us warmin a barstool somewhere, We're not all NCO's which short timers claim stands for 'No Chance Outside' the military. A lot of us been to college too, lad. But when you weigh it alongside a Tour 365 in Void Vicious, that pigskin don't mean shit . . . ."

Crazy Craig wrapped an arm around the college boy's shoulder and walked him back over to his girlfriends. "'Course, I've known a lot of bank presidents and professional people who were real friggin' idiots. I'll never figure out how in hell they got to where they're at in life right now. But you take a point man. A point man, he walks out to the side of the rest of the patrol . . . fifty, maybe a hundred meters beyond the bamboo, prowlin' for Charlie . . . a sort of early warning device. Now *that's* a profession that deserves the highest paycheck in the land! But you know how much a point man earns? Just your basic soldier-boy salary. Nothing more . . . ."

"A . . . *point* man?" The youth cocked his head to one side. Crazy Craig sighed in submission: college boy obviously had no perception of life and death in the rain forest. and Crazy Craig didn't have time to explain it all.

"Forget it, kid. don't mean nothin." Craig noticed the blonde girl was sizing him up with those bedroom blue eyes of hers. His face dropped in front of hers suddenly, and they all but rubbed noses. "And I don't rape Vietnamese women," he added. "I got more *honies* over There than I can handle." His eyes dropped below her dry swallow. "And I can handle more than *you've* got to offer, baby-cakes." Crazy Craig was hoping for shock and a tear or two, but blondie lifted an unsliced dill pickle from her BLT and slowly inserted it into her mouth. She rolled her eyes for him, and Crazy Craig went temporarily insane.

"Uhhh-*yoh* !" The soldier turned away and directed a pleading voice in Brody's direction. "Drag me outta here, boy! The lady's got me under her spell . . . ."

Graham was leaning against his Volkswagen van when they left the restaurant. Somehow he'd left the restroom without being noticed. Arms folded over his chest, he grinned tightly at the two soldiers and saluted with the wrong hand as they passed.

"At ease, Alpha-Hotel," Crazy Craig muttered the military phonetic for 'ass hole.'

"Aw, fuck me till it hurts!" Brody halted as if he'd walked into a glass wall.

"What is it?" Crazy Craig started to ask, but then he saw the flat tires also. On their rental car. Two of them. Both rear wheels.

Crazy Craig glanced back over a shoulder, but Graham was gone. *The asshole stayed just long enough to bask in our reactions*, he decided. "That motherfucker . . . ."

"I knew we shouldn't have put that VIETNAM—I'VE BEEN THERE decal on the bumper. That's the only way he could have made it as our vehicle." Brody slowly shook his head from side to side, then dug down into a pocket rustling coins about as he searched for the car keys.

"Then you agree . . . ."

Brody whirled around, but Crazy Craig had not taken off after Graham yet. "Well, we've got no positive proof, actually. It couda been, . . . remember that beer bottle I ran over back there . . . ."

251

"What are you—some kinda goddamned highway patrolman or something? whatta ya mean, 'positive proof'? Scrote-face back there punched-out our fuckin' tires, Treat."

"We don't know that for certain. It *coulda* been the bottle . . . ."

"You're tryin' to tell me a friggin' beer bottle took out both rear tires The *rear* tires, Treat? No way. Maybe—and this is getting fuckin' astronomical, but maybe both side tires. But not the back ones. Not from one lousy beer bottle. No way, *Jose!*"

"Okay . . . just hold onto your hostility for a second. Maybe they only let the air out . . . ."

"'Hold onto my hostility?' What kinda goofy shrink talk is that?" Crazy Craig walked over and kicked one of the tires. Air was still hissing from an obvious knife slit along the side.

Frowning, Brody glanced up the block. "Well ther's a gas station right across the street. You start changing that side there's a spare in the trunk. I checked. I'll double-time over there and see if they repair tires. I just hope they're open . . . ."

"Me?" Crazy Craig backed away a couple steps, palms raised. "Change *that* tire? No can do, GI!" He turned and started back toward the cafe. "We got some young, energetic *college boys* around here somewhere who I know will be just *delighted* to volunteer their services, even if it's the first time they *volunteered* to do anything in their lives!"

"Wait a second! Hold on." Brody caught up with him. "I don't want any trouble. You know how Neil Nazi is when it comes to trouble with the law. If the cops pick us up for smashin' face, they're gonna turn us over to the MPs, and we're talkin' either Fort Benning or North Carolina MPs, and those fuckers eat nails for breakfast. They're gonna boot us around a little before they ship us back to Nam. And if worse comes to worse . . . ."

"If worse comes to worse," Crazy Craig took over. "They'll send some rookies over from the Academy. Fort Gordon's just down the road a ways, you know. Now *that*

252

could be . . . *fun.* "

They had the tires repaired within a half hour, and as Crazy Craig finished mounting the first one, he wiped sweat from his brow with bruised knuckles and glanced over at the hippy van still parked where he'd last seen it. "College boy's still in there feedin' his face."

"Just pretend they're not there." Brody sighed. He wanted to kick ass and take names too, but the colonel was notorious for coming down hard on troops who got in trouble on their R&R's or stateside leaves, and he wanted sergeant's stripes, not an Article-15 reprimand in his packet.

"I don't know what's happened to your . . . your backbone lately, Brody," Crazy Craig complained as Treat slipped the second tire on and began releasing his frustrations by swinging the lugwrench around at blinding speed as he tightened the bolts in place.

"Cut me some slack, pal, okay?"

"I mean . . . are you fucking bucking for acting-Jack or something?" 'Acting-Jack' was Army slang for probationary buck-seargeant.

"Something like that . . . ."

"I knew it." Crazy Craig let a tire iron bounce off the pavement noisily to emphasize his point. "Another goddamned lifer in the making! What ever happened to the good old days when everyone was drawin' grids across pinup, short-timer calendars, savin' the nipples and snatch for last, and—"

Brody thought he heard something like the crunch of metal against bone. He jumped up just in time to see Graham and two of his friends striking Crazy Craig over the head from behind with long boards. Before The Whoremonger could even react, Crazy Craig, appearing like he was about to drop forward and collapse, sprang into action.

Using his thick wrists as the fulcrum, he propelled his jump boots up off the ground, knocking back Graham and one of the other students. Rising above the third youth, he blocked the swinging board with his arm. Brody winced as wood splinters unleashed a spray of blood, but the sight only seemed to invigorate the other GI. With his elbow, he broke the student's nose as he knocked him off his feet. Moaning, the youth rolled around on the ground, cupping his face in his hands, but didn't get back up.

"Come on, lowlife scumbags!" Crazy Craig challenged the other two as he slipped off his brass belt. Slowly, he twirled it around and around.

Glancing down at the student with the broken and bloodied face, one of the youths retreated back to the restaurant, but Graham charged, raising the board as if he were planning to bat a home run out of the ballpark.

Crazy Craig dodged the swing easily, side-stepping out of Graham's path as he rushed by. Pivoting, and bending to the left slightly, Craig's right boot flew up in a *ju-jitsu* kick. It caught Graham in the gut, but he did not double over as his opponent had intended.

Yelling like a madman, the college student whirled around, charging again, but Crazy Craig blocked the swing this time with a sharp, jabbing strike of his fist, and the already cracked board broke in half, leaving a long, spear-like splinter. With some ceremony, Craig removed his jacket and draped it over a motorcycle. "Aw, fuck me till it hurts," Brody muttered as the youth charged, using the board now like a lance. If only this were any other time. In The Nam, he'd have an M-16. Back on the block, he'd have a .38 in the glovebox. Now, all he had was his fists. And he wasn't in the mood to break any knuckles today. Brody slowly began moving to Graham's blind side, but college boy was quick. He charged for the third time, and Crazy Craig was unable to fend off the attack this time. The ten inch splinter ripped through his brown poplin shirt, tearing a chunk of flesh from his right breast.

Eyes bulging with rage now—it had just been a contest of martial arts skills to the soldier up until now—Crazy Craig disarmed Graham the punk. He jerked the board out of his hands and, like a pugil stick, flipped it around. Then he slammed it against the college student's cheek, stunning him.

254

Graham staggered for a moment, but his eyes quickly began to clear. Happy the fight was not over, Crazy Craig threw down the board, slipped in his own blood, then rushed up and tackled Graham.

The two rolled around on the blacktop for a minute or so, then Graham found himself victim of a chokehold, with Crazy Craig's forearm across the youth's throat and his wrists locked behind Graham's left ear.

Grinning triumphantly, Crazy Craig squeezed. He squeezed long and hard, refusing to show mercy, and soon Graham's eyes rolled up into the top of his head and his tongue dangled from a slack lower jaw.

"Okay, Craig!" Brody's boots appeared beside the soldier's smile. "Contest's over. Cut the punk some slack and let's beat feet outta here!" A faint siren could be heard growing in the distance.

"I'm gonna *cut* his fuckin' *head* off!" Crazy Craig promised, squeezing tighter. His own eyes bulged now, as did the veins along his neck and temples as he applied more pressure, and Graham began to turn blue.

"*OKAY!*" Brody knew it was time to save Crazy Craig from himself. He tried to pry the bigger soldier's arm loose, but without success. Words were obviously useless— the GI was drunk on adrenaline—so he pulled an old *tae-kwon-do* secret from his bag of tricks.

Brody grabbed Crazy Craig's little pinky finger and pulled. He pulled hard, but the move was having no visible affect on his buddy. So Brody tried Step No. 2, which is an even better trick, as far as many *karate* enthusiasts are concerned, and he twisted Crazy Craig's thumb back. *Twist it hard! Don't play with the damn thing, Private BRO-dee!* He heard the voice of an old drill sergeant on his hands and knees beside him as he wrestled with another recruit during the hand-to-hand combat classes. "Twist it hard—like you wanna break it, boy!" The instructor's words became his own. "I wanna hear somethin' *snap!*" slipped out too.

Crazy Craig's grip loosened, and he suddenly let out with a growl. "Okay!" He rolled away from Graham, trying to pull free of Brody. "*Jesus,* Treat!"

255

Brody was not apologizing. "Get in the fuckin' car!" he ordered the bigger man as he checked Graham's bruised and swollen throat for a pulse.

"Is he . . . ." Crazy Craig was slow in responding.

"Congratulations, you idiot." Brody's anger was obvious.

"He's dead?"

"As dead as they come, asshole . . . ."

"Good riddance, prick."

Brody glanced up at Crazy Craig. "What?"

"Fuck him, man. He wasn't worth the price o' salt in the blood I love over this abortion . . . ." Crazy Craig wiped his hands off and turned away.

"Jesus, Craig . . . ."

"College boy can suck Satan's cock now for all I care . . . .*Good riddance!*"

They could hear its motor roaring now, even though the police car was still quite a distance away.

"Let's get the fuck outta here," Crazy Craig muttered, climbing into the passenger seat.

"Are you kidding?" Brody rushed over to the door.

Crazy Craig was holding his hand against the puncture wound over his breast. "Do I *look* like I'm kidding?" Brody could tell by the sound of his voice the earlier jab with the splinter had not punctured a lung.

"They'll hunt your ass down, Craig. If you run, they'll send the dogs after you, and they won't ask any questions until *after* all the gunsmoke clears."

"Read my lips." Craig was tired from the fight, and running out of patience. "Get . . . into . . . the . . . car. . .or shut . . . the fuck . . . up."

"If you stay, you can plead self-defense," Brody reasoned.

"You gotta be kidding."

"This is GI country—they'll believe you. *I'm* your witness!"

"Shit." Crazy Craig slid across the seat and behind the steering wheel. "Sayonara, pal. It's been fun."

Brody winced as he started up the car. "At least let me

256

get you to a hospital . . . ."

Crazy Craig was feeling the effects of shock now. He started to pass out from loss of blood. The horn went off when he leaned against the steering wheel.

Brody quickly opened the driver's side door and pushed Crazy Craig back into the passenger's position. "I need time to think." Brody was feeling panic take over. "I'm heading back to the city . . . to a hospital. I can come up with a story by the time they . . . something about I lost my cool and left because I was afraid you were going to bleed to death if—"

"They'll have cops waiting for us at all the hospitals soon as they find that slab o' cold meat back there, dummy . . . ."

"Then what the flyin' fuck do you propose that I do, Sherlock?" Brody burned tire rubber screeching out of the parking lot, and he headed away from the sound of sirens.

"I . . . I got kin nearby." Crazy Craig's head dropped back against the seat. "I can stay with them for now."

"What happens when they learn they're harboring a . . . murderer?" Brody kept his eyes on the road as the speedometer hit ninety.

"You're the one claims I'm so innocent." But Crazy Craig sighed. He was out of breath, unable to argue. "Just keep driving this direction on Highway 20. I'll tell you when to turn off . . . ."

It wasn't until over fifteen minutes later, when Brody noticed a soldier home on leave, hitch-hiking at a highway on-ramp, that he remembered Crazy Craig left his Class-A's jacket back at the scene of the 'crime.' The jackets had nametags on them, and if Crazy Craig was like most other GIs, he kept a spare set of military orders tucked away down the inner pocket. Orders which had his old unit and new destination written all over them, not to mention his name, rank, and serial number.

As Brody watched the memorial ceremony, his thoughts shifted from Crazy Craig to the Chaplain giving a sermon. The Army priest's jeep, freshly waxed and without a dent in it, stood on a knoll behind him. Brody wondered how, during that incident three months ago where the MPs chased them through Plei Me in it, Nervous Rex and Stormin' Norman managed to return it to its rightful owner undamaged. He wondered what kind of story the Green Berets came up with, or if they bothered to come up with one at all.

The fog was finally lifting, and shafts of sunlight piercing the overcast fell across a stretch of woods beyond the perimeter, creating an illusion that reminded Brody of Georgia. And he thought about Crazy Craig again . . . .

The police tied Crazy Craig to the death of Graham the campus activist, of course, and a homicide warrant was issued for his arrest, but somehow Brody was never connected to the crime. His story to CID investigators that he hadn't seen Craig again after the funeral detail apparently held water. Brody spent several weeks holding his breath, afraid the photos of himself would be shown to witnesses at the scene, but no one from the police department ever took his picture for a photo line-up, and the only other photograph of him the Army had floating around was an old Boot Camp shot in which he looked like someone else altogether. Brody was glad he joined several other daring recruits and had his hair completely shaved off back in BCT.

Crazy Craig kept his promise and never returned to Vietnam. Last Brody heard, the deserter was living somewhere in the wilds of Florida's Everglades—that American jungle that closest approximates the rain forests of Indochina. Brody wondered if he was still having the nightmares. The ones where he believed he was God and could fly over the battlefields without using a helicopter gunship.

A warm breeze was dispersing the mist now, and it carried some of the Chaplain's words to Brody.

"These men did not die in vain . . . ."

Brody felt a chuckle rise in his chest, but his lips remained grim as he watched a magpie ascend from a distant treetop.

". . . For freedom and peace in South Vietnam . . . "

The magpie began swooping about wildly, and Brody could see that it had taken to chasing a dragonfly.

". . . We pray for these men's deliverance unto you, O Lord . . . ."

A dragonfly, or perhaps a hummingbird . . . .

"We will never forget them . . . ."

Brody pulled a pack of made-in-Saigon Blue Ruby cigarettes from the pocket of his flak jacket. Normally, he did not smoke. But lately he was having strange dreams. They were nightmares, really—there was no getting around that. Nightmares about Void Vicious and helicopter crashes and severed limbs dangling from tree branches. Nightmares in which his words and even his thoughts were in fluent Vietnamese.

CHAPTER 24

"*Ouija,* tell us what the outcome is going to be . . . ."

"You have to be more specific," one of the soldiers in the dark underground bunker snapped.

"Okay, okay! Ouija, tell us what the outcome of this battle with the VC is going to be . . . ."

The plastic triangular indicator glided across the gameboard balanced atop the knees of two soldiers facing each other. A half dozen troopers were clustered around them, watching as Em-ho and Wickman tried to keep their meaty fingertips on the small disc.

Lee had been carrying the Ouija board around in his pack ever since a cousin from Little Tokyo enclosed it in a care package filled with rice cakes and chocolate-covered cherries. Lee loved chocolate-covered cherries.

Lee was not sure how the Ouija board worked exactly. The polished brown paper board was about one and a half by two feet in size, with mystical symbols printed in the corners, numbers zero through nine across the bottom, and the alphabet across the top. A frightening-looking eye decorated the center of the board. A plastic indicator, with three strips of felt along the bottom, was placed on the board, and the two participants sat across from each other, the board resting on their knees, and their fingertips resting on the edge of the indicator. A small plastic circle with a pin through it comprised the most important part of the indicator, for after each question was posed to 'Ouija,' the pin, after roaming the board for a few tense seconds, would stop over a number or letter, and then another and another, until an often cryptical answer was spelled out. Ouija — pronounced WEE-GEE by most players of the occult-lovers' pasttime—was the title given to whatever representative from the spirit world decided to come forth, possessing either the indicator, the board, the players, or a combination of all three. Most players elected to take no chances, and called on a dead relative to help them out, but periodically unknown ghosts and even an occasional evil spirit wanted to play the game. Lee's relative wrote him to be very careful. "Mother made me get rid of the game-board," she said. "Mother claims the Devil himself controls the board. Well, you and I know that's a crock, but she wants it out of the house, and I couldn't bear to part with it . . . I mean, I couldn't just throw it away. so I'm sending it to you, cousin. Please take care of Ouija, whoever he or she is. When you return from Vietnam, I will be older, and then you can convince Mother to let me keep it. Explain to her that throwing the board away would cause more havoc than just hiding it in a trunk somewhere—you know how feisty Ouija can get. I swear, sometimes I think it can read my thoughts . . . ."

There was considerable debate as to just what powered the Ouija board. Skeptics claimed it was energy from static electricity between the indicator's felt-tipped legs, and the polished surface of the board. At best, they believed, it's your subconscious at work . . . the power of the brain over mind and matter. Lee believed neither of these two explanations. Ouija had told he and his cousin too many things they could not have known on their own.

The first time they used it, for instance, the spirit identified himself by name. A long, complicated name neither of them knew. Lee's cousin had a pad and pencil beside the board, and Ouija was very patient. He spelled his name out again—this process took nearly five minutes alone—and the cousin wrote each letter down for later

262

reference. When the cousin asked the ghost why he chose to come to them, the answer was simple: "I built this." They were sitting in a small supply shed in their grandmother's backyard, which had been converted into a playhouse for the young children of the family. Cousin scribbled his answer down again, exchanging confused looks with Lee. The indicator refused to move when Cousin asked where Ouija was from, but when she asked where he was born, the name "Yakotaw" was spelled out very slowly. Cousin asked Ouija what he looked like. the answer was rather chilling, "No flesh."; Lee took over, and asked the forbidden question, "When will I die?" Again, the indicator refused to move, then slowly, after several minutes, it started sliding toward the "Goodbye" corner of the gameboard. "*Where* will I die?" Lee quickly changed the question slightly. The indicator slowed to a stop, paused, the meticulously spelled out the words "Play Me." Lee locked eyes with his cousin and said, "Play Me? We *are* playing on you," but when he glanced back down at the board, the indicator was resting in the "Goodbye" corner and refused to answer any more of their questions. Cousin wanted to call on another spirit to take over the Ouija's duties, which was a common practice among the gameboard's enthusiasts, but Lee declined. He was mentally exhausted. Dark clouds had rolled in over the neighborhood during the session, and he felt like he was suffocating in the small shack. He needed some air. He needed to get away from the Ouija board for a while.

When he questioned his grandmother about the answers Ouija had provided, she did not look angry, only amused. But what she told Lee the teenager found shocking at the time: the name given by Ouija was a great uncle of Lee's, who had died several years before Lee's birth. He had built the shack Lee and his cousin were playing in. The uncle was from the old country, and had been born in Yakota, Japan. Grandmother had no idea why Ouija would end the session with the words "Play Me," and suggested they throw the board away because the old uncle they had conjured up had never been anything but a headache anyway . . . .

Play Me . . . .Lee's memory played itself all over again as he watched Don The Brick Wickman's gigantic hands slip off the small indicator again, interrupting the game. *Plei Me* . . . .

"Come on, Brick," someone in the cramped bunker complained. "How the hell are we supposed to get any answers out o' this thing if your paws keep slippin' off the—"

"Don't say 'hell' in front of Ouija." Brody sounded serious, and several of the tired soldiers found the energy to laugh.

Play Me . . . .*Plei Me* . . . .

"You guys are gonna have to start all over," Larson grumbled, ripping the page out of his pocket notebook. He crumpled it up and tossed it back over a shoulder.

"What was the fucking question?" Wickman asked, irritated by the delay they had the gall to blame *him* for causing.

Lee was staring down at the letters on the gameboard, unmoving. *Play Me* . . . .*Plei Me* . . . .

"Em-*ho*!" Brody reached down fron his perch atop a sandbag ledge and slapped the top of Lee's helmet. "Wake the fuck up!"

"Don't say 'fuck' in front of Ouija." Snakeman Fletcher made fun of Treat's earlier rebuke.

"If you perverts wanna talk dirty," Wickman blew a huge cloud of smoke from his cigar down into Lee's face unintentionally, "then ya better start spelling it out so you don't offend—"

"Spell it out?" Brody laughed, pointing down at the letters on the Ouija board.

Wickman tucked his chin in slightly as he compressed his lips. "Uh . . . disregard my last, over and out."

Ashes from the cigar fell onto the polished board, and Larson quckly swept them aside withthe edge of his hand. "Jesus, Brick . . . ."

"Hey, you guys quit gangin' up on The Brick." Zack was there too, his broad back blocking escape as he leaned back

264

on elbows along the steps leading up to the surface.

"Just ask the question again." The Professor belched, and reached down for his bottle of lukewarm beer.

"Okay, okay . . . ." Lee refused to believe that two words his dead great-uncle's ghost told him five years earlier were now starting to make sense. He had asked Ouija where Lee would die, and the answer had been "Play Me." Could it be that death did not improve one's skills at spelling, among other things, and that Ouija could not be blamed if he was unfamiliar with specific Vietnamese villages or hamlets? Was Lee actually going to meet his demise in this godforsaken strip of water buffalo manure?

"*Lee!*" Several of the men called out simultaneously, and Krutch The Stork tossed a crumpled Budweiser can at the private.

"Okay . . . okay! what is the outcome of—"

"Start every question out with 'Ouija,' you dipshit!" Wickman blew smoke in Lee's face again. Ths time it was on purpose.

"Right. Ouija, what is the outcome of this . . . this . . . ." He looked up at Wickman questioningly. "Siege? Is that the right word?"

"Christ!" Wickman nearly bit through his cigar. He flexed his shoulders dramatically, and asked the question himself. "Hey, *Ouija-san*, old boy . . . listen up!" The Brick glanced over at Brody and winked. "What's your opinion regarding the outcome of this here clusterfuck we seem to have gotten ourselves into here at Plei Me, taking into account you're being privy to Military Intelligence from a higher source and all that?"

The indicator glided about the gameboard swiftly, like a skilled skater on ice. The Professor could barely keep up with the letters Ouija was spelling out. "Nho Nguyen?" he asked Wickman, after it slid to a stop in the "Goodbye" corner.

Leaning back slightly to show he was still semi-skeptical, the Brick cracked a wide smile on either side of the cigar. "No win." He pronounced the Vietnamese carefully, and it came out souding very, very English. "Looks like we got us a fucking 'No Win' situation here at Plei Me, gentlemen . . . ." Lee looked like he was about to have a heart attack. "But worse than that, we seem to have latched onto a Veeyet-nuh-MEEZZZZE Ouija !"

CHAPTER 25

Major Minh put his fist through another panel of plywood to emphasize his point. The few members of his immediate staff who were not still out in the field glanced back and forth at each other apprehensively. The attack on the Plei Me Special Forces camp was not going as planned.

"We should have taken that outpost last night!" Minh flung a map case across the underground bunker. "We should be in control of Pleiku right now, this very moment. But what are we doing? We're staring at a progress map on the wall of a hole in the ground, when I should be preparing to accept the II Corps commander's surrender!"

The unexpected arrival of seven Huey gunships and two Cobra assault helicopters had disrupted Minh's plans to effect a swift and total defeat of the Strike Force tribesman guarding the Green Beret camp. He knew the ARVN command would send a relief column as soon as the alarm went out, and Minh's people had been prepared for the routine Air force strafings. But heavily armed choppers with Airmobile troops onboard had not even been a part of his worst-cause scenario.

Presently, he was keeping the residents of the camp pinned down by use of a constantly shifting team of expert marksmen. The weather had cooperated, delaying the arrival of med-evac slicks until the last couple hours, and they had been driven off with the truckload of captured L.A.W. rockets Gen. Chu Huy Man had delivered to him. Minh's people were fairly inexperienced with the Light Anti-tank rockets, however. They weren't designed for plucking aircraft out of the sky, and none of the Hueys or Cobras were downed.

Minh had hundreds of North Vietnamese Regulars on the road to Plei Me, fighting with the relief column that had been dispatched from Pleiku. The Arvins were pinned down and he was confident, would be annihilated long before additional assistance could reach them. Only then could he proceed to Pleiku for the big prize.

First, he had to deal with Plei Me, though. His men were spread thinly between all the targets—it was a grand plan, indeed, and he would have to wait until dark. But Minh had a surprise or two up his sleeve.

One of them was Junglerot Jody.

Junglerot Jody had been an aging, burnt-out whore from Pleiku City, until Major Minh resurrected her. She would always have a sensuous, firmly toned body—at least for anther ten or fifteen years—but her face looked like it had met the business end of a *baht* bus and Minh had been working several days now, adding just the right finishing touches.

Junglerot Jody's real name was Tran Thi Joang, and she was in her early to mid forties, but she had the chest of an eighteen-year-old varsity cheerleader. Junglerot Jody was the kind of girl you'd never take home to mother, and would only take to bed if she wore a paper sack over her head. Most GIs, whose company she had been frequenting since the GIs were French and not American, learned to endure Jody's looks because of the quality of her body. Her nickname came from her complexion problem and rotten disposition, not the quality or cleanliness of what she was selling. But Minh was working on all that. He had two women from the medical corps locked in an earthen cubicle with Junglerot Jody, fixing her face with a satchel of cosmetics straight from Paris. When the NVA nurses finally presented her to Major Minh and his underground

268

staff, the communist officer was ecstatic.

Junglerot Jody was beautiful!

Not only were her flaring thighs complemented by the miniskirt and her jutting breasts visible through the Fredericks of Hollywood see-through blouse, but Junglerot Jody no longer needed her paper sack.

When Major Minh approached Tran Thi Hoang and realized she was wearing a half- inch mask of make-up, he decided he would continue calling her Junglerot Jody, but he wrapped an arm around her shoulder and cheerfully told her his plan anyway.

Junglerot Jody would be Plei Me's version of America's dumb blonde. Minh would arrange for the snipers outside teh CIDG compound to hold their fire, and Jody would cruise up to the front gate on her sputtering Honda-50 and tight haunches, totally oblivious to all the shooting that had transpired earlier. In true Saigon slug tradition, Jody would shake her chest and display just the right amount of leg. With lips painted bright red and shaped like the hole in a doughnut she would ask the gate guards if the defenders of Plei Me were possibly in need of a quickie, which they always were, because *Co* Claptrap had been killed by a mortar during the first hour of the attack. Junglerot Jody would tell the Strikers she was having her Fall Sale, and ad-lib from there.

"Will never work," Jody said simply, after listening patiently to Minh's plan for more than five minutes.

"Why not?"

"GIs no want *boom-boom* after battle. Too soon. They will run me off."

Minh's plan involved a sort of Trojan Horse strategy without the horse. While nobody would be hiding inside anything: they would all be concealed along the treeline. As soon as the Strikers deactivated the minefield and opened the main gate to let Jody in, Minh's soldiers would storm the camp in force.

"These are Green Berets." Minh insisted his plan would work. "They make love best when bullets are flying. To them, *boom-boom* in a free fire zone is more important than napalm or Willie Peter."

Junglerot Jody gave Major Minh a Do-I-look-that-stupid look. Tired of watching the major stare at her cleavage, she folded her arms over it. "The *Strikers* will run me off, not Green Berets. The Strikers no like *boom-boom* on Honda-50. They think I am lowland Vietnamese. They think I am from Saigon."

"You will go, and that ends our discussion."

Jody stood her ground. "I refuse to do it."

Minh drew the automatic from his web belt holster and placed it against Jody's forehead. "You do not have a choice in this matter."

"I see." Jody didn't seem very concerned about this latest development.

"I'm sure you will do a fine job." Minh smiled.

"If I do a 'fine' job, I will be dead."

"Show some optimism, my dear. You have the worst attitude of any woman I have ever met."

"I have managed to survive because of my attitude."

"Or in spite of it." Major Minh watched the nurses walk from the cavernous chamber into a maze of subterranean passageways.

Jody turned to follow them, but Minh cleared his throat loudly, and she hesitated. "Before you leave," he said. "I would like a demonstration of your . . . skills."

A slight grin crept across her features. Junglerot Jody was beginning to feel at home here after all. She began unlacing the belt on her mini-skirt.

"No, not that way." Minh motioned for Jody to drop to her knees. Then he pulled down his zipper.

CHAPTER 26

"Jus' like home . . . ." Treat Brody listened to thunder rumbling in the distance, and the peculiar manner in which it was clashing far away, in Ia Drang Valley, reminded him, for some reason, of rainshowers in L.A.'s Chinatown. *They* had always followed this strange crackling and sucking thump of a show, too.

"Incoming?" Snakeman glanced over at the Professor, who professed to have better hearing.

"Naw," Larson muttered. "Outgoing." It didn't really matter. They were safe in their underground bunker. But Brody's smile slowly disappeared. *That* was the difference: artillery mingling with the heat lightning.

Lee was still asking the Ouija board questions, but The Brick had traded off with Hal Krutch, the warrant officer everyone called Stork. The Stork was the most mellow chopper jock in the First Cav.

"Ouija, is Charlie gonna attack tonight, or tomorrow, or not at all?" Em-ho asked seriously, but Krutch couldn't keep his laughter in.

"I can't believe this," he said. "We're askin' a *WEE-gee* or whatever when the hammer's gonna fall? Why don't we just saddle up and—"

Several gunshots rang out as he spoke—a full magazine on rock-and-roll, at least. Down by the main gate. "This is

271

it!" Brody slammed a banana clip into the well of his M-16 and rushed toward the sandbag steps leading up to the surface. Zack scrambled out of the way, drawing the pistol from his holster at the same time.

The men in the bunker were all Airmobile troopers. The commander of Plei Me had authorized them to get four hours sack time in because he wanted them to help man the perimeter after dark. They all wholeheartedly agreed to help in any way they could, but they were spending their four hours with the Ouija board.

Junglerot Jody was right. She never made it through the front gate. She never even got to proposition any of the guards.

One of the Strikers recognized her as she approached on her puttering motorscooter, both shapely legs balanced over the left side. He recognized her as being the lady of questionable virtue who left him with a permanent case of the drips and, in a war zone, the only way to rectify an error like that was by M-16 jury.

The Striker thought she was just passing by. Twenty feet before she got to the camp access road, he fired the entire thrty rounds into her, knocking her back over one side as if she'd struck a wire strung across the road with her throat.

When Brody and the others got up to the fenceline, the Striker was standing over her bullet-riddled remains, firing another magazine worth of shells down into the core of what face was left. A second Montagnarde was using his hands, arms, and pantomime to recreate how Junglerot Jody's beautiful legs had flown feet up before she disappeared over the side of her Honda-50. The motorscooter traveled another fifty yards down the road without her before running down an enbankment, where it crashed into a tree. The Striker thought it was the funniest thing he had seen in quite a while.

"She Numba Ten." He nodded solemnly, after Treat and the others cast looks of disgust his direction. "VC fo' surrre!"

"Looks like she was unarmed to me," Larson muttered to Krutch.

"No kill with AK-47," the guard explained. "Kill with clap!" Lips scrunched up, he lowered his eyes and shook his head from side to side, then walked down through the punji sticks to assist his friend.

And that was when the barrage fell across the camp. Brody counted thirty mortars or more striking within the perimeter before he made it to the first bunker.

"Well fuck me till it hurts," he muttered as several more soldiers dove in on top of him, but the complaint could not be heard above a roar peaking outside. A roar of war cries. War cries and screaming, and isolated discharges that quickly erupted into nonstop automatic weapons fire and another all-out attack.

"Let's go!" Brody was yelling now, too. The mortars had stopped, and if they didn't act fast, the camp would be overrun.

Several waves of sappers clad in black pajamas, loin cloths, and satchel charges were already slamming bamboo ladders against the coils of concertaina atop the fenceline, and racing up them. That was exactly what it looked like to Brody: a race. He groaned, thinking *Not again!* then flipped the safety to AUTO and began firing at the closest, doped-up guerrillas.

He sprinted from the bunker to a row of sand-filled oil drums, where Lee plopped down prone in the clay beside him and began shooting too.

Both soldiers watched triple tracers signal an empty magazine, and as they changed clips together, Lee exchanged worried looks with The Whoremonger and forced a grin. "Ouija said there'd be days like this!"

CHAPTER 27

There were not only 'bombs bursting in the air,' as the American Anthem goes, but a ring of trees were on fire all around the Special Forces camp. Beneath flares floating on the night mist, tracers were arcing back and forth on both sides. Viet Cong guerrillas were hanging from barbs in the concertina—many missing arms, legs or both . . . some missing even more—and bangalore torpedos were blowing out several sections of fenceline. Only row upon row of feces-lined punji sticks were holding Charlie back. The stakes and the claymores.

"We're in a world of hurt now!" Lee was the first to spot a North Vietnamese NCO standing in full view on the far side of the wire. He was in the middle of a clearing, and had just pulled a L.A.W. open, extending the tubes for firing.

The NVA sergeant was pointing the Light Anti-tank Weapon right at Brody's people, and as Lee stood up to get a better shot at the communist, a round from one of the treetops struck his helmet like a sledgehammer. Lee went down, but he wasn't out.

"What the fu—"

"You okay, Em-ho?" Snakeman was beside Lee, as Brody zeroed in on the Vietnamese with the rocket launcher. Lee appeared to be shaken, but uninjured.

"You're gonna have a hell of a bruise on your noggin come morning." Fletcher was not laughing.

"He's lucky he still has a head!" yelled Zack, as Brody brought back his M-16's trigger.

"I just hope I *make* it *to* morning." Lee pulled his helmet off, looking for the bullethole so he could run his finger through it—like in all the Vic Morrow *Combat* episodes— but the tracer had only ricocheted off the steel pot, without penetrating it.

The NVA sergeant hesitated, lowering the L.A.W. to adjust his sights, and that was all the time Treat needed. He unleashed the entire magazine of twenty rounds on full-automatic, and watched the sizzling red tracers cut the guerrilla leader in half as he slammed in a longer banana clip holding ten more rounds.

As the communist crumpled backward, the shoulder-launched rocket soared skyward in a wild climb, out of control.

It passed up between two South Vietnamese Air Force jets that were swooping in low to drop napalm and thousand-pounders on the enemy positions, disappeared into the belly of some heavy storm clouds drifting over the battlefield, and exploded with a ferocity that seemed to create a sudden if brief downpour.

"The L.A.W. is the Law!" Fletcher cheered with a raised fist as they all watched the smoking chunks of fiery shrapnel arc back down to earth. Brody glanced over at Snakeman, expecting to see the usual So-what? grin, but a Rebel flag greeted him instead—the one Elliot, who was gazing up at the technicolor blast, wore taped across the back of his helmet. Brody knew there were mortar shells that were so sensitive they sometimes detonated within clouds dense with rainwater on their way to the target, but he had never heard of a L.A.W. doing that.

"That was wild!" Shawn Larson forgot, for a moment, that he was the unit's pacifist.

"Can't say as I've ever seen a L.A.W. do that before," admitted Krutch.

"Anybody get a bead on that sniper?" Fletcher yelled

276

above the roar of jets dropping their loads.

"What sniper?" Herman 'Hatchethead' Monrovia appeared running from a bilowing cloud of thick, black smoke and dropped into a prone position beside Broken Arrow.

"The one that nearly knocked Em-ho's *Em*-ho off!" Brody, like the others, never saw who fired the shot, but he sprayed the closest treeline with four- and five-round bursts, and the men watched palm fronds flutter down to cover countless VC bodies.

Hatchethead, who had a crush on Webster's dictionary, turned to face Treat and asked, "What the hell is an . . . a . . . .a whatever you called it . . . ." He pulled his pocket dictionary from inside his flakvest, and it was promptly knocked out of his hands by another sniper's bullet. "KEE-riste!" Monrovia buried his face in the clay as tissue-thin pages exploded like pillow feathers at a slumber party.

"Early Morning Hard-On," Snakeman translated as he pulled a frag pin and heaved the grenade with all his might. It sailed several meters beyond the second fenceline but never detonated.

"Oh . . . ." Monrovia allowed a few seconds more to pass then, when no further rounds zinged in, he began scooping up the dictionary pages.

"Does any of this remind youz guys of anything?" Krutch sounded bitter, but he was not talking about the dud.

Brody nodded. The Stork was referring to their old friend back at the Turkey Farm: a sniper who couldn't shoot straight. But also one they were having trouble catching.

Broken Arrow was not thinking about the Turkey Farm, or the Tea Plantation. He was not even thinking about the Golf Course, at An Khe—which *used* to be home. Two Step was staring at the man laying beside him: Hatchethead Monrovia, descendent of an honest-to-God Texas Ranger. The Indian was wondering what Monrovia was up to.

The two soldiers hated each other and, even in a combat situation—where it was said men were only one color in a foxhole under fire, and that was Army green—Broken Arrow could not envision the trooper inadvertently diving for cover beside him.

Another burst of Cong lead kicked dirtclods and slivers of jacketed copper in the Americans' faces, and when Monrovia shielded his head, he found himself staring over at the Comanche.

Broken Arrow saw Monrovia's out-of-focus, uncomprehending eyes, but what he heard was a soothing voice down by the riverbank, telling ten-year-old Chance about the Staked plains of Texas, and the war between the Kwahadi and the Cavalry . . . .

". . . *The Texas Rangers placed many bounties on Chief Quanah's head, raising them in multiples of five . . . even ten as the months went by and the brave Comanche was still at large . . . .*

"*Then one evening at twilight, Quanah was ambushed at his favorite watering hole. Texas Rangers butchered his finest horse out from under him, but there were only four of the horse soldiers for a change, and as he fell to the ground, Quanah fired his rifle—a repeater captured from the new hunters—five quick times, and three of the rangers went down, never to breathe of this earth again . . . .*

"*Quanah engaged the survivor in hand-to-hand combat, as his rifle was broken in the fall and the Ranger's jammed as he was about to kill the Chief. They fought for a long time, until finally, bleeding from several wounds, Quanah snapped the white man's neck with a running leap-kick to the face . . . .*"

Two-Step stared at Hatchethead Monrovia long and hard, never realizing until some time later that he was holding his M-16 barrel against the other American's heart.

Monrovia never noticed at all. And when he finally did focus on Broken Arrow's ashen face, it was not an insult or threat he directed at the Comanche, but a question. "How's it holdin', buddy?"

Buddy? Two-Step did not move at all as another barrage of mortars descended on their position and everyone else ducked. Two-Step just stared at Hatchethead as smoking

278

shrapnel whizzed past overhead and red-hot chunks of metal rained down on them.

Snipers in the trees were really going at it now, but Broken Arrow didn't seem to notice. Shaking his head in resignation, he stood straight up and began walking slowly back through the compound, in the direction of the latrines. Tracers arced in and ricocheted inches on either side of his boots, and a mortar destroyed a sand-filled oil drum only a few meters away, but he did not seem to ntice any of that either.

Hatchethead watched his old enemy disappear in the spreading gloom. Marveling at the Comanche's luck, he could only shake his own head as he muttered, "Fucking crazy Indian."

CHAPTER 28

An undeclared, temporary cease-fire followed several mortar barrages an hour after Brody saw Broken Arrow walk away from Hatchethead, and three hours before the sun was scheduled to rise. The humidity pressing down on Plei Me was keeping a thick blanket of gunsmoke swirling about the jungle floor. The deathly silence was what was keeping the Americans on edge. A popular phrase making the rounds was that, in Vietnam, silence shouts. In Plei Me, it also touched you. Like a vacuum, it tugged at your eardrums, until your eyeballs were bulging, the lack of sound was so 'loud.' For over an hour, Brody watched several different soldiers stare out at the perimeter over their rifle sights without moving a muscle. Not a single whisper broke the noise discipline rule.

A palm frond falling in the jungle hundreds of meters away was a hair-raising event. Someone sneezed, and everyone ducked. A hint of rotors many miles away vanished the moment it was heard. Thunder rumbling on the horizon dwindled to a hiss of wind, and most of the men decided it was artillery despite the heat lighting. Dark clouds passed beneath the moon, and a few raindrops fell heavily across the compound. The drops diminished to a sprinkle, which continued for some time, adding a new noise to the unnerving silence throughout the camp. Without warning, it would grow silent again. And then it would start all over, until Brody wondered if the dawn would *ever* come.

Sgt. Zack later confessed he nearly "dropped a brick in my shorts" when Broken Arrow returned from his mysterious absence, dragging a kicking and screaming Montagnarde behind him. The tribesman had been disarmed.

"Caught him tryin' to go over the wire," Two-Step explained.

"Oh, that's just *Nuoc-Mam*," Nervous Rex explained, ". . . son of *Nuoc-Mam* Mama. He's okay." *Nuoc-Mam* is the traditional fish sauce most Vietnamese use in their cooking. *Nouc-Mam* Mama was the favored supplier of the spice to area villagers.

"But what *were* you doin' tryin' to scale the fenceline?" The Green Beret Top sergeant had taken an interest in the developments and rushed over to the cluster of defensive positions where all the noise was centered.

Nuoc-Mam didn't speak all that fluent English. And *Nuoc-Mam did* speak English well, depending on which Special Forces trooper you talked to. His knowledge of the language depended on whether he was in trouble or not. Tonight he was obviously in trouble, and a friend— a fellow Strike Force Yarde—rushed over to interpret, abandoning his guard tower in the process. The First Sergeant motioned one of the lower-ranking Green Berets to beat feet over to the post until all this was straightened out.

Nuoc-Mam was nonstop chatter, jabbing away a mile a minute. "He say VC woman put curse on him," *Nuoc-Mam's* friend translated, eyes growing large and convincing.

"Curse?" Top was skeptical, but he'd soldiered in the Orient long enough to know he better get all three sides, and study the situation from every angle before pronouncing judgment.

"Woman live ville outside the wire," the interpreter, a Montagnarde in his late forties named Jong, explained. The CIDG compound was a fortified hamlet in itself, with the Strikers' families living with them 'on-post.' The people living outside the compound were more vulnerable to attack from the communists—indeed, it was not uncommon for enemy agents to infiltrate fringe elements of the villes during mass refugee movements—and this often led to disenchantment with the strategic hamlets program and a silent 'disgruntlement' among the 'outsiders' who were not allowed to participate in it.

"Why would she put a 'curse' on *Nuoc-Mam*?"

Nuoc-Mam was answering in rapid-fire pidgin-Yarde even before Jong translated the question. It helped, Top was sure, that most of the Strikers, if not all of them, knew every detail of all the goings-on within the compound. The conversation transpiring now was just a formality. "He say woman old girlfriend who want *Nuoc-Mam* to take her as third wife. *Nuoc-Mam's* Numba two wife say 'No!' so this girl pissed."

"But the curse, Jong," Nervous Rex cut in. "What about the curse?" Thunder chose that moment to rumble in the distance, and Brody exchanged nervous looks with Sgt. Ritter. Coincidence was one thing. They didn't need a lot of talk about spells and curses floating around the static posts now—not with Charlie prowling the bamboo, setting up for his next attack.

"Girl, she daughter of ville *miao*," Jong revealed. The Green Berets all knew the term: magic-man. Wizard. Sorcerer, by night. Simple medicine man by day, going from hut to hut, longhouse to longhouse, curing the people's ills with plants, herbs and ages-old incantations. "She know the magic too. The *baddd* magic."

"The *baddd* magic?" Nervous Rex rubbed his arms from elbows to wrists as a chill ran through him. Any other time, he'd have laughed all this talk off. But there was an eerie quality to these hills at night. A spooky, mystical feeling.

The hills were haunted, it seemed. Be it by ghosts of the dead soldiers, or that evil that has lurked in the jungle a thousand years, or simply superstition, Ritter and Brody and Broken Arrow and the others didn't know. They didn't care. It didn't matter. All that was important was that it didn't single *you* out. It didn't start following *you* . . . didn't target *you* for trouble. And one had better not bring attention on one's self. No, that wouldn't do at all! Having an enemy inflict the evil eye on you didn't help matters at all. When the enemy happened to be the local *miao's* daughter, you might as well give away all your earthly possessions to your best friends, say your prayers to Buddha, spread your feet, bend over, and kiss your ass goodbye. At least that's how the Montagnarde joke went. In the day time.

After dark, it was no joking matter.

"Well was he trying to go after her to off her young one?" Top asked patiently. "Or was he going out into that free fire zone to lick clit and apologize?"

The First Sergeant certainly had a way with words. Both Jong and *Noc-Mam* cracked uncontrollable smiles. "I want ex . . . explain to her," *Noc-Mam* spoke for himself now.

"Now?" Top threw up his hands. "In the middle of a friggin' firefight? Why couldn't you have picked last week, for Christ's sake? We got a goddamned battle with the bad guys going on right now, asshole! I could fucking have you shot! On the spot! I could have you shot for deserting your post!" The First Sergeant slapped the holster on his hip to emphasize his point. "Or I could turn you over to the Strike Force Leader," he threatened. Who was also Montagnarde. And that would be worse than death, for he was a *mean* Montagnarde, who didn't tolerate mixing women and problems of the pussy persuasion with soldiering.

Nuoc-Mam jabbered away at his friend again. "He say he know that, First Sergeant." An extremely sad and repentant face befell Jong. "But it all start tonight.

Not last week."

"What all started tonight?" Top folded his arms across his chest, challenging them both.

Jong swallowed hard and *Noc-Mam* stared at his jungle boots. "First, early night time . . . when sun set, but not dark yet . . . ."

"Twilight," Nervous Rex said.

"Yes. *Noc-mam* walking his sector beneath guard tower, checking the wire." Jong paused for dramatic effect. "Then it talk to him . . . ."

"It?"

"Cat."

"*Cat?*"

"Big cat." *Nuoc-Mam* could not over emphasize his point as his arms spread wide. "Big cat in bamboo."

"It . . . *spoke* to you?" Top asked without skepticism in his tone.

Jong answered. "Yes. Big cat look into *Nuoc-Mam's* eyes and speak to *Nuoc-Mam* . I know people it happen to before. They always die *rikky-tik*, Top Sergeant. Always."

"Well what the hell did the 'big cat' say?"

"Big cat say I no can leave compound again," *Nuoc-Mam* told them. "Big cat say girl make all animal jungle watch *Nuoc-Mam* . Make sure I never can come out past wire again. Because I . . . *dump* . . . I no . . . make romance with daughter of *miao* . Because—"

"That's ridiculous." The First Sergeant scanned the treeline as something in his peripheral vision swayed, but he could see nothing in the bamboo.

"The tiger actually talked to you?" Nervous Rex spoke more like an explorer who'd finally contacted the natives of *Corapouri* rather than someone who did not believe what he was hearing.

"Oh yes," Jong answered for *Nuoc-Mam* .

"Did it have a male voice . . . or a . . . female voice?"

"Talk with eyes," Jong said simply, not expecting this revelation would be a let-down to the Americans.

285

"With eyes and . . . ." He tapped his temple with a finger.

"Telepathy," Brody whispered, more to himself than any of the soldiers standing on either side of him.

"Animal to man?" Broken Arrow asked with a tell-me-another-one cocking of eyebrows.

"The Viets have a word for it." Nervous Rex glanced skyward, seeking out the moon, but a sheet of clouds was racing past instead. Rumbling storm clouds, carrying a sign of things to come as lightning crackled directly overhead, and the sprinkle became scattered torrents.

"What word?" Brody asked.

"It . . . escapes me right now." Ritter grinned.

"That's awful convenient."

"Bit the big one, Whoremonger."

Top wanted to ask Jong and *Nuoc-Mam* more about the girl and her 'evil eye,' so he motioned the Yardes toward his bunker and, as the scattered cloudbursts became a steady torrent of rain sweeping over the camp, directed the Americans to return to their positions along the wire.

The First Sergeant flattened out in the muddy clay as Big Don Wickman's Hog-60 began blasting away suddenly. He looked up in time to see an entire squad of sappers disintegrate in different directions: a head here, an arm and leg there. . . entire, dismembered torsos flip-flopped up into the barbs of dropping concertina wire.

Wickman's fifty-round burst was so devastating that not a single enemy soldier returned fire. A sniper in the treetops sent two or three bullets down at The Brick, but Wickman just happened to be glancing in the guerrilla's direction and caught the source of bright tracer out the corner of one eye. Dropping to one knee and still firing from the waist, he did not waste time and slugs trying to knock the Viet Cong out of her perch, but directed a steady stream of smoking lead at the palm tree's trunk.

286

Less than a minute later, his M-60's barrel was glowing, and the upper half of the tree toppled over, a screaming rifleman holding on for dear life.

Gently laying his machine gun against one of the sandfilled oil drums, Wickman slipped a fragmentation grenade from his web belt and threw it over the fenceline for good measure. The resulting bright flash and explosion ended the moaning beneath the distant pile of broken palm fronds.

"That's it!" The Brick lifted his M-60 up again and fired an entire belt of rounds up in the air. "ONE-MOTHERFUCKING-THOUSAND FOR THE BODY COUNT! OL' Don Has had the last laugh on Neil Nazi!"

The rest of the men on the line exchanged bewildered looks, but Brody began applauding. "I knew you could do—" he began to express his confidence in Wickman when a rocket roared down from another section of the treeline, a tail of sparks, fire and white smoke following it.

The anti-tank projectile slammed into the earth a few meters to the front and side of Wickman as he dove for cover through a shower of billowing fireballs and shrapnel.

CHAPTER 29

Blue mist wandering through the tombstones made it hard to see the words on the marker at his feet, but Treat Brody knew he had the right grave. He had been here enough times before, visiting his old friend. Treat had the words memorized.

MICHAEL SCOT FREEMAN
1946-1960

"I'm sorry, Mikey," his voice echoed between crypts rising on the dark hillside, as an icy wind swirled up from the ocean. "I didn't mean to leave you all alone that night—I swear! I didn't know what happened to you! I looked everywhere, brother! I really did!"

Guilt and sorrow had been a major pasttime with Treat since the unexplained death of his best friend that night they were both fleeing the devil worshipers in Manhattan Beach. He had come to the cemetery nearly every day for three years now—had it really been that long? He sincerely felt Michael's life could have been saved if only he hadn't been abandoned . . . left alone, out in that dark field, to die . . . .

Treat's nights at home were filled with nightmares where he saw Michael lying on his back in a blanket of breeze-swept wheat, eyes bulging, arms outstretched, elbows locked, mouth frozen open as he screamed without sound for help from the stars, hands clawing at the darkness . . . .

"Please forgive me, Mikey! I just gotta know you don't hold me responsible. You have to give me a sign, Mikey. Anything! This can't go on. All I'm asking for is—"

Treat didn't know if Michael was choosing that moment, after all these years, to forgive him, but there came an eerie grating of stone on cement that sliced through the late night stillness. Treat dropped to one knee and placed both hands on Michael's tombstone, but his best friend was not rising from the dead.

The noise came from behind him, and when Treat whirled around, he spotted them. Five teenaged girls and an older woman. An older woman with blonde hair—the middleaged housewife from the Satanic ritual four years ago!

It appeared they were preparing for another ritual. Totally naked, they were all smeared with blood from face to feet.

The blonde—her long hair sticky with matting crimson now—was carrying a bundle, and Treat recognized a child's cry.

He followed them through the graveyard, until they came to a plot Brody recognized: it belonged to an elderly priest who had died only a few weeks earlier. The infant was naked too. Brody realized that when the woman grabbed it by an ankle and pulled it up above her head then slammed it down on the priest's sloping cement tombstone.

As the child screamed from pain, Treat Brody cried out too: the blonde woman he knew to be a high priestess of Satan, was raising a long butcher knife over the baby, and someone grabbed Treat's arms from behind!

"Brody! Hey, Whoremonger . . . come on! Wake up!" Don 'The Brick' Wickman was shaking his elbows. "It's your turn for watch. Wake me up at zero-four hundred, and I'll relieve you again."

Groggy from lack of sleep, Brody stared at Wickman a moment before remembering bits and pieces of the dream. He glanced about, all over the dark bunker, wildly, but there was only the two of them in there . . . down in that pit underground. The Whoremonger and The Brick. No high priestess . . . no devil worshipers cutting off a child's head so they could drink its blood . . . no tombstones rising from the mist. Treat could smell it: he wasn't in California. He was in Vietnam.

"You'll never know how good it is to see your ugly mug," the Spec-4 said, tasting the sweat on his upper lip. With the back of his hand, Brody wiped perspiration from his slick brow, too, noticing for the first time he was drenched, hair soaked as if he'd just stuck his head outside, into the downpour of rain.

Wickman had miraculously dodged the L.A.W., shoulder-launched rocket, narrowly escaping with only a few puncture wounds along one side. If the Viet Cong were planning another surprise attack, the sudden storm's intensity changed minds in the NVA hierarchy: following the rocket incident and the Brick's thousandth kill, the enemy melted back into the bamboo, and the only sound was thunder, heavy raindrops across the tarmac, and the scream of a big cat, somewhere in the heart of the rain forest.

A big shadow fell across the bunker entrance from above, outside. "Brody!" the First Sergeant's voice boomed. "Let's go! And Brick! You too!"

Brody was glad to hear Top's confident voice. Something was obviously up, and normally that would have sent a queasy feeling through his belly, but right now he was just grateful The Brick had pulled him from the dream.

The dreams . . . . Coming to Vietnam had ridded him of them. But now, after all these months, they had ventured across the South China Sea, through the jungle, and found him. When he blinked, Stormin' Norman's face flashed in front of his eyes, and he thought about the pile of bodybags, and how sick he felt

291

inside when the Green Beret guarding them told him not to worry about formalities: just slip ol' Norman's head in with the rest of his body parts, "'Cause ol' Norm . . . he don't give a rat's shit anymore!" Brody wondered if, when he eventually returned to The World, he would have nightmares about The Nam, too.

"What is it, Top?" he asked the tall, lanky man with tiger stripe fatigues and a charcoal-blackened face. The night patrol 'mask' reminded him of the ghost . . . or the 'daydream' he'd had of a ghost in the wire . . . Stormin' Norman's ghost. Looking at the First Sergeant made Brody shudder.

"I've been talkin' to Jong and that character *Nuoc-Mam*, and somethin' tells me if we beat feet on down into the ville—"

"The *ville?*" Brody cut him off. "The ville *beyond the wire?*"

"Yeah. I think we can get some valuable Intel down there about this series of murders. We can go down through one of the back routes—in this rain and with these pussycat suits on, Charlie'd be more lucky to win a lottery in Laos than spot us."

"But, Top," one of the Greet Berets standing outside the bunker entrance beside Wickman started to protest, and the First Sergeant waved him silent.

"I've been talkin' to this *Nuoc-Mam* character the last hour or so," he explained further, "and I think there's more to this evil eye business than he originally told us. At least, I'm pretty sure bookoo was lost in the translation.

"This witchdoctor's daughter he was telling us about . . . well, the way the story goes *now*, *Nuoc-Mam did* want to engage in a bit o' hanky-panky with her, but Papa-san wouldn't allow it: he didn't want his only child becoming the third wife to, in his eyes, a no-account, worthless soldier. He threatened to put a rainforest curse on *Nuoc-Mam's* family unless he stopped attempting to seduce the girl, and when *Nuoc-Mam* complied, she got angry at *Nuoc-Mam* for not standing up to Papa-san, and she supposedly muttered a couple incantations herself, threatening he'd wake one day to find the old family hut history—*poof*!" Top snapped his fingers. "So anyway, there's an angle to this somehow, boys. We gotta get down there and figure out what it is before—"

The First Sergeant tensed as a young Green Beret ran up with a message. He handed it over, but had obviously read it. "'Just as you suspected, Top. Hardcore NVA out there, mixed with a sprinkling of local Cong."

"What are ya . . . recitin' a recipe or something?" The First Sergeant frowned as he read a hand scribbled status report from one of his senior NCOs on the other side of the camp.

"Lotta the North Viets are wearing Victor Charlie pajamas for some reason, but—"

"What about Sergeant—"

The messenger read Top's mind. "Confirmed dead. The team you sent out just reached the crash site. Crew's dead, too."

The First Sergeant lowered his head. "Damn," he whispered under his breath.

They were talking about the Green Beret who had sacrificed his life that first night of the attack. The Plei Me SF camp was supervised by twelve Green Berets, although, technically and officially, fourteen South Vietnamese *Lac Luong Dac Biet* commandos were in charge of the 415 CIDG Yardes, who came from the Jarai, Rhade, and Bahnar tribes. When the outpost was first attacked on October 19th, most of the camp's jungle fighters were doing just that: patroling the jungle. Two Green Berets led a larger-than-normal combat team on a sweep of the northwest area outside the wire, utilizing 85 Montagnardes. The usual five eight-man ambush squads were also in operation throughout the hills outside the perimeter, and there were two encampments of twenty men each on either side of the main outpost, when it was hit by the enemy. Following fierce fighting throughout the night, a flight of medevac slicks arrived shortly after dawn, but, after the first Huey managed to drop off a surgeon, the second was shot down, and the rest forced to abort the rescue mission and return to Pleiku. From the small amount of soldiers inside the compound, who had weathered bullets, rockets, and mortars for the last twelve hours, a haggard squad of volunteers braved an incredible amount of hostile weapons fire attempting to locate the downed Dustoff and rescue its crew. En route, they were ambushed by a North Vietnamese machinegun nest, and forced to turn back. But not before one of the sergeants was seriously injured. In the fierce firefight, he became missing in action and presumed dead due to the witnessed severity of his wounds. The messenger was just confirming what top had sent a second team out to verify. "Death was instant, First Sergeant."

The rolling concussion from a blast twenty-five meters away knocked everyone except The Brick off his feet. When Brody looked up, Wickman was charging a squad of sappers who had blown a hole in the fenceline and swarming through the secondary barriers, onto the camp.

Brody thought he was quick—he could feel a new surge of adrenaline propelling him after Wickman—but several of the Green Berets lying prone around him were even faster. He had to sprint to catch up as men on both sides began firing their rifles from the hip at point blank range.

Tracers zinged past on either side of the Whoremonger as he watched a half dozen special Forces troopers begin pummelling Vietnamese with their fists, and then a sapper was slamming into Brody too!

Rifle knocked from his hands, he grabbed the NVA by the front of his ruck straps and flung him into the barbed wire, only to jerk him back out. Brody hit the soldier with his fist, but he refused to drop his carbine and kept trying to jab Brody with its bayonet.

"Jesus!" Brody nearly vomited when the Communist

294

kneed him in the groin.

"Jesus!" a wide-eyed, terrified opponent repeated the exclamation. It became immediately obvious to Brody he was dealing with a doped-up enemy. The Vietnamese seemed to reconsider as Brody wrestled him off his feet, and the carbine clattered across several other abandoned firearms. "You name *Jesus*?" His head was twisted to one side, like a raving, possessed demon, but the thing that will always remain in Brody's mind was that it sounded like he had a Japanese accent. That he was a Japanese tourist! Sheets of rain pounded down on them as Brody replied.

"My name's not important!" he hissed, sliding the survival knife from its sheath within his boot. "I'm all your bad dreams put together, boy!" He rammed the blade up into the soldier's belly to the hilt, then ripped upward so hard he pulled an arm muscle. "All your worst nightmares, come to get ya!"

Eyes still bulging, the communist's laugh seemed to strike Brody as his intestines spilled out onto the American. He went to his death smiling, and Brody wondered if the heathen knew any English besides 'Jesus.'

"Hey! Over there—*Look*!" All heads turned as the First Sergeant called out.

Nuoc-Mam had joined the fray, and he screamed out above the drumroll of thunder overhead as all eyes fell on the tribesman's ancestral hut. It was sinking!

Nuoc-Mam and Brody and the others tried to shield their eyes from the unceasing downpour deluging the outpost. They tried to get a better vantage point . . . a drying look at what they knew just couldn't possibly be happening. but no matter what angle you were seeing it from, there was no doubt the local wizard's curse was working: the earth had opened up before their very eyes, and was swallowing up the dwelling whole!

While *Nuoc-mam* watched the structure he was born in sink into the muck a hundred meters away, the

295

Comanche and self-styled wilderness warrior Two-Step Broken Arrow prowled the perimeter on the other side of camp. His M-16 slung over a shoulder, the Indian carried his crossbow. Over thirty notches decorated the polished teakwood frame.

He loved walking point in the rain. Especially deep in the rain forest. High strands of concertina separated him from the wilds and the enemy here, but he still got that feeling in his gut as he stalked movement in the distance. He still got that powerful feeling of being in control . . . of being the hunter, and not the prey . . . .

"The buffalo were gone and the 1870's found Chief Quanah and his people more desperate—the new hunters were killing off the last of the wild game . . . .

"Many of the new hunters lived in a fortified and heavily armed outpost known as Adobe Walls. It was a trading post, which Quanah's Kwahadi attacked in force the 27th day of June, 1874 . . .

"The battle lasted three days, and though the Chief led brutal assault after assault, an endless stream of bullets poured from the stockade. Quanah, who had promised never to retreat, knew in his heart this was one battle he could never win . . . .

"Quanah was exhausted. He was defeated morale-wise. He had been shot in the shoulder, and his prize horse was dead.

"He ordered his proud band of warriors to return to the hills, allowing the new hunters to stay on Comanche land. Already, other Comanche bands had surrendered to the Cavalry and Texas Rangers in preceding months . . . .

"Chief Quanah remained a hunted man for nearly a year after the Battle for Adobe Walls . . . .

"But in the summer of 1875 . . . June, it was . . . Chief Quanah and his war council, chests out and chins high with pride, walked in through the gates of Fort Sill, their weapons lowered . . . .

"Chief Quanah, who refused to participate in treaties or bow to the whites since the arrival of the new

296

hunters, had finally surrendered . . . .
     "The long struggle was over . . . .'
     The gentle music of falling rain made Two-Step think
of his mother's soothing voice—the voice she had used
when she told him stories down by the river.
     His mother was long dead now. Life on the reserva-
tion had killed her, pure and simple. There was no use
kidding himself about it anymore. And there was no
longer reason to blame himself.
     A dragonfly appeared in front of Broken Arrow. It
hovered in mid-air, seemingly unaffected by the massive raindrops, and he took it as an omen: dragonflies
were rarely seen *during* a storm.
     An omen, but he was not sure what kind. Perhaps it
was a message from his mother. He did not hear the
crackle of small-arms fire on the other side of camp—
he was still listening to her gentle, reassuring voice.
     Two-Step reached out and the dragonfly landed on
his fingertips. He didn't know if dragonflies bite—his
mother said they didn't; his brother said they might;
and his sister claimed she'd been bitten three times
before her tenth birthday—but he felt no fear.
     He slowly brought his hand closer to his face, hoping
to see something in the bug's strange eyes . . . hoping
to learn something more from this encounter . . .
something more than just the knowledge dragonflies
are so light you can't feel them. But it vanished when he
moved again. Maybe it had only been a figment of his
imagination.
     He walked up to the fenceline and grasped several
strands of barbed wire, making himself a target for the
first time. He squeezed the strands tightly together,
drawing blood, proving this was not a dream, but he
could not feel any pain.
     He felt no pain about his mother anymore, either. Or
about Chief Quanah and his Kwahadi. He felt no
sorrow for any of the Comanche at all, or halfbreeds
like himself. The Vietnamese meant nothing to him.
Neither the Vietnamese, nor their struggle.

The jungle was all that mattered. He stood there for a long time as flares popped over other sectors of the camp. He stood there, silent and unmoving as a cigar-store Indian, sensing movement out in the bamboo, beyond the wire. But no one fired a single shot at him. Broken Arrow was a member of the Dirty Thirty fraternity, but the commies didn't care.

They allowed him to walk away. And Two-Step knew. He knew there was no Dirty Thirty jinx. He would live forever. Just he and the jungle.

He turned and walked slowly back toward the sound of shooting, letting the rain soak him through and through. Hoping it would wash away the guilt and sorrow, but knowing it wouldn't.

CHAPTER 30

Koy was furious. He was using the same words he'd used those nights he tried to seduce *her*. Koy listened to the hunter sweet-talk Pax, a recently indoctrinated village girl from some no-name hamlet outside of Pleiku City or Kontum. She listened as she silently polished her Indonesian-made machete.

"I want only to help warm you, dear," he was telling the girl. "It is late, and we must both sleep, so there is no reason to waste body heat and sleep on opposite sides of the bunker."

"If you only want to help keep me warm"—the girl was young but not as stupid as she might appear—"then why do you insist I remove my clothes?" She was not shedding tears over this, the hunter observed, but smiling—which was equally confusing, since Asian women often smiled when frightened or upset.

"My dear, my dear." He was up against her again, gently unbuttoning her blouse. "You ask too many questions. You want to be a good communist, don't you? You want—"

"You just want to make romance to me," she accused, pushing him away, then pulling the tunic's flaps tightly together. But she made no move to leave. The girl really had nowhere to go. Nowhere except the jungle and the darkness outside. And the caves were high off the ground, in the crags of a steep cliff. She could easily fall and kill herself trying to run away at night.

The hunter could no longer control himself. He grabbed her arm and slapped hard. Tears immediately appeared now.

The girl was bewildered. Angry, confused—and now—in pain. All she ever wanted to be was a fighter in the struggle against the foreign invaders. Her parents had been killed by French soldiers a decade ago, when she was but a child, and all she wanted to do now was avenge them. She would fight for freedom, she told the hunter that first day he recruited her. "I only want to see the arrogant Americans *die!*"

"Now remove your clothes," the communist cadre ordered.

When she hesitated, he brought his hand back again.

Sobbing now, the girl bent over and slid loose-fitting pantaloons over sunken, undernourished thighs.

The hunter smiled broadly, rubbing his hands together. When the girl began moving the waistband of her panties down over her haunches, the hunter could no longer control himself: he wrestled with his own belt, and his trousers dropped in a pile around his ankles.

That was when Koy emerged from the shadows. The girl who was stripping screamed when she first saw the sparkling blade come down.

Its razor sharp edge struck the hunter midway down his backbone, but did not kill him. Before he could scream, Koy slammed the iron handle against the side of his head. The hunter fell to his knees, stunned, and she kicked him over onto his side.

"Koooyyyyy," he murmured, glancing up and recognizing her. "For this you will—"

"For this I will sleep better," she said, reaching down to grab his ear.

"*No!*" the recent admission to the cell screamed, and Koy whirled around to confront her.

300

"You would rather I allow him to rape you?" Her eyes burned with rage.

"It was . . . not . . . rape. It was . . . not . . . ."

"It was not rape?" Koy laughed, twisted the hunter's ear until he groaned loudly. A pool of blood from his back wound was collecting around her toes. "*It was not rape!?* Then what, dear sister, was it?"

"It was not . . . he did not yet . . . ." The girl went silent. Her head dropped until she was staring at her feet.

"No, he did not do it yet!" Koy brought the machete up over her head. "But if I had not interrupted him, he—"

"No, he . . . ."

Koy lowered the blade, but did not release the hunter's ear. "My friend." She pulled back her own blouse slightly to show a deep gash that was healing into an ugly scar. "I *know*. I know what he is like."

"But." Compassion and fear glazed the girl's eyes.

"If we do not end it here . . . if we do not end it tonight, he will violate you, and then next week another innocent . . . and then another, and another, and anoth—"

"Okay!" the girl yelled. "I am leaving! Do what you feel you have to do, but leave me alone . . . . Just leave . . . me . . . *alone!*"

"No!" Koy reached out and grabbed her wrist as the girl rushed past, heading for the bunker exit.

"Wha—"

"*You!* You will do it!" Koy pressed the machete handle firmly in the girl's palm and closed her trembling fingers around it.

"Me!? *No!* Never!" She shook her head violently, from side to side. Tears struck Koy's cheek.

"Do it. Just *do* it!" Koy was stretching the hunter's ear out, and when the girl continued to hesitate, Koy grabbed her hand and forced the machete down in a blinding swipe.

The hunter, though semi-conscious, screamed in pain

as his ear peeled away and clung to the cold steel. Blood poured down onto the floor.

The girl screamed too at the sight of what she'd done—or helped do—and Koy glanced over at the low tunnel leading out of the bunker. But no one had heard. No one was running to the hunter's rescue. The downpour outside was effectively masking all underground sound with a roaring din of raindrops.

"Now the other!" Koy ordered.

"No!" The girl refused, and Koy grabbed the machete away.

"Then watch!" she demanded. "I am not doing this only for myself. I am doing this for you and all the girls to come . . . all the girls he victimized *before* us . . . ."

"I will *not* watch!" the girl yelled at Koy, but she could not take her eyes away as the blade fell again.

Koy did not reach down to pick up the severed ear for a souvenir. Without fanfare, she plunged the machete into the back of the hunter's head, at the base of his skull. "Scrambled brains for breakfast?" She laughed, twirling the handle about in her hand, and the other young woman gasped as more blood squirted out, covering Koy's wrists.

Koy kicked the hunter over onto his back. "Hotdogs for dinner?" She switched to English, disemboweling him with a single slash across the stomach. Koy began chopping up the man's intestines wildly, and the other woman hid her face in her hands.

"How about *satayed* meatballs?" She cupped his testicles in the palm of her hand and brought the machete back, but her audience fled from the bunker, whimpering.

Koy watched the girl flee through the exit, and the enthusiasm drained from her. She pushed the hunter away, ignoring his genitals now, and just stared at the stupid expression on his face. The man's eyes were lifeless now. Steam rose from his intestines and they continued to ooze through the jagged gash, onto the cool bunker floor.

Koy plunged the machete down into the dead communist's heart and left it there. She rose to leave. Relief flooded her, finally, after all this time.

It was done.

The handle on the upper half of the machete continued to swing back and forth slightly long after Koy had climbed out into the rain.

CHAPTER 31

Brody wore his python mask as the First Sergeant led the charge down toward *Nuoc-Mam*'s old family hut. If there was really magic involved here, The Whoremonger reasoned—if an evil eye curse was really responsible for sinking the home into the bowels of the earth, then one had to combat evil with evil, magic with magic. And what could be more representative of evil than his stuffed snakehead? Any demons lurking beyond the wire would certainly be driven off in fear when Treat made his grand entrance. The firepower their squad carried would surely be sufficient to even out the odds where waiting Cong were concerned, too.

They rushed the perimeter shortly after dawn. It was still raining—worse than during the night, it seemed—but all the precautions were unnecessary. The enemy had pulled back. Except for a solitary sniper—who The Brick took out with a three-round burst from his M-60—they met no other resistance.

Nuoc-Mam's hut had not been devoured by demons and swallowed into hell—as the Montagnarde feared while he impatiently waited the two long hours for sunrise—although its roof *was* barely protruding above ground level.

Mud up to their hips as they waded through the flooding waters swirling below the camp perimeter, Brody's people inspected the damage, and found that the overnight rain had weakened the ground beneath the hut's support poles.

That a Viet Cong tunnel happened to be running beneath the dwelling did not help matters: the tunnel had collapsed, and the structure fell down into it.

Several other homes farther down the hillside had suffered similar fates during the night.

Forming a human chain, it took the combined American-CIDG patrol a half hour to get *Nuoc-Mam* down onto the house. By then, several area residents had gathered to watch as the sun came out, slowly burning away the mist and fog. Isolated sheets of rain drifted over the hills now and then, wandering aimlessly beneath confused clouds but, for the most part, the storm was over. The First Sergeant had summoned two additional security teams down to their positions—one to keep an eye on the Vietnamese onlookers, and the other to begin a search of those tunnels which were not flooded with rainwater.

Nuoc-Mam's ancestral home was empty of occupants. After he muddied himself from boot-bottoms to chin, exiting with a heartbroken look, a cry of relief rose from one hillside.

Rifles raised, Brody and the others glanced behind them to find two old women with several children clustered around them—*Nuoc-Mam's* relatives! They had fled the dwelling when the siege of Plei Me began, he learned later, and spent the last few days and nights at a friend's longhouse on the other side of the hill.

Nuoc-Mam spotted someone else in the growing crowd of concerned Vietnamese. He rejoined Brody's people, and pointed her out. Jong translated. "She the one put evil eye curse on *Nuoc-Mam*," he explained. "Papa-san standing next to her is *miao*." The area sorcerer.

"Well, we'll put an end to this bewitching bullshit!"

Brody flipped his rifle's selector lever from SAFE to SEMI, and brought its front sights down on the woman's back as she and her father turned to leave.

"No! *No!*" *Nuoc-Mam* grabbed Brody's elbow, knocking the rifle up before he could fire. "I beg you, Whoreman!" he whispered harshly. "Not do this! Nebbah mind!"

Jong was equally cautious. "If you kill *miao* or his daughter," he explained, "they would become twice as powerful! Their spirits would return to live in the tree beside our longhouse, or in—"

"Nonsense." Brody disagreed.

"Please, BRO-dee!" Jong pleaded. "We handle later. Somehow . . ."

He didn't look very sure of himself.

"Somehow," Brody said simply. "Shit. You guys have enough trouble with the Cong. I'm going to put an end to this crap about curses once and for all. Mr. *Miao* will understand the business end of an M-16, I'm sure. Me and Mista colt are twice as powerful as any magic herbs he's got stashed up his daughter's *ying-yang!*"

And he was off, trotting up the hillside through the sliding mud and slippery puddles, before the two Montagnardes could stop him. *Nuoc-Mam* wondered if Brody was aware he was still wearing the python mask.

He caught up with the *mjao* and his daughter a couple minutes later.

"Hey! Hold up, asshole!" he called out, and though the woman slid to a stop and turned to face him with a contemptible scowl, the old man kept walking, carefully picking his steps down through the debris-littered trail.

"Who you call 'asshole'?" The woman spoke surprising good English, he discovered. and she was shockingly beautiful—high cheekbones, dark mysterious eyes, long jet-black hair . . . everything you could want in an exotic Oriental mistress. Shockingly beautiful, except for her expression. She was trying to intimidate Brody with the evil eye routine. The 'look' just made him laugh, and reminded him of an old Italian movie he'd seen before coming to Vietnam. She did not appear frightened by the python mask.

Ignoring her for a moment, he fired a single shot down at the ground in front of the descending *mjao*. Jumping back as if the earth itself had spoken, several seconds passed before the old man realized the exploding dirt clods were caused by a bullet and not a competitor's magic. He glanced back up the hillside, fixing an angry gaze on the American.

"He s almost deaf," the woman snarled.

Still ignoring her, Brody motioned for the *mjao* to hurry back up to his location.

He moved closer to the woman as the *mjao* struggled to climb back up the slippery, boulder-strewn trail. The woman was clad in black pantaloons and a loose-fitting blue blouse decorated with faded crescent moons. It was buttoned to the throat, and Brody pressed the muzzle of his rifle along the top of the stiff collar. "You speak very good English." He applied increasing pressure with each word, but the woman's fierce expression did not waver.

"I learn from book. You must know enemy to defeat enemy," she said simply.

"You are VC?" Brody challenged her. "Is that what you are so bravely telling me, *Co*?"

"I am Jarai girl." She spat at his boots defiantly. "Daughter of Jarai *mjao*. If you are not Jarai, we hate you. We hate Vietnamese. We hate communists. And we hate Americans."

"The Yarde Strikers don't seem to hate us," Brody countered. "They appear to be particularly affectionate toward the Green Berets, and—"

"Strikers stupid. They enjoy your *scrip*. That is all. They forsake their people for American money."

"They are defending your people from—"

"They defend those living within the strategic hamlets. None others."

"And what about *Nuoc-Mam*?"

308

"Nuoc-Mam?" She was obviously not familiar with the nickname, and Brody didn't know the Yarde's proper Montagnarde name.

"Your old boyfriend." He motioned over his shoulder, up the trail toward the hilltop, where he knew Jong and the others would be gathering to watch. "What about—"

"He is coward. He no can stand up to my father on my behalf. He no longer exists."

"Fine," Brody responded. "I ain't no fuckin' match-maker, but—"

"Must you always curse?" she interrupted him, throwing her chest out slightly.

Brody responded by jabbing her throat hard with the rifle barrel. She began coughing, and he gently knocked her off her feet with the M-16 butt. The woman dropped onto her bottom in the mud.

Brody stuck the rifle barrel in her ear. "Now listen up, little Miss Mischief," he said softly, the sound of her father's footfalls growing behind him. "You say *Nuoc-Mam* no longer exists. Fucking fine! That means you and old papa-san there," he motioned over a shoulder with his free fist, "lay off the poor guy. No more evil eye. No more mountain magic. Just cut the crap, okay? Knock off the bullshit or me and Mista Colt," he slapped the rifle's front handrest, "are gonna return to Plei Me. To *bury* you and—"

The *miao* let out a terrifying screech when he saw what was happening to his daughter. "Aw, fuck . . . ." Brody mumbled as the old man, ignoring the M-16, began dancing around him in tighter and tighter circles, singing a strange incantation in high-pitched lyrics. Glancing up the hillside, Brody noticed Nervous Rex and the others were silently laughing, while *Nuoc-Mam* and Jong and two or three more Strikers stood with grim, worried looks on their faces.

"Listen up!" Brody fired a short burst into the air, but the *mjao* ignored him, and continued dancing. He seemed particularly upset by the mask Brody was wearing.

He moved beneath the boughs of a large tree and began dancing even faster once inside its shadows.

"What the hell's your papa-san up to?" Brody removed the barrel from the woman's ear and pointed it at the *mjao*. "And if I don't get a good answer, I'm gonna bust a cap on the bastard's head, then we'll *see* how strong his magic is!"

A streak of fear passed through her eyes as she realized Brody meant every word of his threat. "He talk to tree spirit," she said. "He ask tree spirit to take over your mind and—"

"Oh really?" Brody rushed over, grabbed the old man, and flung him out of the shadows into harsh sunlight. He whirled around and fired the remainder of his banana clip into the tree, ejected the spent magazine, reloaded and fired off another thirty rounds, jabbed the trunk repeatedly with the rifle's bayonet, then began clubbing the branches overhead with the weapon's butt, until several fell to the ground.

Brody jabbed the tree with his bayonet, danced around in little circles, stabbed away again, then left the rifle sticking out of the trunk and began running his hands over the sap oozing from all the wounds. Still singing the lyrics from the latest James Bond movie *Thunderball*, in pig-Latin, he began rubbing the sap over his face and chest, then yanked free the M-16, inserted a fresh clip, and filled the treetrunk full of hot lead and smoking tracers again.

The *miao* was mesmerized by Brody's strange behavior. Slowly . . . cautiously he moved closer to the American, trying to hear every word being uttered. When he was only a couple yards from the doorgunner's back, Brody whirled around and screamed, "OO-yae I-day, OO-day Aw-May!" He moved his extended forefinger in a circular motion in front of the old man's face, then jabbed the *miao's* nose flat, and resumed stabbing the tree.

The Montagnarde magic man turned to his daughter, terror in his eyes, and screamed out a torrent of

310

confused questions in their native tongue. The girl seemed equally bewildered by Brody's chant, and, unable to provide a translation to the pig Latin, had to fight back tears as her father flew into a frenzy—it appeared this foreigner had just put a curse on him. A curse the old *miao* had never seen before. A curse he had no remedy for!

"He want to know what you do!" she yelled, moving closer to Brody, then stepping back when he rushed forward, leering at them both like a madman possessed by demons.

"I put curse on him!"

"*What?*" she was crying now as her father jumped up and down, demanding an explanation.

"If he does not apologize to *Nuoc-Mam*, and if he does not allow you to become *Nuoc-Mam*'s woman, and if he does not can his magic man act and all the other crap—the spirits of all the dead white men who roam the rain forest around Plei Me will bang at his doors and walls every night after dark, and he will never be able to sleep until . . . he . . . *DIES! Can you fucking translate that?*"

The woman did not waste time answering Brody, but launched into a torrent of Jarai he could not understand. The *miao*'s eyes grew even wider as she explained, and when she was through, he swallowed hard, tried to wipe the hardening sap off Brody until the American pushed him away, then began bowing repeatedly, over and over.

All the way down the hillside.

"I do not believe you have the power to do all that." The girl had recovered somewhat from the sideshow.

"Oh, an *educated* peasant, eh?" He jabbed the M-16 muzzle into her belly. "Fine. I'll finish off papa-san with my magic, and cancel your ticket with *this* if I have to come back."

She backed off the rifle barrel. "Father says he is moving to the next province. Where they have no Americans."

"Good."

"He does not admit your power is greater than his, but he does not want to be around crazy people who have . . . *dinky-dau* in their heads."

"And you, Miss Hard Ass?"

"I go with my father." She excused herself with a frown and started down the trail.

"No." Brody raised his rifle in front of her. "You go *up* trail," he instructed.

"What?"

"You go up to that man in the tiger-stripe uniform. the handsome one, who—for some reason *I'll* never figure out—has googoo eyes for your body or something."

"No." The woman refused, but there was some uncertainty in her voice.

Brody gave her an easy way out. "Do it or die."

Hesitating for only a moment, she replied, "If you insist."

"I do."

He watched her climb up the slippery trail and, in the distance, *Nuoc-Mam* start down through the boulders and mortar fins and unexploded bombs. "You two deserve each other," he called after the girl, and she paused to stare back down at Brody.

Winking, she said, "Thank you, GI. *Cam on*." The tears were flowing freely now, but they seemed to be tears of joy and happiness.

Brody removed the python mask. "For what?" he asked softly, unsure she would even hear him as several helicopters passed by overhead.

"For free me." She smiled. "For free me from my father . . . ."

She continued climbing, and Brody watched the two of them embrace a couple of minutes later.

Grinning with self-satisfaction, he looked down at his M-16 and rubbed its rear handle-sight affectionately. "You did good, boy," he said to the weapon. "Damn good . . . ."

312

As if in response, the rifle's dust cover snapped shut by itself.

CHAPTER 32

As the sizzling tropical sun reached its zenith, it became apparent the North Vietnamese and Viet Cong were retreating. Plei Me was now saturated with gunships and air support, and the relief column that had been ambushed outside Pleiku was now only a few miles away.

A skycrane helicopter was roaring into camp as Brody's people gathered around *Pegasus*, preparing to return to the Ia Drang Valley outpost. The skycrane had a bullet-riddled Huey suspended beneath it—the medevac a Green Beret sergeant had earlier sacrificed his life trying to get to. The skycrane was undoubtedly filled with bodybags too. Brody lowered his eyes as the monstrous craft dropped to a hover a hundred meters away, and Strikers rushed in to unstrap the cables and chains covering the Dustoff like spiderweb.

"Well, it's been fun." Brody offered Nervous Rex a sarcastic half-salute, then turned to wave at those members of his First Cav unit who would be remaining at Plei Me until the Brass was sure the area had been secured: Chappell and Nelson—the newbies; Cordova and Two-Step—the vets; and Abdul Mohammed—the resident loudmouth.

"Hey, not so fast!" Sgt. Ritter protested. "I'm comin' with you!"

Brody's eyes lit up. "DEROS?" he asked, shaking Nervous Rex's hand.

"Naw! Just an R&R."

"Honolulu?" Brody's mandatory frown of late transformed into an ear to ear grin.

"Naw, thought I'd investigate Sydney . . . ."

"Australia?"

"Yeah. Ol' Stormin' Norman had nothin' but good things to say about the pussy down there. Bookoo blondes—and the genuine article, he claimed. None o' that phony California crap."

"Yeah . . . ."

"Oh, no offense." Ritter remembered Brody was from Los Angeles.

"None taken."

"Yeah . . . I need some time away from The Nam. from time to time to refind."

"I know what you mean . . ." Brody wondered if Ritter would bring up his membership in the Dirty Thirty. Or Treat's.

"A man needs to look at life from a different perspective now and then."

"Yeah . . . ."

"Just to make sure he's not goin' native on foreign soil, you know?"

"I think I know what you mean, sarge."

"I make a point of doing this every now and then." He winked over at Brody. "Otherwise, this land can bewitch ya, right?"

"Right, sarge . . . ."

"But I'll be back," he insisted. "I *always* come back. Vietnam is where I want to die. Eventually . . . ."

"You're talkin' *dinky-dau* , now, sarge . . . ." Brody dismissed the small talk with a wave of bruised knuckles.

"I just can't see gettin' buried somewhere where it's cold, Treat. I just couldn't handle gettin' buried under a

316

lot o' snow."

"I hear ya, sarge. I can identify with *that*."

A tall soldier carrying an MP-40 was running over to them from the vicinity where the skycrane had touched down. He looked like he'd lost thirty or forty pounds recently. His arms were tanned dark, but the patch of skin where his flakvest was unbuttoned appeared very pale. His hair had been streaked by the Asian sun. The youth wore mirrored sunglasses. "Hey! Can I bum a ride with you guys back to Pleiku?" he asked, breathing hard from the sprint. "Our skycrane's down for a half day due to repairs that came about all the sudden like in the form of a couple AK rounds from the ground . . . ."

"Hairy," said Nervous Rex.

"Really."

Zack leaned out of Peg's hatch right then and acknowledged the request by saying, "All aboard who's goin' ashore," as if they were leaving a sea of terrible memories and emotions, and returning home for a rest. He motioned Ritter and the skycrane crewmen up onto the skids.

"We got room," said Brody. "You can catch a transfer at the Turkey Farm, and they'll take you into Pleiku City."

"Great! Hey, don't I know you?"

Brody paused as the rotors overhead began slowly twirling and the turbines kicked in with a high-pitched squeal and whine. "Deadmeat, right?"

"Hey-*hey*! Right! How's it goin' dude?" 'Deadmeat' turned to face Sgt. Ritter. "*Our* bird was the one ferried The Whoremonger in here to Plei Me his first trip to the camp a few months back. Ol' Whoremonger, here," he slapped Brody on the back, "claims he saw a chick down in the wire—a naked broad with big boobs!" Deadmeat erupted into long-drawn-out laughter, then turned back toward Brody. "That was a good one, Whoremonger! My crew's been gigglin' about it ever since that day!" Moving closer, he lowered his voice. "But we still haven't spotted no VC beauties in

317

the buff down there," he taunted Treat.

Brody was about to utter a retort when a flurry of shots from the distant treeline rang out.

"Snipes!" someone on the ground shouted as a single slug tore away Sgt. Ritter's lower jaw.

"My God!" Brody screamed, already covered with crimson as blood sprayed forth from the grisly wound and *Pegasus* began to ascend. "*Rex!*" He bolted toward the Green Beret, but Wickman was already beside the NCO, trying to stop the bleeding with a palm across the gaping crater. The Brick was big, but blood still pumped freely around the edges of his hand as he applied direct pressure to the injury, waiting for someone else to break out a first-aid kit.

"We're airborne!" Lee didn't seem to notice all the commotion, he'd been so absorbed in securing a seat aboard Peg and getting out of Plei Me alive. As they passed over the barbed perimeter fenceline, rising above the treetops without taking any additional sniper fire, he heaved his Ouija board out through the hatch and watched it flutter down into the green jaws of Void Vicious. "I'm alive!" he yelled as other men scrambled to save Nervous Rex Ritter. "The Ouija was wrong: I made it outta Play Me-Plei Me! Ha-*Ha*! I'm alive!"

"Get us to a field hospital!" Wickman was yelling up at the cockpit. glancing back at the carnage in the cabin, Krutch nodded somberly, flooding the rotorblades with more power.

"*Whoremonger!*" Deadmeat was suddenly yelling too.

"Whoremonger . . . over here! *Come here!* It's her! The girl! I see her—the naked girl!" He was rapidly unslinging his MP-40.

"Wait . . . *wait!*" Brody grabbed the submachinegun out of Deadmeat's hands. "Lemme do it! I'll get her!"

He leaned out the hatch, and there she was, crawling under the strands of concertina again—but this time *away* from the camp. Brody couldn't make out her face from this altitude—they were seventy-five to a hundred

318

feet above the treetops now—but she *had* to be the same one.

Oiled down and naked, such a shapely body—the long black, hair. The only difference this time was that she was dragging an AK-47 after her, and he couldn't help but wonder if she was the sniper who shot Ritter.

Brody leaned into the MP-40 as he unleashed a steady stream of shells down at the startled woman. He aimed for her breasts, watched the first slugs kick up clay several yards above her head, and quickly adjusted his aim until the last five rounds in the magazine ripped her in two at the waist.

"Got her! You *got* her!" Deadmeat slapped Brody on the back so hard he nearly fell through the hatch. "But what a waste o' pussy, sport!"

"Hey!" Brody pointed down at the outer perimeter. "Look! Look, you guys!"

A large brown, short-haired mongrel had sauntered over from the edge of the jungle and was ripping the entrails of the woman out with its teeth as it wagged a stub of a tail.

"*Choi-oi*!" Larson yelled over Brody's shoulder. "It's *Choi-oi!*"

"It can't be!" Brody turned toward the cockpit. "Hey, Stork! That's *Choi-oi* down there! We gotta go back for *Choi-oi!*"

Choi-oi was Echo Company's mascot. A mut of indigenous beginnings and dubious pedigree, he had been kidnapped by a disgruntled housegirl back in Ia Drang, at the Turkey Farm. The housegirl had demanded a hundred dollars for the dog's safe return, but before Brody could raise the money or investigate the matter further, they were being scrambled for this rescue mission to Plei Me.

"He'll be okay down there, Whoremonger!" Krutch responded dryly. "The four-legged bastard's originally *from* Plei Me, remember?"

"*Choi-oi* musta escaped!" Snakeman decided "Beat paws back to the Turkey Farm only to find us gone, so he headed home to his Green Beret buddies!"

"It's probably not even *Choi-oi*," Krutch called back over the loudspeaker. "It's probably the bitch that hatched him!"

"Or *Choi-oi's* papa-san," Lee offered seriously.

"Besides, we gotta get Ritter in front o' some medics rikky-tik!" the Stork added.

"Corky and Two-Step are still down there," Snakeman consoled his best friend. "If it's really *Choi-oi*, they'll take care of him until we're all reunited!"

"It *is Choi-oi*, Elliot."

"Fine . . . fine! I believe you, Treat!"

The clearing containing the maze of sparkling wire vanished below them, to be replaced by a thick carpet of multi-hued treetops as *Pegasus* climbed higher and higher.

Brody The Whoremonger was not thinking about the woman with the shapely body he had just killed. Probably not . . . . *Never did get a really good look at her face* . . . .

All he cared about was his dog. *Choi-oi* was all that mattered to him anymore.

"Hey, Brody! You're bleeding, bud!" Snakeman touched his arm, and the Whoremonger winced.

"Just a flesh wound," he muttered, staring down through the hatch at the jungle below. "Don't mean nothin.'"

Just a fleshwound! A splinter of lead from the bullet that tore Nervous Rex's lower jaw away had ricocheted into Treat Brody, reminding him what pain felt like. Reminding him how vulnerable he really was. Reminding him he was only human.

The wound had hurt badly those first few minutes—despite the adrenaline rush—and all the visions of invincibility and godlike stature that came with his thirtieth enemy kill quickly drained from the young warrior.

"You can slow it down," Wickman called up to the cockpit. "Sgt. Ritter is gone."

Tears filled Treat Brody's eyes. He kept them locked on the rain forest canopy rushing past below, but soon he could no longer see the void for the tears. He wanted to go over to Nervous Rex and hold the Green Beret sergeant in his arms. He wanted to say goodbye to the man, but he seemed frozen against the hatch. He could not move from the swivel-mounted machinegun that seemed to stare down at the jungle, mocking its power.

Brody considered suicide as he realized he was the only member of the Dirty Thirty Left. He and Crazy Craig. And Crazy Craig didn't count anymore. He contemplated flinging himself out the hatch, down into Void Vicious, but the thoughts slowly left him the further away from Plei Me *Pegasus* carried him. He just crouched there, clutching the hatch-60 in one hand and Deadmeat's submachinegun in the other, and stared down into space.

The whoremonger stared down into space and thought about *Choi-oi*. All he wanted was some peace and quiet, and some solitude.

Just Brody and his dog.

As the mongrel snarled below her field of vision, Koy screamed her life away. She stared at the peaceful, quiet clouds drifting by noislessly above, floating away, abandoning her. She could not hear the birds any longer, but the sky, uncaring as it was, turned a deeper blue, comforting her, it seemed. And then the growling dog tugged again, and she felt her intestines sliding out of the cavity where the bullets had ripped her in half. Koy screamed again as the sky began to go black at noon.

The dedicated Viet Cong guerrilla never knew what hit her. She never saw the gunship, or heard the rotors and machinegun. She had been concentrating on the razor-sharp barbs scraping against her breasts as she slid along in the mud, then suddenly she was being torn in half, and a dog was feeding off her insides.

But Koy knew she was dying. There was no doubt

about that now. There was no sky above any longer. Only the face of the man she loved, floating in the heavens, smiling down at her.

"Come back to me, Treat Brody," Koy held her arms out as the flapping of rotorblades faded in the distance. "Please come back for Koy!"

But her only answer was the sound from the thirsty mongrel as its tongue lapped at the pool of blood draining from her heart.

EPILOGUE

During the battle for Plei Me, an American Air Force A-1E Skyraider was shot down over the Special Forces compound. Brody's people saw the pilot parachuting from the flaming aircraft, but he was never found. Another plane went down shortly thereafter, but the Green Berets rescued its pilot, and twelve hours later, on October 22nd, a Special Forces unit known as Project Delta, led by Major Charlie Beckwith, broke through to the outpost, after two days of vicious jungle fighting alongside two companies of the ARVN 91st Airborne Ranger Battalion.

Major Beckwith assumed command of the camp, and sent several patrols back out to mop up pockets of enemy resistance in the surrounding area. One such squad, led by Captain Thomas Pusser, was ambushed by a North Vietnamese machinegun nest. Pusser and twelve South Vietnamese were killed. Dozens more were wounded in action.

When supplies ran low inside the camp during the latter stages of the battle, American Air Force planes dropped pallets of food and ammunition down into the compound. Two men were killed when a pallet landed on them. Another pallet crashed through the messhall roof, which was seen as a godsend in contrast to the earlier tragedy.

Thanks to Lt. Colonel Earl Ingram's 2nd Battalion, 12th Cavalry artillery unit, which quickly positioned itself in support of the Vietnamese Rangers who were intercepted on their way to Plei Me after leaving Pleiku, the communist ambush was broken. Nearly two hundred North Vietnamese and Viet Cong were killed in the counter ambushes—mostly by Ingram's cannons. This allowed the M41 tanks and M8 armored cars from the ARVN's 3rd Armored Cav Squadron—supplemented by the 1st Battalion of the 42nd ARVN Regiment, and the 21st and 22nd ARVN Ranger Battalions—to continue on to the besieged Green Beret camp, but they did not arrive until October 25th. By then, the battle for Plei Me was over.

Military Intelligence advised First Cavalry Division Commander (General) Harry Kinnard that the communists had moved only five miles west of the Plei Me battleground, and were regrouping. Gen. Kinnard promptly requested permission from the Saigon Command to finish them off, and the reply he received from General Westmoreland included, ". . . find, fix and defeat the enemy forces that had threatened our Green Berets at Plei Me . . . ."

The new tactical area of operations became the Ia Drang Valley, which covered 965 square miles of dense jungled mountains—an area the size of Rhode Island, but with only two dirt roads cutting through it. The enemy had picked the right spot to lick their wounds: a river snaked through the western portion of the valley, providing them with water.

Meanwhile, as main force American units were beginning their sweep of the Ia Drang, NVA Commander of the Western Highlands, General Chu Huy Man, decided on November 10th to launch a second attack against the Plei Me special Forces outpost on November 16th.

He would use the three units at his disposal: the 32nd, 33rd, and 66th NVA Regiments. Each was roughly the size of an American brigade of three battalions. His initial attack, using Major Minh's 33rd Regiment alone, had resulted in the North Vietnamese being driven off with heavy losses. The staging area for his rebound, Gen. Man decided, would be a base camp he had at the foot of the Chu Pong massif in Ia Drang Valley.

General Kinnard directed 3rd Brigade Commander Col. Thomas Brown to sweep the heavily wooded region south of the Ia Drang river—a command which would bring the troops in direct conflict with Man's NVA. While the 33rd Regiment was regrouping in the valley after its initial defeat at Plei Me, the 66th NVA Regiment—newly arrived from the north—grouped on both sides of the Ia Drang a few kilometers to the west. Ten kilometers further west, the 32nd Regiment was taking up positions on the northern bank of the Ia Drang river itself.

There was a problem, however. Gen. Man knew that his second assault on the Green Beret outpost would have to wait for the arrival of 120mm mortars and 14.5mm twin-barrel anti-aircraft guns, which runners had advised him were now coming down the Ho Chi Minh Trail from Hanoi.

Lt. Colonel Harold Moore, Commander, 7th Cavalry of the First Division, was instructed on the evening of November 13th by Col. Brown to begin an airmobile assault on the Ia Drang Valley the following morning. The gunship blitz would be followed by search and destroy foot patrols in the area through November 15th. Moore's troops were located just south of Plei Me when they received these orders. "Fire support will be provided by two 105mm howitzers at Landing zone Falcon, east of the target area," Brown advised him.

When North Vietnamese Major Minh learned the Americans were landing hundreds of helicopters in the Ia Drang in preparation for a massive assault on the area, he urgently conferred with Gen. Man about these most recent developments.

Both men agreed, the Plei Me CIDG compound could wait. They would concentrate all their efforts on the Ia Drang Valley, and destroy the green sea of parked gunships where they sat.

But the Battle for Ia Drang is another book in itself . . . .

November 19, 1965
Somewhere on the 'Turkey Farm,' Ia Drang Valley, South Vietnam

There was only one package waiting for Specialist Fourth Class Treat Brody when he returned from fighting the Ia Drang campaign. It was a small parcel, with no return address, but a Florida postmark.

Inside, he found a short one-page letter, and a cigar box. The note was dated one month earlier. It was from Crazy Craig's girlfriend.

Dear Mister Brody,

Craig is dead. He committed suicide last month. I won't go into the details, but it was a death befitting a soldier. Craig never really left the army, Mr. Brody. Or, rather, it never left him. It finally . . . the memories . . . they finally just became overpowering, I guess. And now he's gone. I only found his note a few days ago. It doesn't explain anything. Only how he missed you men so much . . . how he felt he could never get on with his life until Vietnam was over . . . until that part of his soul he left over there in the jungle came back to him. He made a list of things he wanted me to send you. It was not very long. They are enclosed. I only hope this package reaches you. I pray to God you are still alive.

Before he killed himself, Craig told me about you. And Nervous Rex, and the others. He told me about the Dirty Thirty. But I don't believe any of it. I hope you don't either, Mr. Brody. Void Vicious can't hurt you unless you believe. That was Craig's problem. He believed.

He believed in Vietnam, and what he was doing over there. And look where it got him.

The note was unsigned.

Brody folded it up carefully, disappointed it carried no traces of perfume from a woman back in The World.

Inside the cigar box he found Crazy Craig's medals. There was a cracked and faded photograph of the three of them posing together on a gunship somewhere: Brody and Nervous Rex and Crazy Craig. A copy of bloodstained military orders authorizing him to escort a fallen warrior back to the States. A tiger claw necklace . . . .

That was all. All that remained of Crazy Craig. At least, all that he cared Brody to have.

A shadow fell across Brody, and he looked up to find Fletcher standing in front of him. "You're blocking the sun, Snakeman."

"You never struck me as the kinda dude who *needed* rays, Whoremonger. Anyway," he sat down beside Treat just as the doorgunner contemplated rising, "I'm beatin' feet down to Vung Tau, buddy. Doctor's orders. I'll bet if you brown-nosed a bit, Leo would let you come along. Hell, you got thirty days on the books—I just checked. You better take 'em before *They* take 'em away!"

"Something's been bugging me for the last couple days, Elliot." Brody stood up and stretched. "Ever since we ended this Ia Drang shoot'-em-up." Even now, Koy's innocent, frightened face seemed to float in front of his eyes.

"Oh yeah? Like what?" Fletcher sounded like he didn't want to hear it.

"The jungle's not so important to me anymore, Snakeman. I don't know what it is . . . what happened to me over the last few weeks, but I just don't care about goin' out on another mission . . . I don't care about ridin' Peg into the fires of hell, you know?"

"That's natural." Fletcher dismissed the talk as soon as he heard Treat begin. Snakeman had heard it all before.

"All I want is some peace and quiet. I wanna find a little bungalow beside a river somewhere and just snuggle up next to a woman and sleep forever!"

"Don't go talkin' 'bout no *deep* sleep, Treat!" Fletcher imitated Clarence Crump III, but Brody wasn't laughing.

"I wanna rest my face against hers, kiss her ear, drink in her fragrance—the fragrance of a *woman*, brother. A real *woman*. And join her in her dreams. That's all I wanna do . . . ."

"Where you gonna find a real *woman* around here?" Snakeman sounded skeptical.

"Not here." Treat Brody responded, heading toward the chopper pads to hitch a ride. "Plei Me."

"Plei Me?" Snakeman did not sound as enthusiastic.

"Right. There's a woman down there I have to search for, Elliot. I'm gonna take my thirty days of leave time and I'm going down to Plei me, and I'm not coming back until I find her . . . ." Koy seemed to be smiling down on him as he spoke.

"She must be pretty special." Snakeman shook his head from side to side in resignation.

"She really is." Brody smiled at his best friend, tears welling up in his eyes. "She's a *very* special person. She's all I ever dream about anymore . . . ."

GLOSSARY

AA   Antiaircraft weapon
AC   Aircraft Commander
Acting Jack   Acting NCO
AIT   Advanced Individual Training
AK-47   Automatic rifle used by VC/NVA
Animal   See Monster
AO   Area of Operations
Ao Dai   Traditional Vietnamese gown
APH-5   Helmet worn by gunship pilots
APO   Army Post Office
Arc-Light   B-52 bombing mission
ArCOM   Army Commendation Medal
Article-15   Disciplinary action
Ash-'n'-Trash   Relay flight

Bad Paper   Dishonorable discharge
Ba Muoi Ba   Vietnamese beer
Banana Clip   Ammo magazine holding 30 bullets
Bao Chi   Press or news media
Basic   Boot camp
BCT   Basic Combat Training (Boot)
Bic   Vietnamese for "Understand?"
Big-20   Army career of 20 years
Bird   Helicopter

BLA   Black Liberation Army

Bloods   Black soldiers

Blues   An airmobile company

Body Count   Number of enemy KIA

Bookoo   Vietnamese for "many" (actually bastardization of French *beaucoup*)

Bought the Farm   Died and life insurance policy paid for the mortgage

Brass Monkey   Interagency radio call for help

Brew   Usually coffee, but sometimes beer

Bring Smoke   To shoot someone

Broken-Down   Disassembled

Buddha Zone   Death

Bush ('Bush)   Ambush

Butter Bar   2nd Lieutenant

CA   Combat Assault

Cam Ong   Viet for "Thank you"

Cartridge   Shell casing for bullet

C&C   Command & Control chopper

Chao   Vietnamese greeting

Charlie   Viet Cong (from military phonetic: Victor Charlie)

Charlie Tango   Control Tower

Cherry   New man in unit

Cherry Boy   Virgin

Chicken Plate   Pilot's chest/groin armor

Chi-Com   Chinese Communist

Chieu Hoi   Program where communists can surrender and become scouts

Choi-oi   Viet exclamation

CIB   Combat Infantry Badge

CID   Criminal Investigation Division

Clip   Ammo magazine

CMOH   Congressional Medal of Honor

CO   Commanding Officer

Cobra   helicopter gunship used for combat assaults/ escorts only

Cockbang   Bangkok, Thailand

Conex   Shipping container (metal)

Coz   Short for Cozmoline

CP   Command Post

CSM   Command Sergeant Major

Cunt Cap   Green narrow cap worn with khakis

Dash-13   Helicopter maintenance report

Dau   Viet for pain

Deadlined   Down for repairs

Dep   Viet for beautiful

DEROS   Date of Estimated Return from Overseas

Deuce-and-a-Half   2½-ton truck

DFC   Distinguished Flying Cross

DI   Drill Instructor (Sgt.)

Di Di   Viet for "Leave or go!"

Dink   Derogatory term for Vietnamese national

Dinky Dau   Viet for "crazy"

Disneyland East   MACV complex including annex

DMZ   Demilitarized Zone

Dogtags   Small aluminum tag worn by soldiers with name, serial number, religion, and blood type imprinted on it

DOOM Pussy   Danang Officers Open Mess

Door gunner   Soldier who mans M-60 machine gun mounted in side hatch of Huey gunship

Dung Lai   Viet for "Halt!"

Dustoff   Medevac chopper

Early Out   Unscheduled ETS

EM   Enlisted Man

ER   Emergency Room (hospital)

ETS   End Tour of (military) Service

Field Phone   Hand-generated portable phones used in bunkers

Fini   Viet for "Stop" or "the End"

First Louie   1st Lieutenant

First Team   Motto of 1st Air Cav

Flak Jacket   Body armor

FNG   Fucking new guy

FOB   Fly over board misson

Foxtrot   Vietnamese female

Foxtrot Tosser   Flame thrower

Frag   Fragmentation grenade

FTA   Fuck the Army

Gaggle   Loose flight of slicks

Get Some   Kill someone

GI   Government Issue, or, a soldier

Greenbacks   U.S. currency

Green Machine   U.S. Army

Gunship   Attack helicopter armed with machine guns and rockets

Gurney   Stretcher with wheels

Ham & Motherfuckers   C-rations serving of ham and lima beans

Herpetologist   One who studies reptiles and amphibians

HOG-60   M-60 machine gun

Hot LZ   Landing zone under hostile fire

Housegirl   Indigenous personnel hired to clean buildings, wash laundry, etc.

Huey   Primary troop-carrying helicopter

IC   Instillation Commander

IG   Inspector General

In-Country   Within Vietnam

Intel   Intelligence (military)

IP   That point in a mission where descent toward target begins

JAG   Judge Advocate General

Jane   Jane's Military Reference books

Jesus Nut   The bolt that holds rotor blade to helicopter

Jody   Any American girlfriends

Jolly Green   Chinook helicopter

KIA   Killed in Action

Kimchi   Korean fish sauce salad
Klick   Kilometer
KP   Mess hall duty

Lai Day   Viet for "come here"
LAW   Light Anti-Tank Weapon
Lay Dog   Lie low in jungle during recon patrol
LBFM   Little Brown Fucking Machine
LBJ   Long Binh Jail(main stockade)
Leg   Infantryman not airborne qualified
Lifeline   Straps holding gunny aboard chopper while he fires M-60 out the hatch
Lifer   Career solider
Links   Metal strip holding ammo belt together
Loach   Small spotter/scout chopper
LP   Listening Post
LRRP   Long-Range Recon Patrol
LSA   Gun oil
Lurp   One who participates in LRRPs
LZ   Landing Zone

M-14   American carbine
M-16   Primary U.S. Automatic Rifle
M-26   Fragmentation grenade
M-60   Primary U.S. Machine gun
M-79   Grenade launcher (rifle)
MACV   Military Assistance Command, Vietnam
Magazine   Metal container that feeds bullets into weapon. Holds 20 or 30 rounds per unit
Mag Pouch   Magazine holder worn on web belt
MAST   Mobile Army Surgical Team
Med-Evac   Medical Evacuation Chopper
Mess Hall   GI cafeteria
MG   Machine gun
MI   Military Intelligence
MIA   Missing in Action
Mike-Mike   Millimeters
Mike Papas   Military Policemen
Mister Zippo   Flame-thrower operator

Miao   Central Highlands witch doctor

Monkeyhouse   Stockade or jail

Monkeystrap   See **Lifeline**

Monster   12-21 claymore antipersonnel mines jury-rigged to detonate simultaneously

Montagnarde   Hill tribe people of Central Highlands, RVN

MPC   Money Payment Certificates (scrip) issued to GIs in RVN in lieu of greenbacks

Muster   A quick assemblage of soldiers with little or no warning

My   Viet for "American"

Net   Radio net

NETT   New Equipment Training Team

Newby   New GI in-country

Numba One   Something very good

Numba Ten   Something very bad

Nuoc Mam   Viet fish sauce

NVA   North Vietnamese Army

OD   Olive Drab

OR   Operating Room (Hospital)

P   Piasters

PA   Public Address system

PCS   Permanent Change of (Duty) Station (transfer out of RVN)

Peter Pilot   Copilot in training

PF   Popular Forces (Vietnamese)

PFC   Private First Class

Phantom   Jet fighter plane

Phu   Vietnamese noodle soup

Piaster   Vietnamese Currency

PJ   Photojournalist

Point   The most dangerous position on patrol. The point man walks ahead and to the side of the others, acting as a lookout

PRG   Provisional Revolutionary Govt. (the Communists)

Prang Land a helicopter roughly

Prick-25 PR-25 field radio

Profile Medical exemption

Psy-Ops Psychological operation

PT Physical Training

Puff Heavily armed aircraft

Purple Heart Medal given for wounds received in combat

Purple Vision Night vision

Puzzle Heart The MACV HQ building

Quad-50 Truck equipped with four 50-caliber MGs

QC Vietnamese MP

Rat Fuck Mission doomed from the start

Regular An enlistee or full-time soldier as opposed to PFs and Reserves, NG, etc.

REMF Rear Echelon Motherfucker

R&R Rest and Relaxation

Re-Up Re-enlist

Rikky-Tik Quickly or fast

Rock 'n' Roll Automatic fire

Roger Affirmative

ROK Republic of Korea

Rotor Overhead helicopter blade

Round Bullet

RPG Rocket-propelled grenade

Ruck(Sack) GI's backpack

RVN Republic of (South) Vietnam

Saigon Capital of RVN

SAM Surface-to-Air Missile

Sapper Guerrilla terrorist equipped with satchel charge (explosives)

SAR Downed-chopper rescue mission

Scramble Alert reaction to call for help, CA or rescue operation.

Scrip See **MPC**

7.62   M-60 ammunition

Sierra Echo   Southeast (Northwest is November Whiskey, etc.)

Single-Digit Fidget   A nervous single-digit midget

Single-Digit Midget   One with fewer than ten days remaining in Vietnam

SKS   Russian-made carbine

Slick   Helicopter

Slicksleeve   private E-1

Slug   Bullet

SNAFU   Situation normal: all fucked up

Soggy Frog   Green Beret laying dog

SOP   Standard Operating Procedure (also known as Shit Output)

Spiderhole   Tunnel entrance

Strac   Sharp appearance

Steel Pot   Helmet

Striker   Montagnarde hamlet defender

Sub Gunny   Substitute door gunner

TDY   Temporary Duty Assignment

Terr   Terrorist

"33"   Local Vietnamese beer

Thumper   See M-79

Ti Ti   Viet for little

Tour 365   The year-long tour of duty a GI spends in RVN

Tower Rat   Tower guard

Tracer   Chemically treated bullet that gives off a glow en route to its target

Triage   That method in which medics determine which victims are most seriously hurt and therefore treated first

Trooper   Soldier

201 File   Personnel file

Two-Point-Five   Gunship rockets

UCMJ   Uniformed Code of Military Justice

Unass   Leave seat quickly

336

VC   Viet Cong
Victor Charlie   VC
Viet Cong   South Vietnamese Communists
VNP   Vietnamese National Police
Void Vicious   Final approach to a Hot LZ; or the jungle when hostile

Warrant Officer   Pilots
Wasted   Killed
Web Belt   Utility belt GIs use to carry equipment, sidearms, etc.
Whiskey   Military phonetic for "West"
WIA   Wounded In Action
Wilco   Will comply
Willie Peter   White phosphorous
Wire   Perimeter (trip wire sets off booby trap)
The World   Any place outside Vietnam

Xin Loi   Viet for "sorry about that" or "good-bye"
XM-21   Gunship mini-gun
XO   Executive Officer

'Yarde   Montagnarde

ZIP   Derogatory term for Vietnamese National
Zulu   Military phonetic for the letter Z (LZ or Landing Zone might be referred to as a Lima Zulu)

A LETHAL COCKTAIL OF VIOLENCE,
DEATH AND BLACK HUMOUR . . .

The Secrets of Harry Bright

JOSEPH WAMBAUGH

Nothing much lived in the desert around Mineral Springs.
Just lizards and motorcycle gangs and a few dopers.
A corpse with a bullet hole in a burned-out Rolls Royce was
kind of unusual.

For a homicide cop like Blackpool this was a case to pass on to
some other poor sucker. Except he'd been hauled out of LA
by the victim's own father. Told to handle it personally as a
private commission. And promised a nice fat backhander at
the end of the day . . .

'So much energy . . . a detective no other writer could have
cooked up, a resolution no other could have ordained'
NEW YORK TIMES

0 7221 8914 1 GENERAL FICTION £2.95

Also by Joseph Wambaugh in Sphere Books:
**NEW CENTURIONS
THE BLUE KNIGHT**

Sphere Books 436 Proof 1 10.2.87 Opus Lazer 25648 F48 File 20

His latest bestseller…

CYCLOPS

CLIVE CUSSLER

Dirk Pitt didn't go looking for adventure. It found him easily
enough. His chance witnessing of an airship disaster and
gruesome discovery of the fate of the crew set in motion the most
nail-biting chain of events of his career.

But it was when he found his trail leading towards a fabulous
treasure hidden fathoms deep in the murky depths of the ocean
that he realised he was onto something very special indeed. For
somewhere in the raging waters lay the legendary lost lady of El
Dorado, the golden prize that had already lured thousands to
their graves…

0 7221 2756 1   **ADVENTURE THRILLER**   £3.50

From the bestselling author of DEATH WISH comes . . .

HOPSCOTCH
BRIAN GARFIELD

Before his enforced retirement from the CIA, Miles Kendig
thrilled to the cut-throat strategy of pursuit, the
red-blooded rapture of out-witting his opponents, the
subtlety of human conflict. Now, with the demands of
everyday life so easily accomplished, he felt empty, lifeless
and unwanted.

'You belong in the rubber room' they told him. But Miles
knew he was the best. He would show them. Both East and
West were terrified by his crazy plan. And this was going to
be Miles Kendig's last chance blaze of glory . . . if they
didn't nail him first!

'Brian Garfield is a natural storyteller'
NEW YORK TIMES

Also by Brian Garfield in Sphere Books:
NECESSITY
DEATH WISH

0 7221 3820 2   ADVENTURE THRILLER   £2.99

A top secret SBS mission during the Falklands
War soars into explosive action . . .

SPECIAL DELIVERANCE

ALEXANDER FULLERTON

In the war-torn, storm-swept South Atlantic, a small band of
highly-trained SBS experts embark on a vital secret mission: to
sabotage Argentina's stock of deadly Exocet missiles.

The dangers are unthinkable: the coastline is exposed and treacherous,
the missile base is surrounded by vast tracts of open land, they must
infiltrate and destroy without ever being detected. Some say it's
impossible . . . but no one underestimates the SBS's lethal capacity.

And one man, Andy MacEwan, an Anglo-Argentine civilian recruited to
the team as guide and interpreter, has more than the success of the
mission on his mind. His brother is a commander in the Argentine Navy
Air Force and there is no love lost between them . . .

'Good rollicking stuff – full of tension and highly authentic on SBS
technique'
TODAY

'The action passages are superb. He is in a class of his own'
OBSERVER

0 7221 3719 2   ADVENTURE THRILLER   £2.99

'It tears like a burst of tracers through the field of
Vietnam War literature' Dale A. Dye author of
PLATOON

SYMPATHY
FOR THE DEVIL

KENT ANDERSON

No acid or grass for Sergeant Hanson – he's army issue all
the way, even in his choice of drug. Young Hanson's a
professional, trained to be as hard as a clenched fist, as
quick as reflex muscle, and he's found his true home in the
Special Forces in Vietnam. He's brutal without apology. It's
his job, and he does it well. He and his buddies Quinn and
Silver are superb soldiers. They know how to kill, and, if
the time comes, they'll know how to die. And there are
many ways to die in the infernal cauldron of the Vietnam
War . . . some you couldn't even begin to imagine . . .

'Chilling and authentic . . . A riveting portrayal of hard
times survived by hard men who cling desperately to each
other – and little else' Oliver Stone, Director of
PLATOON

0 7474 0014 8   WAR FICTION   £3.50

A selection of bestsellers from Sphere

FICTION

THE LEGACY OF HEOROT	Niven/Pournelle/Barnes	£3.50 ☐
THE PHYSICIAN	Noah Gordon	£3.99 ☐
INFIDELITIES	Freda Bright	£3.99 ☐
THE GREAT ALONE	Janet Dailey	£3.99 ☐
THE PANIC OF '89	Paul Erdman	£3.50 ☐

FILM AND TV TIE-IN

BLACK FOREST CLINIC	Peter Heim	£2.99 ☐
INTIMATE CONTACT	Jacqueline Osborne	£2.50 ☐
BEST OF BRITISH	Maurice Sellar	£8.95 ☐
SEX WITH PAULA YATES	Paula Yates	£2.95 ☐
RAW DEAL	Walter Wager	£2.50 ☐

NON-FICTION

FISH	Robyn Wilson	£2.50 ☐
THE SACRED VIRGIN AND THE HOLY WHORE	Anthony Harris	£3.50 ☐
THE DARKNESS IS LIGHT ENOUGH	Chris Ferris	£4.50 ☐
TREVOR HOWARD: A GENTLEMAN AND A PLAYER	William Knight	£3.50 ☐
INVISIBLE ARMIES	Stephen Segaller	£1.99 ☐

All Sphere books are available at your local bookshop or newsagent, or can be ordered direct from the publisher. Just tick the titles you want and fill in the form below.

Name _____

Address _____

_____

Write to Sphere Books, Cash Sales Department, P.O. Box 11, Falmouth, Cornwall TR10 9EN

Please enclose a cheque or postal order to the value of the cover price plus:

UK: 60p for the first book, 25p for the second book and 15p for each additional book ordered to a maximum charge of £1.90.

OVERSEAS & EIRE: £1.25 for the first book, 75p for the second book and 28p for each subsequent title ordered.

BFPO: 60p for the first book, 25p for the second book plus 15p per copy for the next 7 books, thereafter 9p per book.

Sphere Books reserve the right to show new retail prices on covers which may differ from those previously advertised in the text elsewhere, and to increase postal rates in accordance with the P.O.